THE
COMPLEAT
LEE WULFF

SELECTED BOOKS BY LEE WULFF

THE COMPLEAT

A Treasury of Lee Wulff's

Illustrations by Henry McDaniel

LEE WULFF

Greatest Angling Adventures

LEE WULFF

Edited and with an Introduction by
John Merwin

T·T TRUMAN TALLEY BOOKS / E.P.DUTTON / NEW YORK

Published in the United States by Truman Talley Books • E.P. Dutton
a division of Penguin Books USA Inc.,
2 Park Avenue, New York, N.Y. 10016.

Published simultaneously in Canada by
Fitzhenry and Whiteside, Limited, Toronto.

Library of Congress Cataloging-in-Publication Data

Wulff, Lee.
    The compleat Lee Wulff: a treasury of Lee Wulff's greatest
angling adventures / edited and with an introduction by John Merwin;
illustrations by Henry McDaniel.
       p.   cm.
    "Truman Talley books."
    ISBN 0-525-24796-3
    1. Fishing.   I. Merwin, John.   II. Title.
SH441.W77   1989
799.1—dc19   89–1089
                                                                 CIP

DESIGNED BY EARL TIDWELL

1   3   5   7   9   10   8   6   4   2

First Edition

Grateful acknowledgment is made to the following periodicals,
where portions of this book previously appeared:
The American Sportsman: Chapter 22. *The Atlantic Salmon Journal:*
Chapter 9. *Collier's:* Chapter 5. *Country Life:* Chapter 15.
Esquire: Chapter 24. *Field & Stream:* Chapter 7. *Gray's Sporting
Journal:* Chapter 10. *Outdoor Life:* Chapters 4, 6, 43. *Outdoors:*
Chapters 1–2, 17–18, 23, 34. *Rod & Reel:* Chapters 12–14, 16, 20,
25, 29, 32–33, 35, 37–42. *The Roundtable:* Chapter 11. *St. John's*
[Newfoundland] *Evening Telegram:* Chapter 28. *Saltwater Sportsman:*
Chapter 26. *Sports Afield:* Chapters 3, 8, 21, 30–31, 36. *True:* Chapter 19.
Chapter 27 originally appeared as the introduction to *A Handbook of Fresh-
water Fishing,* published by Frederick A. Stokes.

Contents

Contents

Introduction

A few years ago I sat down to write a profile of Lee Wulff and faced an impossible problem: I simply couldn't characterize the man in a short sentence or two at the beginning. I solved the problem then by writing a short editorial note for starters, much as I'm doing now. The contributions of this eighty-four-year-old gentleman to angling have been so many and so varied that even a book such as this can only highlight a few of them.

One might begin, I suppose, with that now-famous phrase of his: "A good gamefish is too valuable to be caught only once." An apt statement, for it reflects the wide acceptance of catch-and-release fishing in recent years. Except the statement isn't from recent years. It comes from Wulff's *Handbook of Freshwater Fishing*, which was published in the late 1930s, at a time when releasing fish was exceptional—if not eccentric—behavior. It was almost four decades later that catch and release began to be widely accepted, not only among fly fishermen but among all fishermen, for all gamefish species. If anyone can claim modern parentage of the movement, it's Lee Wulff.

As we sat talking on a cold, January day, he added, "There was a corollary to that, which was: 'The finest gift you can give to any fisherman is to put a good fish back, and who knows if the fish that you caught isn't someone else's gift to you?'" A fine gift, to be sure, and one that he gave all of us. That early emphasis on catch-and-release fishing, made frequently and often loudly during the intervening fifty years, has benefited each of us directly.

Anyway, that's one way to begin. Another is at the beginning. Lee Wulff was born in Valdez, Alaska, in 1905. I had heard that for years, but never heard why. So I asked him. As he explained, his grandfather came from Germany to New York in the 1870s. His father was born in Brooklyn. His mother was Norwegian, had come to New York as a small child, and was living in Staten Island. Although his father met his mother in New York, he left for the goldfields of Alaska before things progressed to the point of marriage. Eventually, the young Norwegian girl made the trip from Brooklyn to Alaska and married Charles Wulff. It was, as their son explained, "quite a trip for a little lady at the turn of the century."

Charles Wulff found no gold, but did find work as a contractor, sheriff's deputy, and, from about 1909 to 1915, as a newspaper publisher in Valdez, which is, according to my atlas, a little more than one hundred miles east of Anchorage. In 1915, the Wulff family returned to Brooklyn, where Charles had inherited an interest in a retail coal business. After five years, the interest was sold, and the family moved to San Diego, California, where Lee finished high school, and then earned a civil engineering degree at Stanford University in Palo Alto. Civil engineering, he explained, "because my father never knew an engineer to be out of work.

"But," he continued, "I didn't really care too much about it. When I got out, I knew I wasn't going to be an engineer, so I just took what money I could scrape up and went to Paris to study and become an artist."

"That's a pretty big jump. Why?" I asked.

"Well, I was one of two people in our engineering group who ever went to a museum or an opera or anything like that. I felt at that time that engineers mostly went out in the bush, and they didn't have any amenities—the arts and so forth— available. I felt that an artist had a wide scope. A farmer could talk to any other farmer in the world, while most people were limited to their own age-group and their own income group; an artist really had no limitations. He talked with anybody. I had a little talent; so, I thought, I'll be an artist. I went to Paris to study and spent a year over there, which was all I could afford, going to the various art schools and studying and taking trips and sketching."

There is within Lee Wulff's description of making a career in art quite a summary of his subsequent life. He is, in my experience, keenly interested. Not necessarily in something specific; just plain *interested*, with an interest that transcends both nationality and social status.

After a year in Paris, he went to New York City, where "I struggled through a number of jobs, finally getting into advertising and doing very well. Then the Depression suddenly took the legs out from under most of us, and I went from a very fine salary of $100 a week down to $35, [working] for the Du Pont Company.

"I probably wasn't mature enough to realize the full scope of the Depression, but I didn't think I had the heart to run a business and do to people what businesses were doing to my friends. I thought finally that time and money are essentially equivalent: If you had time, you didn't need money. I thought that if I have my own time, if I buy my time back and live that way, I should have a good life."

And so Lee Wulff went out on his own, making more money designing packages for Du Pont as a free lance than he did on salary. After leaving them, "I did commercial artwork and some illustration, some photographs. So I had a good income again, but I still figured I'd lost the heart for business. I started writing a little book about fishing, and lecturing with a friend—a man named Victor Coty, who had started to lecture and make movies. I got started filming with him."

Wulff had learned to fish while still very young, in Alaska. During the New York City days, fishing represented an important break in the continual search for work that every free lance knows. In the manner of urban anglers everywhere, Lee Wulff left the city on weekends to explore the nearby streams—in this case, the Ausable, the Beaverkill, and other famous waters of the Adirondacks and Catskills. His companions on these trips eventually made their own marks as well—one was John McDonald, who became a noted writer for *Fortune,* and another was a young physics teacher named Dan Bailey. Their angling friends included the Catskill fly tiers Reuben Cross and both the Dettes and the Darbees. Wulff and Dan Bailey started a short-lived fly-tying school in a room behind a restaurant in Greenwich Village.

Wulff had been fishing for most of his life, but the professional side of his angling didn't start until then, in the 1930s, partly by design and, apparently, partly by luck.

In 1936, fishing for tuna out of Wedgeport, Nova Scotia, Wulff landed the largest fish of the season. This earned him a coveted place on one of the teams in the first International Tuna Tournament at Wedgeport the following year, 1937. This was the forerunner of all modern angling competitions, and Wulff again took the trophy tuna, which may also have been the largest taken in the world that year. The attendant publicity brought a job with the government of Newfoundland that entailed opening up their tuna fishery, writing stories, filming, and general public relations work. And all the talent, interest, and experience began to take on a focus as broad as it was, in some ways, well defined: Lee Wulff, Outdoorsman.

It has always been my feeling that the *outdoorsman* label refers as much to image as to activity. No one could dispute Wulff's standing as an outdoorsman in terms of activity: he hasn't done it all, but he's done most of it and, likely, far more than you and I put together. And his appearance is right, too; he looks like an outdoorsman: tall, lean, a little craggy in later years. As a short, fat kid, he might never have made it.

In speaking of his early filming days with Coty, he described his role on film as "fisherman," something that would appeal to the outdoor heartstrings of a large audience. "I was his [Coty's] fisherman, and, of course, the most important thing about making fishing films is being able to catch fish. So that demanded the ability to catch fish and to *look* like a fisherman, as it were. To look a little bit special, a little bit as if you had stopped by Abercrombie & Fitch, but not as if you were precisely a classical fisherman. Somebody else could say, 'Well, I could—I will—be like that. I would fish like that. I would wear those things. I would look like that.' "

I suspect that Wulff might be a little embarrassed by that outright theatrical approach now, but perhaps not. He was and is a very pragmatic man, and he was in the business of selling movies. And they sold.

In some ways, the film-and-lecture business was good. "I got a fee for promoting Newfoundland, but it wasn't specifically for making movies, although I did lecture with them. It was disappointing [to me] that John Jay, who was doing lecturing on skiing at about the same time with about the same quality film, . . . got all kinds of fees and things because the ski people were homogeneous, [whereas] I did the fishing clubs and so on at much lower fees. The one good source I had was the Chicago Executives Club, probably the best platform in the country, and I would draw the biggest crowd every year—twenty-seven years in a row.

"Yet the other men's clubs, even clubs like that, never picked up on hunting and fishing as a subject. I would get a thousand people in the Hotel Sherman [Chicago], where Nixon [as] vice-president, or General Bradley, or somebody else . . . wouldn't draw more than two hundred fifty people. It was a very popular thing, and so I made films sometimes just for that, making sure I had a new program every year."

The filming and lecturing continued and grew, and, as Wulff explains, "When fishing finally got to television, I had the first network fishing show, on CBS's 'Sports Spectacular,' which was a combination hunting and fishing show, and I had the fishing part of it. It started me off on television then for the next few years, through 1964. In '64 I was on CBS and also on ABC's 'American Sportsman.' From then on I was with 'American Sportsman' for about ten years. I produced those first ABC shows, and then they wanted to bring them in-house, so I became a field producer or sometimes the talented fisherman." His talent as a producer was no less noticeable; a wall of television and film awards in the Wulffs' house attests to that. Even now, his forty-year-old fishing movies are fresh and bright and even awesome.

I hadn't wanted to interrupt that train of thought but

was aware that we'd skipped a great many things. So we backtracked, and I asked questions. In 1937, Lee Wulff was living in New York. In 1939, he moved a then-new family upstate to Chappaqua, and two years later moved again to the banks of the Battenkill River in Shushan, New York, near the Vermont state line, where he lived for nearly twenty years.

About that move, he said, "I didn't want a child of mine to grow up in the city. A kid in the city has no place of his own. He's always with you or with older people, whereas in the country he can go off and be by himself, have his own life, his own area, his own decisions to make. He can holler and he can do what he wants."

Wulff recalls that in the fall of 1940, when he moved to the Battenkill, the fishing was excellent and the fishing pressure relatively low. By the time he moved to near Keene, in south-central New Hampshire, in 1961, the pressure on the Battenkill had increased dramatically and, he says, spin fishing had substantially reduced the river's large stock of brown and brook trout.

Keene, he said, "is an hour away from New York by plane, but still two hundred miles from New York in the country. You can get off a plane and start hunting woodcock from the airport." It was while living in New Hampshire that he met and subsequently married Joan Salvato, the former national fly-casting champion now better known as Joan Wulff.

In 1978 came another move, to the Beaverkill River, not far from Roscoe, New York, in the Catskills. As he told me, "It [the move] was in order to set up a school here. Joan is a natural teacher, a very fine teacher, and probably the best caster for her weight ever. We felt that between us we could put together a school that would have not only good casting instruction, but a good fishing philosophy basically. So we moved over here to have the school.

"I'd come over the year before [1977] to give a lecture to the Eastern Federation of Fly Fishermen Conclave in Roscoe, and I hadn't been to the Catskills to fish since the early days of the thirties, when I came here all the time. It was almost like coming home; there were people in waders walking around on the streets. I was talking to an audience that had a good feeling and who knew instinctively what I was talking about. I think I gave one of the best talks I've ever given because of that audience. And we decided this was where we should have our school."

After a year or so of getting organized, constructing a school building, working on the ponds, and so forth, their fly-fishing school opened and has been increasingly successful. It's unique in many ways; for example, it is the only major school not associated with a tackle manufacturer. But where else can you go to a fly-fishing school with Joan and Lee Wulff?

Once again in a simple conversation we had skipped about a hundred things I was eager to know about, and we backtracked further. Probably no living man is directly responsible for so many important fly-fishing innovations as Lee Wulff. I'll describe some of them, but I was most interested in the kind of thinking that had produced them in the first place.

"I've always tried to go back to the beginning; not to start halfway up, because the bricks you build on, if they aren't true, everything above them isn't solid. I think [Edward] Hewitt was an inspiration, because even though Hewitt was wrong a lot of the time, he thought in ways that no one had ever thought.

"I made the first fly-fishing vest, in 1932, and I sold it. As I sold the next one and the next one, I made improvements. It had a great advantage, but to many people it looked ridiculous—wearing a vest over your clothes instead of under them. Vermont fishermen, for example, wore a wading jacket, and their pockets got wet when they waded deep. The wading jacket was really to keep water from splashing over their boots. This [fishing vest] changed that; it was simple and comfortable."

For the sake of space, I have to skip many parts of Wulff's life that deserve better treatment: the invention of the Wulff dry flies during the late 1930s; a long friendship with Dan Bailey;

the development of techniques to photograph striking and jumping fish while playing them himself. The 1950s saw his design of the first modern palming-spool reels (that Lee Wulff Ultimate, prototype by Stan Bogdan, manufactured for a short time by Farlow, in England); the development and patenting of plastic-body flies (to which the customary materials could be attached easily without thread); flies with wings of looped hackle; flies built on flexible tubing, which could be fished singly or in series if a larger fly was needed; the Fly-O (designed for safe, indoor fly-casting instruction and practice); and, very recently, the unique Triangle Taper fly line. These are just a few bits of Wulff history.

I was curious about his reputed affinity for shorter-than-normal fly rods. As most readers will recall, he became well known for taking Atlantic salmon on fly rods as short as 6 feet, at a time when heavier rods of 9, 10, or more feet were considered essential. But some people asked at the time why he didn't use a rod even shorter than 6 feet. As he explained, "Well, I had already gone and caught a fish [salmon] with no rod at all [only a reel, casting by hand], just to prove that if you were good enough you could do it with skill alone. I used a six-foot rod because that was the smallest rod I felt I could use without feeling handicapped in some way by not having enough cushion to play a fish or whatever. Six feet was where I arbitrarily set a limit."

"You wound up," I said, "with a reputation that in a lot of quarters continues to stick: being an expert on short rods, period."

"Well, that's one of the unfortunate things that happens when people read only half of what you say. . . . To me, the little rod was a challenge; it's not a better way to fish. There were some advantages, such as when you handle your own fish [a short rod lets you tail a salmon more easily], which people didn't do before."

"So it is," I continued, "perfectly all right if I fish for salmon with a nine-foot rod?"

He smiled. "It's a perfectly sensible way to fish."

Here's another question I'd wondered about for some time, together with Wulff's answer.

"You know," I said, "in many ways you have been described—by yourself as well as by others—as nontraditional and profiting thereby. What value is there in a fishing tradition? Is there any?"

"Oh, yes," he answered. "It works. It may not work quite as well as something else, but it works. It is a way to fix a pattern. The [bad] thing is that once you say *this is the way*—well, you close your eyes."

I haven't touched on his flying days, which aren't over, and which spawned countless fascinating stories. I've said little about his monumental efforts in the conservation field, where, for example, he was largely responsible for the recent creation of the Atlantic Salmon Federation, an international group formed primarily from the combination of the Atlantic Salmon Association and the International Atlantic Salmon Foundation. It is a new, united front to champion the cause of salmon conservation and management. I haven't described how our many conversations have been as much about fine art or gardening as about fish and fishing. I have to skip that and more, to tell a story or two before finishing.

To tell one of them, I have to break a long-standing rule of my own: I dislike writers who persist in name-dropping, and I have spent years blue-penciling same. I can't tell this story without doing just that, however, and ask a little indulgence.

In March 1983, Joe Cullman and Gardner Grant threw a testimonial dinner for Lee Wulff at the Anglers' Club of New York. Seventy-five of his friends were invited; people whom he'd helped and people who had helped him. All during dinner, people who were familiar with different portions of his life stood to give brief presentations. Ernie Schwiebert emceed and, for example, Curt Gowdy talked about the "American Sportsman" days, and Angus Cameron and Ed Zern, among others, added their comments. It was truly a wonderful thing to behold, this testimony to the "Royal Wulff," where captains of industry, writers, fishermen, hunters, and others joined in an evening of toasts and tributes. It was also humbling. I went so far as to steal one of Nick Lyons's cigars, which made me feel a little better.

Anyway, toward the end of the evening, Wulff had to stand at the head table and say thanks. He did so very quietly and briefly, with a voice that trembled gently and with a tear or two on each cheek. That instant was one of the loveliest things I've ever seen.

It was not, however, the most impressive thing I've ever seen him do. That has nothing directly to do with hunting or fishing. A few years ago, we sat on a sunny slope behind his house, where he, at seventy-seven years, was busy grafting small apple trees, no more than a foot high. It was a quiet time, and we talked quietly about apples, the woods, the clearing, the land, what trees did what in the spring. He was as much a small boy discovering the world as an old man who had seen it all. Who, I wondered, would eat those apples, decades from now?

Have you ever walked by a hole in a hollow tree and wondered what was in it? I think of that in trying to find one simple way to characterize Lee Wulff. The poet Robert Frost once compared technology's evolution to the activity of a small boy poking sticks into animal burrows simply to see if anything is there. The same thought might explain, in part, the evolution of Lee Wulff.

We'll trace parts of that evolution together in this book, from his thoughts on conservation more than fifty years ago to his current efforts at having Atlantic salmon achieve legal gamefish status. We'll fish—and learn thereby—with Wulff for everything from trout to tarpon. We'll go through our tackle together, and get his suggestions about what we might do better. After the fishing, we'll think and talk quietly about where we've been.

And through all of this we'll have no better friend and teacher than Lee Wulff.

JOHN MERWIN

Dorset, Vermont
February 1989

Book One

TALKING
TACKLE

Lee Wulff has been an angling innovator in tackle and tactics for more than sixty years, and even now the flow of ideas seems unending. Every time I talk with him he's trying out a new one on me. In this section he explains the origins of his world-famous Wulff dry flies and many of his other fly patterns. We stand witness to the time he jumped off a bridge while wearing chest waders to prove that he—and anybody else—need not drown as a result.

And here we find him urging us to use shorter rods and lighter tackle to catch more and larger fish, not (he says) because shorter rods are necessarily better, but because working through the challenge will make you a better fisherman. Palming-spool fly reels are common these days, but they're a Wulff innovation. We'll find out why in this section and much, much more.

1

Experiment
in Waders

This is one of Lee Wulff's most famous stories and, in the forty-odd years since he wrote it, has become an oft-cited part of American angling lore. The notion still persists, however, that falling in while wearing chest waders is tantamount to drowning, in spite of Wulff's having proven otherwise. I have heard the discussion often in various fishing camps, usually accompanied by one or more sordid examples, but now someone almost always interjects: "Remember when Lee Wulff jumped off the bridge?"

Taking a popular angling notion and either expanding it greatly or proving it untrue has been a hallmark of Wulff's career. It is a theme you'll find throughout this book, to the ultimate benefit of your own fishing as it has been for thousands of others.

It was a thrilling tale and this is the way it went:

The old guide reached for an ember from the fire and stood hunched over, lighting his pipe. Then, exhaling the first sweet clouds of aromatic Beaver in a long breath, he joined his grotesque shadow on the ground and leaned back against the pack basket to continue his story.

"There was two of us guiding this old sport from New York down on the Grey River and we was camped a couple of miles below the falls. Like I told you, the fishing was poor but we was taking a salmon now and again, mostly at the Falls Pool. Well, this feller spotted a big fish in the pool where he was hard to reach casting from shore. Nothing would do then but we must take a canoe up through the rough water to the Falls Pool so he could fish over the big one in proper style and comfort.

"He was a big, heavy feller and oldish with white hair but pretty strong just the same. He had everything fancy with a special fishing jacket that had a place to hold his rod while he stooped over to tie his shoelace, and gadgets and pickets for almost anything you could think of. He carried scissors and a special leader snipper and a spare reel that I s'pose added some weight to the upper part of him fer what come later. He had on them high waders like you're wearing and hobnailed wading shoes that was specially made in England. He always liked to wade best, but after he spotted that fish he quit wading 'cause be couldn't reach him right unless he got into the canoe. He'd sit in the front of the canoe for hours casting his fly over that old walloper of a salmon but the fish never paid no heed to it.

"I was ashore boiling the kettle 'bout noontime when the thing happened. You see, the falls was running pretty heavy and there was a lot of suction right under 'em where the water was boiling and swirling up. We always tried to keep the canoe down toward the tail of the pool but it was hard to fish the fly right from that location and he was always urgin' us to let her slide up a little closer to the falls so he could fish across the current instead of up into it. We'd sit at the stern and jest hold her steady with the paddle, sometimes Art, sometimes me.

"I guess Art, that was the other guide's name, was a little careless this time, 'cause he let the canoe slip in too close to the falls just as that fish took it into his mind to rise to the fly. The sport half stood up off the seat in his excitement, and that

5

throwed the canoe off balance. Next thing I saw the nose of the canoe was heading straight in under that falling water and Art, he hollered and jumped clear of the canoe. I'll never forget watching the old feller disappearing into that rush of white water and the canoe going down into it with him.

"Art couldn't swim no more than I can, but I got a long sapling that was handy on the shore and waded out as far as I could and reached it to him. He was at his last gasp before I got him in to shore. About a minute later the canoe come up toward the tail of the pool, busted almost in half. And then we could see this feller's feet sticking up in the big eddy just below the falls. The air in his waders was floatin' him upside down and he was struggling and strangling 'cause he couldn't get his feet down to get his head up.

"Pretty soon he quit struggling and we could see his hobnailed shoes going 'round and 'round in that eddy, easy-like, and we knew he was done for.

"There wasn't nothing Art or me could do, with the canoe busted and neither of us able to swim, except go down to the village for help and bring up a dory to get out to where he was. So that was the end of that poor feller.

"I sure never would wear those high waders for anything in the world. That feller was a strong swimmer and he never had a chance. Yes, sir! I can close my eyes and still see those wading shoes of his going 'round and 'round in that eddy. . . ."

A ghastly death to consider, isn't it? I've heard the same story, with but slight variations, from California's Merced River to Newfoundland's Grey River. I'm a confirmed wader man, myself. I used to wade wet without regard to depth of water until I started to take the ads in the sporting magazines seriously. Since then I've worn waders and none of them ever seemed quite high enough. Little wonder that after listening to a wise old guide tell a story like that one, those who wear waders vow to take no chances henceforth. But you can relax. The story is pure hooey. You can wear waders and still weather the storm. You, too, can fall in and live to tell it.

Twenty years ago I was a fairly good swimmer. Since then I've been in swimming only a few times a year. In 1920 in a burst of youthful exuberance I dove off a bridge some twenty feet into the Merced River but in the last twenty-odd years I haven't dived from anything higher than the gunwale of a motorboat. So when I stood on the iron framework of the bridge that spans the Battenkill a mile above my home I felt just a teensy bit foolish. It occurred to me that I should have made some mathematical calculations checking on whether or not the amount of air in my waders really might be sufficient to hold me head-down once I hit the water. I could have figured the thing out in a few minutes, even with my rusty mathematics.

It also flashed through my mind that I could have tried swimming in my waders as an intermediate step instead of beginning with a dive into fifteen feet of broad and steadily flowing water. It came to me then that if something did go wrong, Allan, my nine-year-old son, just able to swim, and my one-hundred-pound mother, who never was much of a swimmer anyway, wouldn't be able to do much to rectify the situation. They were taking the picture and there was no one else to help within a half a mile. And lastly, I wondered why I hadn't conceived this sudden urge to prove a point in mid-summer when the water was warm, instead of in October when the water the Green Mountains of Vermont was sending down under the bridge was pretty close to freezing.

I was dressed in the same gear I wear while fishing. My boot-foot waders, held up by suspenders, had the drawstring tied in order to lock in the air. After all, if I left the top loose, some of the imprisoned air might bubble out and lessen the floating powers of the waders and, consequently, save me. As a matter of fact I'd first considered jumping in from the shore but on second thought had decided that some of you readers, seeing a picture of me entering the water at a low angle, might have said, "He fudged! He let a lot of air out of the top of the waders as he went in."

By going in with a vertical dive I felt I was making the conditions as hazardous as they could possibly be. The maximum amount of air would be trapped in my waders. My fly-fishing vest was on over my woollen shirt, although I had emptied from the pockets everything that would be damaged by water. I figured I was neither better nor worse off than

I would be if I fell in while fishing. The water was swift enough to make swimming difficult and plenty deep enough to drown in.

I remembered the time I'd waded out too far in a swift flow and it had taken me down through a long pool, but I'd managed to stay upright and touch bottom now and again as the current swept me along. Of course, there had been no air in my waders then, because the water pressure against them as I waded gradually out toward their limiting depth had forced all the air out of them and made them cling to me as snugly as long winter woollies. Still, it had been enough of an experience to give me a moment's pause. Maybe I'd been lucky that time.

My dive was no masterpiece. I did go in head first, though my wader-clad feet followed at a sloppy angle. The water was cold. I could feel its strength as it closed around me and swept me along over the dimly sunlit gravel of the pool's deep bed. My momentum, together with the angle of my hands and the arch of my back, swept me around in a neat curve and my head popped up out of water almost as quickly as you could say "Arnold Robertson." The midday sun was shining smack into my eyes with a friendly warmth. My mouth was free to drag in all the pure country air my lungs could hold, and my feet were floating nicely but with no tendency whatever to push my head under.

With an ease that made my earlier suspicion of failure completely ridiculous, I swam over to the shore. The air in my waders was probably just enough to give my legs a little buoyancy after supporting the weight of the waders themselves. As I swam, a little water worked in past the drawstring and took away some of this buoyancy, but it made swimming no more difficult and no less comfortable.

That short swim was surprisingly pleasant. After the first shock of meeting the water, it didn't feel so cold and I seemed to swim almost as fast and as easily with the clothes and waders on as I do in a bathing suit. Maybe the broad felt soles of the waders served as swim fins and gave me a little extra speed. At any rate I swam ashore to bury forever the myth of those wading brogues going 'round and 'round while the man beneath them slowly gasped out his life.

My waders, when dry, weigh just six pounds. If I'd worn wading brogues over stocking-foot waders instead of the boot-foot type, there would have been less danger of my feet coming to the top, for, obviously, the more weight on my feet the less floating effect the air in the waders would have. If I'd gone in with the drawstring loose and let the waders fill with water, they obviously wouldn't have floated any part of me.

Just for fun I did let my waders fill with water later and swam along with no difficulty because, ever since Archimedes made his naked dash through Syracuse shouting "Eureka!" every schoolboy has known that objects under water weigh only the difference between their weight and the weight of the water they displace. Submerged and filled with water my waders weighed a lot less than six pounds and no matter how much water I let into them, that water had no weight beneath the surface and hence could not handicap my swimming.

So wear your waders with a gay spirit, fellow anglers, and worry not about falling off logs into deep water while wearing them, or of wading to more than their depth in a vain effort to reach a fish so large that a good bath is a small price to pay for the privilege of putting a fly over him. But wade with care, even so, for wading is an art and there is always the possibility of accident while traveling fast water, whether decked out by U.S. Rubber or Hodgman or unadorned in your buff.

Two dangers have always concerned me while wading and will continue to be bright in my mind so long as I follow the flowing water afoot. I know that I can swim well enough to get to shore in any river. My greatest concern is that I might fall and strike my head against a boulder. Unconscious, my ability to swim would be of small help.

A foot caught between two rocks in swift, deep water spells a serious problem. I believe that I'd have strength enough to pull it out, and breath enough to keep me going until I did. Either I'd try to get my wader foot loose or I'd break my suspenders free at the buttons and pull myself out of the waders. It may sound difficult, but I'm convinced that it would be simple enough (anybody want to bet?).

To break a leg or sprain an ankle while wading shouldn't be fatal. One can swim well enough with the arms alone even if both legs are disabled. A broken arm is not enough to disable a fair swimmer or to stop him short of reaching shore.

All this presupposes that the wader can swim. If he can't, things will be a little tougher for him but they are still far from hopeless. If he's swept into deep water, the same current that sweeps him in should sweep him out if he can manage to stay afloat or catch an occasional breath, even if only for a short time. If the water is swift but not over his head, wading skill is far more important than swimming ability, and a sense of balance is more valuable than a knowledge of swimming in a spot where swimming is foolish, anyway.

If you can't swim and want to fish deep and dangerous water, wear one of the smallest life belts. You'd be amazed to see how little in the way of inflated rubber or kapok will float a heavy man. No! If you're going to drown while wading it will not be because waders are dangerous, but because of a heart attack or by being knocked unconscious or because of the one factor that causes more fatalities in accidents than any other—panic!

I didn't mention panic in my own worries because I think I've covered in my mind most of the types of wading trouble I'm likely to encounter. When and if I do encounter them, I figure I'll be too busy to go into a dither. I've been through a few tight squeaks and invariably my mind goes to action rather than helpless fear. But if you aren't the type to be calm and collected in a crisis, and if you can't swim, then friends, be careful.

But forget for good and all that foolish fear that chest waders will turn you upside down and send you to your just reward if you make a misstep near deep water. It isn't so, and I think I've proved it.

[1947]

10

2

The Left Hand
Is the Right One

During the 1700s and until about 1860—the period during which fishing reels came into widespread use—all fishing reels looked more or less like bait-casting reels (although bait-casting reels per se weren't developed until the 1820s) and were designed to be cranked right-handed while being used on top of the rod. After the Civil War fly casting as a method became more popular, and fly reels designed to be mounted under the rod were widely developed. Unfortunately, the right-hand-wind design persisted, and to this day generations of fly fishermen cast right-handed and then switch hands to be able to wind right-handed as well, even though most modern fly reels can be simply converted from right- to left-hand winding.

During the 1940s Wulff was the fishing editor for Outdoors *magazine, and in this particular essay suggested that his readers start winding left-handed for a variety of still-excellent reasons. At the time it was revolutionary, and although many anglers have since followed his advice, you'll still see right-handed crankers from the Beaverkill to the Beaverhead. If you're among them, it's time to switch!*

People who have seen me fly fishing are often surprised when they see me whittle or write or do anything that requires manual dexterity. They are surprised because they expect me to be left-handed. It is the old, old story of everyone else being out of step. I'm right-handed and I reel my fly reels with my left hand. Here's why:

Being right-handed, I hold the fly rod in that hand while casting. It's not that I can't cast left-handed; I just do it a lot better and more easily with my right. That makes sense. When it comes to playing a fish, the strength required to hold the rod is far greater than that required to turn the reel handle, so I use my stronger arm for the job requiring more strength. That makes sense, too.

However, most fly-rod anglers switch their rods from their right hands to their left when playing a fish in order to reel with their right hands. They do this because their left hands are clumsy and aren't trained for the manipulation of small things like reel handles. This idea has some logic behind it because it saves the necessity of training the left hand to reel, but it means that when playing a big fish, the left hand tires easily and because of that the fish may be lost. It also means that the rod must be changed from hand to hand whenever a fish is hooked. In contrast, with left-handed reeling, the rod always remains in the right hand, the strong hand, where it belongs.

Left-hand reeling (for the right-handed fly fisherman) is much more important with large fish than with small ones. With the little fellows the problem is one of maintaining a delicate pressure. There is seldom much line out and no great strain is put on the rod either to restrain the fish or to hold a long line clear of snags. With the lunkers it's different. It takes real muscle power to handle the rod properly then, and even a strong right arm is likely to wind up pretty tired after a 5-pounder has been brought in.

A right-hand reeler often finds his left hand too tired to hold the rod up when it is playing a big fish and, as a result, changes his rod back and forth during the battle in order to give that left arm a rest. The fact that this change must be made is proof that the left hand just isn't up to the job. That's why many fly rods for big fish are made with a detachable double grip so that they can be rested against the body as an aid to the weak left hand. If you reel left-handed, you won't have to bother with a double-grip fly rod for big fish.

On the basis of pure logic the rod should always remain in the right hand, both for casting and playing the fish. I switched over to left-hand reeling so far back that I can't remember the switch, but I've converted a number of fishermen to my way and they've made the change with little or no difficulty. Some of them switched while in the midst of fishing for salmon or big trout. Others have had a chance to limber up their left hand with some reeling practice before they tried it out on the stream. The latter is a safer, surer way.

A half hour's practice out on your lawn for three evenings in a row will work wonders. Even sitting in your favorite armchair with only the butt joint of your rod, reel attached, in your right hand and your left hand turning the reel handle will soon familiarize you with the movements needed and quickly build up the necessary muscular strength.

The only drawback to making the change is that some reels are designed to be used with the right hand and have line guides or special drags or clicks to work best that way. For left-hand reeling the reel must be placed on the fly rod so that the reel handle is to the left when the reel is below the rod. Left-handed reels are obtainable in such cases, and when there is no line guard the change can be made from right to left hand simply by removing the line from the reel and rewinding it in the opposite direction.

During these war years [This chapter was first published in 1946.] I've been using a right-handed reel equipped with a line guard for my left hand by simply ignoring the line guard and passing the line out of the other side without a guard. The effectiveness of a line guard, incidentally, is something not universally admitted. I know a number of fishermen who have removed them on the grounds that they do more harm than good in guiding the line onto the reel.

In starting to reel left-handed, many fishermen have a tendency to hold the reel handle rigid and move the rod and the rest of the reel around that central point as a pivot. The

13

reeling is accomplished, all right, but it's pretty awkward. However, this phase, if it develops at all, will soon pass and the left hand will adjust itself to its new task and function smoothly. I urge you to give left-hand reeling a thorough trial. I know that many of you will be converted and will find that fishing and playing your fish will become pleasanter, easier, and more effective.

This business of left-hand reeling is not suitable for bait casting, because then the reeling is likely to consume more energy than the actual casting does. The bait-casting rod is normally held against the body for the reeling, which requires a change of hands from the rear grip to the front one. Since the grip of the hand on the rod must be changed anyway, it is easier to change from the right hand on the lower grip to the left hand on the upper one with the butt pressed against the body and the right hand reeling than it is to change from the right hand on the rear grip to the left hand of the foregrip and then back again to the right hand on the foregrip with the butt pressed against the body and the left hand reeling. Thus left-hand reeling in this sport would mean an extra motion on every cast plus the cost of a left-handed reel, since no level-winding bait-casting reel can be switched from right- to left-hand winding satisfactorily.

Only if the fisherman holds his rod with his right hand on the lower grip both in casting and reeling (a tiring business in case you've never tried it) would left-hand reeling have the same advantage here as it does for the fly fisherman. Few fishermen have the hand and arm strength to do this for any length of time. For all those who hold the rod against the body for reeling, the strong, well-trained hand is the one they should apply to the reel handle.

[1946]

3

How to Use Dry Flies for Atlantic Salmon

Both Edward Hewitt and George LaBranche helped to popularize dry-fly salmon fishing through their books published in the 1920s, Hewitt having been introduced to the sport by Colonel Ambrose Monell, who was taking Canadian salmon by this method as early as 1912. In what may have been the earliest North American account, Theodore Gordon alluded to this approach in a 1903 Fishing Gazette *article, describing his tying of dry flies for a Restigouche angler.*

But no one before or since has had a greater influence on salmon-fishing tactics than Lee Wulff, and that includes the dry-fly method. Not only did Wulff develop the most important salmon dry-fly patterns (a story told in Chapter 10), he has, through his books and articles over five decades, been the most important factor in making dry-fly fishing for Atlantic salmon accepted worldwide. Here, then, is an important tutorial from the acknowledged master.

Not too many years ago I could go to almost any salmon river with the foreknowledge that no one else would be using a dry fly. The ability to fish either wet or dry gave me a distinct advantage over other anglers, for salmon that had resisted everything in a long list of wet flies often would rise to a floater on the first few casts. Confirmed wet-fly men, seeing the pioneer dry-fly anglers taking fish under conditions where all wet flies were scorned, soon took up the floating fly as a second method.

The results were not always so fruitful as they had hoped because dry-fly fishing for salmon also has its periods of failure. Not only are there limitations in the times when floaters are effective but certain types of water have special problems, and success varies both with the individual river and with the inclinations of the fish. The generally accepted rule is that Atlantic salmon will not take dry flies when they first enter the rivers on their spawning migrations. This is largely true.

Salmon returning from their sea migrations have their memory of surface feeding dimmed by the saltwater period of their lives, a year or more during which they have taken no food from the surface. While they are in salt water, all the food they take swims through the water in the manner of a wet fly and none of it floats on the surface like a dry one. This may account for some of the salmon's preference for a sunken fly and reluctance to take a floater when he first comes back to the streams. Later on when he's been in fresh water again for a while, the association of his stream location with his early habits as a parr feeding on floating insects reasserts his youthful urge for surface feeding. This is an intangible factor and one that cannot be calculated, but for anyone who knows the habits of salmon and their reactions to similar minor inner urges it is a logical one.

When the water is rough and high and the fish are deep, a good presentation cannot be made with the dry fly, and these are the conditions normally prevailing at the outset of the season. But despite the general rule and the reasons for it, fresh-run fish can be taken on the floating fly. I have taken them as early as June 1 in Newfoundland, with sea lice still clinging to their sides.

I have a simple rule about when to start dry-fly fishing. I fish wet in the early season until I see a fish "porpoise," or make a surface roll that brings the upper half of his body out into the air. This gives me his exact location in the pool and tells me that he's surface-minded. A porpoising fish in the early days of the salmon run is duck soup for a properly presented dry fly. Later on, when the salmon porpoise much more freely, these surface rolls will not have the same significance. Also, in the early season, if I can determine the exact position of a fish as indicated by a jump or swirl at my fly, I may present a dry fly to him when the wet one fails. The biggest handicap to dry-fly fishing in the early high water is the difficulty of presenting the fly to enough fish.

Dry-fly fishing is most successful when the water is low and the fish are concentrated in groups in the pools. There are two factors involved in this fishing and they work out this way. A wet fly when cast covers, let us assume, the fishable width of a small river. The fly lands on the far side and swings all the way across the flow to the near side, covering at least 40 feet. During the same period of time a dry fly cast out on the same water would drift not more than 10 feet downstream from the point at which it landed. The wet fly as a consequence reaches four times as many fish as the floating feathers. When the salmon are scattered over a wide area, the advantage is always with the wet fly. Later on in the summer when the water drops and the salmon tend to congregate in small groups in known locations, the dry fly in its short float will be presented to as many fish as a wet fly on its full swing because most of the wet fly's travel is through barren water.

The speed of the water is the second factor. A wet fly moves faster than a dry fly in order to cover more water but the dry fly occupies an important place in the salmon's vision for a longer period of time. The wet fly moves in contrast with the objects the water carries instead of at their identical speed and is therefore more conspicuous. The wet fly is first glimpsed out of one eye as it approaches, then just ahead as it passes, and finally going away on the other side. The dry fly, difficult to distinguish amid the ripples, debris, and surface foam that convey it, approaches head on and disappears into the salmon's area of blindness behind him.

When the waters slow down and lose much of their surface motion, the dry fly becomes more conspicuous and increasingly effective. This speed of the water is in direct ratio to the speed of the dry relative to the streambed.

The speed of the current is only one of two factors with the wet fly. It is affected by the pull of the angler through his tackle as well as by the movement of the water. The angler's pull normally is used to impart speed as well as direction but the tackle can be used to slow down the movement of a wet fly in relation to the streambed. Even if the tackle is not used to slow the wet fly it still helps maintain it in a better position for the salmon to see and rise to it than the dry fly, for which, in swift water, a salmon must make a downstream rush.

The clearer the water, the better for dry-fly fishing. It has been my observation that rivers with peat-stained waters are not so good for dry-fly fishing as those that are clear. In the early season almost all the northern rivers run dark brown with peat stain coming from the runoff of bog water in their drainages. Some of them carry the brown stain all through the season but the stain is less noticeable once the main flow comes from springs instead of runoff. It is at this point that most streams reach their peak for dry-fly effectiveness. Anglers who have had successful dry-fly fishing on a clear river may suffer a rude shock when they try the same flies on a dark one.

The salmon's interest in a wet fly seems to taper off as the season progresses. It may have sudden revivals after heavy rains but wet-fly effectiveness generally shows a persistent downward trend as time passes. The interest in the dry fly, in contrast, seems to build up consistently until the end of the season; and for this I have no explanation beyond those already given. It is pertinent to add here, however, that though the interest continues to build up, the chance of hooking a fish on the dry fly reaches a peak some weeks after the wet-fly peak and then drops off because of the particular penchant of the Atlantic salmon for making "false rises," a subject that will come up for considerable discussion later on.

Salmon, I believe, rise to a dry fly out of a restless impulse coupled with their memories of the thousands of floating insects they devoured while spending the greater part of their lifetime in the rivers as parr. They rise out of a memory of all surface flies and very rarely in the manner of a trout that is feeding on a particular hatch of insects and seeking an exact imitation. The effective salmon dry fly should look like an insect but it need not look like any special insect; it should have the quality of looking like *all* bugs instead of just one. Consequently, few dry flies are needed for fishing for Atlantic salmon. I like to have a variety of shapes and sizes but I do not consider minor variations in silhouette and coloring important.

A good selection might include some bivisibles (#6–#10), some White Wulffs and Gray Wulffs (#4–#10), a few Black Gnats (#10–#14), and some spiders (#14–#16). To this basic groundwork may be added any patterns that lend confidence to the angler and distinction to his fly boxes. A high-floating, durable fly has a big advantage in salmon fishing as it requires less attention and can be fished cast after cast when the pressure is on and a time-out period to re-oil the fly might upset a campaign of consistent casting to which a certain salmon should succumb.

When a trout fisherman refers to a *rise*, he means that a trout came up and took, or tried to take, his fly. When a salmon angler uses this same term he means that a salmon moved up to *look* at his fly, perhaps taking it but more likely turning away short. A trout, moving up close to take a fly, rarely turns away short of taking it. With a salmon, a fish that may never have seen an artificial fly before and is much less schooled in the detection of insect "fakes" than the trout, the reverse is true. More salmon are hooked after one or more false passes at the fly than are connected with on their first pass at it. Time after time a salmon may rise to the dry fly falsely before taking it, and in many instances he will rise and rise without ever opening his jaws.

As a result of many hours of stalking, I've had a closeup view of hundreds of salmon rising to my own and my friends' dry flies. At a distance of from six to ten feet I have watched them ease up gracefully from the bottom, with their mouths locked shut, to push a dry fly up into the air on the tips of their noses. I have seen them put their chins up over the fly and

19

sink it with the same maddening deliberation. They will sometimes swamp a floating fly with their tails; more often than not they will simply come up below it, materializing as if out of nowhere, put their noses up to within an inch of it, and then turn downward again, leaving the fly bouncing madly on the rumpled surface of the water.

The false rises made by salmon have thrown a good many inexperienced dry-fly anglers off the track. Salmon rises are rare, and on many rivers two or three a day is considered good. Consider the novice angler's situation. He has heard conflicting reports on the timing of his strike. One acquaintance has told him he must strike quickly, as soon as he sees the rise. Another has insisted that a strike is not necessary and that the fish will take the fly down with him and hook himself. Still another may insist that a salmon's rise is like that of a deliberate old brown trout and the strike should come as soon as the fish has the fly in his mouth and starts downward.

When the novice gets his first rise he strikes quickly—and misses. Next time he tries striking a little later—and still he misses. Finally, he lets the salmon take his fly down with him and feels a gentle tug but fails to hook the fish. In each one he has done the wrong thing and is still no closer to the solution of when to strike. His first two rises were false and he should not have struck at all, but in the excitement of seeing so large a fish boil up under his fly he was unprepared to make a thorough check on that little matter of making sure the fish actually took the fly. His third rise was a good one and because he failed to strike he also failed to set the hook.

The dry-fly angler should always strike his salmon when the fish closes his mouth on the fly. The dry fly, without drag, is always fished with some slack in the line. This slack must be tightened and enough pressure added to drive the hook into the flesh beyond the barb. The salmon tends to spit out the dry fly soon after taking it. In my own tests those fish that took the fly and were given slack were rarely hooked.

Salmon do rise to a dry fly much in the manner of an old brown trout. They like to come up under the fly, suck it in, and go down again. With the suckdown the fly is usually safely in the salmon's mouth before the angler can verify its disappearance. Salmon rise in many other ways, the most spectacular of them being the head-and-tail rise in which the fish opens his mouth an instant before his jaws break the surface. He takes the fly, closing his jaws on it, and rolls on over into a downward drive that brings the upper half of his body above the water and shows a large part of his tail as he submerges.

This is his most deliberate rise and—unlike the one in which he sucks the fly down from beneath—is the one that offers the greatest tendency to strike too soon. As a rule, salmon are deliberate risers and no matter how swiftly they must move to reach the fly, they tend to take it gently. But this is not always the case and some salmon will take the dry fly on their way out of water on a clean, high leap, a rare spectacle that once seen can never be forgotten, and I have even recorded this type of rise on movie film.

Some salmon have a habit of waiting until the dry fly has drifted over them and passed on down into their blind area. Then, turning with a rush and almost always making the turn away from the angler, of whom they are already aware, they come around downstream to take the fly. They rush at the fly, openmouthed, heading downstream and toward the angler, already turning back at the take to complete the circle to their former lie. I am ashamed to admit how many times in such cases I have lifted the fly right out of that cotton-white open mouth without giving it a chance to close.

I know of no more exciting moment than the false rise of a salmon, no moment in the sport that requires greater control and judgment. The angler must have keen enough vision and must watch his fly so closely that he can determine whether the salmon really takes the fly or just comes up alongside and opens his mouth, missing the floating feathers by a fraction of an inch. If the fly is taken he must strike; and if that great fish, suddenly appearing after hours of inactivity, does not close his jaws on the fly, he must not twitch his rod arm even a little bit but must hold steady and let the fly drift carelessly on its uninterrupted path.

Such control is far from easy but it is essential to the taking of many of these curious fish. If the fly is yanked away at the false rise, the fish will usually sulk and come no more. If the fly drifts on and the salmon keeps returning to look it over, sooner or later he can be brought to the steel.

The Atlantic salmon essentially cares not for food on his return to the rivers and he needs none. He may take a dry fly on its first pass over him, he may rise a dozen times and then take it, he may rise twenty times and lose interest, or he may not rise at all. Salmon have not the wary brown trout's aversion to the dragging dry fly. They do not find "drag" unnatural, and some anglers make a practice of fishing for them that way. My experience leads me to believe that the dry fly is far more successful when fished in the conventional manner without drag and I fish it just as I would for brown trout with emphasis on the timing of casts and consistently uniform delivery. However, before giving up on a sulky fish I often drag the fly across just in front of him, sometimes pulling it under the surface just over his nose, and these tricks have been rewarded by some savage rises.

One of the advantages of dry-fly fishing is that more than half the time a sharp-eyed angler can see his fish before he hooks him. The easiest way is to fish the dry fly across the stream. Then the least effort is required and the stripping of line is held to a minimum. The fly floats in a path abreast of the angler and not decidedly toward or away from him. From this position it is possible to see the flash of the big fish as he rises for a look at the fly. In this respect dry-fly fishing for salmon differs from fishing the floaters for trout.

The trout angler looks only for rises that actually show a fish breaking the surface; the salmon angler must look for flashes of the fish well down in the water. Failure to spot these interested fish, whose presence may be given away only by the slightest flash or shadowy movement, often means the difference between success and failure. For of a dozen salmon in a pool, many of which may be porpoising and leaping, the one most likely to take the fly is the one that shows restlessness when it passes over him.

A salmon may rise only a foot from the bottom and still be two or three feet under the fly on his first show of interest; but if the angler sees him, he has found a likely prospect and is on his way to some sport. This is an important phase of dry-

fly fishing that few anglers have yet mastered. Remember—
salmon do not always look like salmon. Sometimes all one
sees is a bit of white under his chin or the light spot on his tail,
or the white slit of his open mouth or a combination of mouth
and tail, correctly spaced. It may be the shadow, often more
conspicuous than the fish himself, that gives away a salmon's
location by its movement.

The dry-fly angler from his position abreast of the fly has
a better chance of locating these likely prospects than has the
wet-fly fisherman. The wet fly is presented to the salmon well
downstream from the angler, and the fish that move toward it
are pointed toward the angler at the time, exposing not the
silvery length of their bodies but the small, head-on view.

Under these conditions they can rarely be seen and usually remain unidentified unless they make a noticeable swirl
as they turn away from the fly, and the angler, unaware of
their presence and location, fails to concentrate on that spot
and so fails to connect. My experience in locating fish under
the dry fly has improved my ability to spot these slight movements and so had added to my wet-fly effectiveness.

The same tricks that will fool wary brown trout are
worthwhile when used for salmon. Long, fine leaders will
bring more rises. Casting a downstream loop so that the fly
reaches the fish before the filament does is important. The dry-
fly fisherman should work upstream, so that his dragging fly,
returning from each cast, passes over the heads of the fish he
has given up as a bad job and not over those farther upstream
that he still hopes to catch. In dry-fly fishing for salmon there
are no rules that cannot be broken. The floating fly can be
fished upstream, across the current, or downstream. Salmon
may take it with drag or without, or they may finally succumb
to it when pulled underwater on the retrieve.

A leader of from 12 to 14 feet is average for salmon on
the dry fly and it can taper down to a fine end ranging from
.013 to .010 of an inch. When the fish won't cooperate on that
basis keep adding tippets and making the leader longer and
finer, up to your ability to land the fish. There's no point in
hooking fish that are certain to be lost because to do so may
eliminate a chance at them another day. My limit in fineness

for grilse (5-pound average) is 4X and for the larger fish of 10 pounds upward, 2X. Below that limit I believe my chances of bringing in the fish are not worth the risk of missing a possible rise that might come anyway if I continue with leaders of the same weight and strength. The novice should use a point or two coarser to give himself a chance.

Single-handed rods are preferable for dry-fly salmon fishing because they simplify the stripping of line so essential to that type of fishing. There is a lot more casting to be done with the dry fly than with the wet, and a rod that is light enough to permit long periods of fishing is to be preferred over one that tires the arm quickly.

A detachable butt is wise for the confirmed right-hand reeler, but being right-handed I use my right hand to hold the rod *all* the time whether casting or playing a fish and reel with my left, or weaker, hand. This is the best utilization of normally developed skills, I believe, and permits me to move about freely while playing the fish and to hold the rod higher, shift its angle more readily, and generally have better control of a hooked fish.

There is probably no sight in all fishing more exciting than the rise of a salmon to a dry fly. The playing of any species of fish tends to fit into a pattern and follow a certain routine if you catch enough of them. But the rise of an Atlantic salmon is so varied and unpredictable that there is never any routine about it. A salmon that will keep fooling around with my dry fly, showing a definite interest and giving me an occasional view of his silvery bulk without letting me tag him, presents a problem so intriguing that I would rather find one such fish to work on than several that will whip up and latch on to the fly the first time over.

The angler-versus-salmon duel with the dry fly is, to my way of thinking, the most exciting thing in all angling. It may go on for hours—or for days—and it can be a most exasperating as well as a most satisfying experience.

[1951]

4

The Riffling Hitch

This chapter describes a wet-fly method that Lee Wulff found in the Newfoundland backcountry during the 1940s and subsequently added to the salmon fisher's lexicon worldwide. A wet fly fished as described here makes a small surface wake as it swings across the current and may thus elicit a strike when other methods don't.

As Wulff predicted when he first publicized the riffling hitch, its use has become transcontinental and not solely for Atlantic salmon. The northwestern steelhead that enter their spawning rivers through the fall— so-called summer-run fish—are often more aggressive than their winter-run brethren and are more apt to respond to flies fished near the surface. The riffling hitch can be especially effective for these fish, as many a transplanted salmon angler has discovered to his immediate satisfaction.

The riffling hitch was hidden away in the Newfoundland wilderness for over a quarter of a century, but now the idea is spreading to other salmon rivers—and to other fly-rod waters as well. It is time that the method, its origin, and something of its special effectiveness should be described at length.

This particular technique, which borrows from both wet- and dry-fly procedures, promises to become a third distinct method of fly fishing, suited not only to Atlantic salmon but to trout, black bass, pickerel, tarpon, and perhaps other gamefish where water conditions are right.

The riffling hitch began at Portland Creek, a short, broad river on Newfoundland's northwest coast that has consistently led all the other rivers of the province in the average weight of salmon since the establishment of fishing camps there. It empties on a rough stretch of coastline, forty miles from the nearest harbor. Since Newfoundland's travel until recently has either been by sea or by rail (seventy miles distant), this lack of a harbor has meant almost complete isolation for the few settlers in the area. Before 1946 only a handful of anglers fished the river. One of them was Arthur Perry.

Arthur cannot remember back beyond the time he started to fish. And with Arthur (who never married) fishing has always come first. I met him in 1943, when three of us landed at Portland Creek in one of Uncle Sam's seaplanes. We had scarcely carried the mooring lines ashore when Arthur arrived on the scene, though it was a full mile from his summer lobster-fishing shack. He was, he informed us, the aircraft spotter for the area. Convinced by the U.S. markings on the aircraft that we weren't Germans, and noting our fishing tackle, he offered to take us fishing—and did.

The district was settled long ago by West of England fisherfolk, who drop their *h*s and pronounce *f* like *v*. So it was that after eyeing my wet fly as I finished tying it to the leader Arthur said, "Better let me put an 'itch on it for you, sir. To make it rivvle."

I must have looked very blank, for he continued, "If you don't put an 'itch on the fly it won't rivvle, and if it doesn't rivvle you won't get any salmon."

Still thoroughly puzzled I said, "I don't get it. Show me what you mean."

Whereupon Arthur picked up the fly in his gnarled hands, put a loop in the leader just in advance of the fly, deftly threw it up and over the eye, then pulled it tight to form an overhand knot (*not* a hitch, strictly speaking) around the shank of the hook at the base of the head. Then he did a repeat, tightening the second knot just beyond the first. After inspecting the results he passed the fly back to me with a flourish.

"Now, sir, it will rivvle and I believe you'll catch a salmon," said Arthur.

I had fished more salmon rivers than Arthur had years. Many a guide had watched openmouthed as I hooked a salmon on a fly he thought fantastic or landed it on a slender split-bamboo stick he knew was ridiculous. In the past guides had said, "They won't take a fly in salt water," so I caught them there on flies, or "They won't take dry flies here," and I took them on dry flies. Carefully I loosened the monofilament and undid first one loop and then the other.

"Arthur," I said, "the Turle knot has been working satisfactorily for a long time. We'll try it that way."

Arthur shook his head sadly, as if watching a small child at a picnic, who, advised by his parents to be good, goes right on being naughty. He shook his head frequently that afternoon as we fished our way down through that marvelous mile of river toward the sea. Finally, at the Low Rock salmon lie, the last fishing spot above the tidal rise, Arthur could hold back no longer. "We've fished all the best lies, sir," he explained. "I know it's a little hearly but there's got to be some fish in the river where we fished. But you won't catch any without an 'itch."

So I threw the loops over the eye myself, drew the leader tight, and passed the hitch to him for inspection before casting to where the deep water swirled high and slid on over the low rock. When the fly came in on the retrieve, it rode the surface like a miniature aquaplane, the black head and eye of the fly riding the crest of a tiny wave and a rippling V spreading out in its wake. It swung in the familiar path a wet fly takes, passing just above the ridge of water pushed up by the rock. The rising water rose a little higher, then parted as a big salmon broke the surface and rushed at the fly. His strong jaws closed on it, and I had hooked my first fish on a riffling fly.

My conversion was neither immediate nor complete. Mine is a Missouri frame of mind, and when Arthur declared that the *only* way to catch a Portland Creek salmon is with a riffled fly I was sure he must be wrong—because the men who had fished the wet fly conventionally either weren't very good at it or had fished the wrong flies. On the trips that followed I fished with both the normally tied and the hitched fly and found both effective. The hitched fly, however, although fished less frequently, took more fish, and I had to admit that it not only was much more fun but had several other advantages.

The turning point came on an afternoon when the cool wind was blowing up from the sea. I had fished the stretch above the Low Rock and reached a lie where another group of rocks curved upstream in a U. In Portland Creek the salmon make a habit of lying ahead of instead of just behind the rocks. I can think of no reason for this except that when the ice jams up against the larger rocks, the churning current, working underneath it, digs out a deep hole on the upstream side. Much of the river is shallow and without pools, with the depressions in front of the larger rocks holding most of the fish.

Fishing had been slow and I had covered several good lies without a rise. I was ready then to stick at this one good spot and succeed or fail there in the half hour remaining. I fished the wet fly, attached normally, under the surface in the accustomed manner. I tried #4s, then #6s, and finally #8s. I watched closely, for if I should miss the almost insignificant gleam of silver as a restless salmon moved slightly under the passing fly I'd fail to make the necessary dozen or more identical casts that would bring him to the hook. I was alert to what happened, though it was unexpected.

As the #8 Jock Scott swung its arc—with the fly just beneath the surface, where the salmon usually like a wet fly best—it happened that a leader knot several feet ahead of the fly was just creasing the smooth surface and sending out a small V of wake as it did so. A salmon drove up from the depths and struck that leader knot, insignificant as it was in contrast with the fly. If the riffled knot would draw a rise from the fish, I decided, so would the riffled fly. My fingers threw the hitches on the Jock Scott, and on the second cast a salmon hit hard. Ever since that moment I have fished the hitched wet fly more than the conventionally sunken one of Portland Creek.

No one now at Portland Creek claims to have been the originator of the riffling fly, but this is the accepted story. Long ago warships of the British navy anchored off the stream and officers came ashore to fish. They left a few old-style salmon flies, which had a loop of twisted gut wrapped to the straight-shanked hook to make the eye.

Soft and pliable when in use, the loop enabled the fly to ride more smoothly on its course and avoided the stiffness and canting that accompanied any solid attachment of the stout leader to the fly. But the gut loop grew weak with age, and many a goodly salmon, when hooked on an old and cherished fly, broke away with the steel and feathers. So to play safe, anglers often gave away old flies. To most recipients they were Trojan horses. Only to the Portland Creekers were they a boon.

Quickly realizing that a salmon hooked on a gut-looped fly was likely to break free, they made sure the fly would stay on by throwing those "hitches" around the shank behind the wrapping. The fact that the fly skimmed instead of sinking bothered them not in the least, for they were practical fishers of the sea. They fished the flies on spruce poles with makeshift reels or none at all. They cast them out and drew them back. And because they had no proper flies with which to fish they developed a new technique.

Now, instead of lying in pools of deep water, most of the salmon in Portland Creek are in relatively shallow water and close to the surface. When they lie in the depressions ahead of the rocks they may actually be lying at a lower level than the streambed all around them, which restricts their field of vision. The river surface is usually ruffled, and this makes a sunken fly less conspicuous than it would be in smooth water. Perhaps the additional commotion made by a riffling fly is just the extra something required to make a salmon rise, for the Atlantic salmon doesn't feed in fresh water and need not take a mouthful of anything from the time it enters the rivers till it leaves again.

In 1946 I established a fishing camp at Portland Creek and many famous fishermen have since come to marvel at the number of salmon in so short a river—and to learn the effectiveness of the hitched wet fly.

The making of the hitch is important. Arthur Perry, in common with most Portland Creek guides, makes his so that the monofilament pulls away from under the turned-up eye at the throat. This will make both the double- and single-hooked flies ride correctly (hook down) on the retrieve. Such a hitch is effective on standard salmon-fly hooks with turned-up eyes but awkward if the eyes are turned down.

I use the same throat hitch for double-hooked flies, but with my favorite—the single-barbed iron—regardless of whether the eye turns up or down. I shift the hitch 45 degrees to one side or the other, depending on which side of the current I cast from, so that on a crosscurrent retrieve the fly will always ride with the point on the downstream side. This position seems to give it much better hooking and riding qualities.

Using this method, it's easy to learn how to fish *any* wet fly correctly, whereas it usually takes years before you can watch the water under which the fly is traveling and guess correctly just where it is and at what speed it is moving. Too much speed or too little will not draw a salmon's interest. The perfect speed is the speed at which a hitched fly riffles best.

If the speed of the retrieve is wrong, the hitched fly will either throw spray or sink below the surface. If one of these things happens a strike is most unlikely. Because the fly is visible at all times, the angler can slow down if he sees the fly making spray, speed up if it starts to sink. Almost without conscious effort he learns to maintain his fly at the right speed through fast water and slow, matching the speed of the retrieve to the water the fly is in. Through crosscurrents and eddies, on glassy glides, the lifting or lowering of the rod to speed up or slow down the retrieve soon becomes automatic.

And thereafter it's not difficult to match these tactics to a sunken fly, which, though still invisible, can now be readily imagined as it travels through the likely water. I think it is largely because of this that the guides of Portland Creek have been able to teach novices to catch salmon almost as well as old-timers.

With the riffling hitch, fish are hooked just as readily and held just as securely as when the fly is tied on in the conventional manner. And they're so sold on it at Portland Creek that 95 percent of all the wet-fly fishing done there is with a hitched fly.

It's worked out well on other salmon rivers, too, like the Humber and the River of Ponds. Having had sea-run brook trout at Portland Creek hit the riffling fly savagely, I wasn't surprised when even the sophisticated brownies of my home stream, the Battenkill of New York and Vermont, rose to the skittering feathers. Eastern brook trout have long been taken by dragging the dropper fly on the surface while the tail fly sinks underneath. With the hitch the solitary tail fly riffles by itself, an especially good method for fishing for the more wary brookies.

The first black bass to take a hitched streamer of mine, a hefty Hudson River smallmouth, gave me a thrilling rise. He hit it just as hard as he'd have hit a spinner-and-streamer combination, and he did it on top of the water where I could see it. After all, our grandfathers used to skitter with a long cane pole and a strip of pork rind and there's not much real difference between the two methods. The hitched fly is, of course, designed for stream fishing, requiring a certain speed to keep it riffling. But with greased line and leader this can be managed even on a lake or a very slow-moving stream.

I find myself using the hitch more and more instead of normal wet-fly fishing simply because it thrills me to see a fish break the surface in his strike. As compared with the dry fly the riffled fly moves faster, because it moves across the flow as well as with it. A trout or salmon can wait until the dry fly comes to him, then quietly rise up and suck it in. With the riffling fly the fish must not only rise to but *catch* the fly; and a big salmon, in doing so, rolls up a wave of water ahead of him one never forgets. The same goes for bass, pickerel, and tarpon—each must poke his nose up into the air and show himself with at least as much flourish as if he were after a dry fly.

Are skittered dry flies as good as the hitched wet fly? Experience at Portland Creek denies it. Granted that the hitched fly stays up only because of its motion, the fluffy dry fly rides at a different angle and height, and develops little wake.

Like any new method, riffling the wet fly will be especially effective where the fish have seen a lot of flies presented in the old way. That is why the original dry flies, which were essentially only greased and floating wet flies, brought such remarkable results when first used over trout and salmon, and why long, thin floating bass bugs—shaped almost like streamer flies—made such wonderful catches. It was not because the design or shape of the fly was so different—that came later—it was the new approach.

Various sorts of insects skim across the water instead of flying over it or swimming through it. Water spiders, bugs, and striders or skaters, as well as stalled-out land bugs, slide their way over the ripples and eddies. Many an injured minnow flutters his way across the pool, nose breaking into the air and tail lagging downward, until a gamefish takes him down. Hence to imitate such action with a riffled fly is both natural and effective, and it doesn't cost a nickel. To make your wet flies more effective and to make the strikes more fun, simply follow Arthur Perry's advice and put an 'itch on them.

[1952]

5

The Lost Art of Fishing with a Worm

*At one point during the several days we spent reviewing
material for this book, Wulff held up a manuscript and
grinned: "We have to have this one!" You might well
wonder why he who may be the world's best-known fly
fisherman is so enthusiastic about this worm-fishing
chapter, and I think I can explain just that.*

*Wulff has made a very successful angling career
based in large measure on an iconoclastic approach to
angling tradition, and in the modern view of many
there is nothing quite so iconoclastic as a worm. It's
also worth noting that this chapter originally appeared
in* Collier's—*the late and great general-circulation
magazine—on April 16, 1954. It thus was directed at a
larger (and worm-fishing) segment of the angling public than Wulff normally reached in the outdoor media,
and it appeared early in the spring when an old trout's
fancy turns to worms.*

Let's have a standing ovation for the worm, the lowly little
critter who is all things to all fishermen. No other single bait
is so adaptable, as much at home in all fishing circles—or so

33

maligned. When a man takes his son fishing for the first time, what do they use for bait? A hundred to one they use worms.

Or take the veteran fisherman who has spent two unsuccessful weeks fishing with dry flies for landlocked salmon. On the last day of his vacation, when he's wondering how he'll explain an empty creel to the folks at home, what do his thoughts turn to? Worms—surefire, never-fail worms.

Yet, when that fisherman puts aside his fancy flies and tries for his salmon with a worm, he has a guilty feeling. Chances are, he did his very first fishing with a cane pole and a worm, but now, he feels, he had advanced beyond such crudities. Besides, he has been listening to the whispering campaign that is always going on against the worm; he has come to believe that worms are unsportsmanlike because the fish can't resist them.

That's poppycock. It's true that almost everything that swims in fresh water, from sunfish to salmon, seems born with a taste for worms. But it doesn't necessarily follow that all you have to do is drape a worm on your hook, toss the rig into the water, and brace yourself for the inevitable strike.

Any fish can resist any worm if it's served up to him in a haphazard fashion that arouses his suspicions. Fishing with a worm can be a real art, requiring every bit as much skill and finesse as snaking down the driest dry fly.

It's high time fishermen stopped looking down their noses at the worm as the fishing accomplice for children and beginners. The fact is, fishing with a worm can be just as simple or just as difficult as you care to make it.

Why wait? Likely as not there's a supply of the new secret weapon bait within 100 feet of you at this moment. Dig them up and try them out.

The worms most often used in fishing come in two models, regular and king-size: the earthworm and the night crawler. Earthworms abound in almost any rich soil; now you'll have no trouble finding them. Night crawlers take a bit more effort. They get their name from their fondness for leaving their burrows to crawl abroad on nights when the earth is wet with rain or dew. Hunting them is almost as much fun as fishing with them. Most experts go forth equipped with a dimmed flashlight and tennis shoes. You spot your quarry and advance quietly until you can grab it up.

Now that you know how to get your bait, let's shift perspective for a moment and assume the fish's point of view. If we can better understand what appeals to a fish, we'll have a clearer idea of the worm fisherman's problems.

As a fish, you have certain known characteristics.

1. You're mad for worms.

2. A good deal of the time you're hungry. And even if you've just had a big dinner, you're not above grabbing a between-meals snack if it's attractive enough—or if you just want to make sure nobody else gets it. *But . . .*

3. You're suspicious; you've got to be or you don't live long. You play everything safe, especially tidbits that don't look just right to you.

Maybe you're primarily a lake- or pond-dwelling fish, like a panfish or a largemouth bass or northern pike. If so, you rarely see worms except those washed into the water by the runoff of rains. They're either sinking to the bottom or already on the bottom when you spot them. And because worms can't swim, they're wiggling frantically, trying to get out of their unfamiliar aquatic atmosphere.

But what if you're a river fish? Then your worms will come twisting and turning downstream with the current. They may be bouncing along the bottom or they may be caught in the swifter upper currents.

In each case, the situation and the circumstances may vary; still, a pattern does emerge and it offers the secret of successful worm fishing: for best results, your worm must arrive in the fish's dining room as if he just happened along naturally. And, with very few exceptions, he should come on the scene full of pep and wiggle.

Your task as a fisherman is obvious. Now, how do you accomplish it? Let's get technical.

First, use small hooks. The exact size, to be determined by experimentation, will depend on the size of the worms you use and the kind of fish you're likely to catch. Your tackle box should hold hooks in a range of sizes. Start off with a very small hook, say a #12. If you get strikes but fail to hook your fish, shift to the next larger size and try again.

Your object in using a small hook is twofold. It's easier to conceal the hook—you don't need to thread so much of the worm onto it to hide it from the fish's suspicious eye. And you allow the worm more freedom of movement to cavort—and thus to advertise his presence. He'll live longer, too.

Next, use a long leader of the daintiest practical size. Again, experimentation will have to be your guide. Just don't try to land a 10-pound largemouth bass using a 2-pound-test leader—unless you are more skilled than most of us.

Be dainty when you put the worm on the hook, too. Your aim is merely to disguise the hook and hold the worm on it. Don't bunch up the worm. On a small hook, it is only necessary to slip the point and barb under the worm's so-called collar, a ring of thickness about one third of the way back from his head. On larger hooks, when you have to put on more of the bait, loop the worm. But always leave both ends free to wiggle.

Above all, keep a lively worm on your hook. When a worm shows signs of tuckering out, replace him with a fresh stablemate from your bait can. You may have to bait up every five minutes or so, and you'll go through a lot of worms that way—but you'll catch fish, and that's what you're there for.

So much for your terminal rig—the part of your equipment the fish sees. Now comes the all-important factor—technique. How can you best deliver your worm to the right spot?

The first consideration is what gear to use. Tom Sawyer's old cane-pole-and-bobber rig will still catch fish; it's been doing so for generations and will continue to do so for generations. But more advanced equipment is easier to work with and more efficient, and more fun. The exact type of rig to use depends largely on where you fish.

For simply paying out a line and letting your worm drift downstream on the current of a cascading mountain brook, fly-fishing equipment is in a class by itself. The relative rigidity of the line and its ability to float make it ideal for navigating around rocks and rapids with a minimum of snagging.

Plug- or bait-casting equipment or a spinning rig can be used the same way, but they're not so well suited to the job.

If you move to a pond or lake, and casting is the order of the day, a fly-fishing rig is out of place. Even when practiced by an expert, fly casting—with its whiplike snap—usually tears a worm off the hook. Tossing out a worm with a bait-casting outfit is even more impractical; the worm just doesn't have enough heft to go anywhere.

Not so with spinning. You can take a single earthworm on the end of a spinning rig and send him across the water for a surprising distance.

If you've a fondness for trolling, you can't go wrong with any of the three types of equipment. You need to be governed only by your personal tastes.

And for so-called still fishing, either on the bottom or with a float, both spinning equipment and bait-casting outfits are suitable.

Now you're ready for the payoff—the actual delivery of the worm. Success or failure hangs in the balance; all your preparations, however elaborate, will be wasted if you miscue now.

Just remember that you'll get the best results if you always fish your worm as if he weren't on the end of the line. Make him look natural.

If you're casting, flick him out onto the water easily. Your technique should allow the worm to drop cozily onto the water with the least possible fuss—as if he had lost his footing and fallen into the water accidentally.

If you're trolling, try a spinner ahead of the worm. Just ease along. Occasionally vary the speed of the boat, which will change the level at which your bait travels through the water.

If you're still-fishing, know your good spots and let the worm (a lively one, of course) rest on the bottom. If you're in weeds, use a bobber to hold the bait above the weeds and in sight of the fish. Lower your rig into the water gently, and move it around occasionally to cover the most territory.

If you're fishing a stream, float your worm downstream. But don't hold him against the current; no fish ever saw a worm battling upstream. When you reach the end of your line, reel in and send your worm off on another downstream junket.

Patience is your guide in fishing with a worm. Go slow. Take it easy. The worm is a natural bait and should be fished in a natural manner. If you've rigged your tackle right, your worm will bear a lot of scrutiny before the fish wises up to the fact that you're on the other end of the line.

Now, if the action is slow, there are some added tricks that will increase your chances of a strike. Try these:

Chum. Use the old saltwater technique of piquing the fish's appetite by tendering him bits of food before sneaking your worm in among them. Small chunks of worms will work fine—even crumbs of bread, if you're short of bait.

Dump clods of dirt into the water. In both streams and lakes, you'll at least attract the attention of the fish. You may fool them into thinking there's been a small landslide and they'll be looking for food to follow in the wake of the sod.

Stir up the bottom. If you're fishing a stream in hip boots or waders, use your feet to overturn small rocks. This will serve much the same purpose as the clods, and you'll also kick up tiny aquatic life, thereby alerting the fish downstream that dinner's on the way.

In fishing with a worm, as in fishing with anything else, never forget: angling is the most unpredictable of sports. Fishing rules are made to be broken. There are times when a whole worm will be refused, but half a worm or less will be gobbled up. There are times when you will excite the fish and stimulate them to strike if you cast your worm with a great commotion, instead of stealthily. But before you break the rules, *know them!*

All right, you're in business. Have fun, and if anybody sniffs at you when you open your little pouch of worms, be quick to quote the words of the immortal Izaak Walton, perhaps the greatest fisherman of them all. In *The Compleat Angler*, published in 1653, recalling one good day's fishing, he comments with satisfaction: "The last trout I caught was with a worm. . . ."

[1954]

6

Throw It Out There

In this era of lightweight graphite rods and space-age reels, America's conversion to light-tackle angling is surprisingly incomplete; many fishermen are still over-gunned for the fish they seek, to the detriment of their own sport. More than forty years ago when Lee Wulff first started preaching the light-tackle gospel, the situation was even worse as long, heavy rods and stout lines were the norm, even for stream trout.

This essay details the many virtues of short, light fly rods—an aspect of the sport pioneered by Wulff—and was written almost forty years ago when fly-casting instructors told one to cast as if a book were being clamped between one's elbow and torso while casting. As the late Arnold Gingrich once noted, Wulff literally "threw away the book" in fly casting to make new and lighter tackle a pleasure to use.

Fly fishermen have long believed that very light rods are not only hard to handle but won't make long casts. That used to be true, but modern techniques have made the featherweight fly rod much easier to use and have increased its range greatly. Important in these techniques is full use of the arm in casting.

Some fifteen years ago, in writing my *Handbook of Freshwater Fishing*, I described fly casting much as everyone else did, emphasizing movement of the wrist rather than of the arm, and warning against bringing the rod back much past the vertical on the back cast. At that time I had only limited experience with featherweight fly rods of from 2 to 2½ ounces (scale weight of the complete rod). But since then consistent, season-long fishing with such rods has convinced me not only that light rods are practical but that the best results will be obtained with them when full use is made of the casting arm. Limiting the rod to the vertical point on the back cast, I've found, hinders rather than helps the cast.

In a recent article I described casting a fly line without any rod at all [see Chapter 7]. A GBF fly line can be cast from 30 to 50 feet by hand. The fly line, which is pliant and of relatively large diameter, is the big factor in all fly casting. A good fly line can be cast with any rod or with no rod at all; but ordinary bait-casting, spinning, or trolling lines cannot be cast even by the finest of fly rods. So let's start with the line and progress from there to its best use with a matching rod.

In casting by hand alone, you must treat the line as if it were a rope. A rolling motion of the hand will send a loop rolling down its entire length. A sharp lift of the arm will pick up 20 or 30 feet and straighten it out behind you; but a twist of the wrist, as used in normal fly casting, has practically no effect. Somewhere between the old style of casting and the casting of the line by hand alone lies the best casting motion for very light rods.

In the traditional method, length and stiffness of the rod provide the casting power. And because the combined weight of the longer rod and the line-filled reel is great enough to make full-arm movement fatiguing, casting is achieved by wrist motion. (Almost every fly fisherman has been told that the perfect caster can hold a book against his body with the elbow of his casting arm while he's in action.) But with short rods the limited power of the wrist simply isn't great enough to throw a light line.

The full-arm casting that would be hard work with a 9-foot, 6½-ounce rod is light work with a 6½-foot, 2-ounce rod. And similar casting distance can be achieved with the latter by application of a new principle in fly casting that I'll discuss presently.

A second factor favoring the use of lighter gear is the improvement of rod materials in the past quarter century. The impregnation of bamboo with Bakelite and the development of fine rods of steel or of glass fiber have given us lightness *and* durability. Perhaps glass fiber has the greatest strength for its weight, but I still prefer a certain delicacy that's combined with power in split bamboo, especially when Bakelite impregnation makes the rod vastly more long-lasting.

In light rods it is the continuous casting, rather than the playing of fish, that causes deterioration and breakage. I enjoy casting and always work my little rods relatively hard. And I cast them to the limit of my strength whenever there's a particularly distant spot I want to reach. In the past I could count on only about one month of life for a very light rod. Now they stand up, season after season, with practically no breakage.

A third factor lengthening the casts of short fly rods is the forward-taper fly line. Its advantage over the old double taper comes only when the line really begins to stretch out, and 35 feet or more are off the reel. Then the lighter line gets extra distance with the same amount of effort. Extra distance over a normal cast isn't so important with the usual 8½- or 9-foot rod, but the long "shoot" permitted by the forward-taper line makes it possible to reach out to all normal fishing distances with a rod of 7 feet or less.

Obviously, the casting power of any fly rod is mainly limited by the weight of line it will handle in the air. And weight for weight you get more line out with the feather-weight outfit. However, there is a weight limit for any outfit. But supposing it's reached at 55 feet, say, you can still add length to the casts, and yet not overstrain the rod, by using a long leader and learning how to snap it out.

Long leaders (mine range from 10 to 25 feet) will extend

the line's maximum casting distance by about 80 percent of their length. Under the old elbow-at-side casting motion it was difficult to straighten out a leader, but with the full-arm motion—aided when necessary by a sharp pullback of rod arm, line, or both—a very long leader can be straightened out completely.

My casting motion resembles that of a pitcher throwing a ball. I start the back cast with my arm stretched forward, bring it back in a slightly underhand swing until the line is stretched out full length behind me, then catch the weight of the line, with my rod arm as far back and as high as I can get it, at precisely the proper instant to drive the line forward and down to the starting point. The light rod lifts it and directs it, but essentially it is the power and movement of my arm in its speedy drive that sends the line sailing forward.

The rotary effect of this line motion in a *vertical* plane has a number of advantages. First, the line tends to come in on a low level and go out on a higher one, lessening the chance of a tangle as part of the line drives forward while its end is still moving back. In standard casting, tangling is normally averted by making the casting motion an elongated oval in the *horizontal* plane.

Often there is an obstruction on the bank, which limits the back cast and thereby limits the forward cast as well. But by bringing the line in low, and lifting it upward as it completes the back cast you get good clearance above the ground or water at a point where you need it most. Thus you can get a full back cast at practically all times. When, under the same circumstances, the tail end of the back cast is lower—as it must be in the orthodox cast, when the line stays on a fairly level plane throughout—it seriously affects the length of the back cast and, consequently, the forward cast.

Another advantage of a high back cast is that it makes the forward cast easier. The force of gravity is always with us and it is easier to throw a line down than up. The forward cast from a high back cast is downhill, therefore easier and longer, pulling out many more feet of line.

Still another advantage of the high back cast is that it makes the forward cast low. A low forward cast leads to better fishing. It is more accurate, because the point of aim of the cast is closer to the water it is to land on. There is no gentle drifting down of the fly to the surface from a point 6 or 8 feet above it. (When such a drop is desirable it can always be managed.) And casting a fly to within a few inches of its point of contact with the water is helpful when the wind is blowing. A strong breeze will blow any light fly and leader away from where you want it to land if there's much space between it and the water.

The low cast, essential for accuracy in a wind, is good at any time and worth using as a matter of normal form instead of only on special occasions. I've observed friends who were having difficulty casting in strong winds. They could shoot a very limited amount of line into the wind, and of course that's all that's necessary when wind-roughened water prevents the fish from seeing an angler at a distance. Almost invariably they'd put their false casts to within a few inches of the point they wanted to reach. But then they'd let habit take over on their final cast, ending it several feet above the water, and the wind would blow it anywhere from 5 to 15 feet away. I showed them how to make their final cast exactly like a false cast, down to the water, and drop the rod forward the instant the fly reached the aiming spot, just over the water. Doing that they could cast accurately into the wind, and they took fish.

To save effort, the pickup of the forward cast should be made with a typical roll-cast motion, pulling the fly to the surface, then picking it up immediately for the start of the back cast. This is a good laborsaving trick used by many fly casters. The angler with a featherweight rod will often have need of it.

Short rods will not pick up as much line as longer ones of the same proportionate power. This means more line must be retrieved before the successful pickup can be made. Overloading the rod on pickup usually spoils the chance of a good cast and, in the long run, is more work than the extra left-arm movement required to bring another yard or two of line inside the guides.

The angler's grip on the rod is, I believe, important. With

the conventional wrist movement, a grip in which the thumb rests on the top of the cork works very well. With small rods I lay my forefinger out full length on top of the rod for best results. This affords greater and more delicate control. It puts my hand at an angle where its overall grip on the rod is stronger and my wrist becomes a continuation of my arm rather than a loose joint.

Conventional casting calls for smooth, easy movement. Fly casters have long been judged by smoothness of line flow and easy grace of movement, even where changes of direction are involved. But all this goes by the board when you're using a featherweight rod. I drive out my casts with every ounce of power I can muster, seeking maximum speed. I depend on perfect timing to let me use my strength and speed for the necessary fraction of a second when the direction of line travel is changed. Here, as in the case of a baseball player, one uses maximum strength and speed to move a light object. The need for snap and speed in getting the ultimate out of featherweight tackle cannot be overemphasized. Conventional casting with a light outfit will get moderate distance, but only coordinated speed and power will make it compete with standard outfits in covering the water.

Few anglers realize how fast a fly line can travel. Once I made stopwatch tests of the time required to straighten out back casts and forward casts. I ran the tests on my 6½-foot, 2-ounce rod and my 9-foot, 5-ounce rod. The amount of line off the reel in each case was the same, 55 feet, and each leader was 10 feet long. I made several runs of ten complete forward casts and back casts during which the fly traveled 260 feet ten times, or a total of 2,600 feet of movement.

The average time for the featherweight outfit was 18.4 seconds, which was a rate of travel of 96 miles per hour. Peak speed is much higher, since the fly has to come to a stop and change direction at the end of each forecast and back cast. The average time for the 9-foot fly rod was 23.1 seconds, or a rate of travel of 76 miles per hour.

Most fly casters are convinced that it takes a heavy line to force their cast out into the wind. That's malarkey! The solution is simple: send the line out with much more speed than the wind it faces. The featherweight rod with its higher speed will actually do a better job than the more powerful but slower outfit.

The featherweight rod should have a good deal of stiffness in the butt and be light in the tip. Here the so-called parabolic actions are not useful, because they have a pendulumlike swing. In the old casting method this swing reduces the problem of timing, because the parabolic rod tends to settle into a rhythm easily felt by the angler and easily followed by him. However, such an action hasn't the "life" to deliver the drive necessary for a maximum cast with a light rod. Its virtues are smoothness and ease. I like a fly rod that takes the maximum amount of change of pace and delivers its full power in the shortest possible time.

Let's consider the tapers of lines and leaders, prime factors in casting. For my 2-ounce and 2³/₈-ounce two-piece fly rods I use an HDF taper. Admittedly the HDG taper would add length to my casts, since the lighter-running G line, with its smaller diameter, would permit a slightly longer shoot. Were I casting in a gymnasium or only on windless days the G would be satisfactory, but under actual fishing conditions— which often include strong and gusty winds—the G is likely to tangle.

Wind will whip the hand-held coils of light line around the reel or hand during the retrieve, causing an occasional jam at the first guide after a sudden strike and run by a big fish. The F line is large enough in diameter to resist this tangling, and I find the sacrifice in casting distance worthwhile in saving more fish.

Most leaders have too small a butt diameter. A perfectly smooth continuation of the taper from the belly of the line right down to the fly calls for the butt of the leader to match the forward end of the line in weight per foot. Inasmuch as the specific gravities of most lines are similar to that of nylon monofilament, the diameters should be approximately equal at the juncture. Such heavy nylon rarely breaks and is slow to wear out. A long leader must frequently be drawn into the guides and I recommend splicing a section of heavy nylon or a 12-foot monofilament (knotless), tapering from .020 to .010

[inch], directly to the line. Lengths of finer nylon can be added as needed.

In these high-speed casts with featherweight rods the leader tends to straighten out well at the end of the cast. But if there is any doubt about it, a quick pullback from the out-stretched-arm position at the end of the cast will flip the leader out straight. A pulling in of the line through the guides at the same instant adds even more snap, and although both actions reduce the length of line out beyond the guides, the difference between a curled-back leader and a straight one more than makes up for the loss.

To illustrate this, try casting with a 20-foot length of ordinary clothesline. You will see how easily the pullback at the end of the cast whips the line out straight. While you have the clothesline handy, straighten it out on the floor, holding one end in your hand with arm upraised. Lower your arm, then give a short, quick yank. You'll notice how the sharp movement carries all the way through the slack line and makes the far end move. Therein lies the secret of the dry-fly trick with the featherweight rod. If, by contrast, you lift your arm to full height again in a slower movement, the far end of the line will not move at all.

A line movement of only a fraction of an inch will set a small dry-fly hook. Once set it will not fall out, so a moment or two of slack means nothing one way or another. With 60 feet of line and leader drifting slackly downstream, a quick movement of the rod butt toward the angler will set the hook, regardless of whether the rod is lifted or left pointing directly toward the fish. In any case, once the hook is set the rod should be raised to cushion the shock of the fish's run, which will quickly take up the slack.

Striking by rod lift is bound to be slower than the "yank" strike. The spring of the rod, which is so useful in absorbing the sudden surges of a fish, now absorbs the sudden power the angler puts into his strike. It slows down all action, and in many cases none of the movement of the strike ever reaches the fly or fish. A little line movement is worth a lot of rod lifting.

Because the casting of the ultralight fly rods depends on

movement of the arm rather than the wrist, a number of variations are possible. When faced with a solid wall of foliage behind him an angler standing on a six-foot beach or slab of rock can coil 40 feet of line and leader at his feet (working backward from the fly) and straighten it out in front of him with a quick snap of the roll-cast type.

The line can be cast in a big vertical oval with its center well in front of the rod by varying the speed of the rolling arm motion. This keeps the line almost entirely in front of the caster, and as long as he has the feel of the weight of the line in the air he can pick the right time on any circuit to shoot the fly out 30 feet or more.

Many of the ideas proposed here contradict existing opinions. They are practical, however, and the proof of their efficiency is something I demonstrate every day I fly-fish.

Featherweight rods really do feel like a feather in your casting hand. They require a minimum of casting effort, and with one you can fish all day. When you become accustomed to such a rod, the standard outfit feels stiff and clumsy. The light rods do call for better coordination, but once you understand the need for the high back cast and perfect timing, proficiency comes quickly. And with it comes a pride no heavier tackle can ever give.

[1953]

7

Spare the Rod and
Prove a Point

*In this chapter Wulff recounts yet another of his
famous exploits—fly casting for and catching an
Atlantic salmon with no rod at all. The thinking here is
vintage Wulff: as a hypothesis, take an angling concept
to its extreme; see what factors apply in the extreme;
and then see how these factors might apply to more
"normal" angling.*

*So in 1946, when he'd already established his
advocacy of lighter-than-then-normal tackle, he tried
eliminating the rod entirely in fly fishing for salmon,
hoping thereby for greater insight into why a rod is
necessary in the first place. In this and other instances,
his achievement was so dramatic that it sometimes
overshadowed what he was trying to demonstrate.
Don't let the surprises in this chapter make you miss
the lessons!*

What I wanted to get was absolute proof with regard to how
essential the rod is in playing a fish, especially a fish on a fly.
I've sat in on sessions with other anglers before the fire in
fishing camps and doodled on angling banquet tables while

the subject of how light a rod should be or should not be has come up for the full round of discussions. Like most other factors in angling, this one is a thoroughly debatable issue and one that gets its share of attention. And, as is usually the case, there is much more debating than actual research. So I've gone a distance in making up for that lack, leading me to an interesting experiment and some final conclusions.

Fishing for bass, muskie, trout, and the rest of the American freshwater gamefish has contributed to the experience on which I base my conclusions in regard to the use of light rods; the use of light tackle for the big fish of the sea has given me an understanding of the playing of all fish that I could never have attained without it. For this chapter, however, I'm going to use the Atlantic salmon to illustrate.

The Atlantic salmon, when fresh-run from the sea, are not surpassed by any other fish in fresh water as testers of tackle and angling skill. The length of their runs, due to their life in the sea, is attested by the amount of line required on the reels of anglers who seek them, beginning around 150 yards and going upward. They are fish of the open water that depend on their speed and strength for freedom. Weeds and snags are seldom encountered, and the battle is one of space and constant motion. The final factor is their stored-up energy, sufficient strength to see them through almost a year of starvation.

In playing a fish, the rod acts as a cushion to soften the shocks of the fish's movement on the weakest part of the tackle, which is usually the delicate leader or the grip of the hook in the fish's jaw. As a secondary measure, it acts as a lever with which to guide the fish or move him in a given direction. In considering the length of the rod in comparison with the hundreds of yards of line out when playing a marlin, for example, the length of the rod becomes insignificant.

Long ago, when I began fishing for Atlantic salmon, I used a 9-foot, 5-ounce fly rod. All around me were two-handed weapons, wielded almost exclusively by men who firmly believed that salmon couldn't be played successfully on rods like mine. My experience with the 5-ounce rod led to the eventual use of my lightest trout rod for salmon—a two-piece

7-foot, 2½-ounce rod. In those firelight and banquet-table discussions many experienced salmon fishermen still held that the 2½-ounce rod, even more than the 5-ounce rod, was incapable of handling a determined salmon and that a good "sulker" would leave me helpless.

But in 1940, the first year I used the 2½-ounce rod, none of my fish gave me special trouble, and they came in at about the same speed as on the 5-ounce rod. An 18-pounder was my largest fish of that season, which still left room for the doubters to say, "You're just catching small ones. A 30-pounder will show up your small rod."

Then, in 1942, a 30-pounder clamped down on my fly and was landed in twenty-six minutes without difficulty. More than a dozen salmon of over 23 pounds came in on the light fly rod without trouble in that season and the season that followed. I still felt that anglers placed too much emphasis on the rod's importance in the playing of a fish and that the use of a light rod depends more on the angler's skill than the fish's toughness. So I determined to make a test that would prove my point beyond the shadow of a doubt, that year, in 1943.

I decided to land a salmon with a standard fly-fishing tackle except that I would use no rod at all. To do this I might have trolled a fly behind a canoe, which would have made the hooking of a salmon a relatively simple thing. But I wanted to do it by fly casting, and to do that I needed a certain type of pool to work in. Finally, I found one that suited me.

A tall man with a good, long casting arm can cast a fly for some distance without a rod. When you stand on a smooth floor, it's simple enough to cast a standard fly line thirty feet or more by hand. The pickup is easy from a polished floor, but not nearly so easy from the water. What I needed was a salmon pool with a rock at its head on which I could stand to cast with salmon lying near that rock. In addition, I needed a steady flow to straighten the line out quickly and hold it near the surface for an easy pickup. These conditions were all met by the Seal Pool on Newfoundland's Southwest River.

The water bends in close to a big rock at the head of the pool and grows deeper as the streambed hollows out with the slowing down of the flow. There, in the deepening water, the salmon lie. My tackle consisted of a #8 low-water type Dark Cahill, a 6-foot leader of about 2½-pound breaking strain, an HCH nylon fly line, and 120 yards of braided nylon backing on my 3⅜-inch fly reel. That was all. The short leader was a concession to the need for keeping the fly near the surface; a longer leader is more difficult to cast. The pool had not been fished earlier that season and I hoped the fish wouldn't be too wary.

I took a long time in getting out to my position on the rock. My movements were slow and deliberate, and I remained motionless on the rock for a little while before I made my first cast. Then, holding the reel in my left hand and using my right arm for a rod, I began to cast while Private First Class Carl Lowe of a U.S. Army Search and Rescue Unit manned my camera and Charlie Bennett, guide extraordinary, looked on.

My first cast took the fly out about twenty-five feet, and it swung in a good arc on the retrieve. On about the third cast a fish swirled behind the fly and took a good look at it. He must have seen me in my exposed position on the rock, too, because he failed to rise again, and eventually I lengthened line and fished the water below his position. After a dozen more casts another salmon rose, taking the fly in his mouth just far enough to be pricked but not hooked solidly as the line tightened.

Reeling in, I slid down from the rock to wade ashore and give the water a rest before trying again. Near the shore, I slipped and went to my knees on a jagged rock, tearing my waders at the knee.

By the time I had taken off my waders and hung them up to dry, it was time to try again, so I waded out to the rock, this time without benefit of waders, to make a second try. The rise was not long in coming, and I found myself fast to a flashing, leaping salmon that was off on a good run down the pool to the deep, slow water. My reel went over to my right hand and I let the fish take line freely. He wound up the run that carried him well into the backing with a couple of tumbling leaps as a final flourish and swung into the current again to work upstream toward me.

51

Then my left hand moved up to where my right hand was held high in imitation of a fly rod, and the fingers picked up the reel handle. I took in line. It was almost as if I'd been using a light rod as far as the effect on the fish was concerned. I moved my arm forward and back to help take up slack or give line speedily. The nylon line, resilient and springy, helped my arm and body movements in absorbing the sudden shocks at the salmon's end of our connection. Slowly the backing came back onto the reel, and the fly-casting line began to pile up on top of it. The salmon's first wild run and his sudden rushes had been safely met, and from there on his movements would be more predictable.

I took in line when I could, gave it when I had to, and dropped my playing arm when the salmon broke water in his spray-scattering leaps. There was, as I had anticipated, little difference in playing a fish in this manner and playing one with my light fly rod. From long experience I sensed when his runs would start and when they'd end and when he'd roll and go into a sort of underwater dance with its attendant head shaking. Each time I was ready with the move to neutralize his action. In seven minutes he had unwound his bag of tricks and found none that worked. He was in close and groggy.

In this sport of catching fish I like to do the entire job myself. A fish is often tricked into coming within reach of another individual who snags him with a gaff, which does not give a true picture of the ability of one man to take one fish on certain tackle in a certain amount of time. I wanted to leave no loopholes; so I decided to land this one the hard way—by myself and by hand-tailing without the benefit of gaff, tailer, or sandy beach.

Charlie had been making grunts of satisfaction on the bank. Carl, who had alternated between taking pictures of me on the rock and trying to get the fish in the air on one of his leaps, moved in closer as the range of action narrowed down.

The salmon was visibly weary. He had run and leaped himself out, just as any other fish does when properly played, tiring himself with his own efforts, not being killed by the leverage of the rod. He headed in under the rock, and I leaned far out over the edge to put on the pressure required to make him angle off into the open water again. The current picked him up and swung him sideways, the long, silvery line of his belly flashing in the dull light of approaching evening. He came in again, and I held his head higher so that he slid against the rock on a slant that led him to the surface. The solid rock jarred him when he struck it and he whirled away, half leaping. When he stopped, I put the pressure on and led him in again.

All the line and part of the leader had passed in through the line guard of the reel when I shifted it from my right hand to my left and went down on one knee. With my right hand I reached out to let my fingers get into position to close on the narrow point at the base of his tail. At the right moment I clamped down in a hard grip and held.

Some anglers claim that this tail grip has a paralyzing effect on the fish's spine. Whether this is true or not, I know that most fish properly hand-tailed offer little resistance and don't begin to kick up much fuss until the grip is released and they drop to the earth or to the bottom of the canoe. This fish was like that, quiet until I dropped him on the sandy shore.

He weighed almost 10 pounds, and the time it took to bring him in was just shy of ten minutes. This was, I believe, the first time this feat had ever been performed, and it leads to inescapable conclusions. The first of them is that a rod is not essential to the proper playing of a fish. Instead, the rod is more nearly essential in casting the fly within reach of the fish.

Few of the thousands of salmon I've seen could have been hooked without the aid of a rod, but the great majority of them could have been landed, as that one was, without a rod. Therefore, in choosing the rod the skilled angler should make his choice on the basis of the casting distance required rather than the size of the fish that must be handled on it.

As for a fair evaluation of the rod's position in fly fishing, it depends on the stream to be fished and the individual who is doing the fishing. The rod must be capable of getting the fly out to the water in which fish are lying. One man may need a much longer rod than another who is a better caster. A tall man has the advantage over a short one in the use of short, light rods.

The rod is of great aid in taking up slack quickly when playing a fish and in absorbing the shock of the fish's sudden starts or in giving adequate slack for his leaps. The less capable the angler is in sensing these maneuvers of the fish in advance and the poorer his powers of coordination in making the necessary adjustments, the longer the rod he will need to make up for that lack.

To be able to fish with a very light rod or no rod at all is an achievement, but it doesn't prove that the use of the very lightest possible rod or no rod at all is a sensible way to fish. The rod to choose is one that balances the individual's skill, his need for long casts, and the amount of fatigue he wants to put up with in his fishing day. If he casts hour after hour through the long days of June, a light rod with line to balance is a blessing. He can wind up at twilight with his arm as fresh as when he started. His sacrifice will have been in passing up the chance of reaching fish that the extra distance of a longer rod would have reached, or the slight advantage he'd have gained in leverage to guide a fish or keep the line free from obstructions while the fish was being played.

The ability to get around in a stream to the proper playing position determines to a large extent what sort of tackle the angler needs. Those tough sulkers become just ordinary fish when the fisherman stays downstream of them and keeps the pressure on them to a point at which they're using up energy rapidly, whether they stay in one spot or move off. For the angler whose canoeman doesn't want to bother to move him to the right position or to the man whose legs and wading ability won't get him around the stream in good shape, a rod of fair length and tackle of fair strength are necessities if many fish are to be saved.

It all boils down to individual ability, and even in the case of the most gifted angler, there is a limit to the lightness of the rod, which is dictated by casting distance required and wind that must be bucked or other casting difficulties. If an angler insists on fishing with a rod that is too weak to give him an opportunity to reach a number of fish roughly equal to that reached by his neighbors, he's handicapping himself, with his only possible gain lying in being able to cast for a longer time.

If he wants to prove he can perform a certain light-rod feat, the thing to do is to accomplish that feat enough times to satisfy himself about his ability and then settle back to use the tackle that will give him the greatest pleasure yet won't cut his chances of hooking fish. And these conclusions, I believe, hold for all types of angling.

[1946]

8

The Truth About Long and Short Rods

By the 1970s, after almost forty years of praising short, light rods in print and demonstrating their effectiveness, Lee Wulff had acquired an international reputation for his use of short rods. Unfortunately, this led many people to believe he felt longer rods had no place in angling—something that to my knowledge he never said.

That popular impression, however, was—and is— persistent, and so this essay was written in 1977 as a means of setting things to rights regarding when a long rod might be more appropriate than the shorter ones Wulff made famous. As he puts it here: "The complete angler uses both."

In the beginning, all fly rods were long. They were long because the available materials, the solid woods, lacked the swift resilience that modern types of casting call for. Anglers did much of their fishing then with a single cast, picking up and retrieving the same length of line cast after cast, with no false casting. The long rod, working a line as long as or slightly longer than the rod itself, covered the near waters very well. The fish were plentiful and unsophisticated, and long casts just weren't as necessary as they are now. Gradually, rod materials improved and casts lengthened.

My first rod, given to me back in the teens of the century, was 9 feet long and made of greenheart with a lancewood tip. My second was a split bamboo of the same length, and today's anglers, picking it up, would have exclaimed, "Spaghetti!" The lines used then were relatively light. Bass bugs and heavy flies were yet to come, and the heavy lines needed to control them were used only on very long salmon rods (16 feet and over). Casting was as likely to be by the "Spey" or roll cast as to be overhead.

Split-bamboo rods came of age in the 1920s. Tonkin cane, superior in its weight-to-stiffness ratio, replaced the softer bamboos. Dry-fly-action rods, which were simply stiffer for a given length and weight, came into vogue. With them came heavier lines and longer casts. The forward-taper fly lines that lengthened the casts still farther followed in the 1930s.

These changes showed up most obviously on the Atlantic salmon rivers of the East, where the new, stiffer split-bamboo rods only 9 feet long and weighing only 5 or 6 ounces could, in capable hands, cast as far as the 12½- to 19-foot "salmon" rods made of the old limber materials. There was consternation in the salmon-fishing fraternity when people discovered that it wasn't necessary to own an expensive "salmon" outfit, and when the new breed of trout fishermen, equipped with the improved bamboo fly rods, started crowding *their rivers* and catching salmon as well as they could.

Arguments flared. Just how long did a rod have to be to catch an Atlantic salmon? To prove that very short light rods would take them, I eliminated the rod completely and, casting by hand with the fly line, hooked and landed a 10-pound salmon by playing the fish directly from the hand-held reel. My point was that the proper length and strength of the rod is determined only by the skill and inclinations of the angler. It can range from a telephone pole down to none at all.

The most recent trend—back again toward longer rods—has come about for two reasons. First, the increasing popularity of weighted-nymph fishing, which is now recognized as very effective; second, the appearance of graphite rods on the market.

You can drift weighted nymphs just off the bottom through pocket water that you could never fish well using unweighted flies or nymphs. The gradual realization that a large percentage of trout are found in this type of water, and the recognition that drift control (rather than long casts) is the key to success, are bringing long light rods into great favor. With them, the fisherman has better control over the depth of his drifting nymph. He has less line lying on or in the water as he fishes. If his rod's action is very gentle, he can feel or see the tip vibration at the strike much more readily than if he were using a short rod, in which case much of the line would be lying in the water or on the surface.

On reaching a favorite western trout stream, the angler may face this decision: Will I fish with weighted nymphs and bounce the bottom, knowing I'll have the best chance of catching fish, or will I count on some surface activity and fish with dry flies, streamers, or unweighted nymphs? In addition to giving him a better capability with deep nymphs, the long rod requires less skill in controlling streamers and wet flies. The short rod will be pleasanter to cast and give him just as good a chance with dry flies, but it will probably cut down his catch if he has to change to weighted lures.

Because of their extremely light weight for a given strength, the new graphite rods take less strength to hold up and control. A 9-foot rod of a given action that used to weigh about 6 ounces may now weigh less than 4 ounces. Graphite could well become the material of the future, as important a change as split bamboo and fiberglass that gave us the power we needed to make short, light rods effective. Graphite will give us the lightness to make long rods easy to work with.

One factor in the energy required in fly fishing lies in the total weight of the single-handed fly-casting outfit. The angler must hold it in the air with his casting arm the whole time he's fishing. The lighter the package, the less work he performs. This simple fact has always favored light rods. By reducing the weight of all lengths of fly rods, graphite helps make the longer rods less work to hold up through hours of casting. The new graphite rods also make light rods even lighter and less tiring.

The *longer* and *stiffer* rods using lines of sizes 9 to 11 give the best control of a heavy fly. They let an angler drop a bass bug into a pocket amid lily pads 40 feet away and then pick it up after only a foot or two of movement. The rod can be 9 or 9½ feet long or perhaps even longer if the angler is physically able to handle it. Long stiff rods and heavy lines do call for greater strength than shorter, lighter ones, and an angler should choose between them on the basis of his casting abilities and endurance.

It is not always the longest and stiffest rod that casts the farthest. The distance depends largely upon the individual and the tackle's balance. A short light rod in capable hands will cast as far as a much heavier one. Casting is kinetic energy, the energy of motion; and the power involved is measured by the mass (the line in the air) times the square of the velocity (mv^2). In other words, a line moving at 1.41 times the speed of another line twice as heavy has the same energy as the heavier line and casts as far. I can cast about as far with a light 6-foot fly rod by reaching high speed as I can with a 9-foot rod and pure power. In developing a line of fly rods some years ago for Garcia, I found that my casting distance with any of them, from 6 feet through 9, came out about the same. In a test of actual fly speed back in 1953 I found that the fastest average speed I could get for a fly with a 9-foot rod was just under 76 miles an hour. With a 6-foot rod I was able to increase the speed to over 96.

It is important to realize that casting techniques for small rods and long ones are quite different. The short powerful strokes a long rod requires simply will not develop the speed it takes to cast as far with a light rod. Short-rod casting calls for full-arm movement and a high, developed speed. Once understood and practiced, the full-arm cast becomes relatively effortless and daylong casting with a short rod is far less fatiguing than with a longer one.

In discussing the merits and capabilities of long rods versus short ones, it's necessary to compare rods of similar action. The rods shouldn't change character as they change length or else the comparison isn't valid. The 6-foot rod we're considering is essentially the top two-thirds of the 9-foot rod. (I'll make it plain in what follows when I make an exception to the norm.)

Long rods, like the 9-footer and over, will do many things for the angler:

1. A long rod will give him better control of his fly in the fishing path it follows. The longer his rod is, the better he can guide his line around rocks and through eddies on short casts.

2. He has better control of the speed as well as the course of the fly. He can speed it up or slow it down by raising or lowering his rod, and he has a greater capability to move his fly laterally.

3. He can mend line more easily with a long rod, thereby giving his fly a better drift or a longer free float.

4. He can control the fish he's playing better because of his increased lateral control, and he can lift or roll the line over rocks that are farther away than a small rod can handle. (Obviously there's a point beyond which rod length has no effect on a fish.)

5. He can keep his back cast higher, which is an advantage when there are bushes or obstructions behind him.

6. When he's sitting in a boat or a canoe, long casts are easier with the long rod, and the rod's length keeps his false casts higher in the air and away from the boat and other people in it.

7. If he has a suitable line, he can roll-cast farther because of the larger diameter of the loop he can put into the cast.

8. When playing a fish, the angler's cushion against tackle breakage is greater. There are many more milliseconds in the time it takes for a 9-foot rod to bend down to a fish's swift run and come to tight pressure. The 6-foot rod calls for much swifter reactions.

With all these advantages for the long rod, why would anyone ever want to use a short rod?

One thinks immediately of small streams where trees

hang over the waters and there's a limit to the length of rod one can cast without striking foliage. Yet most fly fishing is done in relatively open water, so let's consider that area as basic.

The work involved in a day's casting can be considerable. When I used to cast all day long with a 9- or 9½-foot rod, I developed wrist muscles like a fencer. It was hard work. Now, when I cover the same water over the same period of time with a 6- or 7-foot rod, I never grow tired. For those who aren't overly muscular, casting becomes more pleasant and less tiring with the shorter rods.

The sheer length of a rod, even if it's made of graphite and very lightweight, becomes a factor in casting. The resistance of pushing a rod through the air while casting increases exponentially with its length whether or not the rod is thin and willowy—just as there's more resistance and more work required to throw a big, fluffy dry fly than a very small one. The number of guides on a long rod is greater than on a short one, and each guide takes its toll of drag on the line as it goes shooting through on the cast. It's harder to develop line speed with a long rod not only because of its air resistance but because of additional guide drag.

I feel very close to the fish I play with my short delicate rods. In taking many big Atlantic salmon (up to 27 pounds) on #16 single-hook flies, I sense not just their movements but the *way* they move and perhaps something of their inner feelings as well. It is almost as if I can feel the heartbeats. I do not believe that with a 9-foot rod I could play these fish so well or sense so completely just how, and when, they are tiring.

The small-diameter lines used with short rods also have their advantages when you're playing a fish. They offer less drag when held across the current, or when they're pulled through the water by a fish in his wake on a fast run. What this reduced drag means is that smaller hooks and finer leaders, which fool more fish, can be used safely for big fish in heavy water. All too often, when you're up toward the edge of your tackle's strength, it is the pull of the fish against the drag of the line rather than the angler's pull at his end that gives a fish his freedom.

Just as the long rod gives greater control when playing a fish at mid-distance, the short rod gives greater control when playing a fish in close. Since most fish are lost either when first hooked or when they're almost ready to be landed, this becomes very important. To bring the fish in to a net or for a hand release with a 9-foot rod is a gymnastic exercise. Most fishermen are forced to use heavier leaders in order to do it, or they have to reach up and take hold of their long rod in the middle, with the reel end dangling free. It is true the long rod offers no problem if the fish is going to be beached or there's a second member of the fishing team on hand to take the fish in a net. Yet fishing is more challenging when the angler lands a fish all by himself. Fish also have the greatest chance of survival when they're never handled—when the angler simply takes out the hook by hand or with a pair of pliers and sets the fish free while it's still swimming.

The final minutes of playing a fish are crucial, and the control a short rod gives is really amazing. The first time a good fish I was playing ran between my legs I was talking to a friend standing on shore nearby. Before I reacted consciously, I'd let the tip of the rod and then the rest of it follow the fish between my legs and I had picked it up again on the far side to continue the playing. Since that day, at our fly-fishing schools I've often let fish do the same thing to demonstrate the short rod's advantage when playing a fish in close. The short rod lets an angler handle his fish with ease and with dignity.

On a windless day an angler can control a heavy fly on a short rod if his timing is perfect, but in the real world of gusts and breezes, it takes a heavy line and a short or heavy leader to control a heavy fly or bug. In a windy situation, or if the timing of the cast is the least bit off, the weight of the heavy fly will override the directional power of a light line and spoil the cast. Where bass bugs or heavy flies must be cast, where long pickups of line must be made and where, as in fly-fishing for tarpon, a fast, long cast with a heavy fly must be made, no intelligent angler would say that a short rod is anything but a serious handicap. When I fish tarpon and when I fish bass bugs, I use an 8½- or 9-foot rod with enough backbone to throw a #10 or #11 line. Short-rod fishing is best with flies that are essentially as light as a feather. The bulkier these "light" flies can be made, the more chances arise to use short rods.

Wind is one of the fly fisherman's great problems. Heavy lines at good speed will penetrate the wind, whereas lighter lines need greater speed to penetrate as far. Small rods *can* give that greater speed and the short-rod fisherman can develop the ability to cast well into the wind.

With long rods an angler can drop loops or wrinkles of slack on twisting water to give a dry fly a longer float. Although the long rod may do it more easily, the short rod does it just as well. There are techniques of casting and sudden stoppage that will drop piles of line where the angler wants them, and once the short-rod angler learns these techniques he can equal the long rod's performance.

In at least two articles I've read concerning the advantages of long fly rods, the authors have compared them with big-game fishing rods. I believe this is an unfortunate comparison. Big-game rods are designed for pumping *in* line and therefore must be very stiff. In pumping, the angler lifts the rod high and then, as he drops it swiftly toward the fish, he is able to reel in a yard or two of line before repeating the maneuver. If he uses a limber rod, he is reeling against the spring of the rod and gains less line than if it were stiff. If he lengthens the stiff rod, his leverage will be reduced and he will not have the strength to lift the rod against the fish's pull. Most important, big-game rods are made for trolling, not for casting. They are designed basically to resist bending in *only one direction*. To compare a heavy trolling rod with a single-handed fly rod is to compare tangerines and turnips.

Once, long ago, someone asked why I used a lightweight 6-foot rod for most of my trout and salmon fishing. I had never thought it out before. "I want a challenging tackle," I replied.

I can almost fall asleep and wake up again between the time a fish starts a run against the cushion of a 9-foot rod and the time the line comes tight on the reel, and I have to take my hand off the handle to give him slack. With a 6-footer I have to be ready the instant a fish starts to move. There's no long cushion of time, no long, slow bending. *That's* way I use a light rod.

At the other end of how light I go, I don't ever want to say to another angler, "You're more effective than I am because you have a tackle advantage." I want to feel that I can do anything any other angler can do as well as he, using my lighter gear and, if need be, making up any tackle deficiencies with sheer skill. That's why I don't use rods shorter than 6 feet when I'm angling for fish that could weigh from 10 to 30 pounds. I need a certain minimum of power to make long casts even though I could play the fish on a shorter rod.

Throughout my life I've been interested in the skills of angling, taking ordinary tackle and trying to do extraordinary things with it. I fish for pleasure and find it in solving difficult tackle problems and fooling difficult fish. I meet a great many other anglers who also fish with light rods for the pleasure and excitement they can give—anglers who are a little more interested in the fun they can have than the fish they bring home. The choice of the length and character of an angler's fly rod is a very personal thing. Long rods are deadlier. The shorter, lighter-weight rods are less work and more fun. The complete angler uses both.

[1977]

9

Points of Contention

As catch-and-release fishing for trout and other species has proliferated in recent years, thanks in large measure to the efforts of Lee Wulff, the question of barbed versus barbless hooks is being debated widely. Some anglers hold that barbless hooks are totally ineffective fish catchers, which isn't the case. Others maintain that barbed hooks inflict too much damage to a fish you intend to release alive. And that, as Wulff makes clear here, may not be the case either.

As it happens, I fish with barbed hooks for trout and salmon unless specific regulations dictate otherwise—in which case I just flatten my hook barbs with pliers. I always use barbless hooks, however, on my bluefish flies because it makes unhooking bluefish easier in light of their vicious teeth. It is also no small comfort to have a big barbless fly passing by my head while casting instead of the harpoonlike alternative.

There is a widespread feeling that barbless hooks are an important conservation tool, and that their use will save a great many salmon that, when released, would otherwise die. Let's check it out.

There is no question that a barbless hook is easy to remove from the jaw of a salmon. It can be taken out with a finger grip. How much faster it can be removed than an otherwise identical barbed hook gripped firmly by the fingers, needle-nose pliers, or a hemostat is open to question. I feel that tests would show the difference in time to be no more than a few seconds. Will those few seconds have a major effect on the salmon's survival? I doubt it.

A barbless hook is likely to remove itself, inadvertently, from its hold on a salmon. In that sense it is a conservation measure: if more salmon are lost while being played, more will reach the spawning redds.

Most people playing fish with barbless hooks tend to play them more gently than if the hooks were barbed. This means more playing time and a more exhausted fish. In fact, most people play fish much longer than necessary to land them. I've read articles with titles like "Catch, Revive, and Release." There should be no need for *revival.* Fish can be brought in consistently with most of their reserve strength intact, so that when released they swim away immediately, enjoying their regained freedom. When an angler has to revive a fish, he has failed to play it as well as he should.

It is in the playing of the fish that we need to call for improvement. Few anglers actually test out their tackle to find out how hard they can pull on a given leader tippet before it will break. Simply tie a leader tippet to something solid and then, with the rod bent at an angle of less than 90 degrees, break it. The safe pull an angler can put on a resting fish will amaze the uninitiated. Few anglers keep their pull up near maximum strength when their fish is quiet or moving slowly. Most fishermen play as if engaged in a tug-of-war with a constant fear of giving line and an equal fear of giving slack. The old rule of "tip up/line tight" prevails. The best results will depend, however, on the angler using his tackle's pressure well, sensing just when his salmon is about to weaken and give ground and when he's likely to take off with a sudden rush. He should play his fish from a down-current position and not try to hold the fish against the current.

Whether or not an angler has this judgment and skill can be indicated by the minutes-per-pound ratio. One minute per pound to land your salmon is like par in golf, a good measure of proficiency. An angler who doesn't achieve this ratio should study playing tactics until he comes somewhere near that range. Such a commitment would be far more beneficial to the salmon than the choice of hooks.

A barbless hook has a tendency to fall out when slack is given, but a barbed hook will not. This *slack* can be a factor that will *shorten the time* a fish must be played. Inasmuch as a dog can be trained and a horse's spirit broken to take a rider, a salmon's spirit can be broken if he can be made to feel that further effort is futile. Skillful play is the secret: instead of constant tension, he's given slack whenever he wants to run, complete slack; when he stops, the maximum pressure is applied. Each time he makes a great effort and feels, momentarily, that he's free, the hard pressure comes again. When his best maneuvers fail time after time, when his best runs and leaps are of no avail, he's likely to accept that further resistance is futile and give up. He'll come to hand with a lot more survival strength remaining than if he's tug-of-warred to complete exhaustion. The judicious use of slack is essential to this playing technique, and slack and barbless hooks do not go together well.

Do barbless hooks *hurt* a fish less? Perhaps they do, although the penetration hurt should be the same and the pulling against the bend of the hook where the barb is not involved will be the same. At the removal of the hook a barb will cut the flesh, the depth of the cut equaling the width of the barb. The width is $1/64$ inch on a #6 hook, $1/32$ inch on a #4 hook, and $3/64$ inch on a #2 hook. A cut of that depth on withdrawal either from your jaw or a fish's would not be a life-threatening wound. For a salmon, compared with the battle scars many of them carry from nets, seals, lampreys, and other predators, I believe it is insignificant. Then, too, a cold-blooded salmon's sense of pain is nowhere near as acute as ours. In the thousands of salmon I've released, I've yet to see a serious wound in the mouth from being hooked.

The key to a salmon's survival after being played is his state of exhaustion. The use of barbless hooks can contribute little to the minimizing of this exhaustion, and if it prevents the use of psychology in the playing it can actually be a negative factor. It would be a sad thing if anglers who continue to use barbed hooks but release their fish while they are still strong and sure to survive were somehow considered less sporting than those who use barbless hooks, particularly if their playing times are longer.

Whenever a salmon needs resuscitation, regardless of hook type, the angler can be certain that he has something yet to learn about playing fish. For the fish's welfare, he should set out to learn it and will only be satisfied when every fish he releases swims away sturdily to a certain survival.

[1985]

10

Some Flies I've Designed
and Fish With

This winter of 1989/90 is the sixtieth birthday of the Wulff series of dry flies, and in that time they have become the most widely used dry flies in the world. There are very few trout dry flies, like the Adams or Light Cahill, that edge the Wulff patterns slightly in commercial sales among trout fishermen, but they aren't used for salmon and steelhead, for which the Wulff patterns are also popular.

Here's the story behind those famous Wulff drys and other patterns Wulff has developed in the intervening years. Not that the process has stopped, mind you. The fly-tying bench at his Catskill home is still a clutter of new ideas, and we spoke on the telephone the other afternoon about a way he has developed for making large-appearing flies on ultrasmall hooks that I'm looking forward to trying. As valuable as Wulff's fly patterns may be, the thinking behind them is even more so for any student of fly patterns, and those thoughts are equally evident in this chapter.

It was the winter of 1929/30 and I was tying flies for the coming season of trout fishing in the Catskills and Adirondacks. Looking over the catalogs of Hardy Bros. and Wm. Mills & Sons to check the accuracy of some patterns, I was struck by the delicate, anemic look of all the dry flies. They were based on the British tradition of slenderness. The bodies were simply wrappings of fine silk or quill over the fine wire hook shank. I thought, If I were a trout, I'd be darned if I'd come up from the depths to the surface to get a single skinny bug like that. For a hatch, maybe, but for one bug?

So I decided to make some heavier-bodied flies, more like the mayflies I found on the streams: the Hendricksons, the Green Drakes, and the rest. Fly bodies tend to become water-soaked and make a fly sink. This may have been why the bodies were so thin, because the floating power of the traditional feather fibers used in fly tying was relatively low. And, when a trout was caught, the slime on the feathers demanded a change of fly or a washing and drying period before that fly was ready to float again. I thought, I'll use bucktail, which is very durable and has great floating power, especially for the tail, which is where most of the weight of the hook is concentrated. Then I can float a thicker body, which I am sure will draw up more fish from the depths.

In my mind was the *Isonychia* mayfly (I didn't know the name then; I just called it that big, gray drake), and the Coffin May, the mature stage of the Green Drake. I made up flies to imitate them with bucktail tails and wings and angora or rabbit's fur bodies. The then-popular Fanwing Coachman was prone to spinning and twisting the leader and the weak tail made of a few fibers of golden pheasant tippet feather didn't have the strength to hold the fly up. It had a bad tendency to sink at the tail. I know a bucktail would do a much better job and that bucktail wings would be just as visible and much, much more durable. So I tied up that pattern in its new form, too.

I used them first on the Esopus in that spring of 1930 with Dan Bailey, my regular fishing companion. Results were dramatic. Hendricksons were hatching and the Gray Wulff was extremely effective. More important, perhaps, was the fact that I caught almost fifty trout on a single fly without having to change it. The White Wulff worked well when the real coffin mays were out and was good as a search fly, especially when light was poor in the evenings. The Royal worked well at any time of the day and had the advantage of being very visible (to the fish, too) because it was both light and dark.

It was Dan Bailey who insisted that I call the flies Wulffs; otherwise I'd have named them the Ausable Gray, the Coffin May, and the Bucktail Coachman. Dan, then a teacher at Brooklyn Polytechnic Institute, was getting deeply into commercial fly tying. We sat down together to work out a greater series of patterns so that he'd be able to sell more of this new type of dry fly. I had already planned a Grizzly pattern because of my success with the Grizzly King in my western fishing. Dan and I worked on to bring out a Blonde, a Brown, a Black, and the rest of the ten patterns he listed for sale.

Fortunately, Ray Bergman was a good friend and he listed the first three patterns in his great book, *Trout.* They were the only dry flies in the book with animal hair instead of feathers and they established the names and opened up the way for the Irresistible (I have a letter from Ken Lockwood, who made the Gray Wulff into the Irresistible), the Humpy, the Rat Face, and the rest of the other-than-feather flies.

That summer of 1930 I fished New York's Ausable for a week. Fish of between 2 and 3 pounds were common in both branches of the stream but Victor Coty and I concentrated most of our time up on the smooth water of the West Branch near the ski jump near Lake Placid. We'd discovered that the tiny rises in those long still-water pools were often made by big brown trout instead of the tiddlers and chubs most fisherman thought were making them. Catching them made us stretch out our leaders, add our finest gut tippets, and move and cast slowly and carefully.

Of course, I had fly-tying materials along with me and we worked out patterns that seemed most like the small insects to which those wary browns were rising. The end result was the Coty Stillwater Light and the Coty Stillwater Dark. They had slightly thicker bodies than the actual insects that were drawing the rises and we felt that made them a little more effective. Again Ray Bergman, who used those I gave him with success on some other rivers, put them into his fly pattern listings in *Trout*.

1932. In the midst of the Depression, I was working in New York City as a free-lance artist. Whenever I wasn't working at art for advertising or illustration, I tied flies to make what extra money I could. The Wulff flies had developed a reputation and I had enough customers to fill out most of my work weeks. Except in the summer when I went fishing, anyway. Top price for flies then was twenty-five cents.

Fishing wet is more effective than fishing dry since trout do most of their feeding underwater most of the time, so I was fishing wet much more than I fished dry. Somehow I got started using a very simple nymph that was just a plain Gray Wulff body without any adornments. Soon I was catching most of my trout on it. I tried to get my customers to buy some. They didn't. Then I reduced the price to fifteen cents each, thinking that a bargain might draw some sales. No one, apparently, wanted to insult the trout they were fishing for with a cheap, fifteen-cent fly. I don't believe I sold a single one of those nondescript nymphs I was finding so effective, even though I finally dressed them up with a couple of turns of peacock herl at the head.

There's a strange sequel to this story. In 1970, at one of Charlie Ritz's Fario Club dinners at his famous hotel in Paris, I sat next to Frank Sawyer, recognized as the premier nymph fisherman in England. In the course of our conversation he asked, "What do you think I catch most of my fish on?"

"A medium-size gray nymph," I replied.

He turned sideways in his chair, fished into his pocket and brought out a box of nymphs. There it was, in his hand, a simple gray wool body on a #12 hook. I held the box in my hand while he dug into his pocket again and came up with another box. "Here," he said, "is what I have to do to sell them. I put a winding of gold tinsel on them and a little darker material at the head." Maybe he was a much better salesman than I or the fact that a lot of people saw him fish helped out. I had tried to sell those nymphs in New York when none of my customers had ever seen them work on the stream.

1935. Frustration was gnawing at me as I fished the Battenkill that day. Fish were rising here and there. Good fish. And I couldn't catch them. I'd tried old standbys with no luck. I'd looked searchingly into the Battenkill's clear water and couldn't see a thing that might interest a trout. Finally I went to a skater and found a trout that would take a dare. He chased it and caught it the second time. Those were the days when we kept fish, and I quickly killed that one and opened it up.

Inside that trout's stomach was a black mass that, when I put it into a small puddle of water on a rock at streamside, disintegrated into a host of tiny black beetles. Those beetles, like icebergs, were 90 percent below the surface, small, black, and practically invisible. I knew what fly I'd tie that evening. I figured a few little wisps of hackle fiber wouldn't put the trout off, so I made a spider turn or two of hackle just behind the eye of a #16 hook, then filled the shank up with a round, black wool body.

That evening I tied a dozen of those Little Black Beetles and was all set for a beetle hatch the next day. There weren't any. In the days that followed I caught a few trout on the beetles just to prove that trout would take them but, in all my fishing, I've never run into that hatch of little black beetles again. I still carry a few with me, just in case. It is incidents like this that make me carry a lot of flies that are just for special occasions and create a need for a vest with a great many pockets.

1947. Atlantic salmon can be most reluctant actually to take a fly yet show a real interest in some of the flies that an angler drifts over them. They will come up beneath a dry fly and pause, inches away, then sink back to their lies near the bottom. They may rise to look at or play with a number of flies yet never take one into their mouths. They may sink them with their tails. They may push them under with their chins while their jaws are locked tightly shut. They may even open their mouths and let the fly float right on outside their jaws as they close their mouths and disappear from view. There can be no more challenging fishing, and sometimes you can get such a fish to take your dry fly. Which one? And why?

Then I think of my flies as piano keys. Each is a little different. Someone sits down at the piano and touches the keys to turn out a beautiful melody. Someone else sits down and fingers the keys and the sounds are discordant. I want to play a melody with my flies that will intrigue the salmon. I may send out a big White Wulff for a few casts. Then a little #10 Gray Wulff. Then a brown Bivisible. Then back to the White Wulff again, first on a cast upstream with a long tantalizing drift down to the fish's lie followed by a cast that drops the fly right down on the fish's nose. Then a skater to say, "Yah! Yah! You can't catch me." I had a wide variety of flies to cast to the salmon but, whereas the White Wulff was at the top of the brightness scale, I had nothing at the very bottom of the scale. I decided to remedy that with a small all-black fly. I called it Midnight, and it was particularly effective right after a big White Wulff had just passed over a salmon on a long, slow drift.

Still 1947. Some salmon anglers seem surprised when salmon rise to a natural insect. It is true that they can't digest any food but if they'll take an imitation of a natural insect why not the insect itself? I was watching a salmon make occasional rises to spent-wing mayflies that were drifting through the pool. The fish was coming up at about five-minute intervals. The rises didn't surprise me, but the thought that here was a type of fly that interested a salmon but that I hadn't made a fly to imitate did. All my flies were designed to float high. I realized that I ought to have one that would lie flat in the surface film to attract fish like the one I'd just seen rising. I needed a fly to drift *in the surface film* instead of on top of it.

I chose to imitate the stonefly, one of the larger and more conspicuous of the salmon-stream aquatic insects, and designed a fly that would just barely float. To fish it, I had to make it land on the surface like a seaplane at a low angle, skidding in to float on the surface tension. If I dropped it in for more than a few inches it would sink. It was hard to see because nothing projected above the surface, but it would bring salmon to the steel when all my other flies failed. And it seemed to draw more of the bigger fish and fewer of the grilse. I used it as a secret weapon for a number of years, then began to give them away. At one club on the Etamamiou River more than half the salmon taken for many years were taken on that pattern, which I named the Surface Stonefly. The members tried to have other fly tiers duplicate that fly and failed. The molded plastic bodies were more or less neutral and didn't pull the fly down as a body of wool or other fibers did. When my stepsons were in high school, I let them develop some customers and they made hundreds of dollars in spending money making up those flies. It is the come-through fly I depend on most in fishing for salmon.

1955. Of all the streamers I made up, some standard patterns and some far-out in color and design, the Black Dace, which is a simple black-headed, black-striped minnow imitation with an orange flair for its pectoral fins, was the most successful. As usual I gave away a good many of the streamers I made, for angling friends to use. The Black Dace is the one that got the most requests for repeats. George Renner, a fine Catskill fisherman, was one of those who says it's his favorite streamer. It's mine, too.

1962. I traveled to Scotland to fish competitively for salmon on the Dee with "Jock Scott," pen name for Donald Rudd, the most widely read writer on salmon fishing at that time. I used my 6-foot, 1¾-ounce bamboo rod, which he labeled a "toy." He used his 16½-foot greenheart Grant Vibration rod. I caught a salmon on a White Wulff dry fly (where George LaBranche had failed with the dry fly), and he caught none. I spent a week of practice on the river before our contest week, to learn the river and to test my flies. I'd written the first article on "hitching" salmon flies back in 1946 for *Outdoor*

Life [see Chapter 4] and wanted to make a special fly for the occasion. I made one with black wings, black body with silver tinsel winding, and a light, bright yellow throat, adding a few long black bucktail hairs stretching out well beyond the bend of the hook. I felt the long hairs would make the fly ride higher in the water when hitched. I called it the Long-Haired Haggis and caught two salmon on it although the gillies and everyone else I showed it to vowed it wouldn't catch *their* salmon. Later on I dropped the long hairs, as they weren't needed when I made the special body for hitched flies that made them ride higher by themselves.

The riffling hitch that I discovered at Portland Creek in Newfoundland, has become an accepted and, in many places, a preferred way of fishing for salmon (and steelhead), but when I visited Scotland again on the Dee in 1970 and on the Spey in 1964, I neither saw nor heard of anyone there fishing with that method. The British are very slow to change.

1963. I caught a tarpon of about 130 pounds (it was released) on the Florida Flats near Loggerhead Key for a film that aired on CBS's "Sports Spectacular." It was on that trip that I made a special mold for a plastic body at the bend of a 4/0 hook that would let me set two pairs of flaring yellow hackles behind a bright red hackle and flanking golden pheasant tippet feathers. It was bright and colorful, more so than most of the tarpon flies of that time and it has since caught a good number of tarpon for me.

1964. On the Moisie River in Quebec a small group of us who were guests of Alain and Marc Prefontaine formed the Sixteen/Twenty Club. To be eligible for membership an angler had to catch a salmon of over 20 pounds on a #16 fly, something that had never been done before. The basic problem I saw was to create a fly on that tiny hook that would be big enough to attract a big salmon. To do it I crammed the shank with Bivisible-style hackles and, for good measure, added a long snoot of bucktail to give it maximum bulk. As it turned out, it also gave the fly a flip-flop action on the surface when retrieved as a skater. Alain Prefontaine caught a 20½-pound salmon that first evening, and the fly became the Prefontaine.

Since then I've caught a great many salmon on that fly, the largest a 27-pounder. The pattern is one of my favorites, one of the most effective. The salmon make dramatic rises when they come for that fly, usually coming at least partway out of the water in their surge to catch it. In 1985 on the Restigouche I caught a 10-pound salmon on a Prefontaine tied on a #28 hook for another first in angling.

1966. I went to the Pacific off Panama to Ray Smith's Piñas Bay Camps to fish for sailfish. I needed a fly that would have maximum bulk with minimum weight. Bucktail and the synthetic fibers that imitate it are heavy. I chose hackles because they're light and when spread out around the shank of a hook they give considerable bulk. To make a baitfish-type fly for such a big fish I needed a long one so I made a tandem, connecting the two 4/0 hooks with a monofilament loop and wrapping the fly not only on the hooks but on the connecting monofilament as well.

The fly was successful, big enough to be tempting and light enough to be easy to cast. I caught half a dozen sailfish on it in my week there and, in May 1967 at Salinas, Ecuador, caught a world record striped marlin of 148 pounds on that fly (the record still stands in 1987).

1967. I married Joan Salvato and our honeymoon was a salmon fishing trip to the Miramichi. I had a number of fly designs I'd made up through the years and carried in my vest but had never given names. The most beautiful of those, in my judgment, was a fly with gray squirrel tail over black squirrel tail for the wing, a burnt-orange body with gold tinsel winding and bright yellow hackle fibers at the throat. When I had time, I put a golden pheasant crest feather atop the wing and behind the body as a tail. It became the Lady Joan. It is an attractive fly, different in color pattern from most salmon flies. And it was effective. Poul Jorgenson put it in his book of salmon flies and it has become a recognized pattern.

1969. Joan and I were giving a trout fishing school for Garcia and the American Sportsman's Club on the Elk River near Steamboat Springs in the summer. In the evenings after fishing I'd tie flies along with other members of the group. As we were about to finish and clean up one night, the discussion turned to the question of the need for the fancy feathers that cost so much. I allowed that most of those feathers were for beauty as we saw it, for our own enjoyment more than for effectiveness with the fish. I went further and said that the stuff fly tiers throw away could make as effective a fly as anyone needed.

Reaching down into the waste materials scattered on the floor I picked up some hackle of the soft, feathery butts of the hackles that everyone throws away, saying, "Here's some poor man's marabou." Then I found enough gray wool to make a body and a tiny bit of bright yellow yarn. From these I fashioned a nymph with a gray body, a yellow tail, and four legs of the soft fluffy gray fibers off the hackle stems. It looked like a crawly thing to me and though the trout didn't have it on their list of known bugs, when it hit the river they felt a real urge to see what it tasted like. Charlie Meyers, outdoor writer for the *Denver Post*, sang out, "I have a name for it! The Wretched Mess." I make it weighted and unweighted, a simple fly of simple materials.

1973. In September I fished at Kulik Lodge in the Bristol Bay drainage of Alaska with my friend Jerry Jacob. The normal method of catching the big rainbows of the Kulik, American, and Battle rivers we fished was to use a weighted salmon egg imitation and bump it along the bottom on the retrieve. We soon tired of this as it isn't a pleasant way to fish with a fly-casting outfit. I decided those rainbows would take a streamer if it were big enough and flashy enough for them to see from their lies near the bed of the stream.

When I opened the little bag of fly-tying materials I'd brought along, I found it was my saltwater kit and not the one with my trout hooks and materials. I took the feathers I'd normally use for tarpon flies and put them on a #2 long-shanked O'Shaugnessy hook with a body of gold mylar tinsel, and we caught more fish on that pattern than we'd been able to catch by bouncing lead. Since then I've caught rainbow and brook trout, northern pike, walleyes, bluefish, and bass on that fly and it has become one of my favorite streamers.

1975. When *Sports Illustrated* gave a party for my good friend Joe Cullman, dedicated salmon fisherman and the man who brought women's tennis to the fore with his Virginia Slims tournaments, they asked me to design a special fly for the occasion. As with the Lady Joan, I reached back into my fly boxes to choose one of the maverick patterns I'd been fishing with. I chose a fly I loved because I'd made it up to represent the light green of the new leaves on a white birch seen against the bark of an old white pine in the sunshine of May. The wing was black, the body was apple green, and the throat was white. A golden pheasant crest feather glistened in the sunshine atop the wing. It has long been one of my favorites and it is with great pleasure that I sometimes write into the log at Runnymede, Joe's camp on the Restigouche, the weight of a good salmon I've caught and list the fly that caught it as a Cullman's Choice.

1977. My friend Bob Kerrigan, who worked for *Gourmet* magazine, wanted to do something special for his boss, Earle McCausland, its owner and publisher. McCausland was a salmon fisherman with water on the York River at the tip of the Gaspé Peninsula. I learned, too, that Wilfred Carter, our director of the International Atlantic Salmon Foundation, was hoping to get a donation from Mr. McCausland, which we needed badly for our work in salmon conservation.

Sports Afield, for which I was a contributing editor, had run an article on fantastic gifts for Christmas. Among them was a fly designed by me that would be registered and could bear the name of the gift recipient. The price was $500. That turned out to be too much, I guess. No one wrote in to buy such a gift.

Here was the opportunity to design a fly for someone that would help a friend and help get money for a good cause. I remembered Scotland as a beautiful symphony of green and gorse and heather. I made a fly with a green and yellow base that would be colorful and, I hoped, attractive to the salmon. A friend of mine was writing an article on salmon flies and he included the Green McCausland in his listings. It caught salmon for Kerrigan and McCausland and their friends, so many that an outdoor writer from Quebec who was writing a book on salmon flies for Quebec called me up to verify the materials that went into making it.

1979. The Stewiacke is a soft, sleepy river, slow and deep, and it lies in central Nova Scotia. It was there in October that I made a film called *Autumn Silver* to show its exceptional late salmon fishing. Bill Bryson, expert angler and assistant director for Nova Scotia's Tourism Outdoors, and Cecil Dennis were our hosts. The weather was warm, the river low, and the fishing lousy for the first few days. Then it rained. What we used to call an equinoctial storm blew in as night fell. Great trees groaned and bent with the wind. The rain pelted down like driven hail. I knew the peat bogs would be flooding and the river, after the storm, would be dark as bitter tea. Inside the camp, warm and comfortable, we tied flies.

I wanted to make something that would fit the rising waters and the mood of the salmon that, next day, should be "on the take." I created the Stewiacke. Bill and I fished it there successfully for the rest of our stay and on other rivers, too, with excellent results.

Our good friend Jim Hill, remembering back to the Christmas article in *Sports Afield*, asked if I could make a special fly for his retiring boss. I could and did. It was Adam's Choice. It is a very beautiful fly, I believe, with a bit of the Blue Charm in it and something of the shine of the Silver Blue. I find it very good in clear rivers. It is like no other fly I know and I fish with it often.

1980. This was the year of the Candy Fly. We were preparing for our second trip to Boca Paila on Mexico's Yucatán Penin sula. On our earlier trip we'd caught both bonefish and permit there. That had been a hurried trip and we'd had few flies with us that were designed for bonefish or permit. I had caught my permit on a Surface Stonefly dragged underwater. This time I'd made up some flies on saltwater hooks that I thought would work.

There are very few things that bonefish and permit eat that fit into the conventional fly shape even though lots of permit and bonefish are caught on flying insect-type flies with wings, body, legs, and tails. Much of their food is in the form of shellfish, which they dig for, grinding up the shells as they feed. I felt that they'd take most any fly to some extent but that if I made one that would, first, ride with the hook up so that it wouldn't catch on the bottom and, second, that would seem to be a crawly thing, big enough to attract attention and weighted to get down near the bottom fast, they'd take it well. A parachute-type hackle gave me "legs" where I wanted them. Next, I wanted a choice of colors that would let me feel comfortable whether I was fishing over clean white sand or varying degrees of vegetation.

They worked. I gave some to a good friend, Keith Russell, to try out in advance. He caught over thirty bonefish with them in a single day and reported back that the bonefish took them just like candy. We called them Candy Flies and designated them Peppermint, Chocolate, Lime, and Licorice.

1982. It occurred to me that with the welding of materials to plastic bodies I could make a better salmon fly for hitching. I could make a special spot for hitching that would make it easier to put on the hitch, make sure it was always in the right place to ride high, would be easy to unhitch, and would prevent the messing up of the fly. All this proved to be true. In one instance Bruce and Susan Waterfall, fishing on the Grimsá in Iceland, caught more salmon than any of the others in their party who were using standard flies for their hitching. The others kept wanting to borrow their flies and when they gave them the flies designed especially for the hitch, they, too, caught more salmon than before.

In 1982, I also suddenly realized that Atlantic salmon

flies were so stylized that a basic premise had been over-looked. It's generally agreed that the main reason a salmon rises to an insect-type fly is the long years of parr feeding in which his basic food has been insects. Salmon flies since time immemorial have been, basically, insect imitations. Trout and parr feed on the same things in the streams, but salmon-fly tiers had neglected one classification that is well known to trout fishermen. They'd forgotten the terrestrials. I decided to rectify this major omission. I made imitations of dragon-flies, moths, grasshoppers, and ants. Again, they proved very successful. The terrestrials filled a vacant space in the salmon fly coverage. The unconventional looped hackle-wing drag-onflies drew wild rises on Mrs. Guests Pool on the Grande Cascapedia when my other flies had failed. The big black carpenter ant, kin to my little trout Red Ant, brought up reluctant fish in the Big Curly Pool on the same river. The moths and the grasshopper had their day on other rivers.

1984. I made a number of refinements in the trout patterns that can be made by bonding materials to plastic bodies. Among them was a small nymph, a fly to fit into the niche usually covered by the Adams or the Elkhair Caddis, a good stonefly nymph and a new and devastating sculpin-type streamer.

For the small nymph I decided to go to a flashy attractor, because most nymphs are realistic and drab. I was able to put bright gold on the plastic body behind the hackle-fiber legs that would give a motion *within* the fly as it moved through the water, a movement sometimes as important as the move-ment of a fly *through* the water. This little nymph can draw interest from the same trout that will strike a brilliant Mickey Finn.

Using a translucent body, something quite insecty but something conventional flies are unable to achieve, I made a caddis-type fly with bucktail down the back and grizzly hackles. It has an interesting look and has been more success-ful than the Elkhair Caddis for me.

The Stonefly Nymph, with its soft materials attached to a

well-shaped body has good fiber movement to give it seeming life. It works better than the earlier stonefly imitations I've made and has become a fly I depend on a good deal in my trout fishing.

The Sculpin/Darter is by far the best imitation I've seen of that type of minnow. It has broad pectoral fins spreading out in true darter fashion. They're made with hackle tips and they move easily yet are very durable. It has a mottled darterlike body with its wing base of gray squirrel tail and its overlying grizzly hackles. It is weighted to sink down into darter territory and is made on a keel-type hook that rides point up, allowing a fisherman to let it rest a moment or two on the floor of the pool before giving it life, a maneuver that is much more likely to draw a strike from wary fish than a standard retrieve.

1986. For years I've been experimenting with flies for that most difficult of fish, the permit. Using the same type body involved in making the Sculpin/Darter but with a weighted hook that won't corrode in salt water, I placed wide brown bucktail flanges just below and behind the head of the fly to give it a broad flatness that might look a bit crablike. I let a badger hackle trail out behind and I covered the back with gold tinsel to give it some flash. On my trip to Boca Paila that year I caught a 15-pound permit and this year I hooked another permit that was even larger on the Permit Fly.

In September, we fished for steelhead on the surface of the Copper River in British Columbia. Steelhead are difficult to bring to the surface. Although they will take a free drifting dry fly, they are much more susceptible to flies that skim across in front of their lies, like a hitched fly over an Atlantic salmon lie. I used hitched flies with a little success. I used heavy hackled, skimming Surface Stoneflies with a little more but both drowned in the rough water where I felt some steelhead would be lying. Harking back to the Prefontaine I put a forward-and-up double snoot on a Surface Stonefly, which lets it skim over rough water none of our other flies came near making. The steelhead (ours ranged from 9 to 15

pounds) took it well. It was the most successful fly at Schmi-
derer's Camp for the rest of the season. I'm waiting now to try
it on Atlantic salmon in rough water where hitched flies tend
to skew to one side and sink and Prefontaines are pulled
under when the leader sinks and the current drags them
down.

[1987]

11

How to Tie a Wulff

Here are directions for tying Wulff dry flies from the man himself. These instructions originally appeared in the Roundtable, *published by United Fly Tyers, a Boston-based fly-tying club. Although Wulff has written at various times about how these flies are tied, I chose the following description because the directions are complete in the text and are not dependent on photographs.*

You'll note that Wulff ties without a fly-tying vise and instead holds the hook with his fingers while tying. He still ties his flies this way, even down to #28 dry flies, a diminutive hook less than one-quarter of an inch long. Commercially tied versions of Wulff dry flies often appear very neat, whereas Wulff's own ties look much more scraggly and buggy, which in his own view makes them more effective for both trout and salmon.

In tying a Wulff dry fly I still prefer to use bucktail, the original material, although calf's tail is somewhat easier to use since it doesn't take the extra time to match up the hair ends and is just about as effective. Tying them in my fingers, my first step is to pick up the hook and start the *dinging* [attaching thread to hook] with a piece of thread long enough to tie the fly. For these flies the thread should be fairly strong, as it takes a firm pressure and a small wall of thread around the base of the wings to hold them in position.

I hold the eye of the hook between the nails or tips of thumb and first finger of the left hand, doing the winding of the thread with my right. When the shank is wound I can either hold the thread in place by pressure between thumb and finger below the eye of the fly or take a couple of half hitches to hold the thread in place.

Next I cover the wrapped shank with lacquer. I like to feel that the flies I tie will stay together for catching a lot of fish and so want the solid body permanence lacquer gives as well as the security against twisting. I use unwaxed thread, as waxing prevents the lacquer from penetrating into the thread. The tail is cut to length and wrapped to the shank. I like a good thick tail to hold up the heavy end of the hook, and having the bucktail run the length of the shank (1X long hooks preferred) starts building up the body as well as making the tail more secure.

Again the thread is clamped between the left thumb and finger, or the head of the fly may be put between my lips to keep the thread from unwinding while I pick up the angora wool, or roll rabbit's fur around the thread to make the body. Normally, I use wool, as it's easier to handle and, seemingly, just as acceptable to the fish. I wind the body from head to tail and back again, shaping it into a natural insect form, winding over it with thread near the head.

The fly at this stage is either held between the lips or the thread is given two half hitches to hold while I cut the bucktail for the wings. I cut it long and then pull out the longer hairs and reset them until all the natural ends are approximately even and the hair is matched up. Then it's cut to length, which is about ⅛ inch longer than the wings should normally be.

The hair is placed, facing forward, at the right place at the head of the body, facing forward over the hook eye. It is wrapped tightly with several turns of thread, about ⅛ inch or less behind the hook eye; then the hairs are lifted, and thread is wound in front of the vertical hair until it stands upright and can be split by windings around the shank and a figure eight or two between the wings. The butt ends of the hair, protruding behind the first windings, tend to give a natural, humpbacked look when the fly is fished.

Next, two saddle hackles are set in with two winds of thread. They face forward, on top of the hook, their bare butts fitting in between the rising wings. The fly, as in all this tying, is still held between the nails of the left thumb and forefinger. A big drop or two of lacquer is then put on the base of the wings to penetrate well and set everything up when it dries. While it is still wet the two hackles are wound. The first wind is through the top between the wings then two or three winds behind the wings and a wind back through between the wings. The hackle tip is gripped between finger and thumb to hold it until ready to tie off. The second hackle is wound entirely in front of the wings and its tip secured along with that of the first hackle. Now the final wind or two at the head with three half hitches to secure things. A drop of lacquer goes at the head and the place where the tail joins the body to make everything secure.

[1974]

12

Fly Reels

Fly reels—and most fishing reels—have a fascination for many that extends far beyond their simple, utilitarian purpose. As one example, I offer a fellow I met when I worked as director of the American Museum of Fly Fishing who had amassed a substantial collection of nineteenth- and early twentieth-century American and British reels even though he had no interest in fishing whatsoever. They were simply well-crafted antique objects whose varied and sometimes bizarre mechanical works offered enchantment to the collector. This collection eventually wound up in the museum, which—as do such other organizations as the Catskill Fly Fishing Center—maintains an extensive collection of antique reels, all to the delight of the public eye.

As in so many other realms of fishing, Wulff has been an innovator in reel design. So-called rim-control reels, in which an exposed reel-spool flange allows manual braking, found their modern reincarnation through Lee Wulff and Farlow, a British tackle maker that first marketed the Lee Wulff Ultimate reel (no longer made) based on this concept. Numerous other American and British makers followed suit, and Wulff's design is now commonplace on modern fly reels by various makers.

Among the fly-fishing tackle basics of fly, line, leader, rod, and reel, the reel is the least important. Why, then, are there so many reels on the market and why are they so expensive?

It is impossible to catch a fish without a fly (hook) and line. It is extremely difficult to catch fish like trout without a leader to fool them into thinking the fly is dissociated with the angler and his line. It is also quite difficult to fly-fish without a rod, although I have done it by hand-casting.

It is not very difficult, however, to catch a fish without a reel. If one can coil the line on the deck of a boat or in a basket worn on a belt, or let the line be carried in a loop downstream in the flow, one can fly-fish successfully.

A fly reel's basic purpose is to hold or store the line not being used either in casting or in playing a fish. Because the reel plays no part in the casting and very little in the playing of the small fish that fly fishermen originally pursued, fly reels were the simplest possible. They are still basically single-action, which means that one turn of the handle produces one turn of the spool. Gears, which would be required to make more line come in with a single turn of the handle, complicate the reel and make it heavier—something to be avoided as the reel must be held all during the casting, and extra weight is more tiring.

With the original reels there was enough friction in the turning to keep spools from overrunning in the rare cases when the fish took line. But as larger and stronger fish were caught, a device called the "click" was installed to give some restraint to the turning and prevent overrun. A *click* is a triangular point, backed by a spring, pressing against a serrated disk centered on the spool stem. By varying the spring pressure, the resistance to turning can be increased or decreased, within a low range.

Most fly reels have clicks, and they actually have a purpose beyond keeping the spool from overrunning. As the angler plays a fish, his reel is below the rod and out of his sight. He cannot see the spool to know how much line is left. The sound of the click, a gentle pulsing at low speed or a veritable scream when the fish runs swiftly, can tell the fly fisherman roughly how much line is going off the reel and how rapidly, even though he can't see it.

Fly-reel spools are narrow, compared with bait-casting or trolling reels, and for the same reason—lack of visibility. In bait casting or trolling the angler can see the spool as he retrieves line and can wind it evenly, so when the fish runs the line will not lift up off the spool, cross itself, and tangle. The wider the reel spool the more likely the line is to tangle. On a narrow spool, even without guiding, there is little chance of a backlash, although it does happen occasionally. The ideal weight-to-line capacity ratio is probably a spool as wide as it is deep. Anglers who can wind line carefully onto a fly reel with a slightly wider spool will have a little less bulk and a little less weight to hold up when casting.

Two things are sometimes done to extend a reel's capabilities. Both add weight and complications. The weight is obviously an added burden, and any complication, such as gearing, increases the chance of mechanical problems. Look at the advantages and disadvantages.

Both add to the cost of the reel. Let's take braking first. It makes it possible for the angler to put a greater strain on the fish mechanically. This is a convenience, but, for a skillful fisherman, not an essential. In my best saltwater fly-fishing catch [see Chapter 22] I took a 148-pound striped marlin on a fly using a 12-pound tippet, a cheap 9-foot glass fly rod without a detachable butt, and an inexpensive Farlow Python 4¼-inch single-action reel with only a click: no brake, no drag, and no multiplying gears. Like many anglers, I brake by using finger pressure—on the fly line as long as it is within the guides and on the inside of the spool after the fly line is off the reel. The bulky fly line and the reel spool can be handled without burning, but the thinner, tougher backing will cut into flesh.

When I began fly-fishing for big gamefish I thought about braking. I could manage it well enough on the inside of the spool but I knew that the greater the leverage of the braking the more powerful it would be. Most brakes worked on a diameter not much larger than the reel's spindle. I wanted one with the maximum available diameter—the outside of the spool. At that time all fly reels were made with the spools inside an outer frame. My first design was to make a section of the outside of the frame free to move, so that it could be pressed against the outer rim of the spool. This worked all right but I had a better idea, namely to open the spool itself to finger pressure. The result was the first finger-control reel, the Lee Wulff Ultimate, made by Farlow. It's an important improvement that may help anglers play fish better. Orvis picked it up with their CFO reels and now many of the reels for larger fish are built that way.

The cost of a good mechanical brake on a fly reel is considerable. How necessary is the brake? How convenient? Obviously, judging by the reel used in the marlin catch (which, by the way, did not have finger control), it is not essential. A brake is convenient and it does give increased pressure against a fish. It should be adjustable, because early in the fight it must be light and later, when the fish is tired and less likely to make a sudden start, it can be increased. This will make the fish work harder and save the possible problem of line overrun or burned fingers, and for most anglers catching big fish is worth it. But are there any disadvantages besides weight and cost?

Yes, one. A mechanical drag cannot be released as quickly as that put on by the fingers. It takes time to release a mechanical drag; therefore the angler cannot play a fish up to the maximum pressure his tackle will stand. A finger can be lifted instantly; the angler with a mechanical brake has to allow a little extra time. If he holds as hard, his fish can break away.

A good method with a mechanical drag is to use it in the medium range and add extra pressure with the fingers, increasing the drag setting as the fish tires but never dialing it high enough to break at a sudden rush. We should remember that the guides in a bent rod add a lot more drag through friction than they do when the rod is pointed directly at a fish.

Lowering the rod reduces drag and has saved a good fish on many occasions.

The amount of line on the reel spool is an important factor both in braking and in retrieving line. It takes a lot more pull to turn a spool that is one-quarter full than it does one that is half full. To give the same braking power, a mechanical drag should be relaxed when there is less line on the spool.

Not only for drag but also in the retrieve is the amount of line on the spool important. If the diameter of the spool is 2 inches it will bring in 6.28 inches of line in a single turn. If it is only 2.82 inches it will bring in twice as much, or 12.56 inches. Some fly reels have an arbor on the spool to increase the diameter of the line. It makes sense if only a fly line is to be used, but I'd rather have that space filled up with backing in case of an emergency. And a reel that holds more line lets you use line of a larger diameter, an advantage both in braking and in retrieving line. What balance will you take between a larger spool and an increase in weight? Decisions, decisions!

The next consideration is multiplying gears, to retrieve line faster. Offsetting that advantage is the weight of the gears, the cost, and the possibility of mechanical failure. A good many people faced with salmon or big saltwater fish choose this route. It can save time in playing a fish and lets an angler put heavier pressure on faster than if he's limited to the single-action retrieve (not forgetting that a slightly larger spool in a simple single-action reel will bring in line just as quickly and may not add any more weight than gears). Fast retrieves are valuable but perhaps not as valuable as some believe.

A trout fisherman playing a 4-pound trout with a 6X, 4-pound-test leader thinks he is using very light gear. He's likely to think, too, that his four pounds of pressure will tire the fish for him and uses his four pounds to try to pull the fish here and there in the pool. Let's go back to the marlin. One doesn't pull a 148-pound marlin around the Pacific on a 12-pound leader. It dawns on the marlin fisherman that his job is to make the fish tire himself and that his pressure is minor until the fish is tired enough to be unable to resist the gentle pressure of his leader. Only when the tackle is heavy is the angler's pressure important in the tiring of a fish. The object is to keep him moving and, psychologically, convince him that resistance is futile. Small periods of rest are not too damaging, and many wise anglers use slack when a fish runs to let him think he's free and then tighten up for the rude awakening, time after time, to convince him that he's not.

What are the overriding factors of value in a reel? Durability is one. Cheap reels are not likely to be as durable as the more expensive ones. If you want a reel for a lifetime you buy one that will last. It is hard to be sure a reel will last a lifetime unless that identical model has been on the market that long. If the materials are time-tested the worry is small. New materials, like plastics, can give trouble. I've had reels that were in perfect operating condition except for a small plastic part that cracked, from age or whatever, and a replacement part couldn't be found.

Not many manufacturers have been making reels long enough for a true age test. The first salmon reel I bought, back in 1933, was American-made and developed shaky bearings after three months of use. I then bought a Hardy St. George. It was "used" then and I used it another fifteen years and it is still in perfect working condition. I have a Vom Hofe that did not get as much use but is also in fine shape. Vom Hofe reels are no longer available. Hardy reels are, and one trusts that they're still made with the same painstaking care and fine materials.

Reels, in a sense, are like shotguns. As far as capability goes, cheap reels may serve as well as the most expensive, at least for a limited time. I've been to hunting clubs where the best, most effective shooters used cheap mail-order guns. Why, then, did so many other members buy Model 21 Winchesters, Greeners, and Sauers? Skill cannot be bought with dollars—but craftsmanship and beauty can. Engraving on a gun or a reel will not make it perform better, but we treasure beautiful things that are a part of our sport. A reel can be a thing of beauty, something we enjoy every time we set it on the reel seat to go out to fish. It will last as long as we do, if it is a good one, and even bring a similar pleasure to our kids. Just looking at it can bring back memories and give us pleasure. It sits well on the mantel and it is easy to carry, something that can't be said of a fly rod or line. It will accept a lot of handling, which can't be said of flies, which, once used, lose some of their beauty even though the rough caresses of the fish they've caught may have increased their charm.

Stan Bogdan is the outstanding American reel maker of our time. A Bogdan reel is a treasure that can be depended on to perform as it should. There are those who say it is a little heavier than it needs to be, but it is a little stronger than most, insurance that it will take much awful abuse. Each Bogdan carries the imprint of the hands of the man himself. It was not turned out in a factory, although my Hardy St. Georges, which I treasure almost as much, were.

Of the many reels now on the market or yet to be made, some will earn their place in history and in our hearts, as have the Bogdans, the Vom Hofes, and the old Hardys. Though far from the most important part of our fly-fishing tackle, our reels are the most durable of all our angling treasures.

[1988]

13

An Angling Challenge

Having known Lee Wulff fairly well for a number of years and having some inkling of how his mind works. I sometimes wonder what he'll think of next. This chapter is one recent answer to that question. Having several years ago managed the unheard-of feat of taking 20-pound-plus Atlantic salmon on #16 trout hooks, he decided to try for a salmon on a #28 hook, the smallest generally available. I and many others would have said that was impossible, but I've learned one just doesn't say that about Lee Wulff. After considerable travail, he succeeded.

Nor was he content with just that. I spoke with him after a recent steelhead trip to British Columbia, where he had tried the same #28 experiment. There was just a little disappointment in his tone as he described taking a 9-pound steelhead on a #28 hook, one pound short of the goal he'd set for himself in terms of the fish's weight.

Many people will regard these accomplishments as stunts without real application to modern angling. But I can assure you that from these experiments will come

*ways and means of fly-fishing that will apply to our
everyday fishing lives. Those who follow Lee's future
essays will be among the first to see just what I mean.*

There are moments an angler cherishes for the rest of his life,
moments that in the remembering always bring a small lump
to his throat and a warm feeling for fellow anglers. One such
moment came for me in Newfoundland's Conception Bay on
the night of August 17, 1967.

For more than a month, over a two-year period, I had
been trying to break the 50-pound-test record for bluefin
tuna. It had been a time of great effort and heartbreak. No one
had ever taken a big northern bluefin on 50-pound line, and
there was a strong feeling in the angling community that it
couldn't be done. My experience till then only substantiated
that belief. I'd hooked seventeen and lost them all. One was
right at the boat after only an hour and a half, and the hook
pulled free. Another came to the boat after eight hours, but
when Captain Ralph LeDrew took the leader, the 350-pound-
test wire broke at his pull. Others were lost at varying points
in the playing: Once the rudder controls broke and the fish
ran off the line and pulled free; one went down into more than
two hundred fathoms and never came up; there were many
hook pulls, and once the line was cut by the propeller. It was
as if Fate didn't want me to catch a northern bluefin on 50-
pound line.

But on that August day, a tuna took my bait at ten thirty-
five in the morning. It was to be my last day of fishing. I was
determined to make no mistake in the playing and to keep
right on top of the skipper so that, among other things, the
line would never touch the corner of the cabin. Northern
boats are often weatherbeaten; I feared that a line grazing the
rough painted wood would fray like a run in a silk stocking,
which might have accounted for one or two of our breakages.
The fish was strong. We played him through the rest of the
long day and into darkness, which came at about nine-thirty,
and fought him on through the blackness until midnight.
Thirteen hours and twenty-five minutes in the fighting chair
without respite or relief. With only a dim cockpit light to see

by, we'd all been on edge for a long time when Ralph LeDrew finally grasped the leader. This time it held. The gaff went home and our big bluefin came aboard.

We were as weary as we were happy during the twenty-mile cruise back to base at Portugal Cove. Only a single light showed up on the pier. We're too tired to haul that fish up to the scales tonight, I thought; it will have to wait till there's help in the morning, and it may lose a few pounds.

Suddenly, when we were closing in on the pier, a deafening chorus of whistles and shouts and automobile horns shattered the quiet of the night. We climbed to the landing for champagne while the willing hands of many helpers brought the tuna to the scales. It registered 597 pounds, far above the old record. The whole tuna-fishing community had come down for congratulations. It was a moment to remember, warm and wonderful.

There have been other records, and each one has brought a sense of satisfaction and of doing what no one has done before, but the fish capture that means as much to me as any other is not a world record, nor will it ever bring the acclaim that world records do. It was one of those things that an angler does on his own to take the sport a little further than it has ever gone before. It's like climbing the forbidding face of a mountain that has never been overcome, just because it is there to be challenged. It is a personal thing, something one believes can be done, and one does it not for the applause of the crowd or the recognition of the record books but for one's own satisfaction and sense of achievement.

It came about this way: At our fly-fishing school I tie a couple of flies in my fingers, without a vise, as I've been tying them since I was nine. One of them is always a Grizzly Midge on a #28 hook, the smallest-eyed hook that one can buy to tie to a leader and fish with. The students are impressed not only with the finger dexterity required but with the fact that a fish can be caught on such a tiny hook. Someone always asks, "How big a fish can you catch on a number twenty-eight?" My stock answer used to be, "A good-sized trout. A four-pounder, perhaps."

But in 1984 I got to thinking: Just how big and difficult a fish can be caught on a #28 fly? What would really impress those students and give them the best idea of the challenges that angling offers?

The answer was an Atlantic salmon. Not a grilse, a one-year sea-feeding salmon, but a multiyear fish of 10 pounds or more, with all the power and speed its sea-feeding and super-storing of energy can give it. I was certain that although good trout have been taken on #28s, no one had ever taken a grilse, let alone a big Atlantic salmon. Back in the 1960s I was one of a little group of fishermen who decided to see if a salmon of more than 20 pounds could be caught on a #16 trout hook. We tested our hooks—Alcocks, Mustads, and all the others—and found that they broke or bent open at less than a 4-pound pull. A few of us finally caught some 20-plus pounders, but after twenty years only four of us had made it. The #16 had remained the ultimate challenge until I decided to try with a #28.

The bite of a #28 hook is less than a ¹/₁₆ inch, and its fine wire can cut like a knife through the flesh of a fish. That small bite would make the hooking of any fish quite difficult, and even if I hooked one I'd never be able to exert even a pound and a half of pressure in the playing. Add to that the worry whether the point of the hook, if it encountered bone or gristle, would penetrate at all, or bend or break off at the lightest pull.

I decided to use 4X, 4-pound-test leaders. The diameter of the tippet would not be an important factor in fooling the fish, for salmon come in from the sea without having been fished for. Four-pound would give me a factor of safety of at least three over the hook and still be strong enough if I cast (God forbid) a wind knot in it. I would fish with both wet and dry flies, but I would count most on skating flies of the Prefontaine pattern, the fly that had been most successful with big salmon on #16 hooks, and on which I'd taken a 27-pounder.

The Prefontaine provides about as much fluff as one can put on a hook, but I needed something bigger than what could be wound onto the shank of a #28. To achieve this, I passed the leader through the eye of the hook, then took two half hitches around the shank to secure it. I carried the tippet on beyond the bend of the hook and then doubled it back, with two knots in it to keep the hackles that would be tied to that trailing bit of monofilament from slipping. I wrapped the hook shank with fine thread and put on the forward-poking nose. Then I wrapped back to the nylon trailing behind the bend and wound on two badger hackles, letting their tips become the tail of the fly. It was barely big enough, but beautifully light and the hook was as well placed as possible.

My first chance to fish for salmon that year was on the Restigouche and I chickened out, knowing that the salmon would likely run from 15 pounds to more than 40. I had no confidence I could hold so big a fish on a #28, and if I *did* hook a 40-pounder—I wanted to land it. My first fishing with the tiny hook was on the Upsalquitch, later on in July. Salmon there ranged from 8 to 15 or 20 pounds, and that was the range I felt I might handle. And there'd be more grilse than salmon, so I could get some practice on the smaller fish. Once I started I would fish with nothing else. To switch back and forth might mean missing the one chance of a lifetime to make the catch.

Fishing was fairly good, and I had a number of rises. The Prefontaine is a special skater, and its bucktail snoot makes it hop around when retrieved. With so small and so light a hook it was especially active, and the fish missed it much more than they got it. It seemed barely to touch the water in its dancing, and as it was not caught in the surface film, it wouldn't suck down into a salmon's mouth as readily as a heavier fly. However, the lightness of its dancing drew more strikes than a normal skater would have. Most fish, when they missed, would come back for at least one more try, and often a fish made six or seven passes before feeling the hook or giving up.

The first fish I hooked was at Two Rocks Pool, where a mirrorlike flow spilled over and splashed on downstream in a wide and shallow race of water. He wasn't on long. His first move was to leap and show himself to be a grilse. His second was to race to the far side of the spillover and go downstream, where a sunken rock in the swift water caught the line and pulled the hook free. The following day I rose several fish and missed them all before connecting with another grilse at Caribou Pool. Here also fish lie just above a swift flow, and the fight was a repetition of the first one, except that this fish was on for several minutes.

I'd learned the first lesson: Try to hook the fish where there's some quieter water at hand to play it in. But when your pools are assigned daily, sometimes there just isn't any easy place to play a fish on the day's beat. That evening I drew Humbug, a long, deep pool with salmon lying at both head and tail. After five slashing tries at the fly, I hooked a grilse at the head of the pool. I was able to stay below it and gradually to bring it down into the deep, slow flow, where the belly of the line did not have the force of a heavy current against it. Once the fish worked up into the tail of the inrushing water, but then it drifted back into the slow flow. This time, my worries about the holding power of the little #28 were groundless. I expected it to pull free at any moment, but it held until Dennis Moran, my guide, could lift the net as I drew the grilse over it. A 3-pound grilse builds confidence, but I wanted a full-size salmon, a fish of 10 pounds, and that would be much, much more of a challenge. That was my last salmon fishing of the year, and the bigger fish would have to wait for another season.

I had a year to think about the project before July rolled around again and, with our school season over, I went to the Upsalquitch, where I felt my chances were best. During the winter I'd come up with an idea I was sure would be helpful.

I had learned much about playing fish on small hooks through my experience with dozens of fish on #16s. I'd learned almost to sense their heartbeats as they decided to run and leap. Learned how to coax them to slow down when they were fresh and wild. How to make them work within the limited pressures I could use to stir them. Learned how to relax them when they were tired, and trick them into swimming in close so I could grip their tails. But perhaps more important was overcoming the difficulty of hooking them on so small a hook.

My idea was to put the hook at the head, rather than at the tail, of the fly. I felt dumb not to have thought of it sooner. That way the hook would have its full bite instead of having part of it taken up by body material and hackle fibers, which would fill in much of the space between shank and point. As a result I found it relatively easier to hook fish in the 1985 season. Not that it was truly easy. Far from it; I still hooked only one out of every seven salmon that rose to the fly.

The first day out I caught a grilse of nearly 4 pounds. Again it was at Humbug Pool, with the advantage of a slow, deep flow. It took nine minutes. The fish, like the first one, was hooked in the corner of the mouth.

The next day I caught another grilse, at Caribou, by coaxing him to stay in the smooth upper water instead of heading down into the rapid run. Then my problem became one of hooking salmon instead of grilse. The river was high and we had to fish from canoes, sharing fishing time with another angler. It seemed as if luck was always against me. My partners hooked salmon consistently but my #28 drew only grilse. Perhaps it was because the salmon gave up after a try or two at the dancing skater, while the grilse often kept rising until they were pricked by the hook or were actually hooked. When the last day of the week came around, I'd landed four grilse and lost many more without ever being fast to a salmon.

On that last morning I drew Humbug again and had high hopes of striking a salmon at the head of that quietest of all the pools. If I hooked a fish there I'd have several hundred yards of smooth water before there was a rushing flow again. But the morning went by without raising a fish. As we came to the tail of the pool on our way back for lunch and to pack for leaving, I saw a salmon roll to the surface and couldn't resist making a cast or two for him. He got the fly on his third try, a 10- or 12-pounder that leaped and immediately raced downstream into the fast water, passing on the far side of a stranded tree trunk and breaking free.

By now the taking of a good salmon on a #28 had become my obsession. I knew it was next to impossible, and that I'd give up the landing of many a good salmon if I fished with

#28s. It was in my thoughts as I drifted off to sleep and there again when I awoke. But I'd caught five grilse by then and that made me certain that, given a break, I could land a salmon. But when would I hook one that wasn't too big and too wild to handle?

I still had another salmon-fishing opportunity, provided by my friend Joe Cullman on his water at Runnymede, on the Restigouche. It is a great, wide river and it was high from a month of rain. All the fishing would be from a canoe, and the steady, heavy, continuous flow would give me plenty of problems.

It was paramount that I have a good man to handle the canoe. Not only must he be skillful but he must join with enthusiasm in this obsession of mine, and *believe* that it could be done and that *we* could do it. Fortune favored me, for the guide assigned to me was Wendell Sharpe, long on the river and wise in its ways, and young enough in spirit to put his heart into something from which the only reward would be the satisfaction of accomplishment.

That first evening on the Restigouche I fished at Wheeler Pool, smooth and steady water hundreds of yards long and hundreds of yards wide. In the high water, salmon were scattered all through it, and it was hard to know where to fish. We tried to place the canoe where we saw fish jumping or rolling. Four salmon came to the little fly with big, heavy swirls. Two of them came a second time, but low and sulky, and none of them felt the hook.

It rained that night, making the river even higher. It was still raining the next morning when Wendell took me up to Deeside Ledge, a dozen miles upstream. In the rain the little skater had to be greased frequently, but it stayed on the surface and I made it do a sluggish dance over the heads of the salmon in the pool. Two of them came for it but failed to feel the hook and wouldn't come back. In midmorning a grilse took the fly solidly. We played it downstream a little way while it jumped and ran till it was tired. The hook held and we went ashore, where I brought it slowly over Wendell's submerged net. He was excited and said something like, "It's hard to believe, but if we can land a little one, given a break we can land a twenty-pounder."

Near the end of the morning a 10-pound fish rushed the fly and was hooked. He made one swift run upstream, leaped, and was free. I reeled in to find that the hook had broken cleanly at the bend.

Midday is a time for rest in the Restigouche salmon camps, but evening found us back at Wheeler under broken clouds, some sunshine, and a little wind. Very soon a big salmon took the fly but before Wendell could get the anchor up he had raced away, slanting upstream to a high leap and, again, the fish was free and I was left with a broken hook.

Before dark two grilse took the fly and both broke away at the end of their first runs.

My log for the next day records a fair day at Wheeler in the morning. The fifth cast hooked a good salmon. I stripped line from the reel immediately and let it slide freely through the guides to put minimal pressure on. Still, the fish broke free just as Wendell got the anchor up. I knew we had to get under way faster and give as much slack as possible until we could get downstream of the fish. Then they could not head upstream with a belly in the line and jump or accelerate against its drag.

Three more salmon and a grilse were on and all were lost, but each was on for a slightly longer time. Wendell was getting faster with the anchor and the outboard motor, bringing us directly downstream of the fish, a point we'd yet to reach with a salmon on.

Evening brought rain and gusts of wind. The fish stayed in a rising mood, and I brought up two salmon and a grilse. The salmon were just pricked, but we got below the grilse swiftly and drifted downstream ahead of it, working it lightly but steadily until I could bring it to our canoe. We were developing a better system.

At the very end of the evening, in the fading minutes before dark, fog started to settle in. There is a magic in the flow of a great river at a time like that. The liquid sound of the water and the lap of waves against the canoe become a very special music. It's hard to see the fluffy skater dancing over the dark, mysterious water at the length of the cast. Eyes strain for the sight of a rise and ears listen intently for the soft sound of a salmon breaking the surface. It is time for the night to take over the river. Time, perhaps, for one more cast—or two.

I heard it first, and then we saw the flash of a silvery body leaping in the mist. Quickly we went through the drill—up-anchor and the pulling of line off the reel. The outboard clattered into life and we moved into position below the fish. We were sure that bright silver we'd seen was our salmon.

Twice more—while we jockeyed downstream ahead of the fish, sometimes with power to maintain light pressure, sometimes with so little power that we lost ground to the river, sometimes drifting free—we saw and heard, far off, the silver and splashing of his leaps. After twenty minutes the fish was tired and we eased it to the shore. The dull beam of the flashlight showed the tired form of the fish as he drifted into the net. Our glow of triumph faded swiftly. The mist and the dusk had fooled us. Our fish was not a salmon but a very large grilse. Wendell lifted it into the canoe.

In 1985 New Brunswick law allowed the taking of grilse but not of large salmon. All salmon had to be returned to the river, unharmed, to rebuild the runs of the large multi-sea-year feeding fish. At least I could keep that fish to mount on the wall of our schoolroom. It was still an impressive fish—for a #28 fly.

The next morning at Wheeler we saw a salmon roll as we approached the pool, and we hooked him on the fifth cast. Before the anchor could be lifted and in spite of the line I was giving, he raced up and across and developed enough drag to break the hook. The fishing was slow then until midmorning, when a grilse finally got the fly after seven wild rises. He, too, broke free. Just before lunchtime a salmon rose to the fly but wouldn't come back. After a dozen casts I changed to a wet fly, which brought a sluggish rise behind it. Changing back to the Prefontaine I swept it over the salmon's head a dozen times or more until finally he rose and was hooked. The anchor came up swiftly. The motor started on the first pull.

The slack I pulled from the rod didn't draw tight until we were downstream.

Wherever the salmon went we followed directly behind him. My plan was to tire the fish by making him back downstream under light pressure. That cuts the flow of water through the fish's gills and, I believe, tires him slowly but inexorably. That fish made no really wild runs, but twice he went far and he leaped four times. Without hard pressure on his mouth, he didn't feel the need to panic. It's strange how consistently fish respond to a light downstream pull by drifting back with it.

An island and a shallow bar in midriver gave us some anxious moments. We couldn't be sure which side he'd go down on. If we guessed wrong and he got cross-stream in that shallow water, I was sure the line would catch on a stone and we'd lose him. We grounded on the bar and I was forced to give him a belly in the line for the minute or two he took to make his decision. Then we moved into the flow behind him. For half an hour we were tense with the fear that every moment would bring the sinking feeling of an empty line. We drifted down through the lower pools: High Rock, Florence, Harriett. Then we were approaching the dock at Runnymede, the main camp. We shouted and Lorne Irving, the camp manager, came down to watch.

He saw the 10-pound salmon come to within inches of the net, and he heard Wendell say under his breath, "God, if I only had the long-handled net we'd have had him." The salmon pulled away from the edge water into the full sweep of the flow. He stopped there and slowly I brought him close in again. This time he crossed over the net. Wendell lifted it and he was ours. A salmon. Ten pounds.

Thirty-one minutes of playing time. Much as I wanted to have him mounted on the wall at the school—to point to, for the question of how big a fish can be caught on a #28—we didn't lift him from the net, but slid him carefully over the rim to freedom.

Released, he swam strongly away to do his share of rebuilding the Restigouche salmon stock. There was a warm feeling in my heart for Wendell, and the thrill of doing something that had seemed impossible. It would call for no fanfare, no listing in any record book. There'd be no certificate to mount on the wall. Not even the mounted fish, or even a trophy picture where he hangs by tail or gills. But that capture is a high point in a long lifetime of developing fishing skills, equaling my 148-pound striped marlin on a fly [Chapter 22]. That record was, until then, my high point.

There are endless challenges to tempt an angler, to lead him into endeavors that test his skill and ingenuity. There are successes and failures. There is always that one step to take that no other angler has taken before. No angler need ever be bored, or think to himself that he has done it all.

[1986]

14

Using
Small Hooks

In the previous chapter, we followed Wulff as he hooked and landed a 10-pound Atlantic salmon on a diminutive #28 hook. Here we learn how flies can be constructed on smaller-than-normal hooks to increase the likelihood of hooking fish on the strike. We find also, as Wulff describes, that small hooks used for normal-size flies may be the answer to those difficult and experienced fish who grow big with old age and sound management in our increasingly popular catch-and-release fishing areas.

I should point out here that Wulff is fishing with #28 hooks and not necessarily #28 flies, as the fly itself may be tied oversized on or adjacent to the small hook. Having devised such a fly, the challenge comes in hooking and landing large fish such as salmon and steelhead on the small and fragile hook, a task that may demand the utmost of an angler's skill in understanding and playing fish.

It's funny how over a period of time ideas come together and mesh. It began with the Sixteen/Twenty Club back in 1964.

107

I'd mentioned to the group that I'd once caught a 15-pound Atlantic salmon on a #16 Spider. Then we began wondering how big a salmon could be caught on such a small hook, and as a result decided we'd have a club of those of us who could catch a salmon larger than 20 pounds on a #16. To date we have four members: Alain Prefontaine, Marc Prefontaine, Lucien Rolland, and myself. I took the small hook idea seriously and to date have caught over a dozen 20-plus pounders, the largest weighing in at 27 pounds. That experience makes me comfortable playing big fish on small hooks.

Thinking in terms of *no-kill* [catch-and-release fishing areas] and the wise trout that live in those waters, trout that have been caught and released time after time on flies, it becomes obvious that those trout, not being altogether dumb, are sure to have noticed that each time they grabbed a bug with a strange, hooklike appendage hanging down at its rear they had a hell of a time with an angler as a result. If they can tell the difference between a well-tied imitation and a poor one, they certainly can recognize and avoid a prominent hook just as a deer can recognize instantly the distinctive head-and-shoulders silhouette of a man. I have a friend who is a white hunter, and by making his charges crawl instead of walking upright he gets them much closer to the game they hunt. Similarly, the wise fish can be fooled more readily with a disguised or smaller-than-normal hook. The ability to play one's fish on a smaller, less conspicuous hook can be a real advantage.

Jump ahead a few years. I'm relaxed and thinking about trout fishing. Into my mind pops the realization that although we'd had artificial worms with which to tempt fish since I was a kid in knee britches, they were hard and thus a giveaway to the fish. It wasn't until the soft plastic worms came along that bass would hang onto them like the real thing and be hooked easily. Translate that to trout fishing. Why not make soft nymphs and terrestrials so that trout would hang onto them as well as bass hang onto the soft worms? I got the idea in midwinter and had to keep it a secret until the following season because if I talked about it to any of my newspaper-writing friends they could have it in print the following day, whereas as a magazine writer I would need six months between the time I wrote the article and it was finally published.

I made up my stonefly nymphs on limp surgical tubing with small, inconspicuous hooks. The flies were soft and would bend double instead of being stiff and hard as any nymph tied on a long-shanked or standard hook had to be. When I drifted them through the trout pools that summer, to my delight I found that the trout would take them and hang on until I tightened up and hooked them. There was no need of a constant sharp-eyed watch on the leader or for a little float on the leader to indicate the strike. So I remained mum until the following winter, when *Sports Afield* published the story.

I used #14 and #16 hooks on nymphs that would normally have been on long-shanked #8s and #10s. I'd started with the hooks at the rear of the nymphs but found I had better luck hooking fish if I brought the hook up to the heads of the nymphs where there wasn't so much material to fill in between the shank and the hook point, which reduces the hook's bite. As expected, I had no trouble landing trout on the #14 and #16 hooks.

Jump ahead to our fishing school. For each class I tie a White Wulff on a #10 hook and then a Grizzly Midge on a #28 in my fingers without a vise, and then the students draw lots for them. Almost invariably the individual who gets the #28 asks: "How big a fish can you catch on a tiny hook like that?"

My usual reply was, "A trout of over three pounds."

Then the thought struck me that I was copping out. How big a fish *could* I catch on a #28 hook if I really put my heart into it? The school was there to teach as much as possible about fishing. I owed it to the students and to myself to find out just how big a fish I could take on that little hook. Atlantic salmon were the most difficult fish I could think of, and they took the smallest flies for their size of any fish I knew. I decided to do the impossible and catch a 10-pound salmon on a #28.

That first season, I caught several grilse of about 4 pounds, but they weren't much bigger than the trout I'd caught, and I felt sure that I could catch a salmon of 10 pounds or more, which would really be breaking new ground. The following season, to the amazement of my guides and perhaps a bit to my own, I took a 10-pounder on the Restigouche, and then, last year, a 12-pounder. The playing times were twenty-five minutes and twenty-eight minutes respectively. It wasn't easy. I lost the first sixteen big salmon I hooked and then landed those two with no losses in between. This past summer there were only grilse in the Atlantic salmon pools I fished over, but on a day in British Columbia, I caught a 9-pound steelhead on a #28 surface fly just to keep in practice.

A #28 hook will break at less than a pound of pull when well seated, but at a half pound under a twisting pull or if the point is not well embedded. I've had more hooks break than bend or straighten. But equally important to the playing of the fish is the ability to hook it. During my efforts for the salmon I realized that the best place for a hook on a fly most of the time is probably *immediately in front of the fly* rather than as an integral part of it or at the tail. Only with tail-nipping fish and with larger flies would the normal tail placement be best. By having the bare hook just ahead of the fly its point is the first thing to strike the flesh of the fish's mouth at the strike, and because there is no fly-tying material on the shank to cut down the little hook's bite, there's the greatest chance of setting the hook. If the body of the fly touches the fish's mouth first, he may, with a quick, spasmodic movement, open his mouth quickly enough to have the hook pull out without the point touching his flesh.

If I simply want to eliminate the telltale bend of the hook and use a smaller one, I can snip off the hook bend and put a small hook into the leader just ahead of the fly with a double hitch of the leader. Even a single hitch will do. One can be fancy and wrap the leader to the shank behind the hitch but I find that isn't necessary, and the hook will be effective even if cocked off a bit with a single hitch.

Now that I feel comfortable with very small hooks, I can make effective soft nymphs and other flies with the hook in advance. Trout will hang onto a fly as small as a #14 nymph with a #20 hook just barely ahead of it. I can use small hooks that will let the flies they're on fool the wise no-kill veterans, and I can make normal-size flies with smaller hooks that will hook better than standard flies. Why didn't I figure all this out back in 1964? It takes time for ideas to fall into place, but when they do they can change our methods of fishing. Small hooks are great. Of course, one has to learn how to play fish well to be able to enjoy their use.

[1989]

Book Two

FROM TROUT
TO TARPON

"Come with me. . . ."

That's how the quiet voice-over of Lee Wulff so often has drawn millions into the action of his many outdoor films and articles. And so in this section we go with him. We're off to the Pacific Ocean, where we'll set a world record for fly-rod marlin. We'll go salmon-fishing, too, with Army Chief of Staff and Nobel Prize–winner George Marshall. After a surprising bout with bluefin tuna, we'll catch our breath en route for giant tarpon in Florida.

We'll fish after dark for largemouth bass, and then head to the north country once more for the wonderful brook trout of Labrador's Minipi region. We'll do a little bonefishing, and then, on another salmon-fishing trip, we'll win a bet we wish we hadn't. The explanation is a little embarrassing, but the story is more than worth it.

15

The Old
'Kill

During the years before World War II, there were several noted artists and writers who lived along the Battenkill in southern Vermont and eastern New York: Norman Rockwell, Meade Schaeffer, John Atherton, and Lee Wulff among them. Rockwell immortalized the people living along the river through years of Saturday Evening Post *covers. Atherton and Wulff, particularly, immortalized the river in their writings. Atherton, whose 1951 book* The Fly and the Fish *remains a milestone, was buried along the river's banks, and even now we tip our hats at a particular pool. Lee Wulff, in this 1940 piece from* Country Life, *pays his respects to his "home" river.*

Almost fifty years later, it is my home river, too. I live nearby and fish the Battenkill often. There are wild brook and brown trout here still, although the average size is smaller than it was in those prewar days. And although I've fished trout from Maine to California and beyond, I still count the 'Kill as the most difficult of rivers. As you consider or recall fishing here, you'll find that Wulff's description in this chapter has held up well over time.

When it comes to trout streams the old 'Kill stands by herself. She starts way up in the mountains and comes sliding down, winding from one side of the flat valley to the other. Her flow is smooth and unruffled even where she strikes in hard against the steep mountains that flank the valley floor.

Oaks and giant elms spread out their green to give her shade and ferns stand deep along her banks. Her flow continues steady through the dry months of the summer by virtue of the height of the mountains she rises in and the timbered nature of the country she follows down. She's a big river, too, but there are no concrete highways coursing along her banks, even though she lies within two hundred miles of the largest city in the world.

The first time I fished it was a long time ago. We stayed with old Merritt Russell in his big house in the fields with the locust trees around it and the most beautiful pool on the river a hundred yards behind it. I remember the spacious rooms with their high ceilings and the charm the old place had. We slept that night on real down mattresses and the blankets on one of the beds, fresh and clean though they were, still wore the leather straps and bells that graced them when they kept the Russell horses warm.

Russell's pool in the morning light was a thing of rare beauty for a trout fisherman. The 'Kill comes down around a long bend rippling over a wide, rocky bed as it edges up to the steep, bold mountain that stands behind the house. As it strikes the solid rise of rock, with its overhanging fringe of hemlocks, it crowds in hard against it and the flow is deep and even for almost a quarter of a mile. The clear water of the stream, shaded by the overhanging branches and mirroring the black of the rocks, is dark and mysterious the full length of the steep shore, and the fish lie there in that long black ribbon of shadow. At the tail of the pool the river splits, part of it clinging to the softening slope of the mountain and the rest breaking away into the meadow to find its depths under the roots of old trees and the cut banks etched by the floods.

Below Russell's the 'Kill winds for miles through the widening valley, through the sleepy village, and on down to the big still water miles below. Beyond the town the flow is deeper and the pools are larger. The trout in the lower water are fewer, too, but they run much larger. Great elms have fallen to the water with the river scouring out the rocks beneath their trunks. At one place three small waterfalls come splashing down a long, sheer face of rock to join the quiet river at the base. Four times in the three miles between the village and the still water the little-used railroad crosses the 'Kill. There is no road that reaches the river there and one seldom finds another fisherman unless it should be one of the villagers who has come down the tracks to sit by the side of one of the pools and let his worms or live bait play idly in the slow current.

There aren't many fishermen anywhere on the whole length of the stream. "Strange!" you say. Not really. The 'Kill isn't an easy river. Its water is extremely clear and its flow relatively smooth. The trout are browns and natives. Taking them in that clear water is a test of skill. It takes fine leaders and long casts for the brownies. The 'Kill is moody, too. For days on end the brown trout refuse to rise. I have seen fishermen come for a day or a weekend and leave swearing never to return.

There are legends that the sawmill upstream poisons the fish, that the state no longer stocks the river, and dozens of other such rumors that serve to satisfy the fishing gentry as to the reason they failed to fill their creels. But the fish are there. Last spring on a day late in June the river suddenly came to life after a period of dullness. In two hours of the late afternoon I netted and released ten fish all over 13 inches and a dozen smaller ones that were all taken from a single pool. Then it was dull again for days.

Those are the brown trout of the erratic feeding. When they decide to feed, the whole length of the river seems to be alive with them. And when they don't feed, it would be completely dead except for the natives. Those natives are a blessing. When the brownies have crawled into the muskrat holes and disappeared, I can go to any one of more than a dozen places and find the natives rising regularly in the still, slow-flowing water and there I can spend hours catching one or two fish on my smallest dry flies with my finest leaders.

Sometimes it takes tippets of fine silk thread that eliminate the glisten and stiffness of a leader to deceive them.

They are small but they are difficult. Except for the early days, the largest native I have taken there was 16 inches. I have heard of a few longer than that but the average run is about 10 inches. When rising in clear, still water I think the native is more difficult to fool than the brown trout. The true test of the sport is the difficulty of taking the fish. If it were just a question of size we should all be out fishing for carp or codfish. I can ask for no greater fishing pleasure than to have before me rising trout that demand of me my utmost skill in order to take them.

The old 'Kill isn't a dry-fly stream in the sense that most rivers are. It has very little in the way of hatches. Its clear, gravelly bed that is so easy to wade doesn't lend itself to insect life. And yet, because of the clarity of the water, I have had wonderful dry-fly fishing on it over a period of years. In the middle of May when the buds begin to unfold there are about ten days of hatches and the river boils with trout every afternoon. But later than that the sight of rising fish, with the exception of natives, is rare. Then I work along, fishing the likely water and hoping that suddenly, as I cast, absorbed in the rhythm of the casting, there will be a sloshing rise and I'll be fast to a brownie that will go anywhere from one to four pounds. I have ranged far for my fishing but I know of nowhere else in New York's open waters where the dry-fly fish will run so large.

The largest fish taken from the 'Kill in recent years was caught by a youngster early in the season of 1930. The lad was fishing the Dutchman's pool with a gob of worms. He had a ten-cent line tied to a long pole he'd cut in the woods. He just threw out his worms and sat down on the bank and waited. When the strike came it was a good one. It took all his strength to get the fish into shallow water. He was all alone and there was no one within calling distance. His rod bent so much that he couldn't lift the fish out onto the shore. Fortunately the hook was embedded deeply and the line held. In desperation he worked the great trout into the shallows again and taking up his raincoat and dropping his rod he plunged in after the floundering fish. He wrapped the raincoat around him somehow and carried him to shore. It was a nice fish. Twelve pounds and 2 ounces.

No one knows how many big fish have been taken there in the last few years. Fishermen come to the 'Kill from far away. They fish and go home. Because there are few places to stay on the river the anglers make their headquarters some distance away from the stream. The people in the village rarely hear of their catches except by chance. Such a case happened last year when one of the local fishermen met a man leaving the stream to get into his car and drive away. The local man asked him his luck. The catch of the stranger turned out to be one fish, but it was a stray rainbow that stretched all the way around the man's waist in his shooting coat. The head showed at one pocket and the tail came out of the other. That fish weighed over 10 pounds and but for the chance meeting the town would never have known of its being caught.

The pool below Buffam's bridge has its quota of big ones. Two years ago a friend of mine stopped there to fish, only to find a group of kids in swimming. They were diving from the bridge into the deep water directly below it and creating quite a commotion. As he prepared to leave, his glance passed the shallow ledge at the head of the pool where the spring comes in and stopped. Lined up in water less than two feet deep and perfectly clear were a school of big ones. Not one in the fourteen was smaller than 3 pounds. The water was low and clear and the fish were already frightened. My friend didn't catch any but it's nice to know that when you fish there you are fishing over dynamite.

Twice while fishing that pool I have had one of those old cannibals try to rob me of the fish I was playing. The first time it was almost dark and all I could see was the swirl and the flash that engulfed the struggling 10-inch fish on my line. I reeled in to find the ragged toothmarks on my fish. The second time it was midafternoon and the water was low and clear. The fish were rising at the tail of the pool. I had already released three natives and one brown. I saw a long dark shadow come down almost to the point of the island with its stony beach where the pool spills over, and swing across to the east bank where the water runs deep under the overhanging trees.

Knowing that he must have seen me, I continued to fish the west bank for a while before I drifted my fly into the shadows under the slanting trunks. There was no answering rise. Between rests I shifted from dry fly to nymphs and streamers and back to dry flies again. A small trout rose ahead of me. I cast to him and when he rose he was hooked. Simultaneous with the splash of his rise I saw the dark shadow slide across the shallow sands and streak off out of my vision in pursuit of the fish on my line. I let the fish run in the hopes that the big one would take him and, perhaps, if I gave him enough time I could hook him.

My fish suddenly went lifeless and swung around below me in the current. He came in like a dead fish and I thought that the big brown must have struck him, although I could see no marks and had felt no strike on the line. As he touched my waders the small trout came to life and went skittering off on the surface. He was 11 inches long and that black shadow that had gone chasing after him had left him paralyzed with a fear that he lost only at the solid contact with my waders.

I have spent long hours on the millpond. The flow is wide between the cut-under banks, from the deep hole at the head to the deeper one just above the low dam. Along the western shore the pines and oaks are thick and high to cast long shadows across the still water. The trout line up near the bank to take the slowly drifting food. Here the fish are mostly natives, except where the water is deepest along the cut banks or under the big elm that leans out over the water with its roots digging down into the stream. Many of the fish in that pool are old friends of mine. I've caught them over and over again. Those are the smaller ones. There are some others that bear the scars of my hooks that, had they been landed, would never have been returned.

Once I located a 5-pounder under an old log near the head of the east bank. I discovered him as I walked along the shore and saw his tail waving gracefully with the passage of the water as it showed below the log. I saw him again several times lying in plain view just outside the log with its tangle of small branches where he made his home. The same fish or another one of the same size was there again the following year until a flood washed the log on down the river. Whenever I passed I tried to tempt him with a streamer or a large salmon dry fly. I never rose him, although once I did have a rise there and pulled a small fish clear of the water in my effort to keep what I thought was the big fellow from reaching the safety of that tangle of branches. I could have taken him at night with live bait or on a gob of worms during a flood, but I wanted him on a fly or not at all. I'm not sorry I didn't catch him. He kept my interest up much longer alive than he ever could have dead.

Woven into the pattern of the old 'Kill is my friend Al. The years have mellowed him and he has a little trouble with the fences I still hop over easily. Each year he fishes the dry fly a little longer but always falls back on the old wet flies he fished the 'Kill with fifty years ago. It is something of a blow to the pride we take in our tackle progress to see the catches Al makes on the same flies and the same short wet-fly leaders he used half a century ago. The Coachman and the Professor, fished under the overhanging fringes on the faster runs, still hold their magic.

We call Al the "Mayor," not because he is the mayor of the village but because we think the title fits his figure and his bearing. The village isn't incorporated and consequently has no mayor, but Al, standing high in the esteem of his fellow citizens, is the postmaster. Postmastering is a fine profession. At three o'clock every day during the season the Mayor is free to go fishing and the chances are 99 to 1 that he'll go.

When a trout strikes the Mayor's fly he gives a quick "Hi!" and strikes back. He has been doing that, he claims, since he caught his first fish. It helps me keep track of how many strikes he's having when I can't see him around some bend, but it's hard on the light leaders I sometimes persuade him to use. One night I spliced his line to some backing as we sat comfortably talking to some friends. When I had finished the splice Al reeled in the line while I sat across the room and let it run through my fingers to keep it clear. When he resumed his talking I tightened up on the line and gave a couple of jerks and a wiggling run in imitation of a native striking. Dignity faded as the Mayor pulled his right hand up in a sweeping arc and yelled, "Hi!" while his chair balanced precariously on the point of going over backward.

I've seen him pull small fish ten or twelve feet clear of the water time after time. He loses a lot of flies that way and he's a sucker for a big fish. I've tried to cure him of that heavy strike but I'm afraid that I never will and even if I did no amount of fish would make up for the loss of that characteristic "Hi!" and the sight of his bending rod.

His fishing has changed a little with the years. I remember, long ago, a day when Al came down to the stream with a long pair of scissors hanging down the front of the hunting vest he uses to carry his fishing gear in. A few days before he had noticed the small pair I carry in my fishing vest and had decided to adopt the idea himself. Sometimes now I find him with another new piece of equipment, a jeweler's glass, which he screws into his eye to see more readily the eyes of the smaller flies he is coming to use.

Now, when it grows dark and there are a few rising fish that he can't take on a wet fly I hear him call, "Hey, Lee. They're rising up here. Big ones. Come on up in a hurry." And I go up to fish while the Mayor spots them and tells me long before I raise them just how long they are and when they were last hooked. That keeps up until it is too dark to see and we walk back to the car in the soft darkness and the rich scent of the fullness of the fields and trees.

There's a thrill in roaming to far streams and fishing new waters. I find new pleasure in the unknown pool around the bend. But there's a deep satisfaction in knowing the old 'Kill intimately, watching its slow changes with the floods of every spring, and having a friend who loves the river as much as I do, who will fish with me or walk along watching for rises and talking of trout in certain spots as if they really were the old friends they seem to be.

[1940]

123

16

Trout Fishing

A PERSONAL OVERVIEW

In many respects, trout fishermen have never had it so good, and things are getting even better. Vast improvements in tackle during the past few decades have made fly fishing for trout much easier and more efficient, although the increased variety of gear has likewise made it more complicated. A growing respect for catch-and-release fishing for wild trout is at least gaining parity with the put-and-take mentality that spawned so many trout hatcheries during the 1950s and '60s.

Lee Wulff has lived and fished through all these changes and in many ways has contributed to most of them. In this chapter he explores some of those changes and the ways in which they've affected modern angling. He also offers here his own definition of fly fishing, which rightly rules out a few of our more novel and new so-called fly patterns.

There has been much debate over when fly fishing started. We know of Dame Juliana Berners's writings in the fifteenth century and that the Romans wrote of fishing with flies in Macedonia around A.D. 300. There has been speculation that the Egyptians fished with flies before the birth of Christ. There is a possibility that the first fly fisherman may have been a bird that antedated all men in being the first to use feathers and twigs to make and use a fishing fly.

In an article in *Natural History*, Horoyoshi Higuchi tells of a heron (*Ardeola striata*), common in both Japan and the United States, that fishes with real flies and their imitations. The heron does not use a rod, hook, and line—preferring to strike with his beak—but he fishes not only with bait but with crude flies that he creates. I quote Higuchi: "It may catch flies, grasshoppers, or cicadas; probe muddy ground for earthworms; pick up leaves, twigs, berries, bark, or moss or simply choose from a nearby miscellany—perhaps a feather."

Like any good angler the heron takes a position where the fish will come within range of his cast. As we did when we were kids, he likes to spot his fish first. Having spotted one he casts the bait or fly to the water and watches. When and if the fish rises he strikes with his beak. Higuchi continues: "An item that fails to attract a fish is sometimes retrieved and reused on the spot or carried off for use elsewhere. On a few occasions I watched herons fashion twigs into suitable lures. If a twig was too long, the heron held it with his feet, broke it in half with his beak, and tossed one piece into the pond." Prehistoric fly making may indeed have begun with the birds.

Between that time and the present there have been many changes in both tackle and techniques. Many of us have read of the early methods of angling and the simple tackle with which the sport started. A few of us have fished with the old horsehair lines and leaders. The first fly rods I made were of lancewood and greenheart. For me, fly fishing began, as an interested participant and observer, seventy-three years ago at the age of nine, and I think many of the most important developments and changes in the sport have come during my lifetime.

It has been a most exciting time for a dedicated angler to have lived. Trout fishing today has been shaped almost entirely by what has happened in that same period. Through improvements in tackle and techniques we grew too efficient as predators, while civilization set about destroying our waters and biologists worked to perfect the synthetic trout. We had to do this, seemingly, in order to learn. We have learned, and are still learning. Trout fishing in America has turned the corner.

I can remember when the best trout fishing meant camping out, and an outhouse was luxury. The best fly dope we had was a mixture of tar oil and pennyroyal, which we thought more often attracted bugs than repelled them. Leaders were of silkworm gut, which came only in short pieces of 8 to 12 inches. They had to be soaked to be knotted. Leaders had to be kept moistened with water or glycerine in order to keep them in condition to tie on a fly or to be supple enough to fish with. The introduction of nylon may have been the most important advance in all of fly fishing. Think of gossamer nylon only .003 or .004 inch in diameter but with a breaking strain greater than 3X gut. If we had to go back to gut leaders and all their problems, an awful lot of today's anglers would certainly give up the sport.

The improvements in tackle have been dramatic. It was difficult to keep the solid wood rods and most of the early bamboos from taking a set. Ferrules were of steel or nickel-silver and had no "give"; the wood bent and the steel did not. This made the waterproofing layer of varnish split and let moisture in. Like spaghetti, a fine strip of bamboo soaked in water can become soft enough to tie into a knot. So when we camped in a tent in days of rain, the wood at the ferrules softened, weakened, and would soon break under the strain of hard casting. Fred Longacre invented the Bakelite impregnation process (later made famous by the Orvis Company), and that insulated the bamboo from water absorption and let it retain its strength.

We had a flurry of development of steel fly rods and one or two of beryllium copper, but when Dr. Howald designed the first fly rod of glass fibers we entered an era where fly rods did not take a set and where they were more pliable and far more durable than ever before. Out of the space program came carbon-graphite fibers, which were lighter and even stronger than glass, and boron, stronger still but not as easy

126

to fabricate into long, slender tubes as graphite or glass fibers. Fly-casting tournaments are a measure of the capability of rods and the materials they are made of as well as of the casters, and casting distances increased dramatically with these changes.

The old rods were all soft-actioned until, in the 1920s, Tonkin cane, a new and much stiffer bamboo, came into the field. This coincided with the development of dry-fly fishing. Stiffer rods were needed to develop fly speed in casting to dry the fly and help it to float. The old soft rods were called wet-fly rods and the newer rods of the stiffer cane were called dry-fly rods. Of course wet flies as well as dry flies could be cast better with the bamboo that was stiffer for the same weight, and the old soft rods drifted off into semioblivion.

The next step forward in tackle and casting—the next headache for our trout—was the forward-taper fly line. I believe the first one was the Hardy Filip line, which appeared in their 1927 catalog. When members of the Golden Gate Casting Club first used shooting heads and monofilament running line in competition at Indianapolis, they cast 20 feet farther than anyone else.

A little later, in 1934, Marvin Hedge brought the double haul to tournament casting, and he jumped the existing record of 125 feet to 147 feet. Because of the increased line speed the hauls could deliver, shorter rods gave the same distance that somewhat longer ones had given and, being lighter and easier to carry, they became more popular.

Glass rods were lighter and more durable than split bamboo. Split bamboo and other wood rods were solid, but rods of fiberglass were hollow. For the same strength they had a larger diameter. In rods of 8 feet and over they had a large bulk and a considerable weight. The newer graphite fibers were much stronger and the rod diameters for the same strength and weight were much smaller. This meant a considerable reduction in weight and rods began to lengthen again, since for the first time rods could be both long and delicate of action.

There is another great advantage to both glass and carbon fibers. They don't require metal ferrules. Since the ferrules of the rod's own material can bend almost as well as the rest of the rod, an angler can use rods with more sections with almost no loss of action. Seven- and even eight-piece rods are on the market. Although I use rods with the fewest possible ferrules when convenient, on plane trips I no longer carry rods that won't fit in my suitcase so I don't spend time waiting for lost or delayed rods in long cases.

Reels haven't changed much. We've had multiplying fly reels since my early fishing. Drags are smoother and better but a skillful angler with a reel from the 1920s can play a fish just as capably as with any fly reel now available. Still, reel designs have proliferated. There are silent reels on the market, too, but I avoid them. Because the reel is down under the rod and the amount of line on the reel is hidden from the angler, I count on the click to tell me what I need to know— how fast I'm losing line and how much I have lost.

The big change in lines has been in tapers. We have many variations of the old double-tapers and many variations also of the new types and new densities. The old silk lines were tapered by varying the number of threads in the line. Since the 1950s, the tapering of lines by varying the diameter of the plastic coating over a uniform base of nylon or Dacron has made them more durable. Silk lines required a great deal of care. They had to be dried off after a few hours of fishing to get them to float, even when coated with flotant. Over a winter's storage many became sticky and could never be restored for further use.

I've mentioned the forward taper, which gave the caster a great ability to "shoot" the line. The Triangle Taper, a single continuous taper for the forward section, usually 40 feet, is a more recent innovation, and it gives greater delicacy, excellent distance, and better roll-casting capability for normal distances.

Fly-line materials are due to change shortly. If a 6-foot leader is better than one that's only 3 feet long, why not make one 30 feet or even 90 feet, the length of a normal fly line? I had one that tapered from 4X up to .055 inch for a 30-foot belly, then dropped back to .032 inch for the shooting section of the line. On a hot day it was a pure delight to cast, and most effective. On a cold day it was like trying to cast a coil of wire. Someday we'll find an almost transparent material both strong enough and soft enough to make a perfect fly line that will eliminate the need for a leader as we know it, requiring only the knotting-on of tippets.

Hooks are far better now, as the trout have discovered. We've come from the snelled hooks of the 1920s to eyed hooks of a greater range of sizes and better design. Flies have changed dramatically. At the turn of the century dry flies and nymphs were just being written about and coming into common use. Obviously, winged-insect imitations didn't really belong underwater and after hundreds of years the fly fisherman finally realized it. (Most of our saltwater flies are still made like insects with *wings*, hackle, a body, and a tail even though there are no hatches and very few, if any, winged insects in salt water.) Almost all the beautiful wet-fly patterns for which the British navy and merchant marine sought feathers all over the world are lost in memory now. Who now knows or remembers what a Wickham's Fancy, a Greenwell's Glory, or a Tup's Indispensable looks like?

We've splurged in patterns and we've accepted new materials that are not the old "feathers for wings and tails and legs, silk or wool for bodies and metal tinsel for sparkle." We're using animal hair and all kinds of synthetics from nylon fibers to Mylar. New designs and categories are running rampant. Some of the nymphs used on our western streams would horrify a conventional old-time fly fisherman, looking as real and deadly as the dragons they resemble.

Those old-time anglers knew little of entomology. Today's fly fisherman is miles ahead in that respect. He's also far better educated in understanding the trout and its food and environment. He knows what hatches there are, when they happen, and which ones the fish like most. And through catch and release he's educated the trout to a great degree, teaching them what's real and what's not, what a leader looks like—and that being hooked on a fly doesn't necessarily mean the end of everything.

Even more dramatic than the change in tackle is the change in fly-fishing techniques. In the days of silk all lines were intermediates (very slow sinkers) that could be made to float if dry and well greased. Weighted flies were rarely, if ever, used because they made casting much more difficult. As a result fly fishing was entirely a surface or near-surface proposition. The fish had to be inspired to leave his lie, normally near the streambed, and rise to the surface to get the fly. Had spinning not come along the trout would have continued to have the sanctuary of deep water and would have remained much more difficult to catch. In the old top-water or just-under-the-surface fly fishing, anglers never devastated trout populations the way it was done with spinning lures, which even a novice could place at almost any spot and any depth in a trout stream.

Trout have no hands; if curious, their only course is to mouth whatever interests them to test it for taste or character. To intercept a deep-water lure, they simply have to move a few inches to one side or the other instead of expending the effort to rise to the surface. Spin fishermen could not only cast metal lures but also live and natural baits, which are most deadly for trout. They could, if they wanted to, even cast a surface fly behind a plastic bubble, but few did. Seeing the spin fishermen's success in sending lures and baits down to the trout's own level in the stream, fly fishermen followed by developing sinking lines and sinking flies. These low-level fly fishermen became more deadly than their surface-fishing counterparts. Trout populations suffered even more, something that was partly offset by the slow spread of the catch-and-release philosophy.

Everything we do to develop new tackle and angling techniques that make fishermen more deadly is anticonservation. If a certain limited number of trout can be taken out of a stream safely, the deadlier—the more effective—the anglers on that stream are, the sooner that number is reached, demanding then either smaller bag limits or a shorter fishing season. We had a better balance when fly fishing was only on or near the surface. Our cure for this imbalance must be catch and release, or something very close to it.

Trout management in my lifetime has grown from almost none to very intensive and controlled. When I was a boy in Alaska, there seemed no end to the trout and salmon in those magnificent runs. But everywhere we took too many and left too few for seed. Our managers made some mistakes. When the numbers dwindled they first thought of setting limits on the daily catches. But anglers kept the big ones to fill out their limits and put the little ones back. Killing the big fish and sparing the small ones to breed changed the character of the runs, reducing the average size of the fish.

Trout hatcheries were next. Hatcheries are necessary and excellent for put-and-take fish, but in developing disease-free, fast-growing, high-food-conversion, cost-efficient fish they lost some of the beneficial characteristics wild trout have. Hatchery fish, force-fed and underexercised, were unable to survive well in the streams; they bred with true wild trout, and the resulting cross had a reduced ability to survive. Our trout streams suffered.

For a long time MSY (maximum sustained yield) was the fisheries' management goal, with no consideration of the quality of the angling it would produce. What anglers really wanted was bigger, wilder fish, and eventually management swung toward big fish, even if not wild ones.

One of the biggest failings of our system is that our managers do not have a stake in the results of their work. In Europe an individual who owns a river makes very sure that his fish are conserved because if the fishing goes to hell he's out a lot of money and value in his river. If our managers, by contrast, make a mistake they don't lose anything. In fact they'll probably hire a larger staff to correct the mistake and end up with a higher-paying job because of it. Unlike workers in business or farming, they are basically civil servants, secure in their tenure and not dependent on doing a top-level, competitive job in order to hold on.

Politics rears its ugly head, and in many cases it is more important to have the governor look good (and be reelected) than to safeguard a heritage for our grandchildren. Since we, the anglers, are an increasing segment of the voting public we

131

can exert a growing pressure on management. Because of that, management is getting better.

Most fly fishermen have great difficulty in defining *fly fishing*. I find it easy enough by realizing that there is not one simple definition but several differing types to consider. First, of course, one has to define a fly.

A fly, I believe, *is a special type of artificial lure made largely of soft material that has no metal or plastic cup or other device to give it an action in the water beyond that which the fisherman can give by movement of his rod and line.*

Once we've decided what a fly is we can separate fly fishing into a number of categories, such as: (1) dry fishing; (2) surface, or just-under-the-surface, fishing; and (3) fishing with sinking lines and/or weighted flies. We can further limit it if we say the tackle must be conventional fly-fishing gear with which a fly can be false-cast a certain number of times at a certain distance. So although any fishing with a fly is, technically, fly fishing, hand-lining a trolled fly or spin-casting a fly and a bubble would then not fit. (I'm sure we moderns get far more technical in our discussions of our sport than the old-timers did.)

One final difference between old and modern is this: when I started fishing we were all looking for a pool or a whole section of a river that could be ours while we were fishing. A companion and I would drive to a stream and one of us would say, "I'll go downstream and you can go up. I'll be back here at dark," and we'd each hope that we wouldn't see another fisherman all day.

It was great, and it still is, to have a good pool all to yourself for as long as you want it. The trouble is there are too many of us and too few pools. So we have to share them. Fortunately, with catch and release, the good streams may become as full of trout as they ever were. They can hold so many trout that trout fishing is becoming social rather than lonely, as it used to be. On Cairn's Pool in the no-kill stretch of the Beaverkill, anglers often stand no more than thirty feet apart, each fishing for several rising trout and each able to converse with his or her friend or partner.

Biologists, both those employed by our governments and those doing research in our schools, have contributed to our understanding of this fish and its environment. They have given us fast-growing fish and hybrid species. They have determined optimum feeding and living conditions. The most valuable studies have been made with wild fish or under actual stream conditions. Studies made in zoos or hatcheries may be misleading, and our angling organizations must always be on the alert.

I remember a report given by a state biologist at a Trout Unlimited meeting who said his tests showed that there was no difference in mortality between trout caught on treble hooks and those caught on single hooks. He was asked if he hadn't made the test in a hatchery, if the fish weren't under 12 inches, and if the hooks weren't at least a #8. He gave a sort of "How did you know?" look and nodded. Had he tested larger trout or used the more common smaller trebles, the fish would have been hooked deep inside their mouths and in the gills, and he'd have had a far different report.

For a long time the cry was, "Kill the big cannibals! They eat the small trout." But it is the big trout that anglers most enjoy catching, and, being mature, they eat proportionately less of the stream's food than the smaller, growing fish do. They're better breeding stock. We're now working back to wilder strains in an effort to obtain trout better suited to our streams. Hatchery fish rarely have the survival capability of the wild stocks.

We are learning to use no-kill on our good trout waters, to keep them as full of wild or acclimated stock as the food supply will allow. These frequently caught trout are both wild and educated, and they provide exciting and most challenging fly fishing.

Hatchery fish do have a place in our fly fishing. Though their survival rate may be low we can put-and-take them in the many streams that run clear and cool and offer good trout habitat in the spring but grow too warm for trout survival in the summer. We can provide these unsophisticated trout for beginners or for those who want trout to take home to eat. Wild trout that are spawned in the streams are cheap, a gift of nature and the trout themselves. Hatchery fish are expensive. We can make them any size the fishermen who catch them want. We can make their flesh pink or red or give it special flavors by changing their diets. It will only be fair to stock them in designated areas, fin-clip them for identification, and require a special license to fish those areas so that those who take these expensive fish home pay for them. We could leave our good trout-producing watersheds in no-kill or slot-size management, which would require only the normal minimum expense for protection that the rest of our fish and game receives.

Fishing, like skiing, has become a sport for both sexes, a sport in which the gear has become much more sophisticated and the lodges far more comfortable. Like skiers, modern anglers spend more time around the fireplace and lunch table in comradeship and discussion, and spend less of their day in actual fishing. It is good to have the ladies with us, participating successfully and often more successfully than we men do in our favorite sport. It is good, too, to have so many fly fishermen, for if we were still just a few, able to have pools to ourselves, we'd lack the political clout of numbers that is giving us better management, cleaner waters, and more and more superior wild trout.

Somewhere along the line we may turn the clock back in fly fishing as we did with big-game hunting, when hunters, finding that scope sights and modern rifles didn't give them the challenge they wanted, brought back bow hunting from the long-distant past. It may be that more and more sportsmen will graduate, as they have from bait to lures, from spinning to fly fishing, or from weighted flies and fly lines to intermediate or floating lines with unweighted flies. Chances are we'll see more waters limited to special types of fly fishing and more anglers taking greater pride in more difficult angling feats.

[1988]

17

Fishing with
the Generals

*Northern military bases depended (and still do) on
hunting and fishing in their immediate areas for recreation. By virtue of his knowledge of the north country
and his growing fame as an angler, Lee Wulff was
sometimes called into service by the military, either to
explore and develop new fishing areas or to be a guide
for military VIPs. On the day described in this chapter,
he was to take a couple of "the boys" salmon fishing.*

*The "boys" turned out to be Army Chief of Staff
General George Catlett Marshall (1880–1959) and
General Henry Harley "Hap" Arnold (1886–1950),
who at that time headed the then-new Army Air Forces.
Marshall eventually became secretary of state and won
a Nobel Prize for his Marshall Plan, which aided
Europe's postwar recovery. And in salmon fishing with
Lee Wulff, General Arnold seemed to continue a per-
sonal tradition of getting the best advice available. He
received his early flying lessons from Orville Wright.*

The morning of June 21 slowly spread its dull gray light and
blotted out the field's landing lights. The water to the west-

ward stretched away to the horizon like a plate of tarnished silver, ending abruptly at the hard line that separated it from the leaden underbelly of the clouds. It looked like rain again. We heard the slushy splash of a tire passing through puddles as a truck went by. It was dry enough at the moment, but there'd been a reddish glare under the gray of the brightening east and there was a soggy feeling to the air itself. I knew the signs: more rain before long. And the rivers were already running bank full with more than a week of rain on the hills behind them.

The C.O. of the base, Colonel H. H. Maxwell, had phoned me the day before to ask if I could come down and join a fishing party of his. "I've got a couple of men coming through here tomorrow who'd like to do a bit of fishin'. How about coming down to join us?" That was all. I'd been back in Newfoundland a week and had yet to put my waders on. I was due to travel down that way in a day or two, anyway. "Sure," I told him. "I'll be there."

Captain Spruill had phoned me half an hour before to be sure I'd be ready and at that moment we were riding across the soggy ground to the Transient Mess where I was due to surround a good breakfast before I joined the others.

I sat down at a table with some operations officers and a navy lieutenant. Spruill said something to the waitress and left. Came bacon and eggs and hot coffee, and we dug in. The navy lieutenant wanted to fish and was asking information. Said the man on my right, "Fishing's pretty punk right now. There are some logs coming down the river and it's so high you pretty near have to cast from the bushes."

I ate and listened and watched as the lieutenant passed over his fly box for the scrutiny of my side of the table. Then Spruill came back and I left, taking the navy out to my gear in the car and giving him a couple of flies with more sting in them for salmon than any of the trout and bass flies I'd seen in his box as it went across the table.

We drove over to the tracks where the railcar was waiting. The sun was up but its light filtered down weakly through the heavy clouds and the spruce and fir trees were more gray than green in its light. The wind was in from the east, just a breath now and then. Fishing was going to be tough. The rivers were too high and the wind was wrong and I wasn't familiar with the stream to which we were going. I went aboard and stowed my stuff. Spruill came back with Jim Sullivan, a Newfoundlander who worked on the base but worked, ate, drank, and slept only to go salmon fishing. We stood outside the railcar waiting for the colonel and the others to come along.

They came in two cars, Colonel Maxwell, another colonel, three two-star generals, and two others on whom there was no need to look for stars. Jim, standing beside me, whistled under his breath. The next moment he was being introduced to the chief of staff of the U.S. Army and the chief of the U.S. Army Air Forces. The thought flashed through my mind, It's a wonder they'd both fly in the same plane. For either one of them to be lost in a plane crash would be bad enough.

Colonel Maxwell, who runs everything mechanical to be found on the base, from airplanes to bulldozers, whenever time permits, settled himself at the controls and the rest of us spread around the car while we headed out the spur on the narrow-gauge tracks toward the main line of the Newfoundland Railway. General Marshall, General Arnold, Jim, and I occupied one double seat.

Those were the early days of the invasion. The party had left Italy the afternoon before and flown the hop across the Atlantic from the Azores that night to reach the base for an early breakfast. They'd decided that half a day's fishing would probably give them more relaxation than anything else, in this brief respite between a checkup on the actual fighting on the two European fronts and returning to the planning and overall direction back at Washington. We talked a little of many things on the way to the river, of the invasion, the war in the Pacific, the mud in Italy ... but mostly we talked about salmon and rigged up tackle and looked at salmon flies. All the while I kept thinking that our chances were slim for good fishing and why, oh why, couldn't they have come when conditions were better.

They'd dug out the best outfits on the base for the party but the wartime tackle situation hit the army as well as the rest of us. I substituted my spare outfit, a 5-ounce, two-piece, 9-foot rod, a 3⅛-inch reel carrying a specially tapered line with a hundred yards of 10-pound-test braided nylon to back it up, for the one laid out for General Arnold. It was scraping bottom to get full rigs for everyone. Jim spliced an end loop on a new line for General Marshall. I rigged up my 2½-ounce, 7-foot rod, which was going to be pretty light for those conditions. We got out at the high bank by the bridge and made final adjustments to our tackle after we'd descended to the level of the deep pool that lies directly under it.

The river is a small one and the salmon enter it early in the season. There was no question that the fish were in the river, as a party from the base had struck good fishing there a week earlier when the rivers first started to rise. But salmon travel quickly when the water is high. Two or three days may make a radical change in the fishing.

The mist was growing heavy and the bare limestone face that rose perpendicularly on the far side of the pool made the water take on a milky look with just a tinge of the green of the spruces glinting in it. As I watched, the first drops of rain came down and made a fluttering pattern on the velvet smoothness of its flow. We spread out along the fifty-yard length of the pool and began casting.

General Marshall, fishing at the head of the pool, broke the ice within two minutes of our arrival. His rod arched and a bright grilse, a small salmon of only one year's sea feeding, fought his way four or five feet into the air and showered a circle of spray on the raindrop pattern. He swept downstream with the current and worked in close to the cliff to leap again. He ranged back into the main flow and bored down into the rocky riverbed. But he'd met a skillful angler and not long afterward the chief of staff beached him gently on the pebbly shore. Colonel Maxwell put him on the keep-'em-alive stringer and anchored it to a log at the water's edge. Things looked more promising. We went back to our casting with a new hope. This, I thought, will be a day to remember.

The lines drifted out lazily through the air and, straightening out, fell to the waters. The small wet flies swam back

Beware that false weariness of the fresh-run salmon. One second his long, blue-backed, silvery body was that of a beaten fish; the next he was racing for deep water at top speed, taking a Silver Grey with him for a souvenir.

"I guess," said General Arnold with a wry grin, "that fish deserved to get away." And I saw no trace of anger in his face; nothing but the pleasure he'd had in playing him.

In the next few minutes I connected with and landed two grilse and added them to the first one, still alive on the stringer. When the others came back, empty-handed, General Arnold was in the act of beaching a grilse that had come up out of the dark, deep water at the head of the pool to take his fly.

Often when the water in a river rises quickly the salmon will take a fly avidly at a certain point in the rise, though scorning them both before that point and afterward. We seemed to have struck that point. There were rises all along the line as the party spread themselves along the pool. Jim fought a grilse at the pool's head while a two-star general snapped his rod at the first ferrule on an 8-pound salmon that had been lying almost at his feet in very shallow water in a little side run at the tail of the pool. Played on the butt joint with one guide only and the rest of the rod seesawing back and forth in the current, that salmon finally came in close enough to slip the tailer up over his tail and tighten the noose on him in its certain grip.

As quickly as it had started, the action stopped. The rain beat down even heavier than before. The river began to run muddy with the red of a clay bank up above. The moment was past and the fishing over. As a group we huddled under the bridge with its scant covering of well-spaced ties. There were no complaints, no cussing, just the good-natured banter that goes with men who are used to taking the weather as it comes.

At two o'clock the railcar came back for us and we relaxed in the warmth of hot coffee and sandwiches. Again we talked of many things as the car swayed along—of other Newfoundland rivers and the right time to fish them, of the marvels of air travel in a world that grew smaller overnight, a new world in which one could leave Italy one afternoon and be in Washington the next night and still have time for a morning's salmon fishing on a Newfoundland river on the way! After an hour's ride we were back at the base and the party was soon flying south to Washington, only six hours away, carrying with them salmon from a Newfoundland river.

What were they like, these men who head our army and its air force? They're the sort of men you'd like to know. It is hard to find words to describe them but the simple, timeworn words are best. They are real and sincere. They might well have been preoccupied with the enormity of the responsibility that is theirs. Instead they brought a rich interest and warmth to their talk with Jim and me, unimportant civilians in a world at war. They are men who know and understand the outdoors and believed that a morning's fishing, even in a downpour, was the right sort of break in what must be an almost continuous time of tension and strain for them. I had a feeling that I could never have had without the experience of that morning, a feeling of intense pride that we, as a nation, had men at the head of our greatest endeavors who were as thoroughly human as your best friend or mine.

In the days that followed, when the salmon were eager for the fly and I was lucky enough to be wading a salmon stream with the sun laying its golden glint alike on the moving water and the lush green mountains that held it to its course, I thought often of the rain-drenched anglers who had expressed a hope of coming back for a longer trip when the conditions were right. I have a sharp memory picture of General Marshall, knee-deep in the river, casting with an intentness that belied his having left a bloodstained Italy only hours before and of General Arnold's subdued grin as he watched that salmon spurt off with his Silver Grey. I'll be forever grateful that it was my good fortune to be with them that morning on the river in the rain.

[1945]

142

18

Black of
Night

In this bass-fishing chapter, we meet the late Al Prindle of Shushan, New York, which was the Battenkill border town where Wulff lived for a number of years. Prindle was the postmaster in addition to being Wulff's close friend and longtime fishing companion. Lew Oatman was another Battenkill regular who became even more famous after his death for his lovely streamer-fly patterns than while he was actually making them. He created one called the Shushan Postmaster that's still sometimes found in fly-pattern books. That also is the title of Chapter 40 in this book, where Wulff recounts his friendship with Prindle in more detail.

My idea had been to lure the old postmaster into my small airplane and fly him into one of the Adirondack lakes for an afternoon of bass bugging. Instead, I found myself at the oars only four miles from home, on the small lake where I kept the plane moored. We were passing it again on our third complete circuit of the shoreline. Al hopefully plopped a bug alongside one pontoon and worked it slowly back into deep

143

water. Nothing happened. And nothing had happened all afternoon.

It was Al's idea. With the summer cottages empty and the normal buzz of outboards just a memory, he felt dead certain we could tie into some of the big bass that occasionally came from this little pocketful of water. "And besides," said Al, "nothing in the world would get me into that flyin' machine of yours."

The sun hung low in the sky and we had every reason to expect the sharp coolness of an Indian summer evening to descend. We might get halfway around the lake again before dark, and now, with October on the downhill half, night fishing didn't hold much promise. A few lily pads grow around the edges of the lake, but not enough to provide good cover. Tall elms and maples line its edges and beneath them the summer cottages crowd against the shore.

We fished the edge of deep water, sometimes tight against the overhanging bushes, sometimes at the edge of a bar that Al remembered. Al dropped the bug lightly beside the float again, gave it a rest period, then shuddered it a few inches to another pause. A largemouth about 9 inches long tugged it under and hooked himself.

He came skittering across the water to the boatside under the influence of Al's good right arm. Reaching down, I shook him free with a flourish and said airily, "Bass. One of those lunkers you were telling me about, perhaps?"

He grunted and we moved along. A big crappie grabbed the bug and then shook free at the side of the boat. At least the little ones were beginning to show some interest. Another undersize largemouth fastened himself to the bug and I set him free. Al's considerable figure doesn't bend quite so easily as mine, so I do most of the bending over.

Al was just saying for the fifteenth time, "There's always a good bass along this stretch of water," when the bug went under with a solid, sucking sound.

Nine feet of split bamboo arched and vibrated as the old postmaster and the fish measured strength. Then the fish came our way. He leaped twice coming in. He dived into the

144

pads and brought a mess of them up to the top with him, but Al worked him free. I slipped the net under him and lifted him into the boat.

"He's a nice bass," said Al thoughtfully. "Maybe we ought to keep this one. It's late in the season and maybe we won't get too many between now and quitting time."

The sun coasted down behind the trees and the new moon started her short arc across the sky. We could hear the smaller fish—bluegills, crappies, pumpkinseeds—popping away at surface foods everywhere about us on the still water, but nowhere did we hear the heavy surge of a surface-feeding bass. We changed places and I picked up the fly rod.

There's a pleasant rhythm to bug casting with the right gear. Give me a rod with plenty of power, a long rod without too much weight but with strength right out to the tip. Just plain casting, picturing a lazy old largemouth underneath that fluttering, struggling bug, watching it and then passing it up just before you pick it up on the back cast, or maybe grabbing, can be richly satisfying when the air is warm and still around you. The insect pests of summer were gone. A couple of ducks dusked in. Still, I couldn't help thinking that we should have been coming in for a landing at that moment after an exciting afternoon of bass fishing in some far-off lake.

Al was saying, "I took two nice ones off that rock there, casting a Dardevle one day last summer. This is real good water and you'd better be ready when he takes it."

It seems to me that Al has taken a big one from every rock and stump, from under every overhanging tree all along the shoreline. His philosophy is one of optimism. If a fish doesn't strike on the first cast, one will surely hit on the second. If not on the second, at least on the third . . . and so on. The longer he fishes, the more certain he becomes that the *next* cast will turn the trick. So Al wasn't surprised when a bass whooshed up and engulfed the bug, but I was.

Realizing that I was a bit late in striking, I really leaned into it. The boat shifted and Al hung onto the oars to steady himself. The rod held its arc and then bent downward, down toward the water until the line began to hiss out through my fingers where I held it at the rod. The fish splashed up and shook, then headed out into the deep water. His leaps were silver flashes in the gathering dusk.

Al slid the net over the side and submerged it. When the fish had spent his strength I slid him above it, half on his side.

Al lifted him in. "Better than three pounds, maybe four," was his verdict. "This was *always* a good shore for bass. There're weeds on the bottom and they like it here."

The light had gone and the shore was only a dim outline. There was still no wind and the warmth felt like August, strange after the cold, frosty nights of the week before. It was like summer fishing but without the hum of insects or the peeping of frogs; a special night, and I began to have a feeling of gratitude to Al for having brought it about.

There'd be other days and nights to come with a wind to riffle the water and send a chill through your clothing: there'd be other evenings to fish if I liked, but none of them would contain this blending of the best of both fall and summer.

The bug dropped, danced its little act, and came back to the boat time after time. Places Al remembered as having yielded lunker fish in the past produced nothing to break the even tenor of the cast and its retrieve. Eventually, as if goaded by some inner force he could no longer contain, Al demanded that I change bugs.

"That dark thing you're throwing around is just black paint and brown bucktail. These bass want something lively and colorful. Let me pick out one for you that's got some color in it."

He spread my lures on the boat seat and eyed them from above the flashlight's beam. He pawed over with his big hands a dozen bugs that had taken fish in the years behind us, spinners nicked by the teeth of pike and walleyes, streamers worn thin and ragged by successful use. He touched them all and finally held up one of Barrett Cass's red-and-white specials. "Throw that thing out there and you'll drive them plumb crazy."

I like to think of night fishing as a mixture of slow, almost silent movement. The dip of oars and the liquid sound of water as they move the last cast a little bit astern, the feel of the boat beneath you and the slightest movement of your partner as he shifts for balance, the faintest rustling of leaves and the twinkle of cottage windows or the occasional sharp stab of a car's bright headlights. Tonight there was added the pungent smell of smoke drifting over from the dry marsh fire still burning under the sod. But all these things merge together and fade when you hear the sharp, wet sound a big bass makes when he takes a bug down under that placid surface.

I could feel Al's tenseness through the rigidity of the boat, then sense his relaxing even before I heard his breath go out. We could both hear the delicate whisper of the tight line cutting through the water and knew the fish had been hooked. We were prepared then for the leap that really shattered the silence of the night.

"Don't lose this one," said Al. "This is the one we came for."

Playing them at night, I picture their movements to myself as I read them through the bend of the rod and the pull of the line. A flashlight may tell you more accurately what a fish is doing, but they'll come in more quickly and won't be half as wild if you can take them in the dark. It's a matter of the sound of a leap and then the angle and arch of the rod.

The size of the line in your fingers is a measure of the distance, judged by the taper you've come to know so well. And at the very end the least faint ripple and its reflection of light or the faint glow of a silvery side or belly mark the fish for you. When using a bass bug there's little chance of a hook hanging up in the net twine, and if you do miss once, there's no harm done. The fish sank into the net on the first try.

I held him up for Al to shine the light. He whistled softly. "I always *said* there was a five-pounder layin' along this shore."

We'd worked all the way round again to the point where the plane was pulled up on the shore and our car was parked. I thought I could catch the faint reflection of light from the little yellow ship.

"Let's make a few more casts," said Al, "just for luck. Uncle Davy and I saw three of the doggonedest, fattest bass that ever swam right along here last week. One of them sniffed Uncle Davy's baitfish but wouldn't touch it. I heaved a frog out and he swam right under it all the way to shore but never opened his mouth to take it in. He'd be bigger than the one we just got. He'd go six pounds or more.''

We moved on slowly. Cars hummed faintly on the highway just over the hill. Now and then a horn honked or a cottage door slammed across the lake. Mechanically I kept on casting, but it wasn't the same. We had a real fish in the boat and that was our evening. If we stayed out the rest of the night we wouldn't improve on it. I was glad I'd come, thoroughly happy and at peace with the world, but ready to quit and far from ready for the sudden and noisy strike that disrupted the soft darkness that hung over the shoreline.

Instinctively I lifted the rod hard. Almost as a matter of routine, I matched the fish's runs with the right pressure, countered his leaps with slack. Neither of us spoke a word as the minutes went by. The fish sloshed up beside us and surged away into the black silence. He drew line from the reel and it whispered away through the guides. We heard him surface a long way out.

"Is he off?" Al whispered.

The bass answered by drawing off more line. Then his strength was spent and he came toward us, shaking his head, backing away and boring down. When he came alongside, raising a slight wake and shining in the faint light, I heard Al's intake of breath and then the drip of water as he lifted the fish aboard.

"That's old Uncle Davy's bass," said Al. "Let me see the two of 'em side by side."

The reflected light from the flashlight's beam showed me Al's smile of satisfaction. I could picture him through the seasons ahead saying to someone, "There's always a big bass along this shore. I remember the time Lee and I were fishing one fall night . . ."

I could look forward with pleasure to having him remind me of that pair of bass next season when we fished again. We'd both had something extra, a dividend on a season already full and finished, which from that instant on became a matter of memory. My satisfaction was at least as deep and lasting as Al's.

A few strokes of the oars set the canvas scraping on the sand beside the plane. I'd flown to some fine fishing, but it was right here at home, too, in full measure when conditions were right.

Especially in summer when the water is low and warm, night fishing really pays off. There's so much commotion and so many fishermen on some of our waters during the daylight hours that I believe a majority of the bass do the greater share of their feeding after darkness falls. The walleye is by nature a night feeder. Big trout follow the lead of the bass and wall-eyes and tend to become nocturnal feeders during warm weather. Only the pike family fail to join in the nocturnal activities, and that, I believe, is because they're blind at night, just as we humans are. I know of no authentic record of a muskie, northern pike, or pickerel being caught by angling when it was truly dark.

If you live only to fish and the bass is your favorite, it would probably be worth your while to reverse the usual procedure and fish through the nights, sleeping during the days. I've tried it and figure it more than doubled my catch in comparison with what I'd have taken fishing only the day-light hours.

I used to start out just about sunset, after a good meal, with a solid lunch aboard the boat, a plug rod and a fly rod beside me. I'd fish through until dawn. It upsets your social life but if you really want fishing it's worth a try. There's no way of knowing for certain at what hour on a given night the fishing will hit its peak, but, by and large, I found most action with bass just after dark, around midnight, and in the pre-dawn hours. Just one angler's experience, for what it's worth.

The fish seem to see just about as well after dark as during the bright sunlight. They'll strike a lure just as it hits the water. They'll connect as frequently with a fast-moving lure. An all-black lure is my favorite for bass at night. There's no question about their night vision and so it seems logical that they'd feed during those hours when the lakes and rivers are quietest and they're safest from their worst enemy, the angler. If the bulk of the anglers fished at night instead of in the daytime, I think it might be the other way around.

There's no special trick to night fishing. Anyone can do it. Although bait will be effective, the angler who uses artificial lures gains most with darkness. The increased effectiveness of artificial lures at night is greater than the increased effectiveness of natural baits. Fishing at night is just like fishing in the daytime except that you handle your tackle by touch alone and the fish move into different waters.

If you're going to cast, you'll want to avoid backlashes. A backlash in the daytime is nuisance enough without adding the extra difficulty of trying to untangle a bird's nest by dim light or none at all. An antibacklash device is a necessity for most casters, and casts should be easy and shorter than normal daytime casting. For safety's sake, if for no other reason, casting should be by the overhead method and not by side-swiping.

On all but the blackest nights your eyes will find enough light to make out the shoreline. You should be able to keep your boat on its proper drift, although every once in a while you'll find your lure landing up on the shore or catching in leafy branches. It helps a lot to know the water you're fishing. A flashlight is a necessity, but don't wave it around any more than you have to.

As far as I know, any lure that will work in the daytime will work at night, but some seem to be more successful than others. I like all-black plugs and white plugs with red heads. Pork-rind lures or bucktail-and-spinner combinations are good, too. All of the surface lures seem to work well at night, especially when the water is smooth. Because of your inability to see them, it's better to avoid fishing in heavy weeds unless you're using a weedless lure.

A good weedless lure will pay off in night fishing even more than in the daytime if the waters you fish are weedy. Many night fishermen settle on a single-hook, weedless lure that they can cast into any water and that will hook and hold fish.

The fly-rod fisherman will probably concentrate on floating lures. I doubt if any daytime thrill for the bass fisherman can equal the silence-shattering strike of a big bass when he takes a floating lure on a still, black night. When the water gets choppy, I think it's smart to fish below the surface, using diving plugs, spinners, and streamers, or any of the deep-traveling artificial lures. Rough water seems to limit the effectiveness of all floating lures.

Luminous lures will sure take fish, but I'm not sold on their being any more effective, night in and night out, than nonluminous lures [see Chapter 38]. There are points that shouldn't be overlooked, though. For one thing, the angler can see them better and if you're a novice at casting and working your plug, a luminous one that you can see will make your fishing easier and your casting more accurate by letting you know just where the lure is all the time.

You'll need a light for landing your fish. Bringing them in after dark isn't as simple as it is in the daylight. Your net should be in position before the light is turned on, and the light should be aimed at the fish instead of the net. Shining the light on the net makes it stand out like a beacon and the fish will do their level best to avoid it.

A dull light that is just bright enough to see by is better than a powerful-beamed job. Then you will have just enough light for the purpose and anything extra helps you little but will frighten the fish a lot. Another point is that you won't have such a long period of adjustment to darkness again after the light is turned off.

Both bass and walleyes will move into very shallow water at night, and fishing grounds that are unproductive during the daytime may become the best areas of all at night. Fish that are deep during the day will swim closer to the surface at night, too. Many a walleye will come to the surface for a floating plug or fly-rod lure that they'd ignore completely during the hours of daylight.

Worms, minnows, and insects work at night, but worms and minnows seem to work best when trolled behind a spinner or cast out and retrieved slowly at a fair depth. Trolling two lines, one with an artificial lure and the other with a natural bait, isn't a bad idea. Be sure to troll slowly. If you find that one method is drawing all the strikes, you can switch both lines to the same type of lure or bait.

[1952]

19

Who Won?

You may have seen photographs of a bass-tournament winner kissing the lunker that earned him first place. Or perhaps a different photo showing someone hugging a dead marlin as it hangs from the scales. These scenes are always a little fatuous and not really representative of true love. However, I do think it's possible genuinely to love a fish, and as Wulff spins this wonderful tale I believe you'll discover just how that can be.

Any good writer, which Wulff most certainly is, may produce hundreds of articles in a life's work, all of them entertaining, informative, or both. But any writer, if he or she is lucky, may in that same lifetime produce one or two stories of breathtaking beauty, which I consider this story to be.

Now that I look back on it I guess it was a swindle from the beginning. I knew the General's character as well as I know a fine salmon's. I should have given the General long odds. We made an even bet. It was a fly rod, to be picked out by the loser.

The General had fished all his life, had landed great

ocean gamefish, one record trout, one near-record muskie. But he had never caught a very large salmon, and he had never fished a Newfoundland river.

He told me I couldn't possibly win the bet if he hooked into a really big, fresh-from-the-ocean salmon. No others were to count.

The bet was this: He'd land the salmon, kill it, and have it mounted for his den. I bet him the fly rod this would not happen.

"You mean I'll never land such a fish?" he said, regarding me with an amused tolerance that must have made junior officers squirm.

I grinned. "I mean you won't hook, land, kill, and have mounted the kind of fish we both have in mind and that occasionally is caught in the Upper Humber River."

That was the bet.

Ten and a half days later, from my relaxed position with my stern on the warm sand and my back curved into a hollow of a stranded log, I could see the whole of Taylor's Pool. Old Nichols, the guide, sat easily on the stern seat of the beached canoe, casual yet aware of every movement in the pool before him. The General stood beyond him in the steady current that came to his thighs, and sent his fly out to the wrinkled water where the deep flow pushed its way over some submerged stones.

The pool began where Taylor's Brook merged its waters with the Birchey Stream of the Upper Humber. The waters were stained brown by the peat bogs in which they rise and the eye cannot penetrate them to a depth of more than three or four feet. The river had the look of a great stream of weak tea moving along on its course to the sea. Light-green marsh grass rose from the swampy shore across the pool. The grass was backed up by the dark green of alders, which in turn were topped by the slender outlines of spruce and fir. Below us the pool was still and dark.

Old Nichols and I, with our minds and eyes, fished the General's fly with the same intentness that he gave it. Even though he controlled its movements and was closer to it, when the heavy swirl showed up where the fly was traveling, we saw it as quickly as he, and sensed as quickly that the fish had either missed the fly or deliberately turned away short of taking it into his jaws.

The wet fly failed to tempt the fish further, but when the General changed to a dry fly and let the current carry it leisurely above the spot where the salmon had chosen to lie, we watched its open mouth break the surface just below the fly and engulf it. The force of the fish's rise carried its back partly out of water and, as it planed downward, the top two-thirds of its tail came into view.

We were prepared to see a big salmon, judging by what we'd seen at the rise, but when the first leap came we all realized that this was an enormous fresh-run female, a fish to talk of for years to come.

The General knew that this tackle struggle would be more difficult than any he had ever had before. The store of energy the fish had brought in from the sea lifted its strength above that of those species of fish that feed from day to day as hunger dictates. The speed that swept the salmon to safety ahead of the seals and otters and sharks was greater, too, than that of any fish that hadn't known an ocean's endless space.

Slowly the salmon moved downstream and the current bellied out the line behind as she traveled up the far side of the pool. Straddle-legged, the General braced back against the current, gripping the loose stones with his wader soles and balancing his weight to let it hold him best. Five times the huge fish leaped as she moved throughout the pool. Then she settled back to her old position behind the rock and shook her head savagely until the General's 5-ounce rod quivered wildly, like a willow in the wind.

A less experienced angler would have lost the salmon when she made her downstream rush. From a finning start she turned up and leapt with a rocket's getaway. She hit the surface swimming and sped on downward through the brown water.

Below the General the water deepened and the alders overhung it. He moved downstream fast, the current pushing him along, until the cold water poured in over the top of his waders. Though he braced to hold his position, the bottom was smooth and would not hold his feet. The flow moved him steadily down with it and the water touched his armpits. The line continued to run off the reel until the backing was more than two-thirds gone.

The green-painted canvas of the canoe touched his shoulder and Old Nichols held it steady with his steel-shod pole while the General, finding a last strength in his long legs, pushed himself a foot or two up from the bottom and fell, facedown, across the seat. In that position, with his left hand gripping the far gunwale and the rod pointed downstream in his right, they followed the fish to the end of her run.

With the backing on the reel again, the angler placed himself below the fish to make her fight the current and the tackle, too. The salmon's gills were moving faster now and the lightning start was missing from her runs. She needed rest to let the strength flow back into her weary muscles. But the General gave her none. Through the torment of the fly's slight pressure, he constantly reminded her that she was no longer free, and her whole being rebelled against it.

Turning downstream again after two leaps that carried her barely above the surface of the water, the salmon passed on the far side of one of those dead stumps spring floods leave strewn along the shallow bars. The General ran the sixty yards through knee-deep water to reach the snag. Lifting his line free of it he found the fish on. Save for the drain of those last two leaps upon her strength, she'd have swum on and broken free instead of turning into an eddy for a rest.

Ten minutes later, flushed, panting, and as weary as any battle had ever left him, the General slid the great salmon halfway out of water on the gravelly shore.

She lay on her side in the shallow water, gills gasping spasmodically. The sun reflected from her scales as if each one were a mirror, outlined by the shadows of its edges. The half-healed scar from some missed leap at a falls was her only blemish. The General stood beside the beaten fish and studied her carefully. Old Nichols kneeled beside him and held forward the short, stout alder stick he'd cut while the fish had been played. One swift blow and the thing would be finished. Old Nichols made a slight motion with the stick in his hand

156

as if to draw the General's attention to it. But the big man was staring at me. There was grimness in his face and his eyes were cold and penetrating. Somehow you do not ever smile at a man like the General when he is looking at you like that. Then he stared down at Old Nichols and shook his head. Dropping to one knee, he drew the fly from its hold on the salmon's upper jaw. With his hand gripping the fish just ahead of her tail, he slid her slowly, gently back into deeper water.

Old Nichols cursed under his breath, an oath of astonishment, as he watched the great fish fade into the brownish depths and disappear.

Believe me, I felt no triumph for having witnessed this fine display of sportsmanship by the General. I felt pretty small.

The General seized my elbow with one of his blacksmith-grip hands and steered me to a fallen tree. He waved Old Nichols over to us.

"Sit down, Lee," he commanded. I sat. And when Nichols arrived and sat, the General said: "I know I didn't beat her alone. Nichols had to come with the canoe and life-raft me."

"That's legitimate," I mumbled.

"Yeah?" he said, scowling. "Without a guide and canoe I might have got myself half drowned and no fish. Never mind that. You won your bet. But I never lost a bet like that before, against one man or many. And I never fought a fish that could swim beside that one, either.

"It's understandable how you were right in judging me—I'm another man, and you've followed me through two wars. But how the hell did you know about that she-devil of a fish? You tell me that, Lee. I don't like unsolved mysteries in any form at all."

I cleared my throat. "Well, I know salmon—they've been a big part of my life—and I know great salmon like that one best."

"That's no answer," the General snapped out at me.

"No, it's really not. But if I tried to tell you the life pattern of such a salmon as you hooked into, you'd call me a liar and a ham, you—of all the men I know."

157

"Tell it just as it is, Lee."

I leaned back on the fallen tree, propping my back against a limb. Considering what had happened so recently, this would be a pleasure.

"Your salmon, General, as an *alevin*, still carrying part of the egg sac from which she had developed, was one of similar thousands that had been spawned by a pair of oversize Atlantic salmon. She looked like all the other millions and millions of alevins that were emerging from the small pockets of water beneath the stones and coarse sand of the Humber's spawning beds, yet not more than one in five thousand was like her. Taking unto herself the characteristics of her forebears she was destined to be one of the monarchs of the river, if she survived.

"She continued to draw nourishment from the dwindling egg sac until it was completely absorbed. Then, less than an inch long but with muscles hardened and hunger active, she became a *parr* and was on her own. Her food was any living thing that came within her reach and yet was small enough to fit within her mouth. Her fear, an instinctive thing, was of anything that moved and was big enough to eat her. She lived and grew between the two forces, ruthlessly striking those living things upon which she could prey and fearfully fleeing those she could not master. Hers was a world in which death was everywhere and mercy did not exist.

"The great bulk of the thousands of fertile eggs of that single spawning pair had survived to the parr stage. They had become a pale cloud of scattered bits of motion on the streambed. Life for them was not yet a matter of individual ability but purely a matter of circumstance. A passing trout chanced to see their movement. The squaretail turned savagely into them. Almost as a unit they darted into tiny caverns of water between the stones for protection, but the trout, by opening his mouth quickly, drew in water from the crevices among the stones and sucked in the small parr, too. He devoured thirty before tiring of the game.

"An eel working upstream from the shallow lake below

passed through them and took her toll of lives. A salmon parr of three years, a fish five inches long, found them and ate dozens. But, of course, your salmon was not one of those to die.

"As days went by she worked her way farther and farther from the shoal of her birth and became more and more of an individual, more dependent upon her own quickness and foresight for food and safety. She was at home then in the twisting currents that made up the flow around her. Her body was covered with its full complement of scales, each growing, ring by ring, as she expanded. Those below were iridescent silver and those of her back were dark brown. Down each side the brown pigmentation extended in a series of narrow transverse bands called finger marks, and overlaying both the silver and brown of her sides was a pattern of bright vermilion spots. Another pattern of black spots was slightly less noticeable in the solid brown of her back. Her tail was definitely forked.

"One day she saw an insect settle to the undulating mirrorlike surface above her and struggle to rise into flight again. Before her mind had fully realized her opportunity, instinct had started her on a wild rush upward. Her jaws closed on the midge and she bent her body downward for her dive. But her speed was too great for that maneuver. Instead, she carried on up into the air in her first clean leap. From then on she leaped often in her surface feeding.

"She spent her first winter under the ice in Birchey Pond, that wide but shallow lake half a mile downstream, clinging to the shore waters where she could dart quickly into spaces between the ice and lake bed too narrow for the preying trout to follow. There, in the greater mass of the past summer's dead vegetation, she found more insect life and better feeding than was to be found in the river itself. The temperature dropped almost to freezing and a strange lethargy possessed her. Even though food was scarcer than in the summer she cared little and hunted for it less. Her scale rings came closer together for the time element between them was always the same and her body was growing little.

"One gray day of winter when she had been idly swimming along just under the ice, a great black shape moved toward her. She swam from it frantically and not until she turned away from its course did she realize that she had not been pursued. She had seen a spent salmon, black, thin, and ugly, a long black skeleton of a fish that had lost more than half its weight through spawning and starvation. Like all salmon, restless fish that they are, the slink wandered the lake aimlessly, waiting unknowingly for the freshening water of spring that would start another change within him. When that change came he would turn silvery again and be possessed of a sudden hunger and would follow the spring floods down to the sea a second time.

"When the slink's coat brightened and he headed downstream to the sea, your salmon also lost her lethargy. Food was everywhere and she fed ravenously again, her speed and fierceness remarkable for her two-inch length. Her second year was a continuation of her first and in it she almost doubled her length. She liked the lake and moved constantly through its quiet waters. Occasionally an urge moved her into the current where the river flowed in, holding a place in the current for a while but each time the urge faded and she returned to cruise the still waters. Most of the Humber's parr were clinging to the current where they swam no more, no less, than she did to hold their stream positions, but they found less food and grew more slowly.

"The warming water of her second spring filled her with a new desire. It was nothing so simple as her need for food or even her selection of the still water as her feeding ground. It was an intangible force that drew her to the outlet of the lake where the brown water poured wildly over the lip to race through the rapids below. Other parr were gathering there, too, in schools, taking a place in the current and holding it.

"Only occasionally did they feed on the passing food. In the end they swam less swiftly than the current and let it carry them backward over the brink into the rough water and, still facing upstream and swimming slowly, they let it take them gradually downstream.

"Almost all the other parr were four years old, but they

had been spawned by smaller fish. Your salmon was precocious and more developed for her age, though smaller than the rest.

"The group was tumbled about in the rough water below the Birchey Forks where the main flow from Aidies Lake comes in, but they all re-formed in groups and moved downstream. There was little hesitation among them now. In the swiftest water they turned to face upstream and let themselves be carried down by swimming forward slowly. Otherwise they turned and swam down with the flow. They kept formation perfectly through the dark and boiling water of the Smooth Rapids, but Bear Reef with its pounding rapids scattered them wildly. Still, there was little change in the content of the group when it re-formed and drifted on.

"At the lip of the Big Falls they hesitated. The pull of the swift current was alarming to them and the heavy vibration set up by the falling water was new and strange. It was more than an hour before the first stragglers let themselves be swept back over the high barrier. By twos and threes the rest followed. The water swept them down through the fifteen-foot drop and released them in a swirling mass of foam and water. Twisting and turning, they were carried on to a smoother flow. Her old group scattered, your salmon joined another school, and continued with them toward the sea.

"Forty-five miles below their starting point they reached Deer Lake. The school of parr moved steadily westward following the northern shore. Within the salmon her urge to migrate was diminishing. She broke formation frequently to feed. Halfway to the outlet of the lake she swung away from the others, all four-year-olds, and let them travel on without her. The pull of habit to revert to her lake feeding of the year before outweighed everything else and there she spent her third summer. Fall found her almost six inches long.

"She began to feed on smaller fish more than before. Small trout, one-year-old parr, and a lesser number of sticklebacks made up much of her diet. Still no insect dared touch the water within her sight. Her rise would be swift, instinctive, certain. It was as if she were a trap that was always set and the sight of a moving insect was the thing that released it. Unless the insect was lifeless or well beneath the surface her rise would carry her on out into the air.

"When winter cooled the water and food became scarce again, the old familiar lethargy returned. This time she fought it. In the conflict of decisions the new one won out. She found the outlet and she moved on downstream alone. The Big Rapids that would have unbalanced her the spring before not once threw her over on her side. Downstream she swam, through the narrowing gorge, over the Shellbird Island shoal where the bare, rock face of Breakfast Head towered a thousand feet above her. There was no heed in her for the cars that moved by on the highway or the trains that puffed along the river's southern shore. Twelve miles below Deer Lake she felt the tides and tasted the strong brine that thinned the brown of the Humber water.

"For days she moved in and out with the tide, feeding well and growing more rapidly than she had ever grown before. At the end of a week her change in color was complete. A coating of shining silver clothed the lower two-thirds of her body covering the parr markings and red spots of her freshwater coat. Her back had turned from brown to bluish gray, but the scattered black spots still showed through it slightly. Nature had prepared her for the sea. Now she was a *smolt*. From above she looked like a part of the blue-green water of the bay; from below she was a hazy silver shadow against the sky. Leaving the brackish water she moved slowly toward the open sea.

"Three years later we find her far out at sea and deep down in water that is never brighter than a twilight. She was stirred to another migration. Six years old now, this was the third time since going to sea that she'd felt that annual restlessness. In her fourth spring the desire had passed quickly. In her fifth she had traveled fifty miles before turning back to the bountiful feeding of the ocean's floor. Like her parents and their parents before them she had held to the sea for three full years and grown steadily. It was incongruous to see her now and think of her early years in the river. After three years of stream life she had come to sea, a parr six inches long and less than three ounces in weight. In an equal time at sea she had become a magnificent salmon and her weight was forty-three pounds. Under a compulsion she could no longer resist she started threading her way upward through the underwater valleys.

"Following the slope of the sea floor, she worked toward shore, still feeding, but restless, pausing little. One night she struck a strange current in which the fresh water had reduced the salinity of the sea. All the next day she followed it, swimming near the surface, feeling the strangeness of the motion of the waves. At night she turned away again, leaving the vaguely haunting traces of fresh water. Thirty-six hours later she struck another current of mixed waters and again she turned to nose up into it. It drew her between a group of ragged islands and on into a great bay. The water pattern was familiar to her now and as she moved deeper into the bay she was joined by other salmon and they traveled in a school.

"Where the currents mixed she held to the major one, tasting in it the bitterness of peat and the remembered taste of limestone in their certain blending. Until then she had not realized clearly that she was headed for the river, but like a farm boy who leaves home at twenty to return at forty and finds the air laden with old scents in a mixture that could nowhere else be duplicated, the big salmon surged ahead, swimming strongly. She ceased to feed entirely, covering the fifteen-mile length of the Humber Arm against the tide in three hours. Then she spent another ten at the river's mouth, moving in and out of the fresh water to soften the shock of the change.

"With her in formation swam more than twenty other salmon. Most of them were *grilse*, or salmon of only one year's sea feeding. They were slim fish with forked tails and a weight of only four or five pounds. Others were mature salmon of two years of sea feeding, sturdy fish with broad, square tails, weighing from ten to twenty pounds. Only two were salmon that had spawned before and were returning from their second pilgrimage to the sea. She was the only three-year maiden in the school, the only one with three straight years of the bounty of the sea behind her, and she dwarfed them all.

163

"As they moved in and out of the fresh water, first one and then another of the school leaped, a maneuver the big salmon had almost forgotten during her years of sea feeding. She leaped, too, unknowing practice for the barriers that lay between her and her spawning bed. On the moonlit floodtide the school entered the river and swam steadily against the easy flow. They covered the lower river as a unit, finding no difficulty in traveling through its lazy waters. The whole school followed her leadership as she paralleled the north shore through Deer Lake's seventeen-mile length. Five miles above the lake they struck the first bad water at the Cache Rapids.

"A few grilse were missing when the school re-formed at the head of the white water and pushed ahead. At dawn they rested, tasting the bitterness of the brown water and feeling the change that had started within them. Their stomachs were shrinking and their teeth were starting to recede into their gums. Within them spawn and milt were beginning to form. Beneath the urgency that had drawn them back to their rivers was an underlying nausea that made all food distasteful and was to remain with them till long after spawning. They rested on the shoal at Harriman's Steady. Settling to the bottom in scattered groups of two and three, they sought out eddies where they could hold their positions in the soothing flow with the least exertion. Two canoes passed over them and they paid them no more heed than they would have to a pair of lazy blue sharks at sea, for few fish could outswim them. As the canoes passed a few feet over their heads they moved aside, and then moved back.

"At the Big Falls less than half the original school was together, but there they joined thousands of salmon who were about to try to leap the high rock face or were resting up from previous failures. Your big salmon was much larger than all but a few of the rest. Her stream days of constant leaping were farther behind her and her bulk was so great that even her superior strength would be taxed to the utmost to make the leap successfully.

"The first day she did not try to leap the falls, but she did make a few practice leaps, moving into the air after a run of

164

only half a dozen feet. Other salmon were going over regularly but the new-old sensation of running water and rocky streambed was still unusual for her in her new size. The river was high and she took a position in the main current near the center of the pool, moving forward a little as the hours passed until she felt the buffeting and vibration of the falling water.

"On the second evening she tried a leap, but it was short and when she fell she struck viciously against the rock well behind the curtain of falling water." I interrupted myself momentarily. "General, did you notice her only blemish, that scar?" The General nodded. "Well, the blow stunned her and she lay still on the bottom for a moment before righting herself. Even as she twisted up and moved into the flow, two eels had been closing in, fresh from tearing out the gills of a grilse that had not revived in time. All through the night she rested near the tail of the pool.

"The third evening found her back in the foamy water beneath the falls. This time her leap was good. From an eight-foot start she broke into the air and traveled twelve feet upward, head forward, to touch the brown water at the lip of the falls and spurt up through it to conquer the fifteen-foot wall of rock.

"Morning found her lying in Taylor's Pool not far from her birthplace. She had hesitated briefly at the Birchey Forks, swimming first to one and then the other. Unerringly she chose the Birchey water and crossed the lake to the upper river. Here at Taylor's Pool she passed on and then turned back, halted by the slight variation in the water above the mouth of Taylor's Brook. She settled comfortably into a lie out there under four feet of water and rested. Overhead, the water moved smoothly in an apparently even flow, but just ahead of the big salmon a rock jutted up from the streambed to mar the steady sweep of water. Behind it the water eddied and swirled and in that churning flow the salmon rested with little effort and yet enjoyed the soothing motion of the water against her sleek and restless body.

"Her teeth were almost completely absorbed into her flesh and they were sore. The spawn within her was growing, too, adding to the nausea that she found in the fresh water.

She still looked much as she had in the sea, but here as well a change was taking place. The silver of her scales was beginning to tarnish, a tarnishing as yet so slight that it could only be noticed in comparison with another salmon taken directly from the sea.

"She knew the need for conserving her strength to survive the three-month period of starvation that lay between her and the spawning time ... and for the long months that lay beyond, if she were to live through them, too. Yet the restlessness of all salmon was a part of her, causing a conflict in her mind. Sometimes, when the idleness palled too much, she lifted to the surface to take a floating leaf into her mouth and then eject it. Again, especially in the evening or at night, she would make a sudden spurt forward, lifting a high wave on the still surface as if to reassure herself that her great strength was still complete. Once, as a small white butterfly passed over her in its erratic flight, she lifted, more in instinct than from plan of mind, in a great surge that took her six feet into the air to capture it. And then your fly came along...."

The General had his pipe clamped upside down and I could see his teeth chewing at the stem. He said nothing for a long moment and then he yanked the pipe away and said: "I think that's the best story I've heard in a year, Lee. It is nature creating a magnificent life, if only a fish. It packs an elemental wallop that is noble. You should tell it to other men. What kind of fly rod and what weight do you want?"

"I wouldn't take a fly rod from a man like you for—"

He cut in on me. "You'll take that fly rod if I have to shove it down your throat in sections!"

I took the fly rod, and now I'm telling the story for other men. Many good fishermen will be familiar with some of it, but mighty few with all of it—with such a sportsman as the General and such an Amazon as that salmon.

[1946]

20

Thin Water and Bright Sun

In recent years light-tackle saltwater fly fishing, especially for bonefish, has become the fastest-growing part of fly fishing. New and diverse areas, such as Christmas Island south of Hawaii and the Caribbean coast of Venezuela, have opened up with the increased demand. Like trout and salmon, most bonefish live in nice places, some of which are described by Wulff in this essay and which add substantially to the fish's popularity.

In thinking of Lee Wulff and bonefish, I'm reminded of a few days I spent bonefishing with Al McClane at Deep Water Cay in the Bahamas. I could see a good fish in shallow water, but the fish was upwind and the breeze was strong. For all my huffing and puffing, the fly always fell short, and I gave up.

"Well," McClane said kindly, "don't feel too bad. I don't think even Lee Wulff could have reached that fish." I'm not sure that would have been the case, but it did make me feel better.

Dave Meyers of Tycoon Tackle was with me in my J3 Cub. We looked down on Grassy Key and the flats beside it from an altitude of about 250 feet. Dave called, "Do you see that flashing?" I turned and saw the bright flashes coming up through a patch of lightly rippled water, flashes as bright as if from signaling mirrors, brighter than those from any other fish I'd ever spotted from the plane.

That was back in 1947 when only a few of us knew that those down-looking bonefish with the undershot jaws could be caught on flies. We circled, landed in a channel, and taxied up to tie the plane to some mangroves near the shore. With our tackle readied we set out, wading and stalking in the general direction in which we'd seen the school. Dave spotted a tail tip moving slowly along with the rising tide. On his first cast he hooked the fish. I heard his reel screaming, but it was erased from my mind when I saw another tailing fish a hundred yards away. We moved toward each other, and when I cast he took my fly. That first surging run of a healthy bonefish on a shallow flat is something to remember, and as more anglers were initiated to the sound of a screaming reel and the brisk bending of their fly rods it became an experience that needed to be repeated again and again.

Our fish, alike as twins, weighed between six and seven pounds. Released, they swam off lazily across the cream-gray marl, mine only after I'd held him out of his element briefly for a candid shot.

Before that year bonefish had mostly been fished for with bait. Spinning, which made the casting of light lures easy, was not yet popular, and they were taken generally on bait-casting tackle. They were known as fast and wary fish that were ideal sport when caught on three-six tackle, 6-thread line (twisted linen, 18-pound-test), 6-foot rod, overall, weighing under 6 ounces.

My first fly rod for bonefishing was a 9-foot, 5-ounce split bamboo coupled with a GAF (#9) line. Within a few years I'd dropped down to a 6-footer of under 2 ounces for an RKO film shot at Fresh Creek, Andros Island, in the Bahamas, a new area then being developed by Swedish industrialist Axel Wenner-Gren. I'd learned by then to get greater speed and consequently greater distance with the smaller sticks. Since then my rods have ranged between these two lengths.

Bonefish at Andros then were quite tame compared with

the bonefish of today. I remember drifting up to an 8-pounder in our boat and having him miss the fly at boatside, then turn around and take it when I cast it back with little more than the leader out of the rod.

Those days of friendly, easy-to-approach bonefish are long gone—unless you can find a new spot where they haven't been fished over before. As more fishermen and more people with shallow-water boats came and learned how to catch them (mostly with spinning gear and bait), more and more were caught; and, because the native people of the Bahamas and other areas like to eat them in spite of their bones, more were kept. In Florida, bonefish were never as plentiful, I believe, as they were in the Bahamas and to the south, but in Florida most fish have been released and few, if any, kept for food.

The Florida bonefish are still there to be fished for. They are there in reasonable quantity, even though fishermen and fishing have increased. Most of them, however, have been caught at least a few times and are smart enough to require fine tackle, a careful approach, and delicate casting. The cream is off many of the close-to-civilization areas in the Bahamas. Where, then, does one go for good bonefish action?

If you don't want to work on those near-at-hand, educated Florida bonefish, you can look for a place in the Bahamas well off the beaten tracks where the flats stretch out for miles and miles, or you can go south to the flats of Yucatán or Belize, or the shores of the islands south of the Bahamas. Come with me now to Boca Paila on the mainland of Yucatán near the island of Cozumel.

Your guide is Pedro, a native Mayan, whose ancestors built the great castles and monuments whose ruins at nearby Tulum are something to see if, by chance, you get a rare cold and windy day that's poor for fishing.

The boat is fourteen feet long, wide, and of shallow draft. There's a thirty-five-horsepower Evinrude on its stern for running, but now he poles you slowly over the shallow flats in less than two feet of water. You stand on the platform at the bow, rod ready and line hanging from the tip to the fly in your hand, and coils spread out on your platform between the first guide and the reel. Your eyes search the water ahead.

A wind blows small waves toward you, and they patter against the hull in a steady lapping sound. Will the noise they make bother the bonefish? Pedro says, "Sí. A little bit. But you can cast far enough." That means he is sure you can cast beyond the spook range of the sound . . . into the wind. He has given you a red-and-candy fly to put on your leader.

The breeze is in from the north and cool, unusual for January and, as a result, most of the bonefish have moved into the channels and deeper water, where they find greater warmth.

Pedro calls out, "Bonefish! Ten o'clock . . . fifty feet . . . going to the left."

You look hard and see nothing, but your fly rod is moving the line, leader, and fly through the air in false casts. You still don't see the fish, but you cast your 50 feet at an angle of about nine o'clock and let it land.

"Behind him," says Pedro, softly.

Then you see him, lazing along, out of range now and going away. How long will it take, you wonder, before you'll be able to see the fish as well as the guides do. Maybe never? No! You have good eyes. In a few days you'll see them better. You'll learn to look as Pedro does and see the slight motion, the shadow on the marl or grass beneath them, even see their own bluish-brownish-grayish shapes against the similar colors behind them. Perhaps if you could stay a month. Someday, maybe. Someday.

The next one is a tailing fish. Nose down, he roots for food and that puts his tail up into your view. You see him as soon as Pedro calls, "Far off . . . tailing . . . twelve o'clock."

You wait then as Pedro poles closer.

It will be hard to straighten out the leader into the wind. At 60 feet you cast and fall about 5 feet short. But the bonefish moves swiftly to the candy fly. Your rising rod sets the hook.

The reel sings as only a bonefish can make it sing. You see the end of the fly line pass out of the rod with the backing behind it. The splice moves on out and vanishes into the light chop 50 feet away.

He fights as only a bonefish fights—speed, speed, and more speed and distance. Then, when he gives up after the fourth long run, you bring him in to circle the boat and finally swim over the net. Pedro lifts the net and holds him for you to look over. "Three and a half pounds." Typical for those southern waters. Pedro slides the net back into the water, unhooks the fish, and lets him swim away.

There's your only bonefish for the afternoon. Three others are too close to the boat before you see them, and they spook before your fly reaches them, and move out of range. Suppertime comes, and you quit, but not without a feeling of great expectations for the morrow. As you slide ashore at the camp and head for a cool drink and a good dinner, Pedro says, "Tomorrow we'll go to Ascension Bay. Bigger flats. No people live there. Many more bonefish. Maybe permit!"

An hour and a half in a bonefish boat is a long run. Halfway in the run you leave the channels and head out across the bay. The sky and the water are clear, clear blue, and they blend smoothly at the horizon with no sign of a shoreline. You watch the birds and look ahead, feeling the continuous pulsations of the boat as she rides over the short, low waves. Ten minutes . . . fifteen . . . then you make out three faraway islands. The water turns lighter, from bluish to pale green, as the bay shallows. At last the bottom is ivory, shallow water over white sand. You slow down and close in on the nearest island.

Roseate spoonbills, roosting in the trees, take flight as you approach. Pedro stops the motor, swings it up, then takes up his pole. The wind is light, the sky clear, and the sun bright. You take your stand at the bow.

You're still stretching your fly line to get the reel kinks out of it when Pedro calls, "Bonefish! Many, many . . . one o'clock, coming this way . . . a hundred feet."

There is a dark patch moving toward you, and you cast as far as you can. In a moment they are all around your fly. You lift your rod tentatively, and a bonefish pulls it down hard.

Your reel sings, and you're thrilled again by the sheer speed of a bonefish run.

"About four pounds?" you ask, as Pedro lifts the net when the long, fast runs are over.

"Four," Pedro nods. "Maybe four and a half," and the fish goes back to scoot away across the cream-colored sand.

That day is one to remember. You see school after school of bonefish, some larger, some smaller than the first one to take your fly. You see a few lone fish that are larger than those schooled up. They're warier, and you don't get your fly to them very well—except once, and that fish's first run wraps your line around a mangrove shoot to let you reel in a broken leader. You saw him well, though, when you cast your fly. "Maybe seven or seven and a half," was Pedro's guess.

The day wears on. You see sharks and rays and a great many barracuda. You see some sawfish, long shadowy shapes on the bottom, fish of the shark family that move away slowly when you pass close by. Your sandwiches are chomped down swiftly. Fishing time is precious on a day like this. Twice, in the afternoon, you see a permit. Each time you fail to reach him with your fly. Pedro spotted them, but you couldn't locate them yourself in time to make even a fair presentation.

To Pedro you say, "Let's fish for permit. Let's stay in the areas where the permit are likely to be."

You find yourself fishing in water that is just a little bit deeper. You look and look until your eyes ache. Finally Pedro puts down his pole and says, "Time to go." You ready yourself for the long run home.

The waves are higher, and you bounce to their rhythm on your seat in the middle of the boat. You get out a light raincoat to protect yourself from the occasional spray. Your bones ache a bit with the bouncing, but your mind is filled with the wonder of the day. Eighteen bonefish hooked—fourteen brought to the boat for release—and those permit. You're already thinking of tomorrow.

For the beginner, a place like Boca Paila can be a dreamland and a breakthrough to bonefishing. The fish are not too hard to catch, and one sees so many that there's a tendency to become an old hand in a relatively short time. The permit are there, too, and an angler who concentrates on the better permit water may well hook one or two on a fly in a week of fishing—while still seeing enough bonefish to give your rod and your reeling hand a good workout. There are tarpon, too, in some of the blue holes and on some of the flats near the mouth of the bay. Then, when you've put in your apprentice- ship, caught a lot of bonefish, and finally landed a 12-pound permit on a fly, you may want to try a spot where the bonefish are bigger and more sophisticated—such as Deep Water Cay at the eastern end of Grand Bahama Island.

The pilot of the Aero Commander that flies you over from Palm Beach may make a wide swing around the lodge to show you the seemingly endless flats that spread out in all directions. You'll strain your eyes, but you'll be too high up to see bonefish from the plane. But you'll know, instinctively, that they must be there, and you'll be eager to get to the ground and out of your city duds and into something you can fish in.

The Deep Water Cay flats hold bonefish with an average size of about 5 pounds. The permit they catch there are big enough to make any permit fisherman think that if he can catch one it could well be a record. There's a catch, though! Those 35-pounders on the wall of the lodge were all caught on spinning gear. The word is out that it's foolish to fish for them with a fly. But you're a dedicated fly fisherman, and you've been dreaming of a bigger permit than the Boca Paila 12- pounder for a long time.

Your guide, Mervin, tells you that it's a long trip to the best permit grounds, and you'll need good weather to make it. Your first fishing day is too cloudy, and there's a good breeze blowing up whitecaps almost everywhere. Mervin takes you to the nearby sheltered areas, fishing here for half a mile—there for only a few hundred yards—and occasionally finding almost a mile of protected shoreline.

Visibility is very poor under the clouds, and you spook most of the dozen fish you see, failing to see them until the boat was too close. Although you can spot bonefish better now than when you first started fishing the flats, you still can't match eyes with Mervin. There are one or two you might have put a fly to if you'd seen them as quickly as he did or as soon as he called, out, but it was only in one of the two brief periods of sunlight when Mervin spotted one a long way off and you made a short but lucky presentation and brought him in for release. It was good to have a bonefish on the line again, but you decide that you'd better sharpen up your casting both as to accuracy and power in order to place your fly better if you have many more days with wind to contend with.

One thing you like, though, is the "guillotine" that Don Dickerson, the manager, has installed on all the boats. It's a U-shaped unit of two-inch pipe that stands at the back of each boat's front platform. You can lean back against it to steady yourself in a wind or in rough water, yet it doesn't interfere with your casting or the spreading out of the line on the deck for that fast, long cast you want to make when a fish is spotted. It's removable, and anyone who feels secure on the platform without it can remove it before leaving camp.

The run to the permit grounds is almost as long as the run from Boca Paila to Ascension Bay, but this time you hug the shore and just seem to go on and on past beaches or mangroves on your port side. Finally, you head out across open water, and again you have that sense of heading into nowhere, for the sky and the sea seem to blend into one another with no line of demarcation. The motor drones on, and you run and run and wonder if you'll ever get there.

You do. With surprising suddenness Mervin slows down and swings the boat toward a shallow white-sand flat with no growth of grass or mangroves to mark it. It is just a shallow flat beside a deep channel that angles off toward a thin line of land off to the southeast. Mervin takes up his pole.

You deliberated quite a while before you chose a fly for this occasion. Inasmuch as the permit here have been refusing *all* the flies the anglers have been casting to them, picking a favorite doesn't seem any wiser than picking a strange one no permit ever saw before. You've started tying some flies yourself, and though you know they're not truly professional, this is a case where professionalism hasn't seemed to work.

You decide on a pink, yellow, and white fly, reminiscent of a Parmachene Belle, you made up yourself. It was the fly that had caught yesterday's bonefish.

Time passes while you watch and watch. Mervin puts down his pole, and you run to another bank, a little closer to the far shoreline. Again you move slowly across the flats, which are a mixture of open white-sand patches and the nondescript tan and brown sea grass dusted with grains of sand.

Mervin calls, "Permit! Twelve o'clock, moving to the left."

You look in vain. Then you see the dark shape moving onto a patch of open white sand. He's big and he's within your casting range.

You cast, and luck is with you. The fly goes out smoothly and for the full 60 feet it will take to drop 10 feet ahead of him and in his path. He surges forward. You tense for the strike. But he goes right on by within a foot of your fly as if it weren't even there and disappears as a fading shadow on a patch of grassy bottom. You turn to Mervin and say, "How big?"

"Thirty pounds. Maybe more," is his reply.

For another hour Mervin poles you along the edge between the shallow water you're accustomed to fish for bonefish and the four- or five-foot depth where the fish would be too difficult to see and where, in any case, your fly would not be as effective. You see one more permit angling away, a hundred feet off. Mervin tries hard to bring you within casting range but fails, and you lose sight of him, then the sun goes under a cloud, and all the bottom goes dark.

You've worked your way to Jacob's Cay, and there on the sand ahead of you is a school of thirty bonefish or more. They cross in front of you at fifty feet, and one of them takes your fly. That is the first of seven you take in the two and a half hours you have left to fish. Two of them you took by wading, leaving the boat while Mervin had a sandwich and a soft drink. Not because he asked you to, of course, but because you wanted to try it to see if it was more fun than fishing from the boat. And it was—until the bottom softened up and wading became like walking over a soft waffle covered with sticky syrup. The smooth, easy travel of the boat was welcome again.

It is smooth this time for the long run home. Slowly, in the three years since your first trip to Boca Paila, you've been realizing that you're really hooked, that every winter when the snow falls and the ice coats northern waters you'll want to be trying for that 10-pound bonefish and that 35-pound permit. The memories of the blue-green of shallow southern seas lying under a warm sun will make the dream all the more tempting. If you can possibly make it, you'll go . . . again and again.

[1982]

21

The Wonderful Brookies of Minipi

As Wulff hoped in this essay written twenty years ago, the brook-trout fishing in Minipi has held up extremely well, largely thanks to the continuation of a farsighted management policy at the camp that allows each fisherman to keep only one trophy trout per week. Having spent most of my life measuring brook trout in inches, I found a recent week at Minipi catching 5- and 6-pounders on dry flies to be an extraordinary experience.

The camps are now run by my friends Jack and Lorraine Cooper, who are not related to Ray Cooper, described here by Wulff as having started the camp at Anne Marie Lake. Access is by commercial jet from Montreal to Goose Bay, Labrador. The round-trip helicopter charter between Goose Bay and camp is part of the week's fishing package. The current address is: Minipi Camps, P.O. Box 340, Happy Valley, Labrador, Canada A0P 1E0.

For years my plane carried me deeper and deeper into the Labrador wilderness as I sought the last strongholds of giant

177

brook trout. I found more than my share, only to see some of the best waters later ruined by overfishing. Then I struck the most fabulous area of all, and as my light rod bowed against the pull of brookies averaging 5 pounds, I vowed to keep this spot a secret until the time when its treasure could be shared without destroying it. That time is now!

Back in the summers of the mid-1950s, when I was flying the only light plane in eastern Labrador, I used to look down on unbroken wilderness for mile after mile. The Indians traveled that wild land occasionally as part of their normal life pattern, and a few prospectors and trappers in search of a fabulous strike of minerals or furs lost themselves in its vastness. Now and then a woodsman traveled into a lowland river basin to evaluate the timber potential, and a few military and bush pilots flew over the area. Some of the bush pilots who loved to fish found time to drop from the skies to the uncharted lakes for a brief holiday. But for me exploring these unknown waters was a major project—and a labor of love.

The air force, with its eyes from the sky, was finding a few choice spots for recreation, like Nipishish, where the brook trout were big and plentiful and all too soon cleaned out. The same was true at Mackenzie—through which the Michikamau poured a massive flow into the Naskaupi and on down to Lake Melville to meet the tides at Northwest River. The brookies and pike were big and fantastically plentiful—for a while.

The rest of the wilderness—from St. Augustine, 100 miles to the south, to Goose Bay, 70 miles north and east; from Seven Islands, 300 miles to the west and northward, forever to the Arctic—belonged to the bush pilots. My Super Cub plane was light, with shallow-draft floats, and I could go in and come out where no other plane could follow.

One summer I scouted fishing sites for the U.S. Air Force. Another summer I evaluated eastern Labrador's sport-fishing potential and reported on it to the Province of Newfoundland. I searched, I fished, I recorded—and I enjoyed. Through all this, one chain of lakes showed up better for brook trout than all the others.

I saw it first while on my way to Dominion Lake. The sun shone on unbroken forests of spruce and fir divided by a chain of lakes at a thirteen-hundred-foot elevation. They lay like mirrors in a breathless calm, insect rich, broken only by the dimples of trout, by the larger circles of diving mergansers and by the wake of an otter swimming near shore. The flow from lake to lake looked perfect. It was deep, with a blue-black sheen of dark peat-stained water, yet occasionally, between the pools, shallow enough for a man to wade from shore to shore.

The connecting rivers were big enough for big trout—many of them. Fast flows tumbled between the shallow lakes, where, from the air, the underwater grass beds showed up in wide areas like submerged golden carpets. I pictured the grass as being heavy with nymphs. In June the green drakes would burst their imprisoning underwater cases and rise in clouds to the freedom of the air.

A float-plane pilot follows a certain routine when he goes into an unknown lake. He flies over the projected landing spot to look down for rocks either breaking the surface or close to it. It's easy to see submerged rocks and reefs in clear water when the sun is high, but the dark rocks under the dark-brown waters of the Labrador peat belt are almost impossible to see, even with a high sun. Under a cloud or with the sun at a low angle, everything below the surface remains a mystery. Then the pilot must estimate the depth of the lake bed from the look of the surrounding country, and no matter how much he knows, he's still guessing.

As I came in over the treetops at the outlet, my mind was filled with impatient wonder as to what I'd find. Would it be as good as it looked? Were the dimpling trout as large as I'd judged from up high? Would there be many?

It took only a few minutes to land, taxi to shore, take out the little fly rod I always carry fully rigged. As usual, I was flying with waders on. I made my cast a dozen steps from where I'd tied the plane, where the running out of the lake first quickened.

No rising fish were to be seen from this earthbound location. I cast and waited to see whether I'd hook a trout or a

179

pike on the retrieve. Instead, I hooked nothing at all, which meant, simply, that the water wasn't swarming with small fish. Then a fish rose within casting distance. In a moment it rose again to my fly. It was a brook trout of over 6 pounds.

I caught four more, all a little smaller than the first. This is consistent with wilderness fishing where nine times out of ten the first fish to take a fly in the best feeding location is the biggest fish in the pool. I kept two.

Going ashore, I poked around and found faint signs of an old lean-to and a piece of snare wire. If I had decided to dig, I felt sure I would have found arrowheads. Then I flew on with the warm, rich feeling of knowing I'd found exactly what I was looking for.

The lakes in the chain were small. Only two were suitable for commercial seaplane operations, although I could fly into a dozen of them with my small ship if it weren't too heavily loaded. And I did—but, except for my confidential reports to the government—for years these waters were my secret.

Labrador had literally millions of lakes—varying in fishing quality from poor to excellent. The angling development, as it came, was toward the headwaters of the Eagle—to such places as No-Name, Park Lake, Muskrat, and Eagle.

Meanwhile the upper Minipi waters were left for me and my friends and as a safe bet for brook-trout movies when I needed them for the Garcia Corporation with Dick Wolff, for the "American Sportsman" television program with Curt Gowdy, and for Warner Brothers with my wife, Joan Salvato.

During these years, I had been doing my best to instigate future protection for these waters. As a result of my reports to the provincial governments of Newfoundland and Labrador, a bill with a definite poundage limit to keep down total catches in the area went through a second reading in the House, but failed in the final vote due to fears that anglers could not afford to have any area of fishing denied them. Another bill for a trout sanctuary also failed.

For forty years I've watched magnificent brook-trout waters go down the drain. The pattern, always the same, is simple. Brook trout, which in the north country require the food of the lakes, consistently congregate at the running water. Take all the fish out of these concentration points, and the entire population of the lakes is devastated.

A second factor—size of fish—works this way: anglers moving into virgin waters take big fish by the hundreds and put the small ones back. It is similar to systematically killing off tall people, putting back short ones, and then wondering a few generations later why basketball giants can't be found. I could cite case after case in Newfoundland alone: Fox Island River, where the average trout in 1940 was 4 pounds or better; North Arm River, where it averaged 6; Western Brook, where it averaged 5. Brook trout now average less than a pound in each of these rivers. No cattle breeder would ever kill off his best breeding stock, but we—in our wild-brook-trout fishing—have done just that.

To be sure, much Canadian water still offers brookie fishing that is superb by American standards. But the spots where 4- and 5-pounders are common, and larger fish possible, are dwindling.

So my hope and my efforts were to set aside a small section of this magnificent Labrador area, where big brook trout are confirmed insect feeders, for a no-fishing sanctuary. It was to be held as a source of study—and a source of supply for stocking other areas—so that the biologists might see how well nature could produce these fish in great size and in great quantity. Nowhere in any *managed* area have I seen its equivalent. Unfortunately, no such major sanctuaries have ever been set up anywhere on this continent. *Game sanctuaries*, yes; but no major wild sanctuaries for fish where none are taken, save for science.

Failing in this effort, I'm glad to report the next best thing: Ray Cooper, a roaming, adventurous Englishman, came to Goose Bay. After a nine-year stint in the British navy and four years at an ionosphere research station in the Falklands, Ray became a woodsman and a trapper. Summers he worked in the bush and for three years was head guide at a salmon club of which I'm a member. Quite naturally, he was trapped by a trapper's daughter, settled down to have a family and sink his roots into the Labrador soil. One winter he trapped in my favorite area and fell in love with it. He named the lake, where I'd set up a camp with Curt Gowdy for the American Sportsman brook-trout program, Anne Marie Lake, after his wife. He and his partner, Bob Albee of Elmira, New York, a friend of mine, set up a fishing camp. They insist on a very limited kill and on fly fishing only.

The main camp takes only six anglers, which, as an old-time camp operator, I know is economically inefficient. But that small number of anglers will never overcrowd the available fishing water. The second camp (now in progress) is made up of tents and can be reached directly by airplane or by canoe and portage over some seven miles of lake and river. At this camp the rule will be to release all fish at the short run between the lakes in front of the camp. This is a direct reversal of the use-it-up policy at some camps that, year by year, forces anglers to travel farther and farther afield to find good fishing.

Fortunately, Ray and Bob are well booked. Their belief that enough good sportsmen are more interested in catching fish than in taking them home has been justified. Their sportsmen go home without a heavy load of brook trout, but they have the certainty of hooking into a 5-pound squaretail on a dry fly. And the persistent or the lucky may easily bring home a trophy trout of more than 8 pounds for mounting. The waters could not be in better hands.

The secret of Minipi's superb trout lies largely, I believe, in the water, which is organically and chemically rich enough to support great quantities of insect life. The lakes are shallow enough to let sunshine reach their beds and warm them into great productivity. The trout, through thousands of years of undisturbed natural selection, have learned to fit into and use their environment.

These deep, full-bodied squaretails of the Minipi waters are magnificent. Their extra-sturdy form can be seen at a glance when comparing them with trout from other watersheds. Best of all, they are mayfly conditioned and dry-fly conscious—unusual in a species where fish over $1\frac{1}{2}$ pounds are normally confirmed cannibals.

The branch of the Minipi water that flows through Anne Marie Lake builds up from the flow out of many high valleys and lakes. Each little pond or long, deep run of water has its proportionate share of brook trout. They grow big and they grow fast. I sent scales from one that went better than 5 pounds to Bill Flick, of Cornell's research team, for a scale reading. Fortunately, he said, the particular scales I sent were easy to read, and the fish had almost certainly reached that weight in five years' time.

The balance between the food in these waters and the need of this particular genetic strain of trout is near perfect. The fact that pike—and big ones—are scattered through the same waters does not preclude the trout's great size and numbers any more than foxes on the wild plains ever eliminated the millions of prairie chickens there. I'd once hooked a 5-pound brookie at Anne Marie Lake and, as I played it, had a pike slash its belly and spill its guts into the stream. I've also seen a swarm of brookies, gathered to feed behind the spawning suckers in a little brook, gang up and drive a northern larger than themselves away from the spawning area.

I'm still sad to think that there cannot be a sanctuary for these magnificent brookies—to live and breed and remain unmanaged by civilization.

Last summer I stopped in to see how the camp at Ann Marie was coming. The main camp had been in use all season, and the outlying buildings and tents were taking on a settled look. I fished the running out of Anne Marie hard by the camp, spending a fruitless hour with a red-and-yellow bucktail that normally was a real killer and then after changing to a small dry fly, drew two good rises and landed a 5-pounder.

Later I flew up over the far western valley and located Bob and a couple of his men, out exploring new waters. They were far up a tributary brook in a pond ringed with timber and too short for my plane. I circled and waved, then headed back to one of my favorite pools, the pool where Dick Wolff had taken his 7-pounder in 1958. "Dick's Pool" looked like it always did. The fish were lying in the deep channel at the outlet of the shallow pond. A dozen trout were rising, and I either lost or released them all on a Scraggly Wulff. With the willing fish chastised, I switched to a big #2 red-and-yellow streamer and brought a dozen more to shore for release. Two of them broke water in clean, rainbowlike leaps. Their average was, as it has always been, close to 5 pounds.

Even though the canoes from Anne Marie must have penetrated that far on several occasions, the fish were still there as of old—mute testimony to the camp's good management and a tribute to the axiom that a good gamefish is too valuable to catch only once. To write of fishing like this is to write of dreams, and yet I have found in several lonely spots I flew to first, pools with a quarter ton of available fish—trout one man could catch in a single day, if so inclined. This superb fishing never lasts and only a few of us who scouted the wild fishing have seen these things. One trapper took 400 pounds of trout out of Minipi for dog food, along with his catch of furs.

Next morning, Bob was back at a pond I could land in, and I flew Ray over there from the main camp. A couple of 3-pounders were frying over the campfire, and Bob's eyes were glowing—with memories of a 9-pounder he'd caught and released back where I'd circled over him the day before.

We fished a slow flow near their tent. It had been ten years since I had fished in this exact spot and it was Bob and Ray's first time. Our flies covered the water but the pool seemed barren. No fish were rising, none would strike. In desperation I cast long and far to where the water rolled slowly toward stillness in the depths and let the red-and-yellow streamer sink a long time. When I started to retrieve the fly, I couldn't. It was fast to a trout. I worked him in till he touched the rocks where I stood. The other fellows gathered around to watch. He was bigger than the one that now hangs over my mantel. For a brief instant—when I first saw him clearly—I considered taking him down to a taxidermist since I was ready to fly on home. My hand touched his back to pick him up, but he was too broad for my fingers and slipped away. I played him toward a sloping rock while my instinct to take him home to mount fought with my cultivated policy of freeing the bigger fish. He scraped the leader across a rock and broke free. I took off—an hour later—without him.

Late that afternoon, halfway across the three-hundred-mile stretch to Seven Islands, I ran into foul weather. The wind rose, the rain poured down, the fog rolled in. My wind-shield was an opaque splatter of heavy raindrops, and all I could see was a small bit of terrain directly below on either side. I flew by compass and that tenuous sight of the ground. Visibility came down to less than half a mile. I had, as always, a tent, sleeping bag, and some food aboard.

I found myself over a pond in a high basin that had been carved out of a wide plateau by the last glaciers. I made ready to go in. The spruce tips were only one hundred feet below my pontoons, and the clouds were misting around me. It occurred to me then that there, on that unknown pond, while I waited out the weather, I might conceivably find a bigger fish than the one I'd lost.

But before my floats touched the water, I saw a glimmer of light under the dark clouds at the far side of the lake. I pushed the power back to cruise and flew on westward through showers and slowly lifting ceilings, hopping over the ridges but keeping one lake in sight behind till I had the next one in view ahead. Long before I reached Seven Islands, visibility was back to fifteen miles.

That unknown pond just might have had a bigger trout in it than any in the upper Minipi basin. So may half a dozen others, as yet untouched, or secret to some lonely flier in the wild and vast north country. But till I know for sure, I'll rate Minipi best.

As of now the trout in this area are safe with Bob Albee, Ray Cooper, and their sportsmen. I hope their wise Fish for Fun policy spreads as other wilderness areas are opened to fishermen. If the government does not allow competitive operators to increase the pressure on these waters and the anglers at the camp do not take more than a certain number of fish (this means an absolute number out of the watershed, not a given number per angler, which is variable), the fishing in the Anne Marie Lake basin, though no longer secret, may always be superb.

[1969]

22

Marlin
on a Fly Rod

Here's what Lee Wulff himself held for many years to have been his greatest of angling adventures—the taking of a record fly-caught marlin. In the twenty-odd years since Wulff's feat, other anglers have taken marlin on fly tackle, but I don't think Wulff's use of such basic fly gear has ever been duplicated. The few fly rodders these days who chase billfish choose at the very least a substantial graphite fly rod and an even more substantial reel with a heavy-duty braking system totally unlike the very basic dime-store tackle Wulff used for his world record.

Wulff mentions in this chapter his hope that more anglers will start casting—as opposed to trolling—to big-game fish in the open ocean. This reminds me of the new and developing white-marlin fishery in the Atlantic off Martha's Vineyard and Nantucket islands in Massachusetts. Here, boat captains are cruising until fish are spotted and then casting baits to the marlin with heavy spinning tackle. Because the fish often seem unperturbed by the boat, it may be only be a short time until fly tackle comes into use here also.

Off Ecuador, in April, the Pacific is often oily smooth. Then, if you leave Salinas and run due west for fifteen miles, until the headland has all but disappeared in the haze on the horizon and the sky and the ocean are wide and empty, you'll begin to see marlin tails and fins breaking the surface. These striped marlin may be almost motionless, with the slow lift of the rollers washing over their partly exposed backs. More likely, they'll be cruising along at anywhere from half a mile up to seven miles an hour. Although marlin are solitary rovers, now and again as many as seven get together, tails and fins showing, as they ease along just under the surface of the ocean.

This Pacific area just off the mouth of the Gulf of Guayaquil probably has the world's finest marlin fishing. Scattered among the hundred or more striped marlin that an angler may see on an April day will be an occasional black marlin of 500 pounds or over and, possibly, a big blue. A small fleet of local fishermen in picturesque lignum vitae–hulled sailboats have trolled hand lines in the paths of the *picudas* for generations, but as yet the area has not been fished hard, either commercially or for sport.

Billfish fall into six main species. The Atlantic sailfish is the smallest and the white marlin next, both weighing normally under 100 pounds. The Pacific sailfish averages near 100 pounds and may run up to more than 200. All three are slender, willowy fish endowed with considerable speed and great propensities for leaping, but they are not comparable in long-range speed and endurance to the three larger billfish species: the striped, blue, and black marlin. These three are sturdier and heavier throughout their length. The striped marlin, smallest of the three (averaging around 150 pounds off Ecuador), goes up to a record 430. The Pacific blues go up to 555. The black marlin tops them all with a record weight of 1,561 pounds. They're all of the same general makeup, with little difference in fighting quality.

To take one of these tough, durable marlin on true fly-fishing tackle, I realized, would be comparable to scaling Everest, an angling feat not yet achieved by any man. I'd taken a number of Pacific sailfish and knew how tough *they* could be. To take one of the top three, a swift and enduring striped, blue, or black marlin would make angling history and stimulate a greater interest in the taking of all the big-game fish of the sea not only by fly casting, but by the other, less difficult casting methods as well.

Marlin will hit feathered lures, and one striped marlin, a 145-pounder, had been taken on a fly by Dr. Webster Robinson, a much-admired angler of Key West. To take his fish, he had used a multiplying reel and a nonstandard fly rod with a butt. Even a very short butt changes the character of the tackle, and a reel handle that doesn't spin as line races out makes playing any fish much simpler. To qualify for the Federation of Fly Fishermen's standard classification, the rod must be single-handed with no butt, the reel must be simple single-action, and the fly must be cast, not trolled, to the fish.

I wanted to prove that ordinary fly-fishing tackle, the sort that is in normal use for bass-bugging the lakes, would (with some extra backing) take a striped marlin, and that drags, multiplying reels, and rod butts are not essential. I chose a glass fly rod made by Garcia, single-handed, weighing only 5 ounces and selling for about $12.

My reel, a Farlow Python (single-action without brake or drag, with only a slight click to prevent overrun), cost about $30. I'd have to brake it with my fingers against the reel spool. My fly line was #10 forward taper with 300 yards of 17-pound-test, braided-nylon squidding line for backing. It added another $20 to the cost. The leader, key link in the tackle chain, costs very little but is extremely important for record recognition. Mine had an 11-inch shock section of 80-pound-test nylon next to the fly, then the section of more than 12 inches in length and maximum 12-pound-test that is required by practically all fly-rod groups for records.

Florida fly-rod groups and the Salt Water Fly Rodders of America insist on less than a foot of shock leader next to the fly (where teeth, mouth, and bill can chafe), while the Federation of Fly Fishermen, largest of the fly-fishing organizations, will allow up to 2 feet, a considerable advantage when fishing for billfish. I made sure that my tackle would qualify for all sets of specifications, even though such a small difference as the shorter shock leader could spell the difference between success and failure.

With me in the boat was Woody Sexton, who has a fine reputation as a guide, angler, and sportsman. Woody didn't normally guide for marlin and had never taken one, but he knows the field of fly fishing, and is a top fly rodder in his own right. Guide and angler must have a close relationship and, when I had worked with Woody on a big fly-rod tarpon in the past, we'd had that. The boat was a fifteen-footer with a thirty-three-horsepower outboard. We were taking light fly-fishing gear in a very small boat out into the largest of oceans, and most of my friends and fellow anglers felt that the striped marlin would be just a little too tough for the tackle and me.

With ABC's "American Sportsman" crew all set to film the attempt, failure would be very distasteful. Ninety-nine times out of a hundred, when an individual sets out to break a world record he fails. The odds against success are long and in this case mine were even longer. I had been counting on two weeks of shooting time, but other commitments had forced "American Sportsman" to cut the time to only one week. Seven days is a short period in which to break a record, and the realization of the cost of the expensive sound crew standing by would add to the pressure.

The previous April, I had caught Pacific sailfish with a fly off Piñas Bay, Panama. Then I'd used a trolled teaser, a ballyhoo without a hook, to draw the sailfish within fly-casting range. Off Ecuador we could do without the aid of trolled teasers, since marlin showed up plentifully on the surface. A month earlier off Ecuador I'd taken an 18-pounder, trolling on a 12-pound-test line, the first ever taken on 12-pound line in that area.

I'd had the advantage of a trolling rod, a belt socket to hold its butt, a star-drag reel, and a 12-foot, 80-pound-test leader. It had taken forty-five minutes. So I knew 12-pound-test would be strong enough to take a marlin, but the strength of arm required to tire him, the capacity to handle line at great lengths and speeds on a single-action reel, and the

189

ability to bring the fish to gaff on fly tackle without the aid of a strong, long leader with which to pull him in those last yards were yet to be proved.

The first day out, we left Salinas an hour and a half after sunrise, and ninety minutes later we sighted marlin fins in a smooth sea under still air. Had we been fishing in conventional fashion we'd have been aboard a fishing cruiser more than twice as long and twenty times as bulky as our skiff. We'd have been trolling, and long outriggers would have projected to each side to increase the scope of the baits that followed in our wake.

There would have been a cabin to relax in for comfort and shade while waiting for fish to strike, rod sockets to hold the rods while the baits trolled, star-drag reels to set the hooks when outrigger slack was used up, and a swivel chair to sit in comfortably while playing a fish.

For fly fishing we needed a boat without a cabin or outriggers, a boat as free of encumbrances for the caster as a rowboat on a lake. Fly-fishing rules call for casting to the fish. They forbid trolling. Accordingly, when we spotted a fish we tried to place ourselves in his path, so that he would pass within casting range and, as he swam by, I'd cast from the drifting boat.

It wasn't easy to reach the right position. Marlin at the surface rarely set a purposeful course. They tend to meander as they travel. My fly was a big one, a 4/0 tandem made with long rooster feathers in a mixture of red, white, and yellow. Woody had dubbed it the Sea Wulff—a bulky fly that cast about as easily as the average bass bug. With the first four fish, we were able to get into position for only one good fly presentation.

The wake of our approach to the first marlin (before Woody put the motor into neutral) was too great for the big fish and, as it hit him, he sank far enough under the surface to be invisible. His tail showed again beyond us when he was well out of casting range. Trying him again with a more careful approach, I placed the fly a dozen feet ahead of him. He showed not the slightest interest. After that, his course became increasingly erratic, and during the long and difficult

190

maneuvering toward a third try we spotted a second marlin tail and decided to try for that one instead.

He came up to us as we lay quietly on the smooth water. He was headed almost directly toward us, and I cast when he was sixty feet away. He turned from his path a few feet to look at the fly and followed it until he saw the boat. Then he slid down out of sight, failing to appear on the surface again.

The third fish was a wild one. He was cruising along swiftly, tail tip showing from time to time. We circled to put ourselves in his path but cut a little too short and the wake was high enough to put him down out of sight. Had we been trolling a fly, it might have passed near him and drawn a strike. Once a fish is out of sight there's not much point in casting, the ocean being as big as it is, but I tried a cast anyway, to where I thought he might pass, but without result.

We left that fish for a fourth we saw lying almost motionless on the surface. He looked big and lazy and unconcerned. We came in very slowly, making almost no wake, and coasted to a stop, motor in neutral and idling. The cast was a long one and the fly dropped beautifully, I thought, right in front of his nose. Instead of gulping the fly down, he took offense and vanished dramatically with a great splashing surge.

We saw marlin every few minutes, it seemed, throughout that day, but if they showed any interest it was merely to swim alongside or under the fly for a moment. I had the feeling the heavy shock leader was spooking them. Woody thought it was the sight of us, since they usually were headed right toward the boat when they moved in on the fly. Once two fish moved up swiftly on the fly at the same time and I felt sure the usual feeding jealousy between fish would cause one or the other to show off by proving he could get the fly first. Neither cared that much.

Time went by. The afternoon breeze came up and the fish tended to cruise a little faster. Waves built up and the tails were hard to see. The only way we could get flies to the fish was to cruise parallel at the same speed and fifty or sixty feet away and cast the fly just ahead of them, giving the fish a quick look as it landed and the retrieve pulled it away. We found three fish curious enough to follow the fly toward the boat, but once they were in close and easily visible, they'd sink down and come up a few minutes later on another course. By three-thirty when we had to start our run back to Salinas, our total sighting for the day must have come close to seventy.

It was hard to believe that we could have seen so many marlin without drawing a strike. In my experience with Pacific sailfish I'd found them much more willing to take a fly. We were deeply disappointed: the cameras hadn't rolled seriously all day and the chances of hooking a marlin, let alone landing one, grew more remote.

The breeze came up earlier the next morning and for the first three hours we didn't see a fin. At eleven the breeze slackened. Suddenly, as if by magic, marlin tails were everywhere. We moved in on fish after fish without getting a good presentation.

We wondered why the fish were so wary. Woody and I had to swing wide as we passed them until we could draw far enough ahead to swing into their paths. If we moved in too far ahead, they meandered off and passed at too great a distance. If we cut in too close our wake sent them down. The sound of the outboard in close may have distressed them more than a normal marine motor does.

The first three fish we were able to cast to were headed toward us. They moved in behind the fly, turned away if I stopped the retrieve, or followed in too close to the boat and spooked if I didn't. The fourth fish was barely within casting range. Luckily, a long cast just reached him. He came up under it, slashed with his bill, and almost in the same motion turned back and took the fly. The time was just noon.

At first he was slow and gentle. He eased along, as if unaware that he was hooked. Once the hook was set, my pressure at the reel was as light as I could make it. I wanted to avoid the swift, raging surges and the long, coursing leaps that would break the leader if he undertook them at the peak of his strength. I hoped to take the edge off his wildness before he fully realized his danger. For a quarter of an hour his only indications of discomfort were a few vicious head shakes.

Little by little I built up the pressure. A school of pilot

whales loomed behind us on the same course. As they reached us, the marlin moved off and I had to increase the pressure a little. So he moved faster and faster, until the click of the single-action reel was screaming and the handle was just a whirling blur. He jumped a dozen times in a run that took him far off, and I could only hope the trailing line and backing would not break the leader's 12-pound strength, even though I was putting practically no finger pressure on the line at the rapidly spinning reel.

The leader held. The marlin sounded. When he ended his dive, my reel was almost empty and the line was going straight down and out of sight. It is hard to know what direction to follow under these conditions. We drifted and waited for several minutes until we could detect a slight angle in the downward sweep of the line. Woody headed us in that direction.

The line was slowly coming back onto the spool. Less than a third of the backing had been reeled in when suddenly we saw our marlin leaping two hundred yards away. Knowing he had brought the far end of the line up to the surface, I could put more heart in my lifting to straighten out the belly. Eventually the tail of the fly line came onto the reel spool.

Twelve pounds is a considerable pressure, but an angler cannot begin to approach his tackle's limit unless both boat and fish are moving slowly and the situation is not likely to change suddenly. I thought I could sense that the fish now would hold a steady course. I increased pressure with my fingers on the reel spool, ready at any instant to lift the finger and release the spool. From this point on, I knew I had a chance to nag the fish with my tackle, telling him he wasn't free, making him struggle.

The difference between playing a big fish with a rod that has a butt and playing one with a single-handed fly rod becomes apparent after about ten minutes of the action. With a rod butt settled comfortably against the body and one or both arms on the grip there's good leverage, and with a little effort the angler can keep up a good strain for a long time. But when the pressure to gain line must be put on by holding the rod and lifting with only one arm while the other hand does the reeling, it takes a well-conditioned arm and considerable endurance. It is for this reason that I was using my strong right arm for the holding of the rod—where strength and delicacy are most needed—and using my weaker, less-trained left hand for the reeling.

Woody maneuvered the boat beautifully. Pressure built up on the fish and occasionally he made more jumps, but his earlier exertions were telling on him, and these leaps were not swift enough to snap the leader. Another long, searching dive took him down until I was again near the end of my backing, and this time he stayed down a quarter of an hour.

At the end of two hours he was back on the surface, really tired. So were we. He set off at a steady pace, about 6 feet under the surface. When we closed to within 30 feet of him we could see him plainly, but when he pulled as far ahead as 60 feet we lost sight of him. A pair of marlin appeared and joined him, swimming parallel courses about 30 feet to each side. We followed him. The idling motor gave a little help, but most of the boat's forward motion came from the tackle's pressure on the fish.

We skirted a big school of mackerel. We saw a solitary shark fin on the surface, but it never came close. The wind lightened and smooth patches of oily calm showed up between wind riffles. We could see our fish often, and occasionally we could see the fly itself. After one of the marlin's periodic gymnastic flurries that ended with particularly frenzied surface thrashing, we swung up close behind him and my heart came into my throat. The leader was wrapped around his bill and the fly seemed to be dangling free beside his head.

I felt like giving up right then. My arms had been aching for hours and sweat was pouring down my back under my shirt. We knew it was only a question of time before he'd shake his head or slide backward in full exhaustion, which would crate slack and either free the leader or draw the 12-pound-test over the roughness of the bill and chafe it through.

If we'd had a typical trolling leader, we'd have had no problem but, tired as the fish was, I had to bring him within gaff reach on that 12-pound leader—while it lasted. Time moved slowly and the fish kept working to the westward. The camera boat crowded up a little closer. The fish was now well aware of both boats and, seeing danger in them, stayed from 10 to 20 feet deep. All the pressure I dared exert wouldn't bring him up. Finally, in sheer exhaustion, he stopped and started to slide backward, tail first. I felt slack for a horrible instant, then he thrashed forward and I had solid pressure again. When we could see the fly once more it was embedded near the corner of his mouth and holding.

It held that way until he came in. He surfaced to thrash a few minutes later, and when Woody closed in I held as hard as I could. He was on his way down again when Woody barely reached him with the gaff back near the tail. Spray flew as Woody held the gaff and rope. I got a glove on one hand and tried to reach the bill. It was too far away. He swung around, head under the boat and tail out flashing. When his head showed up beyond Woody, I raced around, got a grip on his pectoral fin, then his bill. Soon we had him on deck and lashed down.

It was already four-thirty and we were well to the westward, out of sight of land, with a twenty-five-mile run back to the bay at Salinas. We slid in as the sun was setting. The International Game Fish Association representative checked the tackle and the marlin's weight. The scales showed 148 pounds, making him the largest marlin ever taken on a 12-pound-test leader and the first ever taken on the Federation's standard fly-fishing tackle.

As things stand now, most big-game fishing is a static ritual: the captain and crew prepare the baits, find the fish, present the baits, and set the hook in the fish before the angler takes over the relatively simple job of sitting in the chair and playing the fish with tackle that is usually much heavier than necessary. But angling is changing.

Better tackle and better boats are available. Ship-to-shore radios make today's venturesome fisherman safer in a small boat than he used to be in a cabin cruiser. The big-game fishing world, once limited to those with a very considerable amount of time and money, is opening up so that almost any dedicated angler can afford to fish for almost any kind of fish.

For the good of gamefishing in the future we can hope that anglers will start being prouder of the quality of their fishing abilities than of the abundance of their catches. Light-tackle fishing seems due for a great surge in popularity, and fly fishing, as well as other types of casting, is about to spread out from the streams, lakes, and saltwater shorelines onto the deep blue seas.

Casting is a personal game. The rod stays in the angler's hands and he moves the bait in a manner he thinks will be attractive to the fish. He searches out, dreams up, and experiments with lures that will catch more fish for him. We have only begun to think of the lures we'll need when artificial lures become common for all ocean fish, and baits on the oceans become as unacceptable to most anglers as worms on a trout stream. It is more of a challenge to fool fish with an artificial lure than it is with a morsel of food, and it is lots more fun to cast a lure right where the fish will take it than to watch the captain, through his skillful boat handling, place it in the same spot.

Everything points to a new surge of interest in open-sea fishing. Freshwater fishing is limited and most of our freshwaters are heavily fished. Where fishing is private it's expensive. The best Atlantic salmon fishing, for example, can cost the angler as much as $5,000 per week. But the seas are free and open, and in a matter of hours a jet can get you to a spot where the fish are big and exciting. The sea off Ecuador is only one such spot in a world that is three-fifths wet.

[1968]

23

Catching
Big Trout

*Jason, my ten-year-old son, had been coming along
pretty well with his trout fishing, but he'd never seen, let
alone caught, a really big one. Taking a hint from Wulff
in this chapter, we trucked our canoe down to the
Battenkill on a sunny August afternoon when the water
was low and clear. I expected to see enough trout in
floating so Jason could learn something about where
they held in the stream, and, with any luck, we'd see an
old mossback or two for future inspiration.*

*I gently steered the canoe over a wide spring hole I
knew near the bank and we watched along the banks
and bottom. There were a few brown trout up to 16
inches or so scurrying among the logs, and Jason
started to get excited. Then I directed his gaze to a
black-spotted "log" in deep water near the bank, and he
almost tipped us over. The brown trout we were watching was an easy 7- or 8-pounder, one of the few that still
haunts sections of this river. I'd like to be able to report
that we caught him a day or two later, but we haven't—
yet.*

The taking of one big trout may well be an accident, but when an angler takes very large trout consistently, season after season, it is the result of specific skill and understanding. The average fisherman working a trout stream catches average-size fish. The less skillful fisherman usually catches smaller-than-average trout because the younger, smaller fish are not as wise as the big ones and, being easier to fool, they fall prey to poor fishing tactics. The very skillful fisherman, however, does not usually catch larger-than-average fish. He simply catches more average-size trout.

The reason for this is the basic difference between fishing for trout and fishing for big trout. The ordinary expert trout fisherman has all the skills for taking trout, an understanding of their habits and of trout water, yet the catching of big fish requires more than this. The big-trout fisherman must know the stream thoroughly, spending many hours unproductively in scouting for big fish and watching them in order to be at the right spot with a satisfactory lure when one of these lunkers is in the mood to strike. If there are a dozen pools, each of which is capable of supporting a very large trout, he must know which ones actually do harbor an oversize fish and, in general, he must work out a campaign for each trout.

August is a good time to locate these old sockdolagers, and during August there should be a few good chances to take them. The water goes low in midsummer and the holes capable of holding big fish are easy to identify. There must be plenty of water in them and a good hiding place under a cut bank, a submerged log, rocky ledge, or similar cover. Using this hiding place as a home base, a big trout may forage as much as several hundred yards away, always returning to rest and hide when his feeding forays are over.

The fisherman who scouts the stream quietly, walking the banks, spending time on the bridges and high points of look-out during the bright hours when the sun lights up the pools to advantage, will see the big trout. Having located one, he will come back time after time to watch and wait and thus gradually learn the fish's habits and routine. The angler who fishes a pool rarely gets close enough to see these big fish; and, if he does, it is a brief, fleeting glimpse as the trout darts away. The action of the line in the water, the movement of the rod, the splash of waders, or the crunch of gravel underfoot gives notice of the angler's approach.

Big fish like big water and they prefer the wide, deep pools that are unwadable during high water in spring and early summer, but that can often be waded in midsummer when the waters are at their lowest and most trout fishermen have given up for the season. Bright sun and low water leave the lunkers most conspicuous. A good method of spotting fish on the larger trout streams is to use a canoe and come slowly down the river.

By careful inspection of all likely hideouts on a bright day, it is possible to spot about three out of four of the very large trout in an average stream. Spotting big fish takes time and trouble, but without an exact knowledge of where such fish lie there's only a casual chance of hooking one.

Big trout tend to be minnow feeders and, as a consequence, they settle where there are plenty of minnows to prey upon. This usually means the long, deep pools or steady runs where there is a large section of good feeding available without crossing any riffles or shallows; in other words, without leaving the pool. In this respect a long pool of only moderate depth is better than a very deep one that is small in size.

The most important factor in taking big trout is the timing. There are times when all trout, big ones included, let down their guard and feed with little caution. At such times the confirmed big-fish angler will be working a pool that he knows holds a lunker, while the average angler is happy merely to take trout that are larger than his usual average from good-looking water where he feels big trout should be, though he has not actually seen one there.

With a big trout located, or preferably a number of big trout marked down, the angler will want to keep them constantly in mind. If he's a versatile angler with a liking for, and a good knowledge of, all the methods of trout fishing, he'll fish for them fairly often. If the fisherman is a specialist in only one field, he'll find few times when there's much chance of hooking one of these prize fish.

The dry-fly man has the least chance of taking a very

large trout, for the big fellows go overboard for floating flies only a few times a season and can rarely be cajoled into coming to the surface at other times. It is at the time of the first big hatches of the spring that the big ones usually indulge a special hunger for insects and join the smaller fish in surface feeding.

In low water, big trout occasionally take a floating fly, but they're unpredictable in their choice of lure. It is impossible to know in advance whether a #16 spider, a #10 Wulff, or a #2 fly-rod mouse will be to their liking. The rise to the dry fly after the time of the big hatches has passed is a casual thing, the taking of a few flies only as a slight change of diet and not as a regular method of feeding.

The reference above is for daytime feeding. It may be a different thing after dark. Many old lunkers will surface-feed at night with considerable regularity, since on many streams the best hatches of mayflies and larger insects come during the hours of darkness. Taking a big trout on a dry fly at night is an exciting business. To do it, the feeding station of the fish should be known with considerable accuracy.

Feeding positions are regular enough to mark fish within a few feet of the same spot, night after night. The cast should be practiced in daylight so that when actually in the dark there will be a minimum of slack line and leader as the fly passes over the fish. The strike should be made at the sound of the fish as he rises, but when there is very little slack to be taken up, a big fish in a deliberate rise will often hook himself on the dry fly. From that point on, it's a tough, exciting problem to subdue a big trout in a darkened pool. Although there's no longer any need to work in total darkness, the flashlights or headlights give only minor assistance in playing a fish that must be felt rather than seen.

The dry flies for night fishing are usually fairly large, mostly oversize imitations of the type of insect likely to be hatching out. Any large dry fly may turn the trick, as the fish seem less selective at night than in the daytime. The main advantage in having a big fly lies in being able to play the fish on a bigger hook and the heavier leader tippet that normally goes with it.

The wet-fly man is free to fish the water wherever he wishes, since his moving fly is always ready to bite into the jaw of the trout that takes it. The strike need only be a gentle lifting of the rod when the first pressure of the fish is felt. The wet-fly man can wade and fish through a well-remembered pool in absolute darkness, covering it almost as well as he would in daytime fishing. If he's careless he'll get hung up on his back cast or perhaps cast far enough to entangle his fly on the farther bank. Nowhere near as much planning and judgment are needed to wet-fish at night. But fishing with either the floating fly or the sunken fly after dark is a very good way to take big trout.

The nymph or wet fly in the daytime is more effective than the floating fly. It travels closer to the cruising or resting trout and is more akin to the type of food he prefers. Mornings and evenings are best for big fish, and streamer flies or minnow imitations are favorites. Imitations of the larger nymphs, such as the stonefly or crane-fly larvae, are particularly effective. To fish for these big fish with wet flies, the casts should be made to the best feeding spots in their pools, usually the point where the current begins to slow down but before it loses too much of its speed.

This will be about where the water breaks away to turn back into large eddies. Practically all the food the current is carrying reaches this point, and a big fish, when feeding, chooses such a point to look over the entire food layout and take his pick before the smaller trout have a chance to work on it. To move farther up into the current calls for using up too much energy, and to drop back farther would permit other trout to move up in front of him and get the choicest morsels. In fishing for the big ones the casting should be concentrated right on the prime feeding spot. There's little chance of picking him up at any other point.

The worm, minnow, and other natural-bait fishermen take most of the big trout. Just after a summer thunderstorm the angler who has located a big fish can be pretty certain the fish will be in his best feeding spot near his hideout, and a wriggly night crawler, hooked once lightly through the band on a 1X leader, coming down the current to him, is almost certain to draw a strike. The time to fish is from the moment the water starts to rise as the runoff comes into the river with its load of food until the river steadies or until the fish have satisfied their hunger and cease to feed.

A lively minnow moving around near the preferred feeding spot is a good bet, and the minnow fishermen may well spend hours in the right spot. If his minnows stay lively, he can work the same pool for hours at a time with a better chance of taking a lunker than the fisherman using any other type of lure or bait. The minnow is natural to the stream and the big trout's favorite food. A big trout coming up to his feeding station considers it natural to find a living minnow there, whereas the worm—except at flood times—or the artificial lures will almost always be spotted as out of place.

Grasshoppers, crickets, June bugs, and other natural trout baits may draw strikes where worms—which may create suspicion because of the trout's past experience in being hooked on one—and artificial lures draw no response. Big trout are moody. They're big enough to command the best feeding spots and to have their choice of the stream's food supply.

They're swift and strong enough to catch their food in good-size chunks and, whereas the smaller fish may take his meal in a hundred different particles, the big fish is likely to get his dinner in two or three gulps. After he has taken a few fat minnows, however, a grasshopper, a small dry fly, a hellgrammite, or a bucktail mouse may be appealing as a dessert. Don't overlook the field mouse, especially when the banks are undercut. A mouse imitation is good for big trout—and so is a live mouse.

Spinning and bait casting are the easiest methods to use for the taking of really big trout. The heavier lures can be cast to waters beyond the reach of the fly. They may be made to travel deep where they are within easy striking distance from the big fish as they feed or cruise near the bottom. Many casting lures are excellent imitations of the minnows that make up the bulk of the diet of the bigger fish. Metal wobbling lures that have considerable flash work well at slow speeds and are favorites.

Most big trout, as we have said, are caught by fishermen who have spotted them previously and made it a point to try for them at least once each time the stream is visited. The attempt may take only five to ten minutes, but it is always with tackle that will hold a big fish and a lure that should tempt him.

There are times when steady pounding will catch big trout, but I think they are relatively rare. One of them occurred on the Battenkill River in the Vermont section. Meade Schaeffer and Walt Squires located a big brown at the head of a deep run. They fished, using flies only, all that afternoon and were back bright and early the next morning to continue. From a vantage point on the bank the fish was clearly visible as one or the other of them worked on him from a position in the stream. A little before noon the fish came up to take Walt's #14 dry fly and, after an exciting battle, was brought in and beached. That brownie weighed 7½ pounds.

The usual story behind the capture of a big trout is one of constant attempts on each trip to the river and a final catching of the old-timer off guard and hungry. Fishing for big fish is something like hunting big game. There is much patient stalking and study attached to it. Action is not continuous, but when it does come it is truly exciting, and the resulting pictures or the mounted fish stand for years as a measure of achievement and a point of conversation.

[1940]

24

Angling's Charmed Circle

On the cover of the May 1964 issue of Esquire, *in which this tarpon-fishing chapter first appeared, is a large and delightfully provocative photograph of a famous actress. In the upper-left corner of the same cover is an equally impressive—but very small—photo of Lee Wulff holding up a giant tarpon. And on the cover, next to Lee's photo, it reads: "This is the cover we'd planned for this issue . . . then along came Yvette Mimieux." All of which shows simply that it's possible, but not easy, to upstage Lee Wulff.*

It's been well over twenty years since Lee Wulff and others described the hoped-for mark of a 200-pound tarpon on a fly. No one's done it yet, although we hear some hair-raising stories from time to time of such fish hooked and lost, often near the boat after hours of struggle. The record, which stood at about 148 pounds when this chapter was written, is now over 180 pounds. Some fishermen have spent hundreds of thousands of dollars and untold days over the years in hopes of setting a 200-pound-plus record. But keep in mind, should you seek these remarkable fish, that your skill

*and luck will tell far more in the end than the size of
your bank account.*

It is only when all the winter's tourists have returned to the
north and spring's warm breath enfolds the Florida Keys that
the biggest tarpon of all come into the shallow flats and
channels that surround them. They cruise with the tides,
feeding on crustaceans and small fish. Sometimes they circle
slowly, as a group, in a sort of mating dance. Sometimes they
travel a steady course, "rolling" as they go, one fish after
another bringing its mouth, then its head, and finally the
whole upper half of its body above the surface. Very often the
largest fish, which approach or exceed the 200-pound mark,
meander slowly at a five-foot depth, singly or in twos or
threes, working the tide changes. Anglers, seeing them, feel
their pulses quicken. The hand that grips the rod grows tense,
particularly when it is a fly rod with which an ambitious
angler plans to tackle these magnificent fish.

Would you like to enter the charmed circle of anglers
who can manage one of the sport's most difficult feats? Come,
stand beside me on the stern of a sixteen-foot skiff as we
approach Loggerhead Bank. Stu Apte, one of Florida's best, is
guiding you for tarpon. Your tackle is a 9-foot fly rod with a
single-action fly reel (Beaudex) possessing no adjustable drag
or brake, a reel designed for lesser fish. You are reeling left-
handed and the single-grip fly rod will be held in your right
hand all through the tension and struggle of playing a tarpon
if you hook one. You are doing it the hard way and if you
succeed in taking a tarpon of more than 100 pounds you will
have earned the respect of your guide and of all the anglers
who know enough to know that this is one of the angling feats
to separate the men from the boys.

The outboard that drove us out at a twenty-five-mile-an-
hour clip has been tilted up out of the water and a canvas
spread over it to keep the loose coils of fly line, which fall to
the deck at your feet, from catching or tangling on any pro-
tuberance of the engine. We have sighted a school of rolling
tarpon and are trying to intercept them. Between the thumb
and forefinger of your left hand you hold a tarpon fly, an

orange-and-yellow imitation of a shrimp, tied on a 4/0 hook. Between it and the tip of the fly rod in your right hand the leader and a 20-foot loop of line hang down to drag on the water. (Line for fly casting must be off the reel and free to cast out before the cast can be made.) Over the other three fingers of your left hand hang long loops of line that rest on the canvas at your feet. Nearly 70 feet of line are off the fly reel and ready for casting. Somehow you must keep the long loops of line from tangling in spite of the wind and your movements as you watch for the fish. If, when a tarpon is sighted within casting range, you have changed your position and one foot stands on the loose line at your feet, as well it may, the cast will be abortive and fall short.

Stu stands on the bow of the boat and from that point of vantage drives us ahead, stern first, by pushing with a 14-foot spruce pole. It has a *foot*, or broadened area, that keeps the butt of the pole from sinking into the soft bottom when the thrust is made. He has gauged the speed of the tarpon and is poling, all out, to intercept them. The morning sun is still low and there is a fair breeze blowing that will make it difficult to see the fish under the surface when, if we are lucky, we draw close to them. Only the occasional surface roll gives away their position as we stare across the hundreds of feet that separate us.

Suddenly Stu points, and as he calls you see the tarpon underwater. The school has turned and is coming directly toward us. You send the cast out without a tangle and drop the fly seventy feet ahead of the boat just as the lead fish are approaching. You start the retrieve with your left hand by giving a few short, swift jerks to impart to the fly the semblance of life.

The wind is driving the boat toward the fish and they are coming fast. We close in too swiftly. One of the leaders spurts toward the fly, but as he reaches it the looming boat frightens him. With his mouth partway open to take the fly, he turns away short. A great muddy boil comes to the surface where he and each of the other tarpon of the school reverse their course and speed away in retreat. Tarpon in the shallows are as

206

easily frightened as trout in a mountain brook. That opportunity to hook a tarpon has come and gone.

Loggerhead Bank is a crescent-shaped area several miles long that is barely covered at low water and deep enough for tarpon to feed on it anywhere at the flood. Two narrow channels cut across it and the incoming tide pours through them as well as through the broad, deep areas around each end. We choose a position at one channel's mouth where we'll be in the path of any fish coming either through the channel or trimming the edge of the bank where the water slopes off gradually from a few feet to ten or more.

Stu drives the unshod end of his pole into the soft bottom and ties the bow rope to it. As the sun rises higher our eyes will be able to penetrate the water better and the slackening wind will make it possible to cast well in any direction. If the tarpon come by we will see them underwater as silvery-gray-green forms, slightly darker or slightly lighter than the bottom below them, depending upon the angle of the sun. Sometimes the most conspicuous thing about them will be their shadow on the places where the bottom is clean and hard and neither grass nor sponge nor soft marl can absorb it. They are hard to see and all too often an angler's first realization of their presence comes when they swirl and race away.

Half a dozen other boats are fishing the area, too. Most of them are using spinning tackle that lets them cast farther and more easily than a fly fisherman can in spite of any wind, and makes the playing of a fish much simpler. We watch the other boats while we wait for tarpon, for if none of the other anglers shows signs of seeing fish over a period of an hour or more, the chances are that tarpon are not in the immediate area in any numbers and fishing will be better at some other spot.

Stu sees the fish first, a moose of a tarpon, coming toward us from down-sun. He's traveling two or three miles an hour with a lazy movement of his silvery length and his course will take him within seventy-five feet as he passes between us and the bank.

It is time for a quick check of the coils of line in your left hand and the loops trailing to the deck. The fly must drop just ahead of the tarpon as he passes and, since this one is swimming near the bottom, it may take a few seconds to sink to a better sight level for him. A single, relatively short false cast should put you in position to extend the cast to the seventy-odd feet required. A second longer false cast or a third, flaring the fly over the water near him, will spook him and spoil the show. A fly touching the water over his back instead of ahead of him can put him to instant flight.

The moment arrives. You release the fly from finger and thumb. Your muscles move and the fly line follows the rod through sinuous contortions. Finally it straightens out and the fly falls ten feet ahead of the tarpon but a little short of intercepting his line of travel. It sinks slowly. He is almost abreast of it when you give it the first movement. The big fish shows no sign of interest and is passing it by when you give a second and harder pull, moving the fly about a yard. Slowly the tarpon turns and with a sudden rush opens his mouth to engulf the fly. You strike both with a lift of the rod and a hard pull on the line with the left hand.

There's solid pressure and the rod bends almost straight toward the fish. He shakes his head once, twice, three times, then launches himself halfway out of the water in a cloud of spray. He heads out past the boat to reach the deep water. There is slack and you strip line frantically to try to maintain some tension. He passes us at twenty-five feet and speeds on. The tension never comes again. The fly hit a hard part of his bony mouth and failed to penetrate beyond the barb of the hook. The slack and the continued head shaking let it work free. To hook solidly one tarpon out of five is all that one can expect.

Stu morosely reports, "That x#*# fish, #$%&xx*, could have won the tournament for you, xx$#%*$*, and would have made a magnificent mount."

Tarpon are right at the top of the gamefish list, along with the Atlantic salmon and the trout. To offer the sportsman the greatest challenge the gamest fish in the world must be swift and strong. To be most dramatic they should leap when hooked, and a leaping fish is more difficult to play. They should, preferably, be caught in moving water, which adds an extra hazard over the playing of a fish where the water is still. They should take an artificial lure, for the catching of a fish on a piece of the food it normally feeds on does not require the inventiveness involved in luring a fish to something inanimate that is contrived to look edible and alive. The lures these special fish prefer should be very small in proportion to their size, calling for small hooks on which it takes great skill to hold them. They should be caught by casting, for casting requires greater skill and effort than letting a line drag behind a boat or having a bait sit in a single spot to wait for a fish to come by. The trolling fisherman can set his drag and let his mind go far away from the sport, knowing the fish will hook himself. The still fisherman can drowse and dream while he waits for the tug of a fish on his line or the sight of his float being pulled under. The fish taking a natural bait will taste and swallow, often being hooked deep and badly hurt. The fish taking an artificial lure realizes the fraud immediately and, given a second or fraction of a second, will safely eject it. Casting requires constant attention. And fly casting requires a greater ability than either bait casting or spinning. The ability to overcome these difficult sporting problems with the top gamefish lets an angler walk proudly among his peers.

The spin fishermen have a distinct advantage over even the most expert fly fisherman since it is easy to cast farther and more accurately, even in a wind, by this method. Then, too, when a fish is hooked they have a good clutch-brake system on their spinning reels to keep the line's pressure automatically below the breaking point. Those who fish for tarpon with trolling rods, star-drag reels, and lines of 20-pound-test or over have an even simpler job of landing their fish. The particular outfit you fish with now has a simple single-action fly reel without adjustable brake or drag. You will have to apply braking power by pressing a finger against the turning reel spool with one hand while holding the rod with the other. If you apply pressure too quickly blisters will form; too slowly and the reel will overrun, tangle the line, and let the fish break. Why do you use so demanding a reel?

Simply to prove you have the skill to make it do the necessary work.

Your leader, in order to qualify for the Metropolitan Miami Tournament, must include a 12-pound-test segment more than 12 inches long. Leaders are usually made up with a less-than-12-inch section of 80-pound-test nylon monofilament next to the fly to absorb punishment given by the hard, rough jaws. The 12-pound-test monofilament comes next to be followed by a section of 20-pound-test, then a 40-pound-test section where the leader is knotted to the line. The fly-casting line is 35 yards long, bulky and strong, and attached to the casting line is 200 yards of 20-pound-test braided-nylon backing.

A tarpon may take the fly and set off on a sizzling run. The motor may be started but before the boat can get full head-way the fish can pull the line to its end and snap it.

Some tarpon seem just too tough to handle on light tackle. If not too fast at the strike-and-run they may be too determined as "travelers" and set so strong a pace over so long a period it is the angler who is worn down and becomes weak and careless instead of the fish. To hold a fish of record weight (present fly record is 148½ pounds) takes plenty of skill and stamina. Still, that record should not stand too long. There are plenty of fish of more than 200 pounds swimming the shallow waters in season and, with an increasing number of fishermen using the fly, some lucky angler should soon hook and land one. These thoughts run through our minds as we wait and watch for another tarpon to come within fly-rod range.

No tarpon comes by for the rest of the morning. We see one boated and several others hooked and lost by others fishing in the vicinity. Then the action stops and one by one the boats give up and go off to seek out those small, special places where tarpon may feed and which each guide has found and keeps secret. Stu's secret spots prove barren. Late afternoon sees us back at Loggerhead Bank hoping we will strike a few tarpon coming in on the early tide.

Stu shuts off the outboard a quarter of a mile from the

bank and poles stealthily in. As we reach the bank's edge we see three tarpon cruising toward us, all in line. The biggest is at the tail where you can't present a fly to him without spooking the fish just ahead, which would most surely spook all three. Your best chance is the lead fish, the smallest of the three, weighing under 100.

You make the cast perfectly, just ahead of the leading fish. You twitch the fly. He spurns it, passing underneath, but the middle fish surges forward to take it. The line tightens and the tarpon leaps.

You are busy keeping the slack line from tangling as it whips out through the guides and then the reel is singing and your finger is pressed against the metal spool to brake him. Finally the motor starts and you gain back some line as we close up after the long run. You were lucky. When the tarpon leaped and caused some inescapable moments of slack, the hook did not shake free. On his sudden surges, as you follow, you are careful not to let the strain build up to more than 12 pounds. You remember through your trained muscles just how much pressure it took to break that 12-pound monofilament when you pulled in practice tests against a fence at home and you stay 3 or 4 pounds under that pull. When his speed is gone and he resorts to bulldog fighting you finally make him tow the boat and then are able to keep up a steady pressure of nearly 10 pounds. Your arm, never relenting its strong but sensitive pressure through the rod, grows weary but does not weaken. All goes well. In an hour and a half he is ready for the gaff. Normally the guide gaffs the tarpon, using a "killer" gaff with a long handle if the fish is to be kept and mounted, and a "release" gaff, small and easily held in one hand, if the fish is to be freed.

Every part of the play an angler can conduct completely on his own adds that much more to his interest and to his stature among other anglers. This fish is big, but not big enough to win the tournament or to mount. It is the release gaff you pick up as we work to the shallow water where the flow of tide is running as swiftly as a salmon river. You slide over the side, determined to bring the fish within your own reach with what, for most people, is ordinary freshwater-bass fly-fishing tackle, but in spite of the fish's size and the run of the tide you manage it. The gaff grips his chin and you hold him up momentarily for a picture before you shake the gaff free and let him swim away. Stu gives his estimate as 120 pounds. Not a monster. Not within 20 pounds of the present record, but the *greatest sport* can lie not merely in maximum size but in taking the *available big fish* with *extra handicaps* as you have just done.

Stu Apte is probably the best or the luckiest tarpon guide in the Keys. Tarpon caught under his guidance have been at the top of one of the tournament's tarpon listings each year for the last three years and include the present world's record for the fly rod for both men and women. He has an exceptional ability to see tarpon, the energy and judgment to pole a boat swiftly and to make seemingly miraculous interceptions. He has an instinctive ability to know where tarpon will be cruising and particularly when and where tarpon will show up in some of his secret spots. He is as good a fisherman as any of his clients and knows how best to work the boat and give him every chance to hook and save his fish.

He can take a pretty poor angler and, by giving him a spinning outfit and the breaks of downwind casting and expert boat handling, probably help him catch a 100-pounder, perhaps even the biggest tarpon of the season. Such an angler can talk of the monster tarpon he caught, but when Stu Apte and the other knowing guides who work the Keys talk about good anglers they have known, they talk of those who can do it the hard way, of the fly-rod anglers who can handle any big fish well and for whom, perhaps, the biggest tarpon that swims would be neither too big nor too tough.

So you have taken a big tarpon on a fly and it is a source of pride. How else can you set yourself apart in angling? Although there are many ways, most of them will be difficult to explain to your friends and best understood by the angler himself, who recognizes that his own feat was far above the normal effort required in a particular form of angling. Al-

212

though great feats may come in any form of fishing, the easiest way to enter the charmed circle is to fish for the most sporting fish with the right tackle and the qualifying method.

When a wise old brown trout is rising and small-selective, it takes a hell of a fisherman to take him. If the sun is bright and the water smooth, even the finest leader seems to stand out as bluntly as a clothes rope. The successful small fly, a #16, #18, or an even smaller #20 must have the magic endowment of looking alive, though it has not the power to move a single whisker as it drifts freely with the current. The leader, in attaining the fineness of near invisibility, dwindles in strength to less than a pound. The cast must be perfectly placed, preferably falling to the water in a downstream curve, in order to let the fly drift to the fish ahead of the leader and line. The rod must have great delicacy and the playing of the fish must be done with exceptional care. When a trout of 4 pounds has been fooled and played to a finish on a #20 fly, the angler will have recorded a feat that few others have managed and they, too, were master anglers.

When the Atlantic salmon angler fishes the tough, low-water conditions when salmon seem to resist all angling efforts and is able to take a fish of 15 pounds or better on a leader of 3 pounds or less in tested strength, he demonstrates that he, too, has learned to fish exceptionally well. I have taken a number of good fish on a #16 fly and on a 1¾-ounce fly rod (an outfit considered by most far too difficult to tackle run-of-the-mill trout with), but none of them weighed as much as 20 pounds.

A group of us have spent parts of the last two seasons trying to catch a salmon of more than 20 pounds on a #16 (single-hooked) trout fly. So far no one has succeeded, but eventually I am sure one of us will manage it. It is difficult enough to hook salmon that weigh 20 pounds in most rivers on *any* fly and when and if one of us does manage to hook and land one on a #16 he will be doing something in angling that never before has been achieved and recorded. The grip of so small a hook is so delicate only a master player of fish can hope to subdue a 20-pounder. To tackle the job is something like climbing a great mountain . . . because the challenge is there and a man wants to prove he can meet it. The fisherman who is lucky enough to hook the biggest salmon of the season and who lands it on a 20-pound-test leader and a 1/0 fly may brag of his catch and his luck but not of comparable angling skill.

In each of the above cases the greatest credit is due to the angler when he accomplishes the entire capture of the fish on his own. It takes more skill and provides more pride when the angler nets or lands his own fish without the aid of a guide. In that way the fish is captured by an individual instead of by a two-man team. Doing it alone is the hard way. In any case he must hook and play it on his own in order to call it *his* fish.

In big-game fishing it is next to impossible for the angler to do the entire job of capturing a fish. Big-game fishing is a *team sport*. The captain, who sets up the fishing, usually finds the fish, makes or checks the bait, plans the presentation, and directs the playing of the fish. He has the most difficult job on the team and usually has most of the fun. The real thrill for an angler in big-game fishing is being an integral part of a smoothly working team. That requires not only a good knowledge of the whole operation but an intimate understanding of the fish and the moods and the abilities of the other members of the team. Unless an angler can distinguish himself by using light tackle, his participation in the taking of any big-game fish is well submerged in the group effort. Because he has paid for the boat and the crew's time, he may take the liberty of saying he "caught" the fish they bring in, but those who know the score realize the average big-game angler hires most of the brains and skill that accomplish the capture of "his" fish.

This is not to disparage big-game fishing. The capture of big-game fish is as thoroughly a sport as any other type of angling. It is to suggest that the big-game angler should say *we*, not *I*, when telling of his catches. The angler who takes a marlin on 10-pound-test line most assuredly shows great tackle skill. But as with the matador, the tennis champ, the golfer, the fighter pilot, the greatest glory seems to fall to those who go furthest *alone*, either in the crucial moments or for the full game. The 4-pound trout on the #20 fly, the 15-pound salmon on a 3-pound-test leader or the 100-pound fly-rod tarpon on the 12-pound-test leader will, without question, let you lay claim to being an exceptional angler.

[1964]

25

Three of a Kind

Suburban anglers with fireside feet should take great delight in knowing that there is still a glorious and open north country such as made famous in the poetry of Robert Service at the turn of the century. I may yet get there to hear a timber wolf and think back to the old Jack London yarns. And I may wonder on the same trip at a night of northern lights, while seeing the same colors the next afternoon along the flanks of a giant Arctic char or delightful grayling.

In this chapter we join Lee Wulff along the Arctic Circle for lake trout, grayling, and char—survivors in the face of one of the most hostile environments on earth.

Three of a kind. Three gamefish that can take the Arctic's freezing cold. When you get up north beyond the warmth required by the salmon, the various stream trouts, the bass, walleyes, and all the rest, you'll find three rugged species—lake trout, grayling, and Arctic char—all thriving. By inhabiting water least accessible to anglers, this freezing trio offers a combination of lonesome country and very good fishing.

The season may be short and the country often forbidding, but they live in a world that comes alive with a vengeance for the short time between ice-out and ice-in again. It is a world of unusual wildlife and fantastically long days. It is a world to escape to where nature is supreme and man is only a very casual intruder.

The north saves its moisture as snow for nine months or more of the year and then releases it when the hot sun of the Arctic summer burns for its short, bright period. It is a country that can be traveled easily in winter when it is frozen hard—if the traveler can take the cold. In the summer it was almost impossible to travel except by boat or canoe in the waterways—until this century's bush pilots in floatplanes opened it up. They found lots of water to land on, and their passengers found lots of water to fish. The northern bush probably has the greatest proportion of water and fish to the number of anglers who fish it.

The belle of this northern ball is the lake trout. It's an adaptable fish that extends its range far to the south as well. It grows to great size, takes artificial lures well, and is great on the table. Lake trout have given me some memorable moments.

The first came when I was fishing for landlocked salmon in a northern New England lake just after ice-out. I'd been using streamers and had caught one landlocked salmon of about 3 pounds. It was three in the afternoon, calm and warm for spring. A few flying ants and other insects were buzzing by, and I saw a dimple on the surface here and there. I changed from my marabou streamer to one of my then-newly designed Gray Wulffs in a size 10.

The fish were cruising, and when I was able to drop that fly just ahead of a rise, a fish sucked it down. The resultant run at the hook set was unbelievable. The reel complained wildly as the fish sped away toward the lake's center, drawing out most of my backing. My guide moved us slowly toward the fish as it clung stubbornly to its new position. I waited for the jump and great splash to show me just how big a landlocked I'd hooked into. It never came. The fish was a lake trout, a 12-pounder.

As I looked down through the clear water at the lake bed below us, I figured out the reason for that dramatic first long run. Like a bonefish on a flat, that laker had taken my fly in about three feet of water and had raced over a hundred yards across a shallow flat to reach water of a more comfortable depth. That fight was a far cry from the usual lake-trout struggle where the fish is hooked in deep water and simply twists and turns and makes short dashes because it has no reason to believe any other section of the lake will give it a better chance to escape. Early-season lake trout near the Canadian border are like their fat northern cousins only in the early season. As soon as the water warms up they head for the deeper, cooler water to follow their food and find their comfort.

My second lake-trout surprise came in the middle of Labrador where I'd flown in to practically unknown fishing waters at the outlet of Mackenzie Lake, part of a flow in the southern outward drainage of Labrador's great central lake, Michikamau.

The outlet was wide and unwadable. I was working my way along the shore over and around rocks between dog-kennel and full-cabin size, getting strikes from good-size brook trout on streamers. Here, as with each new place I flew in to explore, I had a hope that I'd find a spot where a new world's record brookie would take my fly. This wasn't going to be the place. The fish were running consistently from 3 to 4 pounds.

Then a big fish grabbed my streamer and began a dogged fight. My hopes soared for a stray brookie that might be up in the world-record class. I followed that fish downstream for two hundred yards while it stayed out in the deep central run. I climbed over rocks and under spruce branches or else went around them, up to the top of my waders in the swift flow, to keep within range of the fish. The struggle ended at a deep, swirling eddy where I brought the fish to shore. Again it was a 12-pound laker that had been the source of my surprise—a laker that had left the still waters of the lake to fight the current in search of better feeding on small trout. I hadn't even had a lake trout in the back of my mind, although I should have known that a lake as big as Michikamau and its offshoots, if not blocked by falls, would hold them, although not all the Labrador lakes did.

One of the great far northern lake trout spots is Great Bear Lake in Canada's Northwest Territories. It is generally deep and steep shored. Most of it is a desert as far as food for fish is concerned. Only in the shallower coves or edges where sunlight can reach the bottom is there algae, weed growth, and insect activity for the base of a food chain. Two things are important to consider. One is that the fish's growth in these northern lakes is very slow. Sixty-pound fish were found by scale readings to be sixty years old. When one is taken out, a replacement is more than half a century away.

Second, the production area is so limited that there is no great stock of fish waiting out there in that huge watery desert to swim in and replace those taken out. So the number of big fish available to anglers has plummeted, and there is increasing fishing pressure on the lake's productive areas, most of which are now identified and fished hard.

What is needed and hasn't been forthcoming is a reverse size limit, which will let as many as possible of the big breeders survive and breed. Instead there's a minimum limit, which further reduces the best breeding population. In spite of this, fishing can still be excellent on any given day. Even if lake trout never grew big they'd be a fine sporting fish under northern conditions where they rarely go deep.

If you'll drift your boat or canoe across one of the shallow coves of Great Bear Lake, you'll find a lot of lake trout from 3 to 12 pounds. They'll be visible against the light-colored lake bed when the sun is shining, and they can be stalked like a bonefish on a Bahamian flat.

I have pleasant memories of taking lakers on long casts with large streamer flies. Streamer flies were our best bet, although I caught some on a fly-rod mouse and others on a big, black stone-fly-nymph imitation. And, of course, flashing spoons are deadly for lake trout. As when bonefishing, the sun is a great aid, almost a necessity for spotting these shallow-water fish. But, sun or shadow, the fisherman can cover the water and know that the shallow bays and ragged shorelines are where the fish are.

Second of the frigid trio is the grayling. Grayling can take the cold, but the species has a wide range, perhaps the widest of all three. They're found in places like Yellowstone National Park and were once common in Michigan, where a subspecies used to exist. They're found as far south as the Alps in Europe, and there, under consistent fishing pressure, they have grown to be very wary gamefish.

European grayling are reminiscent of our New England ruffed grouse. Ruffed grouse in the Canadian wilds are quite tame. They can be hunted and shot handily with a .22 rifle. They'll sit on a branch and let a hunter walk quite close before they fly. The New England grouse that have been hunted since the hungry Pilgrims hit the shore are a far different bird. They'll hide under cover, wait until you pass them by, then roar out in an unexpected direction. They'll fly behind trees and behind low stone walls. They'll make a monkey out of a hunter most of the time.

I knew quite a bit about grayling in my native Alaska before I realized how wise and wary their counterparts in Europe had become. I caught them in Alaska in my youth and in the Northwest Territories in later fishing. As a young member of the New York Anglers' Club, I was in the audience when the late, great Charlie Ritz addressed the group. He talked about European fly fishing and had come to the subject of grayling. Looking over the audience he spotted me and said, "Lee, what do you think of grayling?"

The answer I flashed back was, "They're a beautiful, glorified chub."

I'd never give that answer now. Grayling may be simple-minded and easy to catch where they've never seen a fly before, but where fly fishermen have angled for them for generations they can take on all the wariness of the brown trout.

Grayling have small mouths, and while I have had them hit a full-size Dardevle while fishing for other fish, they are most likely to take and most fun to catch on small flies, particularly dry flies. They're a fast-water fish, like the trout, and consequently give a good account of themselves on typical trout tackle. Their high, flaring dorsal is distinctive, and its purplish color gives it a spectacular glow. Like the lake trout, they're good eating, though unlike the lake trout, they're heavily scaled.

Grayling do not grow large. A 4-pounder is a very big one. Twelve- to 18-inchers make up most of the angler's catches, and they're big enough to provide excellent sport. Their range is the northern part of our continent west of Hudson Bay. They're fairly plentiful in the big northern lakes like Great Bear and often very plentiful in the flowing waters of the area. They surface-feed a great deal, and like the trout fisherman who fishes the rise, a grayling angler can often see his quarry feeding, then make an approach and present his fly.

Typical trout flies and trout equipment are all one needs for grayling. If they've been fished for a bit then 2X leaders or finer are in order. Wet flies like a Black Gnat are excellent, and a wet-fly fisherman can cover more water when the fish are not feeding on the surface. Grayling in pocket water make a trout fisherman feel right at home, and often the fishing is better than he's ever had for trout.

The third of the frigid trio is the Arctic char. They're fairly closely related to the brook trout and when in spawning coloration have a comparable beauty. They have characteristics somewhat similar to the brook trout, but grow much larger. They do not take dry flies well, perhaps because of the limited insect life of the north and their long periods of sea feeding. Instead, they are extremely susceptible to wobbling spoons. They can be caught on all ranges of trout tackle, depending upon the area and the subspecies.

I've fished for them in Baffin Bay, where their shape is small-headed, lean, and racy like a very trim, small Atlantic salmon. They're easiest caught on hardware there, where they move in and out of the river mouths with the very high tides of the bay. I tried flies there with little success, managing to hook fish only on a large shrimp imitation, a greenish creation on a #4 hook. Shrimp were coming down that river and entering the salt or brackish water there, and it was a natural food. The fish seemed hungry enough and struck readily at any small baitfish imitation that had a flash of metal. The ice had just gone out of the bay in that very late summer of 1956, and the wind blew in cold from the offshore icebergs.

The fishing at Frobisher Bay for char was fast and furious until a few years later. Then the powers that be decided that the increasing Eskimo population there needed some work to do that was fitting for their heritage. They decided to let them catch and sell the char for their livelihood. They didn't stipulate that they had to catch them with traditional Eskimo gear. They let them use modern nylon nets, and the netting was too deadly for the fish to last. Now there are even more Eskimos and not very many char at Frobisher.

There are char in abundance farther south in Labrador at places like Tessuiak where fish of nearly 30 pounds have been caught. In the fifties when I dropped in on some of the Labrador lakes and thoroughfares north of Lake Melville in my seaplane, I often found char ready and willing to take streamer flies like a Mickey Finn or wet flies like a Silver Doctor. There were char in the lakes and streams south of Lake Melville, but there were brook trout there, too. The brook trout were relatively easy to catch, and the char rather reluctant to take a fly.

The best char fishing and probably the biggest char are to be found in the Northwest Territories. The Tree River, near Coppermine on the Arctic Ocean, or the rivers of Victoria Island to the north are the best known for big fish in great numbers. Unlike the grayling and lake trout, which limit themselves to fresh water, the char are anadromous whenever possible, spawning in rivers and spending most of their feeding time in the sea where food is more abundant. In the sea they take on the protective coloring of all free-swimming ocean fish, dark along the back and silvery on the sides and belly. Reentering the streams on a spawning run they change rapidly to more protective garb, culminating in the bright, red-bellied spawning dress, similar to a brook trout's.

This sea experience makes them a special fish. While they do not jump like an Atlantic salmon they do have a similar sense of space and distance. Their runs are long and swift as if escaping from the seals that sometimes pursue them in the sea. The char are a long way from civilization. Fishing for them is worth the trip.

Once a group of us, convening from scattered fishing grounds at Goose Bay, Labrador, brought in brook trout, Atlantic salmon, and Arctic char. Our hostess prepared a very special fish dinner. Each species was cooked three ways: baked, broiled, and fried. A great deal of tasting and discussion went on and when the verdict came in it was the char that won out, hands down, as best tasting, however cooked.

[1980]

26

Lightning Strikes Twice

Bluefin tuna have always played an important role in Lee Wulff's career and in many ways actually helped to start it. Fishing out of Wedgeport, Nova Scotia, in 1936, Wulff caught the largest bluefin taken that year. In 1937, fishing in the first International Tuna Tournament there, he took the most and largest fish. These events led to his being asked by Newfoundland officials to research and record on film the province's hunting and fishing resources.

So began a career of exploring the north country by foot, boat, and now-famous bush plane, filming and writing of his adventures for an audience that eventually numbered millions of people all over the world. I'm sure the results over the ensuing fifty years far exceeded the fondest hopes of Wulff's sponsors and perhaps even his own wildest dreams.

Although both Lee Wulff and his wife, Joan, have been responsible for a number of world-record bluefin tuna over the years, in this chapter we're concerned not with a record but with something even more unusual: the hooking and boating of a double-header involving two of these giant fish at once!

Although both tuna boats had been fishing without a strike for over a week there was still an air of excitement aboard as we left the mooring in the *Shamrock II*. Boating the big bluefins is an uncertain business at best and there was no way of knowing, that August morning, we were heading into one of the most exciting episodes of the sport.

Conception Bay at the far southeastern angle of Newfoundland is no ordinary tuna ground. Underlying our enthusiasm was one significant fact. For each of the past two years the largest tuna in the world had come from these cool blue depths and nothing less than a 500-pound fish need be expected. We would be trolling over record-making dynamite. We did not guess, then, that it would be something other than the size of the tuna that would make that day memorable.

Reports coming in from Wedgeport told of a blank season there without so much as a single tuna being taken by its anglers. We subscribed to the theory that there are just so many big bluefins in the western Atlantic run and that when they are slashing baitfish at one spot they obviously cannot be doing the same thing at another. Since they had not come in heavily anywhere to the south and we were at the northern end of their run, we anticipated a surge of the big fish into Conception Bay from the sea. (We did not then know that many schools had come in to another great bay a hundred miles to the north where no one fished for tuna or even tried to harpoon them.) We had spotty records of tuna sightings in many places within a sixty-mile radius but it was hard to know whether the "reporters" knew the difference between tuna and somewhat similar "fish" like the pilot whales, porpoises, and dolphins that also frequent that coast in considerable numbers.

The two experimental fishing boats the Newfoundland government had purchased and equipped with trained tuna-fishing crews from Wedgeport were based in Conception Bay, and to change their base would be quite an undertaking. The tuna roam the entire Newfoundland shore. Seen at some point outside the bay on one day, they may not show there again all season. Once in Conception Bay, however, they usually stay on for a prolonged feeding period. The tuna-boat skippers had decided to play a waiting game.

It seemed a good time to watch and wait. Blind trolling had already resulted in the taking of three fish of approximately 600 pounds each. The season was just getting under way. But the first scattering of fish had shown and disappeared, and no one had seen a fin for a week.

Bait was a problem, too. Mackerel and herring, usually plentiful, were scarce. That day at sunrise when the nets were pulled, a lone squid and one small sea-running brook trout made up the entire haul, neither worthwhile for bait. We started our day with one stale mackerel bait and a half a dozen old herring left over from two days before, far from an encouraging prospect.

There were six of us aboard. Al Vardy, whose first tuna, taken the year before, had been the largest for that year from the whole world's waters, was slated to take the chair in the event a bluefin struck. Al, as tourist director for the island, had always had an active interest in promoting the sport, but the capture of that first fish had imbued him with an enthusiasm one rarely finds a man putting into any sort of work he gets paid for.

Harold, Al's fourteen-year-old son, was our sharp-eyed mascot. Rex Herder, a Newfoundlander home on vacation from his work at a resort in the Bahamas, was with us to share the excitement. When the boats were not crowded he often rode one of them, ready to give the crew a hand when an extra man was needed with a gaff or at the wheel.

Elie Pothier and Bill LeBlanc were skipper and mate, respectively. Both were from Wedgeport and both were wise to the ways of tuna and tuna fishing. Elie it was who had skippered the lead boat when the two forty-footers made the one-thousand-mile run from their Wedgeport home to this new and promising tuna spot. Jack Brinton, a local lobster fisherman, was aboard as second mate to watch Elie and Bill and so learn the procedure well enough to skipper his own boat that season.

I was aboard as a photographer, hoping that out of

almost a month of uninterrupted opportunity I'd come up with a movie the province could use in its expanding film program. In the two weeks that lay behind I'd seen one tuna caught, but by the time it had come to gaff the light was gone and my sequences of the playing had no climax and therefore little value. I'd caught one myself on a day when the angler scheduled had failed to show up and we'd gone out just for a quick look around. It, too, had not been boated till near dark when the light was too poor for color. Not that that had mattered, as there had been no one aboard to take my place as cameraman anyway.

Conception Bay is about fifty miles long, twenty miles wide, and has one large island and a number of smaller ones scattered over its surface. The water ranges in depth from slowly sloping sandy or rocky beaches to great holes of more than 100 fathoms, a depth often achieved quite close to shore. That morning, when Elie dipped the thermometer over the side for his daily water temperature check it read 51 degrees when 50 feet down, a reading consistent with those of the two previous weeks.

The lone mackerel swam behind as a trolling bait from the starboard outrigger pole, and all the herring were spaced along a leader on the port outfit with a hook buried in the tail fish to create a "teaser." The teasers often seemed to draw fish in from quite a distance but rarely accounted for a strike.

Of the fifteen fish taken in 1957, the first full season of tuna fishing in Conception Bay, most were taken in the deep water along a steep shore between Topsail Cove and Bauline and it was along that shore we trolled in the morning. Al and Rex put in a good stretch at cribbage in seesaw play. The rest of us scattered around the boat with an eye cocked out toward the horizon and the possible splash of a tuna.

It was a dull morning. Not even a school of pilot whales broke the monotony of the small blue waves, stirring restlessly under a wind too weak to make whitecaps. Sweaters, worn against the predawn chill, were soon discarded. Al stripped to his bathing trunks to fortify his already impressive tan. Several times we passed the *Jean-Anne II*, sister tuna boat from Wedgeport, but each time their signal mimicked ours. Spreading hands indicated no sign of fish. Their baits were as stale as ours and their hopes, like ours, were waning.

Noon called for a brief pause over a sunken ledge to lower a large spoon and pick up a few cod for the daily chowder. Time crawled along slowly. At three o'clock, with the sun slanted well to the west, we left the favored waters and trolled back near the lesser islands off the yacht club.

I was at the wheel when the first strike came and I left it on the instant to dash for my cameras, which were resting in their opened cases just a dozen feet away. I wanted to be up on top but couldn't get there in the confusion, with one hand tied up by a heavy movie camera. The rear of the cockpit was a welter of chaos. Through the moving bodies I saw a second strike boil up beside that first, still-spreading boil. Out of the smother of foam a big tail and the afterpart of a tuna's body flashed briefly. The second outrigger pole bent down, then snapped back sharply as its string, too, broke to let the line run directly from rod to fish.

If there had been a scurry before, there was pandemonium now. One fighting chair, two tuna outfits jumping in their sockets with their lines streaking off, reels screaming, were surrounded by five men and a boy. For the moment the tiller went unattended. The racing fish crossed each other's paths as they streaked away. Bill got the rod out of the starboard socket and passed it over Al's head where he sat in the chair and reached the port side. Elie dove forward to whirl the wheel and sent the *Shamrock* skidding around to port.

As the tuna boat completed its rearward turn the lines crossed a second time and again Bill passed the rod over Al's head.

By this time Al and Jack had moved the starboard rod into the chair's gimbal, and Al had snapped his harness to the reel.

Elie left the wheel, grabbing up a bait knife, and made for the line on the rod Bill, with Rex's help, was hanging onto. A second later that fish would have been free and long gone, but I bellowed, "Wait!" and the shock of my shout plus an urgent need for another turning of the wheel drove him back to the tiller. Cutting one line is standard procedure in case of a double strike at Wedgeport.

I had gained the upper deck and was ready to take some of the action, but I dropped back to the cockpit again, camera cradled in one arm, and reached the scene of action just in time to intercept Elie as he came back a second time, knife brandished, to cut one fish free. His words, "We'll lose them both," were all mixed up with mine.

"We've got nothing to lose but a forty-dollar line," I shouted. "I don't care if it's never been done, let's try it for a while, anyway. If they foul they foul, and even then there's a fifty-fifty chance we can still cut the right line."

Only half convinced, Elie retired to the wheel but the knife stayed in its place on the bait box after that. He swung the boat toward the fish that Rex and Bill were playing, realizing that theirs was the greater need. Just holding a tuna outfit involving a 14/0 reel loaded with half a mile of 130-pound-test line without a harness or belt socket is something of a chore. Put a quarter ton of bucking, diving tuna on the other end of it and you have all the trouble anyone wants.

Harold, on top, was waving his red jacket frantically but though we scanned the horizon there was no sign of another boat. The *Jean-Anne II* had trolled out of sight. None of the yacht club's cruisers had yet come out of the channel, two miles to our west, for an evening on the water.

There was nothing to be done but hang on. Until the two big fish separated themselves by something approximating a mile we had a chance. Elie tried to keep the boat equidistant between the two fish, working first one way and then the other, depending upon which outfit had the most line out. The waves were showing spots of white foam as the breeze freshened.

By the time I had filmed what I felt was the necessary action and could leave my cameras temporarily to help the crew, there seemed nothing left for me to do. Harold, on the top of the cabin, had unearthed some flares and waved one, spitting fiery incandescence, back and forth above his head. Jack worked the fighting chair for Al, who pumped endlessly to gain an occasional few yards of line.

Bill held the other rod while Rex, holding it also, reeled whenever there was the slightest chance of gaining line. Elie was everywhere from the wheel to the chair to the free rod, comparing the line left on each spool and moving the boat accordingly. Both spools were down. The drags were tighter than the anglers had any right to tighten them. Time was running out and each sweating one of us knew it. The ship-to-shore radio, ordered and long overdue, would have made all the difference had it been installed.

The boat rolled in the chop at a standstill. Neither fish was much farther off than the other. Neither reel had enough line left to guarantee a wide swing toward the opposite fish. In a minute Elie was going to get the knife and I wasn't going to make a murmur of protest. I looked at my watch. We'd had them on just twenty minutes.

"Dinty's coming! Dinty's coming!" Harold's voice rang out from above us. We followed his arm with our eyes, but from our lower position in the cockpit we couldn't see a thing. I climbed up beside him and could make out a white speck, coming on, growing larger as I watched.

Doctor "Dinty" Moore was the commodore of the yacht club and no boat could have been more welcome. If only he could make it! Only two days before he'd installed a tuna chair in his *Whitecap,* explaining as he put it in that, while he might someday feel like taking a tuna, it would probably be little more than a decoration. True, it was set low in a deep cockpit and playing a tuna from it would have been awkward. We were praying that we could decorate it with a tired angler for just long enough to finish off the other fish and then come back and pick him up again.

It is hard to shout across the sound of motors and boats with waves beating against their hulls. Signals are easily misunderstood. A week earlier when a tuna had been brought to boat at dusk just off the yacht club channel a whole flotilla of boats had surrounded it. Twice one of them had crossed the line and very nearly caused the loss of the fish. There had been a big to-do about it later at the club and a general agreement that no boat would go in anywhere near a fighting angler. Dinty sheared off, both he and his wife uncertain as to whether the waving and shouting meant to come in or stay clear. They moved inexorably farther away.

In desperation Elie chased them to get within sure hailing distance and Harold and I both made motions in unison for him to come alongside. That time they understood.

Both boats headed downwind and Jack hopped aboard as their sterns lined up. Rex passed the rod over and quickly followed. In seconds he was in the chair and each boat turned away in the wake of a tuna.

The crew and angler could work unhindered now and the *Shamrock* soon closed in on Al's fish. Surprisingly, he was almost whipped. We conjectured about it at length afterward but at the moment we were simply grateful that he came to gaff so swiftly. I looked at my watch again. Thirty-five minutes. Exceptionally fast time.

From atop the cabin I trained a camera lens on the fish as they tried to lift him into the boat. Perhaps in smooth water they might have managed it. There were three of them—and Harold—and it wasn't enough. There was nothing to do but tow him behind and that would certainly complicate things when it came to getting Rex and Jack back aboard with the other rod. They were out of sight in the whitecapped distance. We headed toward their last remembered position.

The *Jean-Anne II* loomed up ahead of us, trolling. We raced alongside, and the mate and one of their anglers came aboard to help haul the tuna in. With the first fish aboard we sped on and found the *Whitecap* heading slowly into the wind. Dinty grinned and waved. The tuna was still fast. He headed the boat downwind and we came alongside. Rex and Jack reboarded the *Shamrock* and Rex climbed over Al's fish on the planking to get into the empty tuna chair.

Rex's tuna must have been a tougher fish or, as it proved, a little bigger. Or else the rest he'd had while Al was bringing his in had given him new strength. It took another twenty minutes to bring him to the gaff. Even then the total time of fifty-five minutes was fairly low. There was plenty of manpower to slide him over the side and when both fish lay together, side by side, in the cockpit, as one we broke simultaneously into a cheer.

Hands were shaken. Bottles of root beer and of another, stronger potion more suited to the moment were opened. The *Whitecap* ranged alongside a third time. Hands touched from boat to boat in cheer and congratulations or came over empty to return with the stuff for making toasts.

It was a gay moment. The tuna flags went up, one above another on our boat and we headed toward the yacht club and the setting sun.

As we slid through the waves on our way in, Elie turned the wheel over to Jack and came to sit beside me. "Sometimes I get excited," he whispered in his Wedgeport-French accent. "I saw lots of tuna hooked, quite some doubles, too, but I never saw two caught before or ever heard of it, either. You were the wise one. You knew our luck. I'm glad."

"I'm glad, too," I said, "for everyone."

Al's fish weighed 544 pounds, Rex's 565, for a total of 1,109. It was Rex's first big tuna. Perhaps the day meant most to him. I know it meant a great deal to Al and the crew to have had a part in so unusual an accomplishment. It meant most of all to me, I think, to be on the spot to film so rare an occurrence in the annals of angling.

[1966]

Book Three

A GAMEFISH
TOO VALUABLE

Someone once pointed out to me that the difference between Shakespeare's Romeo and Juliet *and the modern* West Side Story—*essentially the same plot—was that there's nothing in* West Side Story *worth quoting. I mention this not to elevate Wulff to Shakespearean status (I have to draw the line somewhere!), but rather to point out that of the millions of words written by thousands of people on hunting and fishing in this century, he is quoted more often by far than any other. That, I assure you, is a rare compliment from the American angling public.*

That phrase of his you hear most often—"A good gamefish is too valuable to be caught only once"—was born in this section's first chapter, which was written more than fifty years ago. Ever since then, Lee Wulff has been leading the often-uphill charge to preserve and protect our sportfishing. So in this section we explore his efforts in that regard, from a talk he delivered to a Newfoundland Rotary Club in 1938 all the way to his current efforts at affording Atlantic salmon the protection of formal gamefish status throughout its North American range.

27

To Be Caught
Only Once

*This chapter is the introduction that Lee Wulff wrote
for his* Handbook of Freshwater Fishing *(1938). As
things turned out, it was the most prophetic piece of
writing in modern angling history.*

*Here you'll find—in its complete context—that
oft-quoted Wulff phrase about a good gamefish being
too valuable to be caught only once. Actually, the word*
good *wasn't used until later in the same book. I prefer
the first version, since one man's "good" gamefish may
not be so viewed by another fisherman. The gospel of
catch and release, however, offers much to all fishermen and to all fish.*

Fishing is truly a contemplative sport. Throughout its long
history since the first men on earth, using the crude weapons
of their times, sought fish for food, it has required a concentration and alertness that still lend it charm. It is deeply
rooted in us, this fishing, with its heritage of long centuries of
hungry men, and while our thoughts as we follow the sport
today may reflect the easy moods of our natural surroundings, the basic hunting instinct, the impulse to outwit the

quarry, is always there. The angler's mind, engrossed with the problems of the sport at hand, has little room for the worries that at other times plague him, and therein lies the key to the rare relaxation of fishing.

Somewhere in the wide range of activity between the hard physical effort of wading for long hours against a swift current in a rocky stream, casting steadily, and the indolence of lying quietly in the sun waiting for a bobber to go under, there is a type of angling to suit everyone's mood and everyone's pocketbook. Fishing is fishing wherever it is found. I have come to feel sorry for the angler who limits himself to one type of lure or one species of fish. I have seen the most skillful anglers, who had fished for the whole gamut of famous fish over a wide range of waters, catching panfish with proportionate tackle and enjoying it thoroughly. Whereas some types of angling offer a more difficult problem and the keener students of the sport naturally seek these out, the underlying endeavor remains the same and the brotherhood of angling encircles them all.

Angling's problems are never solved. They rise anew with each new pool and each new day. Silver-haired veterans of countless trips fish with an eagerness that makes it plain that their store of fishing knowledge is still far from complete. My own most prized possession is that love of angling in which I have a pleasant problem that I will never completely solve. I can wish no greater boon for any man. And when my own hair is graying, fortune willing, I hope that I may spend long hours on a favorite stream, watching its changes with the cycles of the seasons and the floods of every spring, finding good fish that I cannot catch to give me pause for thought.

The difficulty lies not in just being able to fool the fish. Their intelligence is far inferior to our own. Deceiving them is a much easier problem than guessing where they will be at any given time under an ever-changing-and-never-quite-the-same set of weather and water conditions. To the fish three things are of prime importance: food, safety, and comfort. If it is food the fish are seeking the angler must concern himself with the kind of food and where they will go to look for it. With that problem decided, he can concentrate on making his lure effective. If it is safety the fish are seeking he must find his fish before he can tempt him. And if it is comfort he must know where a fish will seek it and put his lure within easy reach of his quarry.

There will be no end to angling controversies for there is no one best way for everyone to fish. One angler may take a certain phase of angling and through his mastery of the single side of the game claim fishing success. Among such fishermen are those who fish with but a single lure. Through their knowledge of fish habits and their ability to put their single lure where feeding fish will take it they often outdistance others with more suitable lures but without the same knowledge of fish and fishing waters. There are too many conditions, varying constantly, that must be balanced for any set solution to be devised. The problem itself alone remains constant: to find the fish and make them strike. It is seeking the answer that absorbs years of men's lives and gives them in return the blessing of peace of mind and the health that follows hours spent in the open.

Increasing populations and the decrease in the amount of fishable water due to pollution and the inroads of civilization as we know it have lifted the value of our inland fish for sport far above their value as food. The day of the great catches is passing. Hatcheries, operated by funds from the license fees of anglers, turn out millions of fish to stock the lakes and streams. Over the years the fish have developed a new wariness, angling has become an art requiring great skill, and the catching of many fish is a privilege lavished on the few whose opportunity or skill is great.

There is a growing tendency among anglers to release their fish, returning them to the water in order that they may furnish sport again for a brother angler. Gamefish are too valuable to be caught only once. Fish from the markets, though not so rare, are just as nourishing and just as tasty as the gamefish of our lakes and streams. It seems logical to buy our food fish where they are much cheaper than those we buy for sport by way of license, tackle, transportation, and time— and return our catches to the waters that we, as anglers, hope will always be well stocked.

It is a long step from the day when the fisherman's catch meant life and health to himself and his family to our present day where anglers fish for sport alone. Even the day of the fisherman who consistently hangs up his trophies of the day to brag about is passing, too. Pride in accomplishment will always remain but, seemingly, angling is reaching a new high plane when a fisherman can spend a day on the lake or stream, catching fish and returning them to the water again, unharmed, to come home empty-handed. That angler keeps no trophy to show his fellow men as proof of his prowess but contents himself with the pleasure of a day well spent in the surroundings he loves. He has fished for sport and not for glory. Upon him and those who follow his leadership the future of angling depends.

[1938]

28

A Conservation Talk for Newfoundland

One of the pleasures in putting together a book such as this is being able to include a few things that otherwise would never see the light of popular print. To introduce this chapter, I quote from the St. John's *(Newfoundland)* Evening Telegram *of Friday, October 14, 1938, in which this essay originally appeared:*

"Speaking frankly and as one businessman to others, Mr. Lee Wulff, sportsman, photographer, writer and lecturer, spoke at yesterday's meeting of Rotary on the value of the Game and Inland Fisheries to this country and of the absolute need for their conservation, so that our game resources will not go the way of the buffalo in the United States and become extinct.

"Rotarian Angus Reid, Chairman of the Newfoundland Tourist Board, who had given Mr. Wulff an assignment to take photographs of our game resources, in introducing the speaker mentioned that Mr. Wulff had already made movies of the tuna fishing, salmon fishing, moose hunting, and partridge shooting."

When I first received an invitation to address your club this summer I had planned to come before you as one sportsman speaking to other sportsmen. I am certain that among you there are many who are anglers and hunters. I can be certain of this because our history and our heritage has made it true. We were hunters and fishermen before we were farmers, tradesmen, or manufacturers. In the first days of man on earth his very life depended on his ability to hunt and fish. Without that ability he and his family starved.

Through those early centuries there was bred into the human race an instinct so deep that the late centuries of development has failed to wipe it out even though our need of fish is now supplied by professional fishermen and our need of meat by domestic animals.

Lacking the imperative need of fish and game for food we hunt and fish mainly for pleasure.

I had thought to describe to you some of the thrills that accompany the capture of the giant tuna that are common to these shores or bring you the thrill that comes when his majesty the moose emerges from the woods into an open bog within sight of the hunter. But now, at the end of a summer of following the sports in your country I have come to talk to you as one businessman to another.

Hunting and fishing are my business. I write on them, talk on them, and take pictures of them. More than that, I feel that if I can show sportsmen how they can better enjoy their sport by widening their field of activity or showing them how they can get more pleasure from it, I will have done something that many of us strive for and few achieve—the creating of pleasure for others.

You, gentlemen, are businessmen, representing the business of your country in its many varied forms. To each of you your own business, whether it be baking, banking, or bookkeeping, is your first concern. But everything that affects your country affects each and every one of you. As your country rises and falls you rise and fall with it. If it becomes richer you gain, too, and if it becomes poorer you lose in business opportunity. And so, hunting and fishing are your business as well as mine.

In the United States, with its 130 millions of people, one out of every ten buys a fishing license and one out every thirteen a hunting license, at fees ranging from one dollar to twenty-five. Millions of others fish in the ocean where no license is required. Fishing is our biggest single sport. It has more followers who spend more money on it than has baseball, golf, or any other single sport. Every fisherman and hunter that can be induced to come to Newfoundland spends money here and brings wealth, and a share of that wealth is yours.

The tourist business in the sections of North America that have scenery or sport to offer is one of the most important sources of revenue. In the state of Maine that tourist business is considered the biggest single source of revenue the state possesses. In Nova Scotia right next door, it is one of the principal resources of revenue. And here in Newfoundland is a wealth of sport and scenic material that is practically untouched by tourists. It is a business that can be developed. The resources are here, it only remains for you to capitalize on them.

This is not a myth or fairy story. It is a cold hard fact. Tourist business is big business. It means money and wealth to the country that gains it. With accommodations for tourists, sport and scenery to attract them, and proper publicity to draw them, they will come to Newfoundland. Your Tourist Board, with its efficient secretary, is working intelligently toward that end. The returns will be big but the effort needed to build up a large tourist flow is a great one and all the possible help and cooperation are needed to get it started.

The scenery of your west coast with its high mountains rising from the sea and its long deep bays, is the equal of anything on the Atlantic seaboard, and Bonne Bay and Bay of Islands are more magnificent than any other western Atlantic harbors. Proof of their beauty is attested by the ships Clarke Steamship Lines send along this coast weekly all summer, each booked to its full capacity of from 300 to 350 passengers. If there were suitable accommodations, proper publicity would draw thousands to spend their vacations on your shores.

To emphasize the value of tourist sportsmen as a source of revenue, I can point to the island of Bimini in the Bahamas, a tiny strip of land a few miles long, with only one industry, big-game fishing. Bimini sends annually to the Crown from thirty to forty thousand dollars in taxes alone. In Nova Scotia, deep-sea fishing is considered to mean more than half a million dollars annually to the province in tourist trade.

Newfoundland has a wealth of salmon rivers. The Atlantic salmon is the peer of freshwater fighting fish, a brilliant performer that has become exceedingly rare and is only now being revived in the United States, from which it was all but extinct. As long as your rivers remain unobstructed by dams or unpoisoned by pollution, salmon parr can be stocked in them and there will always be a return of salmon from the sea.

Your lakes and streams are filled with trout, most sought after of all gamefish, and the sea trout that come into your rivers are a splendid sporting fish that has not yet received the publicity it deserves throughout the world of sportsmen.

Giant tuna, one of the finest of angling trophies, come into practically all the bays and harbors of Newfoundland. The broadbill swordfish, highest trophy of all saltwater fishing, is to be found on the south coast. Those of you who are fishermen must realize the thrill that goes with the capturing of a mighty fish of the ocean, weighing upward of 500 pounds, on a thin strand of twisted linen and understand how it will lure anglers on trips of thousands of miles to the far corners of the earth to follow their sport. Nowhere else in the North Atlantic can a deep-sea fisherman pursue his sport amid such beautiful surroundings. Nowhere else will the giant speedsters of the ocean be found in such tiny landlocked harbors. It is hard to believe that the southeast arm of Bonne Bay or Penguin Arm in Bay of Islands are not lakes surrounded by high mountains instead of long narrow fingers of the sea.

Newfoundland's big game, her caribou and her moose, are real attractions to hunters. Witness to this is the speed with which all available licenses for shooting this game have been taken up in the two years of the open season. Ducks, geese, snipe, partridge, and other birds are here in plenty to lure the sportsman for his holiday as well. Duck shooting in the United States has fallen off with the recent scarcity of wildfowl there. Good duck hunting is increasingly hard to get. You are raising ducks here and sending them down to the States for us to shoot because they leave before you open a season on them for your own gunners. If there were an open season on waterfowl, starting before or immediately after the close of the salmon season, it would be possible for the tourist-sportsman to combine his fishing trip with big-game hunting or duck shooting as an additional lure to bring him here.

These natural resources are your country's treasures. They must be handled as carefully as any other business to give a fair return in sport and in dollars. And because it is your country's business it is your business, too. I was surprised to find only one hatchery in all Newfoundland, and that one a privately owned one. The time will come when your streams must be stocked. It is good business to put out small salmon parr and let the ocean send you back a crop of big salmon. There are possibilities that non-native wildlife might flourish and give better sport than the native fish or game.

In the United States we have no heath hens left, no carrier pigeons of the flocks that once blackened the skies, because they couldn't cope with the dangers of civilization. Instead we have ring-necked pheasants that were imported and are wary enough to exist at our very backyards. Our buffalo are gone, and if they were not I doubt if we'd have any place to put them anyway. Instead our deer, wise and wary game, have spread out to take their place. Our imported brown trout will survive where our native mud trout will not, and we are extremely glad to have them in our otherwise barren streams.

The problem of conservation is not a new one. Hundreds of different methods have been tried out as game has dwindled in other more accessible sections. There is a wealth of experience to draw on and, as always, an ounce of prevention is worth a pound of cure. The state of Connecticut, for instance, is preparing to spend a quarter of a million dollars in the hopes of restoring salmon to the Connecticut River, a great stream hundreds of miles long with many branches, that once had a run of salmon as great, it is estimated, as the entire run of Atlantic salmon in all the other rivers of the North Atlantic and that now has none at all.

The fishing, the scenery, the wildlife, all these things are part of Newfoundland's wealth. It is not just the business of the angler, the hunter, and the lover of scenery to see that they are preserved; it is the business of everyone. And, gentlemen, it is a business that will bear watching.

Newfoundland is a country that depends on its natural resources for its existence. The main income is from pulp, fish, and minerals. If your supply of these things should become exhausted, you, as a country, would be very poor indeed. The quantity of minerals in your land is fixed. You guard your pulp stand against fire. The fish in the ocean may be beyond your control to regulate and guard when they leave your shores, but the fish that come into your rivers will survive or perish as a result of the care that is taken of them.

The near extinction of your caribou seems to have been no lesson on the saving of the salmon in your rivers. Your salmon—and I use the word advisedly, because they are a part of the country and belong to no one man or group of men but to every Newfoundlander—are becoming fewer each year. River after river is being given the name of being spoiled as anglers and netters move on farther afield.

I'd like to speak of the conditions I found while salmon fishing as an observer with no ax to grind, no group to favor, other than to hope that through my writings and my pictures anglers will know a wider pleasure in their sport. I have seen salmon rotting on the shore at the falls of the Upper Humber, dead and stinking on the bank or lying underwater with the gaff wounds plainly showing, simply because there is no legal limit to the number of fish a licensed angler may take. The guides who saved them in the hope that they would be able to get them out before they spoiled will be the first to lament when salmon grow scarce and they or their children have no more parties to guide. The anglers who caught the salmon should have known better. They were Americans, I'm sorry to say, and with the lesson of American game scarcity fresh in their minds they should have had enough sporting blood to release all the fish they did not need for immediate use for food.

I have talked to salmon packers who are unanimous in admitting that each year the salmon take in their locality is growing smaller. No one denies that the salmon are going and unless something is done it will be the story of the caribou all over again. I have found that more than half the grilse in the rivers I fished were net marked. Yet the size of salmon mesh is big enough to allow the passage of a grilse, and anything smaller is forbidden by law. How do they get marked? Either by illegal netters or by cod traps. Strangely enough, though salmon nets have a minimum mesh of $5\frac{1}{2}$ inches and may not be placed nearer than a certain distance to the mouth of the rivers, the cod traps may use a $3\frac{1}{2}$-inch mesh, and outside a few local restrictions confined to the Avalon Peninsula, there is no restriction on their placement. I have watched the boats coming in from cod traps and what did they bring? Codfish? No. Not one single codfish but grilse and salmon instead, and when the salmon run has passed these cod traps are taken up. This has been excused by some on the basis that the people are poor and they really need the fish for food. It sounds like a good excuse until you consider that they were poor ten years ago, and probably will still be poor ten years hence—the only difference being that if the salmon are gone they will be a darn sight poorer.

If these poor people are starving it would be cheaper for the government to buy codfish for them than to allow them to ruin the salmon supply of any river. But usually the salmon so captured are not used for food by the men that catch them but are shipped to market and the chances are that the operators of these traps are not the poorest in the community at all.

In speaking of conservation I have been told, too, that Newfoundlanders are *different* and that because someone else finds a certain measure of conservation essential it doesn't follow that they must do likewise. Newfoundlanders *are* different. I admire them for their independence of thought and their courage. But, unfortunately, the salmon are the same whether here in Canada or in the United States. They will stand only so much persecution without suffering depletion. Salmon are a crop just like any other. Before modern man came they hung in a balance of nature. We can't keep on constantly removing them without additional stocking and expect the same number to return year after year. And in addition to the salmon we take ourselves, in many cases we have also protected the natural enemies of the salmon, allowing them to flourish and increase their depredations on the fish. This is particularly true of the American merganser or shellduck and the kingfishers whose principal food is the salmon parr and which, outside of man, are the salmon's greatest enemies.

There is no comparison between the amount of revenue derived by the government for each salmon that is netted as compared with that gained from a tourist for each salmon he catches. Some commercial fishermen pay only $2 for a canning license. The others pay nothing. The angler pays his license fee to the government, and his transportation, board, supplies, and other needs to the community. Sportsmen taking a few fish will provide as much revenue as the commercial fisherman taking a hundred times more, without the certainty of depleting the permanent salmon supply. On rivers where the income from tourists is as great or greater than that from the netting of salmon it looks like very poor business to allow nets to take a quantity of fish great enough to impair the salmon run for future years. *But* that seems to be just exactly what is going on. Twenty years ago, when the salmon run in Alaska was threatened with depletion, government regulation restricted the commercial take to a point where it would not permanently damage the run. Each year the total run of salmon and the fishermen's take were totaled and balanced and a quota set for the following year with the result that the salmon crop in Alaska will always be there to harvest.

No one wants the extermination of the salmon. Neither the anglers, the packers, nor any of you who are businessmen want them exterminated. They belong to every Newfoundlander and no one man or group of men deserves the right to take so many that the yearly run will continue to diminish. With proper care the salmon will last as long as the rivers run.

Boiled down to the basic facts, there is no reasonable reason for allowing the salmon supply of your rivers to dwindle away. Certainly if all the pulpwood were being burned off your hills you'd manage to stop it. As soon as the flames began to rise and leave a black trail behind them you'd be up in arms. But the salmon go quietly with no flames and smoke. Like the caribou suddenly they will be almost gone.

The guardianship of your fish and game is primarily your government's business but it is up to you, regardless of whether you fish or hunt, to make certain that the job is done, for you will be among the ultimate losers if it is not. What is true of the salmon is true of many other things—of all wildlife and even of scenery that may be marred or ruined by thoughtlessness or improper planning.

It is a job of proper regulation and even more of education so that the improvident may realize the value of the resources at hand. It is up to those of us who know the pleasure of fishing for fun and not for food to show it to others and for those others of us who realize the value of wildlife to help those others to save it for themselves. My plea to you is to take a real interest in the proper regulation of your fish and game so that there will always be sport here for yourselves and for those tourists who will come to share your pleasure, paying their way and bringing more wealth to Newfoundland.

[1938]

29

Atlantic Salmon

PROGRESS AND PROBLEMS

Perhaps no man has devoted more energy and time to the conservation of Atlantic salmon than Lee Wulff. He notes in the beginning of this chapter, written in 1982, the happy joining of forces by the two most influential salmon-conservation organizations. What he doesn't say, however, was that he was instrumental in bringing this coalition about and works to this day as a director of the new Atlantic Salmon Federation.

His main thrust these days, he tells me, is in trying to get Atlantic salmon legal status as a gamefish, with all the management restrictions thus implied. This makes perfect sense to me. For one thing, gamefish for the most part aren't sold commercially. The lack of a commercial sale, of course, deprives a poacher of his prime motivation, and poaching is a serious problem for all North American salmon stocks. Commercial salmon ranching, a rapidly growing business, would supply market needs in that event, leaving indigenous salmon stocks sufficiently relieved to rebuild themselves for the good of everyone.

There is good news on the Atlantic-salmon front. The two most important organizations of Atlantic-salmon anglers—the Canadian-based Atlantic Salmon Association and the American-based International Atlantic Salmon Foundation—have merged their efforts. Each will remain incorporated in its own country (to retain nonprofit status), but they have formed a joint committee of six members from each group called the Atlantic Salmon Federation, which will determine policy and programs for both groups. The executive director of the new Federation will be Dr. Wilfred M. Carter. He will also be director of both groups, which will operate under a single staff. Just as the duck hunters of both Canada and the United States work efficiently through Ducks Unlimited, the salmon anglers can now do the same for better salmon fishing.

In March 1981, at the annual meeting of the Atlantic Salmon Association, I was dismayed to find not one official delegate from any other salmon-angling organization in Canada. Joan and I made a swing of public appearances through the Maritime Provinces this year to help counteract this. We drew record crowds. The clubs were able to raise some funds (through tickets and raffles) for conservation work and the expenses of sending delegates. Because salmon management has brought salmon so low, the salmon anglers were ready to join together and take political action.

At this year's meeting of the Atlantic Salmon Association in Montreal, delegates from practically every salmon club in Canada were on hand. They passed two resolutions for presentation to their government's salmon managers and asked for swift action. The first resolution was for the institution of "river harvest," and it was signed by all the representatives.

River harvest means the harvesting of salmon only at the mouths of their native rivers. This method has long been practiced in Iceland, which has had the best management of any salmon-producing country in the North Atlantic. Under this system, each river is managed as an ecological unit. A river whose runs have been depleted for any reason can be given the greatest possible protection in order to get the maximum number of prime spawners to the beds to revitalize it. Conversely, a river that is in excellent shape can be cropped to whatever degree is reasonable.

As anglers can prove that the salmon they catch are more beneficial to society, they can claim a greater share. There should be no taking of salmon from the present commercial share for the anglers without just compensation for losses to the commercial netters. The anglers are ready and willing to pay more in licenses over the years to catch those big fish that the nets have been intercepting in the sea.

Interception of salmon in nets other than at their own river is an indiscriminate harvest and an international problem. American salmon are being intercepted in Canadian waters. Salmon from New Brunswick rivers, where expensive measures have been taken to try to rebuild the runs, are being netted off Newfoundland on their return from sea feeding. Biologists agree that river harvest, the taking of salmon either in the river by angling or, when plentiful enough, in nets below the angling areas at the river mouth, is the best way to manage. Though attaining this goal may be a long, hard struggle, public pressure can make it a reality. As I explained on our lecture tour, we, the anglers, outnumber and can outvote the commercial salmon netters and can override the commercial lobby to achieve fair management. Anglers have consistently been far more concerned with saving the stock for the future than the commercial fishermen have.

The second resolution deals with something I've complained about for years. Because the value of the flesh of the large salmon is a little greater on the market than that of the small salmon or grilse, commercial interests long ago persuaded the Canadian government to regulate gill-net size so that the nets would capture and hold the large salmon while allowing the grilse to swim through and go on to the spawning grounds. No cattle breeder would ever sell his prize bulls for hamburger and breed his runts, but that is exactly what the Canadian government forced commercial fishermen to do. As a result, the average size of the fish in the salmon runs has dropped to an alarming low.

In 1940, while suggesting that Newfoundland start breeding its best salmon stock, I studied the books of Job Brothers, the largest salmon exporters in the colony at that time, and found that the average size of the fish they shipped had dropped from 16 pounds to 10 in that twenty-year period. Anglers I know who fished the Serpentine River in the early 1900s told me that they never caught any grilse in that river in the old days and that the salmon averaged about 20 pounds. In 1940, in one pool, in one morning, I caught thirteen salmon ranging from 12 to 20 pounds. In a recent report, I found that only seven fish over grilse size were caught in the whole season and that the grilse made up 95 percent of the run.

Another comparison may be in order. Consider the poodle. Originally it was the *pudel*, a big dog used for hunting and retrieving. Because it was very intelligent and companionable, people wanted it for pets and wanted it smaller. They bred the smallest dogs and developed first the miniature and finally the toy poodle. After constant breeding, these miniatures and toys breed true; small dogs begetting small dogs. This is happening to Canadian salmon under government regulation.

It is particularly pathetic when one realizes that the salmon parr that become big salmon on two or three years sea feeding before they return to their rivers use no more, and probably less, of their native stream's food supply than do the parr that will go to sea and stay only one year before returning to their rivers as grilse of about 4 pounds. In other words, a suitable river can produce as many or more 12- to 20-pound salmon as it can grilse, bringing back from the bounteous sea feeding about four times as many pounds of salmon. This is a terrible waste, and it is still almost unbelievable to me that Canadian biologists have been standing by without protest and watching this happen ever since the twenties.

With enough public pressure applied toward reversing the government's present policy, and instead taking the small salmon for commercial sale and making sure the finest fish go on to the spawning grounds, we can gradually rebuild the size of the individual fish in the salmon runs. It is gratifying to note that the ice has been broken by the provincial government of Nova Scotia in its angling control of the Margaree (though not by the federal government in its netting control at that river). The province has ruled that the anglers fishing the Margaree's early run can keep grilse they catch, but must return all larger, longer sea-feeding fish to the river to go on upstream to spawn. The federal government in Ottawa regulates all salmon policy in all provinces except Quebec. The controlled provinces must keep their regulations within federal guidelines. The resolution I mentioned earlier received unanimous support, and public pressure will now be exerted to effect this long-needed change.

There is a parallel between the realization of good trout management in the United States and obtaining good salmon management in the Maritimes. In 1938, I wrote in a book: "A good gamefish is too valuable to be caught only once." It took a long time for public pressure to build up. The number of trout fishermen expanded, and their dissatisfaction with poor management grew with their numbers. Eventually in the mid-1960s, catch and release came into being. Since then, from the beginnings in Yellowstone National Park and on New York's Beaverkill, the no-kill pattern has spread all across the nation and is growing. It was obvious long ago, but only now are our managers accepting it wholeheartedly. They were forced to it by pressure from national angling groups such as the Federation of Fly Fishers, Trout Unlimited, and Theodore Gordon Flyfishers.

Only through catch and release can a country that believes in public fishing give excellent trout fishing to an almost unlimited number of anglers. It is our democratic answer to the owned and controlled fishing of Europe, which through good management provides excellent catch-and-take-home fishing for only a few. With good trout waters holding all the fish they can support, no-kill is providing excellent fishing for more than ten times as many anglers as the old catch-and-keep management does on the same river's adjacent water. Obviously, as no-kill is expanded to other productive waters, the number of fishermen who can enjoy it will expand many more times, creating more satisfied fishermen to join with us to secure the best possible future management. And there's no more challenging fishing than for the smart, caught-again-and-again, plentiful fish of these areas.

Catch and release will be one of the many tools salmon managers can use, too. There is no way modern salmon fishermen can catch as many fish as we old-timers did. The number of salmon anglers grows and grows, but the number of salmon pools do not. In the future, we must try to make each salmon we catch be a more satisfying challenge through the use of lighter tackle or because we caught it on a fly we tied ourselves, or perhaps on a fly our companions said would *never* take a salmon. We can try, too, to make many of our salmon give pleasure to more than one angler.

It will take time, effort, and money to achieve our ends. I believe that salmon anglers, like the trout fishermen of a decade or two ago, are ready to organize and do what's necessary to secure better salmon fishing in the future. It will come through support of the Atlantic Salmon Association and the International Atlantic Salmon Foundation and the Atlantic Salmon Federation they have created together. Every salmon river should have a group of salmon anglers to love and cherish it. All the groups should be united to speak with one voice for good fishing not only for ourselves, but for our kids.

There is a third resolution now circulating among the Maritime salmon clubs for signatures; and again, it promises to be unanimously approved. It will insist that the Canadian government get tough in enforcing the law against "by-catches," the taking of Atlantic salmon illegally by means of cod traps and mackerel nets, for example, and that the tagging system, introduced by New Brunswick for angling-catch control, be used to control the legitimate commercial netting.

New Brunswick introduced tagging for all angler-caught salmon with a season limit of fifteen per angler. Tagging is not a new idea. It has been used successfully for steelhead on our West Coast for many years. For Atlantic salmon management, it is a beginning. Tagging gives the best possible control of the catch and is the best tool for catching poachers. It is important that all salmon, taken by any means, be subject to tagging. If only properly tagged salmon may be legally possessed, then poachers of all types, whether they take fish in the sea or in the rivers, may be more readily apprehended.

The essence of good management is numbers. The right number must reach the spawning ground. The right number of big salmon in proportion to small salmon must be allowed to spawn to revitalize the stock. Tagging is a way of making the numbers come out right. It will take pressure from the anglers to make the government institute a mandatory tagging program. It may not be easy, but acting together, we can make it happen.

Unfortunately, managers enjoy complex management. They like to work with many variables. They decide on a season, then on a license fee that is designated to limit fishing pressure. They decide on a daily limit, which means the taking of an uncertain quantity over the course of the season. They are a lot tougher on anglers than on commercial fishermen. They guess and hope they've guessed right.

They could be much more accurate by deciding through their many studies how many fish can be expected to come into a river as an annual run. Then they need to decide how many are needed on the spawning grounds, being a little generous there to be sure they don't get too few. They can estimate the poaching take, which has been just as certain as the salmon runs, and subtract it from the number needed on the spawning beds from the annual run. This will be the number of fish to be taken by angling. When that number is taken, the season should close. If everyone knows and expects that, it will work no more hardship on anglers than any other type of management. As the limiting number approaches, anglers who release their fish would certainly be applauded by those who get to fish on through the days the season can then be extended.

There is an overcrowding problem now at Le Havre River in southern Nova Scotia. On weekends, there are sometimes more anglers sitting on the bank waiting for a chance to fish than there are actually fishing in the pool. Management is working with seasons and license fees and limits as usual and failing to solve the problem, whereas the simple granting of two types of permits would. An A permit would allow an angler to fish Le Havre the first weekend and every other (alternate) weekend throughout the season. A B permit would let an angler fish on the alternate weekends. This would immediately cut the weekend crowd on the river in half. Both licenses would permit fishing during the week and elsewhere as usual.

Another future step should be the elimination of all but single hooks for Atlantic salmon fishing. Single-hooked-flies-only is a good limitation. The use of anything beyond a single hook for salmon, except perhaps in the very small sizes, is unfortunate. They're a sizable fish and easy to foul-hook. A large double hook is heavy and sinks readily to the level at which the fish rest. An angler who deliberately foul-hooks a fish with one, and many do, can say, "I was using legal tackle. The fish made a pass at my fly, and I struck." A warden is powerless to stop this poaching under the present Canadian rules.

Doubles have long been used for salmon for, years ago, everyone believed heavy leaders and a strong hold were essential to holding these fish. Light tackle and dry-fly fishing proved that theory wrong. Like most of the anglers I fish with, I have nothing but single-hook flies in my vest, except for a few #12 or #14 doubles to give me a small blocky shape that's different from the others with which to tempt reluctant salmon. I'll gladly give up this small category of flies for the general good of all legitimate salmon anglers. It would seem that those who refuse to give up their doubles either aren't as skillful anglers as the rest of us who succeed with single hooks or are so obsessed with tradition that they'll sacrifice a lot of fish to snaggers that would otherwise spawn.

On our recent visit to the two major salmon angling groups of Newfoundland (the Salmon Protective Association of Western Newfoundland and the Salmon Protective Association of Eastern Newfoundland), I had the feeling that both groups would recommend the single-hook rule for Atlantic salmon in their province, a good step forward.

* * *

Another way of improving salmon fishing is to return to their original scope the areas in which salmon spawn. There is an illusion that salmon spawn only in the headwaters of their rivers. This may now be true, but it was not always so. Nature's way is a wise and effective one. She once used all the suitable spawning areas. Man spoiled this system.

If a salmon can find his way back to his native river, even to the special branch he lived in as a parr (salmon from each major branch of a river are different), he can also find his way back to the particular pool or river area in which he was spawned. What has happened is that as settlers and settlements took root at the mouths of the rivers, the fishing at these points became very intensive. Even after the main runs had moved on upstream through these lower waters to their own special natal areas, anglers and poachers continued to operate as long as fish were there. Eventually all these lower-river fish were caught out, and since no fish were spawned there to return again with that homing instinct, these waters became barren of spawners, and people accepted this loss and waste of spawning areas as "natural."

They can be brought back by Vibert box or other types of stocking. And this is where no-kill can be helpful. If, after the main run of fish has passed on to their various destinations, no fish are taken from such cleaned-out areas, the stocked fish that settle in there can multiply and establish a lower-river cadre to utilize these presently unused spawning redds. Everything we can do to make for full utilization of the rivers for spawning and make the genetic stock in those streams most satisfying for anglers will make future fishing better.

Notice that I said most satisfying for anglers. There is always a move by governments to hope for better genetic stock for commercial purposes. It is important to anglers that the salmon they fish for will have a good natural tendency to take a fly and particularly a dry fly. Anglers also look for fishes' natural tendency to leap well when hooked. I'm particularly pleased with the Canadian salmon, which take both dry and wet flies well and leap high and often, when I compare them with the European salmon, which have almost no

257

interest in dry flies and leap far less frequently than our Canadian and American stocks.

Much research is being done to try to grow the biggest fish in the shortest time. That's what the commercial salmon ranchers and pen raisers want. If in gaining quick and heavy growth the tendencies that make a salmon take a fly and leap well are lost, it will be a disaster for anglers. Our American hatchery stocks, disease-free and fast growing, haven't been able to survive in our streams and often hurt rather than help our fishing. As an angler, I resent bitterly any use of angler-donated money for research that does not protect the qualities anglers value most.

The pen raising of Atlantic salmon is making great strides. Norway produces thousand of pounds and is now exporting these fish to the United States. Salmon raised in sea pens in Canadian waters are now on the market. I've eaten them and they are as tasty and as valuable on the market as the wild strains. Some anglers hope that they'll create a glut on the market and drive down the price to a point where it will make poaching less attractive. That is a false hope. The market will simply expand as more people learn to enjoy eating salmon, and we can expect that if the price in the expanded market for salmon drops, just as oil prices are dropping at the moment, the salmon producers will get together and cut back on production to keep the price tag at top level, just as OPEC is doing. When the commercial salmon producers tell you their production will aid anglers by solving the poaching problem, just smile but don't believe them. Let them pay for their own research.

A lot of research will come out of the work on salmon in pens. It will be suspect, like any work on fish in hatcheries. They'll be studying fish that are practically force-fed and have to make no effort to survive. We need wild fish in our streams that spend their youth feeding on insects in the streams so that when they return from the sea they'll still have the instinct to take an angler's fly and not look for lifeless pellets or shrimp mixed with oatmeal.

The matter of releasing salmon still comes in for bitter debate. Even though test after test proves that salmon will survive the playing by an angler just as the long-distance runners can run to exhaustion and, in a few hours, be ready to run again and live to a ripe age like mine. If effort to exhaustion *kills*, then every horse that puts its heart into a race should fall over dead at the finish line.

They may give instances of where a played-out salmon has died. I'll admit that a salmon can be played to death, just as it is possible to run a man or a horse to death. It indicates in the case of the salmon that the angler was not a very good one and couldn't bring in the fish in a normal time. Or the angler was insensitive to a worthy opponent, torturing him beyond the normal rules of the game. There is an answer, of course. It is to learn to play fish well, or if the salmon seems tired as he comes close, to cut the leader and let him swim away with the fly. The fly won't bother him much. I've seen salmon climbing their rivers and leaping the falls, showing great holes of red flesh where they'd escaped from the bites of seals. I've seen them scarred with the cuts from nets and the rocks they've struck as they leaped the falls, still going on determined to their appointment with destiny. Catch and release will work, and to kill a lot of fish because a few might die is not in the interest of future anglers.

There are more salmon rivers open to public fishing than are owned by individuals or clubs or leased or controlled by governments. All the rivers of Nova Scotia and Newfoundland and Labrador are open to public fishing. The best fishing is obviously in the private or strictly controlled waters. The governments have not yet learned to manage salmon rivers so that they produce the maximum of fishing. The first objective must be to make the rivers as productive as possible. Then it is time to determine how many fish can be taken and who will be permitted to take them, dividing them, if need be, between anglers, Indians, and commercial fishermen. The better and more restricted the angling is, the more that anglers will pay for it. Rates in Iceland now exceed $2,000 per angler per week and on Norway's Alta it reaches $5,000 and more. Granting "free" fishing, and equal opportunity for a uniform low fee as is now done in Newfoundland and Nova Scotia tends to put the most pressure on the best waters, beating them down to average level or below-the-average level within the province. This is another place where catch and release may keep the river's runs in good shape, giving the anglers the *recreation* of playing many big fish without reducing the river's potential for the future. If, and it is logical that they should be, fees are higher on the better rivers, it not only tends to limit fishing, but also to give more money with which to conserve the salmon. These are problems that will be solved politically to please the electorate.

But today's politicians should not be allowed to reduce the salmon's productivity in order to give today's constituents something extra at the expense of generations to come. Only angler pressure and angler vigilance will protect the salmon from unscrupulous politicians. It hasn't been done, but it can be!

[1982]

30

The Bright Future
of Trout Fishing

*Ten years after this chapter was written, that "bright
future" is increasingly showing in the present as the
management philosophy expressed by catch and
release proliferates. The Yellowstone experience, as
described in this chapter, has gained worldwide publicity, and much of the trout fishing done now in Argen-
tina, for example, is catch and release under rules
imposed by farsighted outfitters. Even some Soviet
anglers, fishing the no-kill Beaverkill in the fall of 1988,
expressed interest in the concept as it might be applied
to their newly developing trout and salmon fisheries.*

*The Yellowstone cutthroat trout described in this
chapter are either a subspecies, variety, or color variation of the only trout species native to the American
Rocky Mountain region (depending on whether you're
a taxonomic lumper or splitter and which biologist's
argument you favor). In any case, their color is a wild-
flower blend of buttercup and lavender with the brilliant red pigmentation under their jaw that gave rise to
their equally colorful name.*

I have seen the fishing of the future. It is superb, available to everyone, and it is free.

Forty years ago, in my *Handbook of Freshwater Fishing*, I wrote that "a good gamefish is too valuable to be caught only once." At that time, it was an expression of a wistful dream. Now, in Yellowstone National Park, it is a reality, a solid basis for good sportfishery management.

Because Yellowstone is under federal jurisdiction, those who manage it escape most of the political pressures that have dogged state fish and game departments since they came into being. The park management was charged by Congress with maintaining the area in a truly natural state. They have taken the mandate seriously. They have allowed no hunting; no natural living thing is killed unless human lives are endangered. The trees live, die, and fall in an environment undisturbed by ax or saw.

Only in fishing has there been any variation in that basic rule, any killing or consumptive use. The park managers began with 2.2 million acres that straddle the Continental Divide and contain some of America's finest trout streams. Free by their mandate to manage with vision rather than political expedience, they have produced the kind of fish populations the Indians might have known. The waters are totally unpolluted. The fish are durable, and completely adapted to their surroundings. The anglers, who come to Yellowstone from all corners of the United States and abroad, are the happiest in the world.

Picture yourself arriving at Buffalo Ford on the Yellowstone River. The day has been warm and the evening promises to be cool and comfortable. The wind is still. You find a dozen fishermen spread out in the two hundred yards in your vision. You test the depth and find you can wade the river without filling your chest waders. Once across, you ease upstream to a long, glassy run. Now you can see only three fishermen on your side of the river and seven on the roadside of the stream across from you.

You see rises in the oily-smooth flow of the run; the trout are taking very small flies on the surface. Most of the anglers are using fly rods, but two are using spinning tackle and casting lures. Any type of tackle is permitted, as long as you use only artificial lures with one hook. That hook may be a single, double, or treble.

You start with a #16 Spider and miss a rise. Although you cover several more rising fish, they spurn your fly, often rising just beside it to take a natural. You retrieve the Spider and clip it severely on top and bottom and try again. You hook a fish that turns out to be a typical Yellowstone River cutthroat 16 to 17 inches long. He fights hard, but stays under water. With your 6X leader, you play him carefully until it's time for a moment of admiration and a quick, careful release. The release is part of the regulations; you have used the fish once, but he belongs to the river.

The trout turn picky again. You reach for your scissors and this time trim the Spider down to almost nothing, leaving only two fibers on each side. You catch three more fish, two about 16 inches long. The third looks like 20 inches as you hold it briefly before release.

There are half-a-dozen fish still rising occasionally within the area you can cast to without encroaching on the anglers below and above you. A few trout come up under your fly and turn down again without taking. You try a #20 Adams and it doesn't work. Then you try a fly Tim Bywater gave you; it's called a Hank of Hair. Just a few fibers of bucktail on a #16 hook. No hackle. No body.

The first fish you cast to takes it. After that one, nothing will come to your fly. The growing darkness encourages you to retrace your steps. You find your way back across the Buffalo Ford while there's still a little light left in the sky.

You have experienced an evening of exacting, magnificent fishing on a stretch of river that provides great sport for 4,000 anglers per mile per year. The regulation that set this stretch aside for catch-and-release fishing with artificial lures only caused anguish among anglers at first. In fact, there was a 50 percent drop in the number of anglers per mile per season. Now the fishermen are back in their old numbers, content with the new rules.

Yellowstone's move into great management started more than ten years ago, under the guidance of a far-seeing conservationist, Park Superintendent Jack Anderson. Anderson had the courage of his convictions; one of his early steps was closing the famous Fishing Bridge to all fishing.

Fishing Bridge crosses the Yellowstone River where it empties out of Yellowstone Lake, at one of the prime spawning areas for the lake's cutthroat trout. Hundreds of fish can be seen from the bridge, many of them resting in long lines in the eddies of the bridge supports.

The bridge was a famous point for anglers to congregate. They fished not only for the cutthroats that rested or spawned near the bridge, but for all those that passed under the bridge on their way to spawn below or return to the lake. The bridge was by far the park's most productive and popular fishing spot. At its peak, it yielded two hundred pounds of trout per acre per year.

It was obvious to Anderson that the cutthroat population could not continue to take the pressure. The typical American habit is to keep the biggest and best of the fish, and return the runts for breeding stock. Given that habit, there was bound to be a net loss, both in numbers of fish and in the size of the individual fish. Most fishery managers would have sought some sort of compromise with the fishing public. Anderson, weighing the evidence, went whole hog and closed Fishing Bridge.

There was a great outcry from fishermen, but good explanatory public relations softened the blow. When the first year of nonfishing arrived, the bridge was lined with fish watchers who seemed delighted just to see the fish and their spawning. The frustrated anglers among them could realize, as they watched, how many fish there were to be caught, either in the lake or in the river below the spawning area. Fishing *is* permitted there, and that's where the fish at the bridge eventually wind up.

Another unpopular regulation also went into effect in 1973. It permitted the taking of only two trout per day from Yellowstone Lake, and those had to be *less* than 13 inches. Park managers saw the need for building a spawning population of large, high-quality fish. Anglers howled, but they kept right on fishing the lake in the same numbers as before.

Although the lake now yields fewer fish to eat, the pleasure of fishing the lake satisfies just as many or more anglers as before the limits were established.

Park managers are constantly examining and rethinking their regulations. The figure of 4,000 angler days per mile per season on the no-kill stretch of the Yellowstone River is a large one. I asked John Varley, a biologist on the park management team, if he thought they might ever have to limit the number of anglers on this stretch. He admitted it might be necessary. When the catch-and-release restriction first became effective and the angling pressure dropped to half, he said, "The grass had a chance to grow on the banks again, and the scene was much more natural. Now we're losing that naturalness again. We'd rather limit the angler's time a little than cut down on the beauty of this place and of the pleasure of fishing there."

Just below this great stretch on the Yellowstone lies the Hayden Valley. Here, for six miles, there is a sanctuary where no fishing is allowed. Hayden was closed to enhance park visitors' chances of seeing wildlife. In this sanctuary the fish are a little more visible, a little less afraid. And from this sanctuary may come the fish necessary to replenish the small losses among the fish on the catch-and-release stretch above. The studies on fish mortality under such rules have had an important effect on the park's regulations. There is something to be learned here, for all of us, because the studies explain the artificials-only regulations that cause so many fishermen pain.

The studies show, among fish caught and released, a hooking mortality of less than 10 percent for lures and flies, and from 30 percent to 70 percent for baited hooks. A study in Yellowstone Lake found no significant difference between barbed and barbless flies (4.0 percent and 3.3 percent respectively). For the baited hooks, mortality was 73.0 percent if the fish had been superficially hooked. Hooks baited with worms were swallowed 55.1 percent of the time; the overall estimated mortality for baited hooks was calculated at 40 percent.

It is interesting to note that the use of landing nets

increased hook removal time and mortality in general. Physical damage from struggling within the net was blamed for the greater mortality. No significant difference was found between the techniques of removing hooks by hand and with pliers.

It was from these data that lures were limited to artificials with one hook, whether single, double, or treble. There are no fly-fishing-only stretches, but because cutthroats are primarily insect eaters, the majority of the trout seem to be taken by fly fishermen.

The fishing regulations for the park are condensed to a single sheet with a map on the back. They include special streams for fishermen under twelve years old. Four streams—Gardner River, Obsidian Creek, Indian Creek, and Panther Creek—are maintained as special areas for young people. They, and they alone, can fish for trout with bait and keep five of them, brookies, regardless of size. There is serious consideration being given to eliminating the bait-fishing areas for the youngsters in 1978, however. The primary reason is that it is contrary to the basic philosophy of low-kill or no-kill. There is a feeling in the park's management that discouraging meat-gathering among the young will pay greater dividends in the long run. And last year, only 400 kids out of 15,800 fishing in the park took advantage of these special areas.

The bill that made Yellowstone our first national park passed Congress on March 1, 1872. At that time, the park contained three cutthroat subspecies, one native to each of the three great drainages. The Montana grayling and the mountain whitefish were the only other fish. At that time, 40 percent of the park's beautiful waters were fishless because of falls and other barriers.

The management began introducing exotics. Brown trout (Loch Leven type) were planted in the barren Lewis and Shoshone lakes in 1889. Brook trout were introduced to the Gardner River system. Rainbows came to the Firehole and Gibbon rivers in 1890. Some German Von Behr trout were also introduced to the Firehole. There were some Atlantic salmon plants in 1909, but they didn't take. Neither did many other exotic, nontrout species. The park waters were great for trout, and fortunately for trout fishermen, the alien species did not flourish.

The Montana grayling, originally a river fish according to biologist Varley, suffered serious depletion in the early days. Only a few survive in the rivers, but the grayling have changed habitat to live as well in some small lakes in the park. One of the park management's main objectives is to reconstruct that species as a fluvial, or river, fish, and bring it back to an approximation of its early abundance.

The cutthroats, which were plentiful in practically all the park's fishing waters, have suffered from the introduction of non-native trout species. Last summer my wife, Joan, and I fished the Blacktail Ponds, small ponds in a wild meadow setting. We caught brook trout. In the beginning, there were just a few rising fish. They were well out from shore, but as dusk settled in, the fish moved inshore and the surface activity increased. The few fish we caught in sunlight were 6 or 7 inches long. As dusk turned toward dark, larger fish began to hit my nymph or streamer, and I released ten fish, the largest of which was 13 inches. It was a pleasant evening on a very accessible but very wild and natural pond. Another angler there, fishing spinning gear, was getting trout for his camper table. The general two-fish limit on all but no-kill waters is expanded here to five trout—if they are brook trout. Five are enough for a camp table.

I found out later from Varley that the Blacktail Ponds had originally been cutthroat waters. The brookies, being fiercer competitors, had taken over completely. I asked if there were any thoughts or plans afoot to return the ponds to the native cutthroats. He said, "Not at the moment, but it might be done by stocking the old, wild strain and keeping some of them while killing all the brook trout caught." That would probably take twenty years or more, about the same number of years it took the brookies to obliterate the native fish that had been there for thousands of years.

I asked John Varley if he'd really like to see the park back to where it was in 1872. He sighed and said, "Yes. But it isn't possible. We'll favor the native species over the exotics whenever there's a conflict ... and we believe the cutthroat is as fine a trout as any other. But in 1872 there was a lot of barren water here and the exotic trout are just too well established, I think, for us ever to wipe them out."

The rainbows, also interlopers, have flourished in many areas. They've done particularly well in the Firehole. To strike one of these flashing fish in this river, while the geysers spout and fume in the background, is one of angling's special thrills. Rainbows, Varley points out, are very adaptable. In the Firehole, they have changed their breeding habits 180 degrees, and now spawn in December instead of in the spring. Rainbows can stand higher temperatures than the browns. The brown trout just hang on in the Firehole, and they haven't changed their life-style one bit. The rainbow has adapted to an environment that will reach 90 degrees F. on summer days. The rainbows are able to spawn in the main stream, while the browns must travel up beyond Old Faithful, or push into some of the small, cooler tributaries to find a natural spawning situation.

Meadow streams like the upper Gibbon are ideal for brown trout. There they find deep pools and undercut banks. The water is slow and the angler needs a lot of stealth coupled with fine leaders and casting accuracy to be sure of success. Small fly hatches are the order of the day, but grasshoppers and large stonefly nymphs are consistent brown-takers.

As I waded up to the tail of a still deep pool on the Gibbon, I looked back across a neck of land to where Joan was fishing, and I saw the antlers of an elk. He was resting in the shade on the small peninsula that separated us. He showed no fear, watching us as we watched him. I stood knee deep in the cool water and moved slowly, casting carefully. I dropped my hopper fly beside a projecting log and was fast to a brown. The elk showed no emotion as I brought the fish in.

The Madison has some similar meadows stretched within the park but most of its water moves with a fair amount of speed. It slides, it runs, it ripples over a rocky bed between the quiet areas where there is weed growth and lots of insect life. The glassy waters call for ultrafine leaders, for the fish are well educated by many captures. The rough water permits coarser leaders and, perhaps, less perfect imitations. They may be hard to catch but the best thing about these catch-and-release waters is that *the fish are there*. The trout populations in catch-and-release waters are likely to amaze anglers who are used to consumptive fishing.

Slough Creek is one of the catch-and-release streams. It has a lazy flow in normal times, with pools much too deep to wade except in the riffles or along the bank sides of the pools. It cuts through a meadow and digs deep caves under the banks for trout to hide in. It runs cool even in midsummer and it's populated by cutthroats and rainbows or hybrids of the two. For years it has been building up its stock of fish.

Two years ago I fished Slough Creek in September. I had just returned from a very successful fishing trip in Alaska. The rainbows in Bristol Bay drainage had run well up toward the 10-pound mark. There had been a lot of them, fish that were in their normal lies and would respond eagerly to any reasonable fly.

To move from a wild, productive Alaskan stream to Slough Creek, where many hundreds of anglers fish in a season, might seem to have been a letdown. But it was not. Slough Creek holds a few trout big enough to match the Alaskans, but most were in the 16-inch to 19-inch range. The difference lay mostly in the wariness of the Slough Creek fish and the quality of the fishing problem.

Cast a fly out to a good lie in a good presentation and the smart Slough Creek trout will not move unless he can't see the leader. If it's a moderately fine leader he may swim up under it to make sure the fly is a trick. Only if the fly is particularly tempting and the leader quite fine will he be fooled.

I caught and released a dozen fish that afternoon, good fish in the 1½-pound to 3-pound range. Some took a grasshopper plopped down at the edge of an overhanging bank. More took a midge on a #22 hook. There were several on #18 nymphs and one took a big black Woolly Worm I worked through, slow and deep. Each was a triumph calling for a plan and a good execution of it. When the afternoon was over

269

I felt a greater pride and satisfaction as a skillful angler than I had on the best day of my Alaskan trip.

Alaska offered the pure enjoyment of wild and untutored trout in completely natural surroundings. Slough Creek was fishing for wild *and wily* fish under very natural stream conditions. The first was typical of the great fishing of the past. Slough Creek was typical of the great fishing of the future.

[1978]

31

No Place
to Hide

*As an experiment last fall on the upper Connecticut
River in far northern New Hampshire, I put away my
fly rod and took up an ultralight spinning outfit rigged
with hairline monofilament having a breaking strength
of about 2 pounds. I had a small collection of wobbling
spoons that were relatively heavy for their short length
and, knowing they'd sink quickly in the fast water,
went to work. The results were remarkable. Trout holding in the deep, fast runs at the heads of pools—trout
that I could never reach with a floating fly line—came
all day long to the spoon as it fluttered near the bottom.
I released all the fish unharmed but left the river feeling
uncomfortable, as if I'd invaded someone's living room
uninvited.*

*I got a similar feeling not long ago on a Norwegian
salmon-fishing trip. Leo Postonen, my Swedish guide,
and I had spent two days fishing an immense pool by
conventional floating-line methods without even moving a fish, although we could see fish periodically as
they moved from deep to shallow water and back again.
I finally accepted his invitation to use a special very-*

271

fast-sinking fly line that would swing the fly 15 to 20 feet deep near the pool's bottom. I did very happily catch (and keep) a salmon in so doing, but am still left with the feeling that somehow I cheated. I remember wondering at the time what my friend Lee Wulff would have thought. And those very thoughts are his basis for this chapter.

John was a banker whom I'd just flown by seaplane from our Castors River, Newfoundland, camp, so that he might leave on the DC-3 from the Portland Creek camp. After we had landed he reached into a pocket, moved his hand around searchingly, and brought out everything the pocket had held. A puzzled look came over his face. His little gold-plated pocket knife was not there. Then, checking his wallet, he found that several bills were missing.

"Look, Lee," he said. "A half-emptied bottle of whiskey disappeared back at camp, but I didn't mention it. I think one of your guides may have helped himself from my wallet. I've had the knife a long time, and I'm careful. Its absence is suspicious, but there's always a slim possibility that I mislaid it somewhere."

I was back at the Castors River camp within an hour, and we searched. We'd never had a case of theft in the years the camp had been operating, and it was hard to believe any of my guides would steal. But one had done so. We'll call him Andy.

Unmarked money can't be traced, but the little knife gave him away. We found it jammed into the moss between the logs beside his bunk. Andy was fired and never forgiven. At the start of the next season, he pleaded to have his job back, but his theft had become common knowledge, and I feared my forgiving it might encourage another. When I refused, he said, "Okay, if you don't give me my job back I'll ruin the Trout Brook."

The Trout Brook, as we called it, flowed into the Castors River—a fine salmon river. It was spring fed and channeled through the gravel and clay in a fairly open course with occasional pools six or seven feet deep.

The Trout Brook was one of the two places in our wide-spread fishing area where I was certain any angler could catch a brook trout of 5 pounds or over. Naturally, I used the brook sparingly, taking few anglers to it, and then insisting that they keep only one or, at most, two fish.

At that time, 1951, Newfoundlanders were not required to buy a license for trout fishing and the limit on trout was 36 per angler per day.

After his threat, we could see Andy, accompanied by his two teenaged sons, pass up the trail to the brook in the morning and return in the evening. On their return, the empty burlap bags the trio had carried up in the morning were filled with trout. I could have given in, rehired Andy, and saved the Trout Brook, but only at the price of the respect of my men, and at the cost of opening up the operation to other types of blackmail.

The trout were vulnerable in that clear, open stream. They had *no place to hide*, nowhere to escape the constant bombardment of food and lures. Day after day, the loads came out as Andy and his boys, waving derisively, hiked past the camp. They caught trout with well-disguised hooks and cut bait, with worms, with flies, and with spoons. When a big one wouldn't take a lure or bait, they probably snagged him with a treble hook. The river was never the same again. It became almost barren of trout. Andy ruined it as he had promised and it was legally done.

The very vulnerability of the fish of the streams, as compared to those of the lakes, is why we, in America, first felt the pinch of diminishing quality-angling resources on our streams. The trout fishing in the settled areas went first. On our beautiful streams every fisherman knew where the trout had to be. In the riffles or the shallows he could see them, and if they weren't in either of those places they had to be in the deeper pools or runs, where a spinning lure or a weighted natural bait could reach any desired spot. In order to survive, any form of heavily preyed-upon wildlife needs a sanctuary or a guardian who watches carefully and gives protection. Every species needs a chance to restore its numbers when the population starts to diminish. Our stream management gave

273

the fish neither, and the streams were the first to fade, while the lakes still provided good fishing.

The increase in our technical capability to catch or eliminate a species outruns our protection and diminishes capability of the fish to recover from our catches.

Perhaps the most difficult and challenging of all gamefish is the Atlantic salmon. In North America the salmon may only be taken legally with an artificial, unweighted fly. As a basic nonfeeder, it takes a fly only because of a little-understood memory pattern or impulse. My earliest experiences with Atlantic salmon had been in Nova Scotia. There the fishing had been only fair, with anglers often outnumbering the fish they sought, and really spectacular catches had become a thing of the past. Ahead of me lay Newfoundland and its relatively untouched rivers.

The year was 1935. Already, at thirty, an unusual angling career lay behind me. My viewpoint, then, was as American as apple pie. I _knew_ the waters belonged to the people. The fish in them were mine to catch and, because I had become a very good fisherman, I felt, quite logically, that my share of fish should be a very good share.

I visited Jim Tompkins's Afton Farmhouse in Newfoundland. It looked out on a small meadow. Across the valley lay the lower end of the Long Range Mountains, and at the head of the valley lay the lake from which the Little Codroy flowed gently through the meadows and woodlots to reach the tidehead a mile away.

The Home Pool, Aggravation, The Widow's Run, Tompkins Nose, and all the other pools were listed on a blackboard on the porch. After each of the better pools, depending upon the number of angling guests at the time, an angler's name was written. This meant that each angler, by rotation, had, for the morning hours of that day, sole use of one of the best pools. In the afternoon or evening an angler might roam the river and fish wherever no other angler was either fishing or standing by to rest the pool.

For the first time my angling was being restricted, not by gentlemanly instincts but by hard-and-fast rule. I wasn't free to cover the river or to make an early start in order to cover much of the best water before anyone else. I felt a strong resentment, especially when for the first two mornings I drew pools from which I did not take a fish. I thought then that, because of the prevailing low-water conditions, there were very few fish in those particular pools. I know now it was because I was still relatively untutored as a salmon angler and had been counting on covering a lot of water instead of, as those conditions demanded, working hard over nonreceptive fish. I still had not advanced to the concept of the angler-versus-salmon duels that could last for hours or days—contests where an angler works on and studies a particular salmon, or group of salmon, with knowledge that leads to success.

In the afternoons and evenings I roamed the river, either with the guide that I shared with my angling companion, Victor Coty, or on my own. I did a little better then but had an underlying feeling that after the morning's fishing most of the fish in each pool had either been turned off or taken out. Though I caught a salmon a day, others were doing better.

The Little Codroy's relatively short, slow, meadow flow, with its lake sanctuary at the head, drew large salmon and 15-pounders were the average.

Grilse were extremely rare in those days when heavy competition from the big fish on the spawning grounds had given these "dwarfs" little chance to breed and survive. The really large fish eluded me. (Later on I was to see another angler's 39-pounder, freshly caught and glistening in the grass beside the Widow's Run, to confirm the size of a fish that, the day before, had risen for and missed my fly.)

Jim Tompkins, sensing my unhappiness, suggested a trip for us to the scenic Grand Codroy, a larger river.

We traveled by train and on a hand-pumped railcar to the upper pools of Six Birches and Seven Mile. The pools were fantastic. We *released* salmon and, though our guides were certain they would die, we marked some with a bit of string tied loosely around the tail and proved a 100 percent release recovery on the following mornings.

Back on the Little Codroy we found the fish still hard to take and, again, the old resentment returned. I wanted the right to fish any water, any time, and catch more salmon than anyone else at the farm. There seemed to be even fewer salmon in the pools and no new fish were coming in from the sea. I was in a troubled mood as my two-week trip neared its end. Through the long afternoon and early evening I fished the river down, missing dinner and skipping around the pools where other anglers cast or "sat the bank" to rest a pool. I worked on down the river until, at sunset, I came to the lowest pool in the river, Spruce.

Casting mechanically, with little hope of a rise, my resentment against the system of "private" morning fishing intensified. Jim Tompkins acted as if he were under the English system and "owned" the pools for the morning. Of course, anyone could fish in Newfoundland waters if they bought the $5 license required, but, on the Little Codroy there was no place else to stay—unless you were willing to bring your own camping outfit and supplies.

Newfoundland, then a colony of Great Britain, did not have a guide requirement for nonresidents as it does now. A lone individual rugged enough to camp out and live alone could take the cream from a good stretch of any river on the island. Why hadn't someone done that, here in the Little Codroy valley, I wondered. I'd camped out in Nova Scotia and we who camped out on the rivers had the best chance to put the first fly of the day over the best pool with its night-rested fish. We'd done it to the discouragement of the more casual anglers who came at midmorning.

I began to question this procedure. Were we, the effective fishermen, who fished hard and free wherever the fish could be found, part of the reason there were so few fish left in Nova Scotia rivers? Did we who gave them no rest and no sanctuary in pools take too many of this river remnant that had not been caught in nets? Did we fish too effectively and too hard?

Of course, I reasoned, the sea nets were to blame. They nearly blocked the rivers, giving little access for the fish. But once a smart, or lucky, salmon reached the river he could find a mate and reproduce unless an angler took him out. That was the key. How many, in actual numbers, reached the spawning grounds? Were the fishermen who last had the opportunity to save these spawning remnants to be judged morally wrong even though they might be technically in the right?

That was the answer! It didn't really matter what the system was as long as enough salmon reached the spawning ground to crowd and even overcrowd the beds with fertile spawn. Enough to fill the rivers . . . and more! Enough to put Darwinian pressure on survival to eliminate the dwarfs and weaklings in competition with the best of the breed.

While my thoughts had been wandering, the pool I was fishing had changed. The water had risen, imperceptibly at first, until I realized it had moved up from my knees, halfway to my hips. My eyes, which had been casually keeping my dry fly under surveillance, picked up a shadow moving just beyond its drift . . . and then another. I cast just ahead and watched a long, sleek fish swim undisturbed beneath the fly. Singly and in twos and threes, salmon came in with the rising tide to cruise the pool. Some settled to form dark gray patches on the reddish gravel of the sunken bars. Others continued to cruise up into the warm, shallow flow at the head of the pool and then, turning, circled back under the shadowed spruce, testing out in each upstream circuit the discomfort and danger of the path upstream.

I cast as swiftly as I could from one fish to another. I kept my fly over fish, the biggest I could see, for as long as possible, yet not one salmon showed any sign of interest. Darkness drew near and I gave up casting just to watch the phantomlike swimming of half-a-hundred Atlantic salmon. I felt a sadness at what I had just realized must come. The salmon were far more frustrated than I. In the long run, they were in mortal danger of being unable to maintain their existence in this, their home river. I realized then, for the first time, that because you were a law-abiding fly fisherman angling under democratic rules, you were still not without responsibility as to the percentage of the fish you took as a group from the river.

Added to my memories of Spruce Pool at twilight are many others. I remember Jim Tompkins, a big rawboned man with big, calloused hands, at a later date when we were both fully aware that the great days of salmon angling in Newfoundland were passing, that the Little Codroy's run was shrinking rapidly, both in size and number. I can still see Jim at the end of a long evening's discussion with tears streaming down his rugged face, knowing that mine could not long stay dry. We wept with our hearts for the salmon river that was dying; a river that he had lived by and loved for his entire lifetime; a river that I had come to know and love.

Jim Tompkins, whose angler guests fished that river, passed on before the river died. He did not live to learn, as I did, of a year in which the total angling catch of his beloved Little Codroy dwindled to a single grilse.

The river itself, as I saw it last, was still the same. The lake at the head was clear and clean in the sunlight. It flowed as it had for generations, though fresh green meadows where snipe still flew and geese came in the fall. There was no encroachment of modern civilization on its banks. It looked just as I remembered it on that first trip in 1935.

The salmon catch is coming up again. Slowly. The Trans-Canada highway crosses at its tidal waters and twists on to its eventual ending across the island at St. John's, bringing far more fishermen than the river can support. The future of the Little Codroy is still far from bright.

Whom can you blame? The anglers who took as many salmon as the law allowed? The poachers who added their catch numbers to the total? Or the wardens who failed to appre-hend them? The judges who failed the salmon when the guilty ones were brought before them and given suspended sentences or wrist-tap fines? The commercial netters who, through overfishing, took too many of the fish they preyed upon? Or management whose job it was to safeguard and keep productive that magnificent resource?

The old view of seemingly unlimited quantities of a species has fooled a lot of well-meaning people. I can recall sitting on the bank of an Atlantic salmon river in 1941 and having a warden supervisor say, "Mr. Wulff, you wouldn't believe the number of salmon that come into this river. The sea is full of them offshore in June. They'll never catch them out."

But they did. They took so many that there weren't enough reaching the spawning beds to maintain the stocks. Then, in 1964, with the fish already established in a long decline, the fishermen of the sea found the salmon's sea sanctuary. The fact that the small stream-spawned fish went down to the sea and disappeared in its vastness had freed them from persecution until they returned to the shore waters of their native rivers or entered the rivers themselves. But when fishermen found the routes of the salmon's travel, then they found the ocean feeding grounds. As a result, salmon catches expanded, as the total numbers dwindled, then plummeted. Now, in most of Atlantic Canada all commercial fishing for the species is totally banned.

This same increasingly effective technology let us find and follow the great schools of fish in the sea, and to entirely eliminate the great herring run of the northeastern Atlantic that was a main support of the Icelandic fisheries. One factor in such a sea disaster was the introduction of nylon nets, invisible to the fish and far more effective than nets of twine had been. Had we limited ourselves to twine we might have saved some of the fisheries we have lost.

Similarly, in the Pacific, our advanced techniques let us find out where the big ocean fish fed in the depths, and let us take them on long lines, speedily handled with new mechanical devices. Meteorological advancements and computer-determined preferences of the big tuna schools of the Pacific have allowed the scientific commercial fishermen unerringly to find the greatest concentrations and capture them. The Pacific Ocean is 256 times as large as Texas (20 times as big as the United States, including Alaska), yet in this great area, Japanese fishing fleets regularly home in on the greatest schools of migrating tuna. Scientists tell us that through tagging we're learning the migration routes of the tuna as they cross the Pacific. It is a simple matter to follow these routes, locate the temperature the tuna like best, and, "Presto!" there are the tuna. Ready, crew?

These swift members of the mackerel family have been on earth since the Eocene period and have changed little in the intervening fifty million years. We can hope they'll flourish for another fifty million, yet we have to recognize our capability of depleting them to the point of extinction. Normally, our restraints tend to be too weak and too slow in developing. Instead of saying, "Let's try a limited use of this new, superior fish-taking device," we, as individuals, just say or do nothing. We theoretically rub our hands together in anticipation and say, "Now we can really make great catches of this seemingly inexhaustible resource."

Our lakes are mere pinpoints compared to the expanse of the Pacific. If the pelagic fish of the wide Pacific Ocean are threatened, then the threat to our lake fish, if we allow full or nearly full harvest, must be very real. These gamefish, the backbone of our angling resources, used to have a sanctuary. We saw them on the surface or in the shallows but when they swam into the depths we couldn't see or follow them. Except in the clearest of waters or in the weedless lakes, it was easy enough for a fish to disappear. Learning to read the bottom was a matter of hours of trial and error, of taking depth measurements with an anchor or a deep-trolled lure. Students of a lake marked charts and remembered where the best feeding places for fish were and at what depth. Such things as the type of weed that caught on a lure when it was snagged were noted and remembered. Learning to know a lake was a long, enduring labor of love.

Then our increasing technology came into play. Outboard motors made it easier to troll, to cover more water. We began to get some idea of where the lake fish hid when scuba divers went exploring and found them in schools at certain depths at certain times. These aids were minor. A scuba diver could, if he found bass, lead an angler to them but, for the most part, anglers still had to rely on intuition or luck.

This no longer is true. A good look at today's bass boats and their equipment shows that an angler no longer needs to be intuitive or lucky. He must simply be able to read and reason. Each of these boats carries a depth finder, an instrument to read the temperature at any depth and another to read the oxygen content at any depth.

Those three things, depth, temperature, and oxygen content, don't tell you where the bass *is* as much as they tell you where he *isn't*. You know he won't be in low-oxygen-content water. You know he won't want it too hot or too cold. You know that he won't want to be on a flat, weedless lake bed if he can find one of the areas of unusual "structure" that a depth finder will show you.

It's easy to eliminate great sections of the lake in that way. Knowing where he won't be tells you where the fish *must be* to be comfortable. The depth reader, taken over the acceptable water, will pinpoint the structure, the type of topography bass prefer. It will put you over the old riverbed at just the right depth. It will show you the drop-offs and sunken ridges that please both the bass and the things they feed on. Go there, and your boat's electronic wizardry may even actually spot the fish for you. With *no place to hide*, these fish can be reached by the well-equipped angler with an endless variety of lures and baits, day after day. Their chances of escaping the ever-growing numbers of better-equipped anglers have grown very small and, with the aid of improving electronics and increasingly effective tackle, the angling pressure becomes more deadly each year.

This great and sudden expansion of fishing areas and angling potential has given many people the idea that these great impoundments are impossible to fish out. They seem endless and inexhaustible to American anglers. Surprisingly, some biologists are quoted as saying, "Fishing pressure can't hurt a big *lake*," even though they read almost daily what commercial fishing pressures are doing to the fish of the *oceans*. But the fishing pressure is building and building. Does it remind you of the statements of the whalers? "The resources of the sea are limitless." "The oceans are so vast that mere man can't deplete them."

It is foolish to try to stop progress or damn the natural increase in our electronic and other capabilities that develops with time. We should not have stopped outboard motors or fiberglass hulls or electric trolling motors at the start. Our job is to learn to evaluate the destructive powers they give and, with wise planning, learn to live with the new, more deadly capabilities they give the angler.

We must accept the truth because our lake fish, like the stream fish before them, now have no place to hide. We may safely expand our fishing and our pleasure, but there are good reasons to go slow in expanding our total kill. The great fishing we now enjoy on these large impoundments is vulnerable—as all wildlife is vulnerable—to overharvest.

The one management tool that can keep us from following the normal pattern and depleting the seemingly inexhaustible supply of fine gamefish in our lakes is the policy of releasing a larger and larger share of our catch. In this way the increased ability to take fish out can be balanced perfectly with the need to keep fish in.

In spite of some resentment against the increasingly popular bass tournaments, their managers have been among the first to realize the necessity of maintaining the stocks of fish. They concentrate large numbers of exceptionally gifted anglers on a particular fishing water. If they were to keep all the limits they catch, the effect would be disastrous. Instead, they have developed a policy of returning the great bulk of their fish unharmed to the waters from which they were taken. This policy provides considerable sport and pleasure for both anglers and audience and will do less harm than does the average quota of fish-keeping anglers that normally fish a lake. At the Miller High Life B.A.S.S. Masters Classic tournament held recently at Clark Hill Reservoir in South Carolina, twenty-six contestants proved their competence by capturing 620½ pounds of largemouth bass in three eight-hour fishing days. Of these, 88.6 percent of the fish were brought in alive and released safely after weigh-in.

The path to ruin is easy to follow. It is slow and often uneven. In the long run, while proponents and opponents argue the relative scarcity and the need for smaller limits, the old outdated catch-and-keep rules still hold. The controls are too little and too late. This has been the pattern with too many of the things we have loved and wanted to keep . . . from haddock to herring, from passenger pigeons to whales. When anyone tells you to catch all you can of any species and *keep* them, using the most modern gear available, you may be certain they're dooming the fish you love to relative scarcity or ultimate ruin.

(This story was written especially for those who read a recent article of mine that questioned our general American management policies. Following its publication I received considerable mail, most of it favorable. In large measure the unfavorable reactions came, I think, from either a misunderstanding of my words or my failure to be explicit enough. For those who have a continuing interest in our management policies I would like to point out that nowhere in the article did I say that I was in favor of private ownership of angling waters or against public angling for our country. Instead, I wrote that Europe's private ownership system was working better than our democratic public one and that, within our democratic view of equal sharing of our fishing and widespread public use, our only chance of equaling the private system's quality was to *release* our fish, particularly the biggest and best. Shortly after my experience at Spruce Pool, I wrote that "a good gamefish is too valuable to be caught only once." I believe it is still worth repeating.

Nowhere in that article did I say we should not keep *any* fish, or that all waters should be managed for the highest quality of sport. I did say that selectively killing off the big fish and putting the small ones back to breed could only result in a dwarfing of this species, and that hand-feeding of trout in hatcheries for many generations would weaken or eliminate their ability to survive under difficult conditions.

I failed to ask one simple question and I ask it now. How does the catching and killing of a good gamefish in his prime of life improve the quality of the fishing within the waters

283

from which it was taken? It means there is just one less fish to catch. The angling quality of the water *must be considered poorer* for its loss. Fishing a half-filled stream can never equal the joy of fishing a stream filled with all the gamefish it can hold.)

[1974]

32

The Old Ways

Even as North American colonists emigrated from a landed aristocracy that controlled, among many other things, the utilization of fish and game in western Europe, they brought with them a concept of field sports rooted in the fifteenth century and earlier. Manuscript fragments in English, German, and French from the fourteenth, fifteenth, and sixteenth centuries clearly show the development of rules and codes of conduct all designed to make the most of both skill and luck in the taking of fish and game.

Unfortunately, this imported attitude toward field sports didn't prevent the decimation of, for example, American Atlantic salmon stocks during the nineteenth century. But I believe it is that ancient attitude of respect for one's quarry that has persisted and is in part responsible for the millions of dollars we now spend in trying to reconstruct those stocks during the 1990s.

A visit to Scotland can take you deep into angling's roots. On our recent trip, Joan and I stayed at two castles that now

operate, at least in part, as inns. Like many such, they were
built long ago by royalty, who maintained them year-round
for just a month or two of use when the sport in their surroundings was at its peak. The castle lands and waters
stretched for miles and miles in every direction. The rich
were very rich and the poor were very poor.

It is difficult to look at these sports in Europe with American eyes and understand them. Fish and game belonged to
the kings and the sport they provided was for the royalty.
This gave hunting and fishing an artificial dignity we Americans have never known. It was part of the Pilgrim's pride that
here every man was a king and that the game belonged to
every man. In Europe, the select few were proud to have the
right to hunt and fish because it marked them as part of an
elite. This continued—in a lesser degree—even as the great
estates were broken up by time and taxes, and the new land-
owners took over the hunting and fishing rights.

In America, by contrast, hunting and fishing were practiced as much by the poor for subsistence as by the well-to-do
for pleasure. Some of the special prestige of the field sports
was lost. As the "government of the people" took over most
all of the waters and much of the land, these sports became a
"right" of the poor rather than a privilege of the wealthy. In
America as well, the taking of the game or the fish, while
holding to some traditions, was subject to many variations
and the "getting" often became more important than the
method used.

But in Europe, methods and equipment were developed
as a fine art. In Britain, for example, Atlantic salmon fishing
reached its peak of tradition and complexity at the peak of
power of the British Empire, in the late years of the last
century and the first years of this one. Britons aboard naval
and merchant ships scoured the world for the finest of
feathers and other fly materials. Skilled craftsmen created
complicated and extremely beautiful fly patterns. They were
so painstakingly tied that today, like the armor and weapons
of knights of old, they are made only by a few dedicated
craftsmen, and they are to look at and to admire rather than
to use. The names of the flies linger on, but a Jock Scott or a

Silver Wilkinson bought in a sporting-goods store today is a far cry from the beautifully crafted symphony of colored feathers, silk, and tinsel of those great days of salmon angling.

We Americans, with our innovations and our dedication to bringing the best of everything—including angling—to all our people, have cut corners on tradition. Our main thought has always been effectiveness rather than preservation of a sport or its traditions. We have simplified and improved equipment. We have developed new techniques and methods.

To visit a castle on Scotland's Spey, one of the world's most famous salmon rivers, and to stay at Tulchan Lodge or Revack Lodge, with their magnificent oil paintings of early owners and of great sporting scenes, to see the reverence with which hunting and angling are still regarded, can be a refreshing experience for an American sportsman. On the Revack Lodge water of the Spey, each beat has its own gillie. That gillie will know his own small stretch of water—and understand the salmon in it—far more intimately than any roving guide can ever know an entire river.

Perhaps there is a fault with British salmon angling, one that is carried over from the great days when angling was most glorious and effective: an unwillingness to change, to try new things. It gave me delight to hook a salmon and to raise two others on a #16 skater, a fly completely foreign to British salmon angling—and to do it even though the fish were dour and the water lower than ever before in the memory of living man.

In 1962 I caught salmon on the Dee, another famous Scottish river, with a technique new to Great Britain—the hitched, or skimming, wet fly. By this time, twenty-three years later, I expected the riffling hitch to be universally known and frequently practiced in British waters, as it is in Iceland, Norway, and, of course, Canada, where it originated. But apparently it is not. Their fishing methods, although well suited to their special conditions, seem old-fashioned to us. They use longer rods and the Spey casts (special roll casts), which we rarely use, may be their most common type of presentation. They often fish beats where the trees crowd in on the river behind them and the space needed for conventional overhead back casting just isn't available. Their salmon, too, are different from those on this side of the ocean. They rarely rise to a dry fly. They don't jump as frequently when hooked. Perhaps most important, the spread of time through which the salmon enter their rivers covers most of the year, sometimes from January to November.

The biggest difference between British fishing and ours lies in their system of ownership and management. Their methods have been seasoned by centuries of experience and through relatively stable populations—compared to our far shorter time period and our constantly expanding population of people and fishermen. Theirs is a system of ownership of waters and fishing rights, whereas ours is based almost completely on public ownership and government management. When an individual or a corporation owns a river, great care is taken to maintain its fishing quality, for if fishing drops off, the value drops, too, and there is a heavy financial loss. When an American river suffers damage or depletion, few individuals and no corporations suffer any financial loss. Instead it is our children who are the big losers, and they have no votes and no voice in the river's control.

On our side of the Atlantic we try to hold down the number of fish taken (by the relatively unlimited numbers of licensed anglers permitted to fish) by restricting the methods, the time of the open season, and the cost of the license. Because our rivers are open to so many anglers, we must have much stricter catch limits than the British have. Actually, they rarely have any catch limit; in truth, they do not need any. The private owners make sure the rivers are not overfished.

I was amused to hear recently that one of the fine anglers' groups of New York had passed a resolution requesting that the British set limits on the number of fish an angler could take in a day or a season. They were upset by reports of a single sportsman taking a dozen or more salmon in a single day! That's pure sour grapes—*If I can't, I don't want you to!* Just because we, under our system of public fishing and heavy pressure, cannot allow it doesn't mean that they can't or shouldn't. The key factor in stream management is *numbers*. If the number of salmon allowed to reach the spawning beds is sufficient, the run will maintain itself. If it is not, the salmon will decline. It doesn't matter at all whether the salmon that are taken are taken by one individual or by a hundred or by a thousand. It doesn't matter whether they are taken by angling or blown up by dynamite. Management is pure numbers. With their time-tested system, the British probably enjoy better management than we do. Our managers don't have the guts to say, "This river can spare X fish to angling; when that number is killed, all angling ceases." Instead they play games with methods, license fees, and seasons, with a slim hope that they have pleased everyone and will still come out with a fair measure of conservation. British owners can manage each river separately to maintain maximum productivity.

A visit to a place like Scotland can be an education for an angler. He may not like the idea of trout or salmon being taken by spinning gear and bait or hardware. He may not like the limitations private ownership puts on angling. But he can learn to understand a different system that has worked well for a long, long time. He can look deep into angling traditions, and he can meet dedicated fishermen and talk with them about their fish and their fishing methods. Anglers, regardless of the system they fish under, have much in common. The love of the sport can take them across the barriers of politics and national goals.

[1985]

33

Catch and Release

Last fall I paid a brief visit to Seventh Heaven, which in this case happened to be an ebb tide chock-full of striped bass within reach of an easy cast. Along Cape Cod's outer beaches, where I happened to be, and throughout much of its range, a "keeper" bass must be 33 inches long or larger and the bag limit is only one or two fish. This recent development ensures that most stripers will have spawned at least once before being killed and that the days of loading one's pickup truck with a thousand pounds of dead stripers from a rare surfside blitz are over.

I looked behind me and saw a man, woman, and small boy watching as I released yet another small bass. The boy watched wide-eyed, and I was glad of that. The woman asked if they weren't good to eat and why was I letting it go. So I explained to her what I just explained to you, adding that small bass are indeed delicious but more valuable alive than dead. The boy's father asked slyly if game wardens ever came along the beach, which made me feel sorry for the boy.

Catch and release has become increasingly popu-

*lar in recent years, even to the extent of having various
symposia devoted to the topic, where its applications
may be debated at length. For all the discussion, many
people still seem to miss a basic and immutable fact:
Once you keep and kill a fish—any fish of any kind—
it's gone. Period.*

The year was 1935 and the river the Grand Codroy in Newfoundland. I was playing my second salmon of the afternoon,
a 12-pounder, bright and fresh. Near us, in a scooped-out
puddle at the river's edge to keep it from drying out, lay my
first one, almost as large. My guide moved forward with the
gaff but I motioned him back, saying, "I'm going to tail this
one and release it."

His face darkened. "It will only die," he said. "It's like
throwing it away, and my kids are hungry."

"I gave you a salmon," I replied. "That should be enough
for a good meal."

"I need this one, too. I've got two kids. Besides, I've got
my dogs to feed. If you put it back it will die and be wasted."

There was a small dead water nearby, a pool 1½ feet
deep and 20 feet across, left beside the main river when the
water dropped. I hand-tailed the fish and released it into that
little pool. "We'll come back in the morning," I said, "and if
it's dead it will still be good to eat. If it's alive I'll put it back
into the river."

Next morning when we returned the salmon was so
lively we had a tough time catching it and getting it back over
the thirty feet of gravel to the river. It's amazing how determined the old-time guides (and most anglers) were to believe
that no salmon, played and released, could survive. Of
course, behind it lay their wanting all the fish an angler
himself did not need.

Another time, we were making a salmon-fishing "short"
for Warner Brothers on the St. Jean River in Quebec. We
usually had some spectators, and all of them were dismayed
and disbelieving when I returned a 30-pounder to the river.
"It will die," they all agreed.

The filming was at a bridge pool where the salmon were

291

easily visible in the crystal water. That particular salmon had a deformed right pectoral fin, which twisted away from its body at a unique angle, making the fish easily identifiable. The citizenry were amazed to see that fish swimming right along with the others the next day, and the next, and so on for a week, until a rain raised the river and the heavier flow beckoned them all upstream.

Through the years I can recall hundreds of such instances, where stubborn people took a lot of convincing that released salmon or steelhead, both big, hard-fighting fly-rod fish, would survive. At my fishing camps on Portland Creek, in Newfoundland, I regularly carried salmon from the camp pool for 100 yards to a small pool beside the cookhouse and released them there. Before we had refrigeration, that was our way of keeping them fresh and ready for the kitchen. (And the incoming guests, of course, were fired up to go fishing when they saw those big salmon lying there in the slow flow and realized there were a lot more like them waiting in the river.) Not one in one hundred died from the playing *or* the 100-yard carry by the tail.

Some voices are now saying that a salmon shouldn't be lifted by the tail, much less carried, if he's to live when released. I'm sure they've never done any research to back up the statement, and apparently don't know that obstetricians routinely lift newborn babies by their feet in recommended exercises. It's amazing how so many obviously ridiculous postulates are made by sentimental people who never really check out their proclamations.

I'll admit it's possible to kill a salmon or steelhead by playing it too long and handling it too roughly, but reasonable care in playing and releasing will give the fish almost certain opportunity for survival. As a onetime cross-country runner, I can remember how we ran till we felt we couldn't take another step, dropped to the grass to rest, and were running again a few hours later. If exhaustion killed animals, then every horse that put his heart into a race would die at the finish line. Salmon or steelhead played with reasonable speed, and not gill-damaged or abused by pulling them out onto the shore or into the bottom of a canoe (where sand and dirt can get into their gills), or holding them out of water long enough to suffocate them, are almost certain to survive.

There are still people who contend that catch and release will not work, but fortunately they are in the minority now.

Catch and release has finally been accepted by governments in Canada as well as the United States. Some seven years ago Nova Scotia decreed that all early-run full-grown salmon in the Margaree River must be released to go on to the spawning grounds, in order to increase the numbers of large salmon. The program was successful. In the last two years Canadian fisheries and ocean-management officials have insisted on catch and release by anglers (not commercial netters) as a way of letting the biggest and best breeders reach the spawning ground while allowing anglers to keep the grilse, which are likely to reproduce their own kind. They are making up, finally, for the decades of management that permitted, even insisted, that commercial netters take the biggest and best stock while letting the smallest fish through to breed.

Catch and release is now revitalizing the Canadian Atlantic salmon runs. Last year on the Restigouche, for example, more full-size salmon were reported on the spawning beds than had been seen there in years. This year indications are that the reports will be even better. That means a brightening future for our Atlantic salmon anglers for the first time in many decades.

Some opponents of catch and release said that if people couldn't keep their salmon, they simply wouldn't buy licenses, and so the funding for conservation would suffer. They claimed that the people who owned the expensive fishing wouldn't open those camps if salmon couldn't be killed, which would put a lot of guides and private wardens out of work. But these things didn't happen. Many of the anglers who opposed it most vigorously have become its strongest boosters. Now when they see a big salmon swim away after they've captured it, and realize that that salmon is almost certain to spawn and put more big salmon into their river a few years down the line, they get the fine, warm feeling that they're making a real contribution to their sport.

The province of Quebec, which makes its own salmon regulations, allows an angler one fish a day, salmon or grilse, on most waters; but where salmon are plentiful it allows an angler to keep more, sometimes as many as four a day. It is reasonable that the harvest should be allotted according to the productivity of each river, with the most stringent regulations in effect where the runs are the lowest. In Nova Scotia, New Brunswick, and Newfoundland, where salmon regulations are determined by the federal government, the angler may not keep a full-grown salmon, and he is limited to two grilse a day. All fish over 24 inches must be returned unharmed to the rivers. (The 24-inch length is an arbitrary definition of a grilse; actually a grilse is simply a salmon that has returned to the river after only one year at sea, but its size may vary, making field determination difficult.) Anglers dare not weigh their large fish for fear of reducing their chances for survival unless they can weigh the salmon in the net, then measure the net and subtract its weight. Most anglers just guess or take a quick measurement and judge the weight from the length. It's amusing to note that under these regulations the average size of the fish reported in the angling logs has increased considerably. A 30-inch salmon, which normally weighs about 10 pounds, is often rated as 15 in the logbook after its release.

"How big do you think it is?" breathes the angler, as he and his guide look at the trophy resting in the net.

"That's a beautiful salmon," says the guide.

"Think he'll go twenty pounds?" says the angler, who hasn't had much experience judging weights.

Instead of saying, "Twenty? That's an eleven-pounder if I ever saw one," the guide mumbles, "He's a real nice salmon, maybe you're right."

The fish swims away and everyone is happy.

It is reasonable to allow an angler one trophy fish a season, and to have one of his allotted tags so designated. That will help bring weights back to reality, and it's likely to happen in 1986.

Some large salmon are still being taken in the commercial nets. The Indians are still allowed large salmon in their quotas. It's patently unfair to let any group take large salmon if the anglers, those who have done the most for conservation, are denied even one fish each. There are still some bugs to be worked out in the regulations. They allow unlimited catch and release until the angler has caught and kept his second grilse. This recognizes that "fishing" rather than "catching" is the essence of our sport. An angler hopes to be able to do a lot of fishing on his vacation; if he catches his one salmon in Quebec, or his two grilse in the other provinces, in the first hour of fishing, he's through for the day—if released fish count against his limit.

Some anglers are against unlimited catch and release because they feel it lets a dog-in-the-manger angler get to the best spot in the pool and stay there all day. Such people do create problems, but I believe they could be solved in a way that doesn't deny people the pleasure of more fishing. A fisherman on public water who is approached by another and asked to move on down the pool could by law be granted only a certain amount of time in which to do so. (Enforcement would be easy because the requesting angler would certainly report any breaches of the law and etiquette.)

Another side effect of catch and release (and the insistence by some river groups that released fish be counted against one's daily limit) has been the use of lighter leaders. Just as the salmon is coming to the net, extra pressure by the angler will break the tippet and set the fish free so it need not be counted as "caught." Some who changed found that the challenge of playing fish on light leaders became more important than making the capture of the fish as certain as possible.

Catch and release has given us fishing where we would otherwise have lost it. Instead of shorter seasons to curtail the numbers of fish taken, we have full seasons with limited takes. It is far better to have fishermen present on the rivers than to leave them deserted for the poachers. Catch and release has proven its value in Atlantic salmon conservation; it has come of age as a management tool.

I see great days ahead for Atlantic salmon fishing. The salmon will be brought back to good numbers. There is a good chance that the Atlantic salmon will be officially named a gamefish in Maine and in Canada, which will secure its protection for all time. Of the $50 million the salmon is worth to Canada each year, $42.6 million is due to angling—and only $7.4 million to the commercial fishery, which takes more than 80 percent of the resource. Salmon are far more valuable to society if caught by angling, and there is no logical argument to prove that Canada benefits by a continuation of commercial fishing. If naming the Atlantic salmon a gamefish in Canada is not a benefit to their society, it will never come to pass; if it is beneficial, it is certain to happen eventually. A great many anglers are asking, "Why not now?"

[1986]

Book Four

QUIET WATERS

We've been through the rapid flows of tackle talk, fishing here and there, and working to preserve the quality of our fishing for the future. Now we've hit the quieter waters downstream in this book, and we've time to take a breath. Here we'll join Wulff as he reflects on places he's fished and some companions along the way.

You'll find a rare piece of Wulff's fiction in this section, and also discover the greatest disappointment of his long angling career. And as we exit through the last chapter, I invite you to share something that surprised me as much as anything I've ever seen him do.

34

The Old-Timer

*Outdoor fiction was a popular part of most of the hunt-
ing and fishing magazines during the 1930s and '40s
when Wulff's writing career had gotten into full swing,
but he wrote very little of it. This chapter is one of a very
few older fictional pieces that I'm aware of by Wulff,
which as far as I can tell has been the extent of his
fiction output.*

*Some local friends will recognize the Battenkill
River in this story. Wulff fans may likewise recognize
the narrative voice as belonging to Al Prindle, the
Shushan, New York, postmaster who was Wulff's frequent angling companion during the years they shared
the Battenkill.*

It seems that the Old-Timer has disappeared from the 'Kill
and every now and then someone has a new idea about the
manner of his passing. Ordinarily, when one of the real
lunkers of his size passes on someone finds his carcass, or
there's a rumor that he was speared, or shot, or even dyna-
mited by one of the local poachers. But there hasn't been a
sign of that big trout since early last season. He just vanished,

300

and lately three fish of around a pound and a half were taken from the slow run of water he used to keep clear of all other fish life.

I don't take much stock in the usual tales of how he might have been killed and eaten by a stray otter or one of the bald eagles they see once in a while, cruising high up over the river. I just let 'em rave on and smile a bit, because it happens that I'm one of the two fellows who know what really did happen to him. . . .

The whole thing was the result of the contest. The same bunch of fishermen have been coming down to Charlie Gunther's Hotel for years, and every Decoration Day they have a contest for the biggest fish. The first one was so long ago that I forget who started it, or why, but there's been a contest every year as long as I can remember. Out of deference to Charlie none of us local fishermen ever fish in the contest, so that those staying at his place have the old 'Kill to themselves. It's a lot to ask of a man to give up his favorite stream for a full day right in the height of the hatches, but there's not one of us that isn't indebted to Charlie for a lot of things. I'm not likely to forget the time he lent me enough to get that specialist for little Jimmy, or that it was his say-so that got me the job as postmaster so that now I finish work at three every day and can put in a lot more daylight on the old 'Kill than I used to.

The bed of the 'Kill scarcely changes from one year's end till the next, and all of us that fish it much know where the big ones hang out. They've all been hooked and lost enough to put a probable weight on them and to locate their hangouts pretty accurately. Although there are some rainbows and brookies in the river, the big ones are always browns. The brookies don't seem to be smart enough to live to a ripe old age and the rainbows always get the cruising urge and pull out downstream before they cross the 3-pound mark.

Some of my pleasantest memories are of sitting up in the big room at Charlie's while his regular patrons were talking over the whoppers and the chances of getting them when Decoration Day rolled around. Lately, though, the thing hadn't been quite the same. An old grouch named Ogilvie had been winning the honors for the past six years, and it got so nobody could say anything around Charlie's place without having Ogilvie contradict him.

Last spring was the first year, too, that Judge Dunn wasn't down. We missed that hearty laugh of his, but a man can't be across the Great Divide and down here, too. Young Dunn was up from college as usual and the rest of the same old crowd was on hand. There was one new man, a pleasant-looking chap named Black, who came up to stay in old Doc Sullivan's room when the Doc found he couldn't make it himself.

The place was filled for the full five days of the long weekend, but because we had a sudden cold spell the first few days, the fishing was miserable and everybody's nerves were a little jumpy. Added to that was Ogilvie's increasingly over-bearing manner and the way he ran down anyone else's methods or chances to cop the prize.

Oh yes, I forgot to mention the prize. It was always a trout rod, and a fine one. Charlie jacked up his prices for that week just enough to cover the fifty bucks for the rod, and believe me those rods have all been honeys: two-piece, 8- or 8½-foot sticks, with enough power to cast the 'Kill and all the delicacy it takes to handle a big brown on 4X gut. And there was Ogilvie with six of them. Every year he brought down all he'd won and most of them he didn't have time to use more than a couple of hours a season but he was too mean to give any away or to lend one out.

He's a good fisherman, all right, and as far as we knew he caught all his fish fair—that is, on flies as the understanding was. Last spring Ogilvie took a particular delight in finding faults in everything young Jack Dunn said and laughing at every idea he put up about trout fishing. The old Judge was the only one of them who could match Ogilvie's sharp tongue, and now that he'd passed on, his son was getting all the spite the old fellow had been saving up over the years.

It was at dinner on the twenty-ninth that the blowup came. Young Jack was getting hotter and hotter under the collar until finally they had some words and it ended up by their making a side bet on those six prize rods of Ogilvie's against the kid's car that Ogilvie would or wouldn't win the contest again. It was a dumb bet for the kid to make and all of us told him how foolish it was. We had him almost convinced to withdraw it when Ogilvie said, "Well, I suppose he might as well welsh now as later," and that settled it. The bet was on. The Judge didn't leave much and I remember thinking how much the kid would miss that car.

Although it was a miserable day for fishing, a few minutes later every one of the dozen of us that were there had picked up our rods and started off to escape the memory of the episode in the only way we could—by fishin'. I fell in step with this fellow Homer Black, the newcomer, and we walked down the railroad tracks together. He'd watched the kid fish some and didn't give him much chance of getting a big one, and neither did I. In fact, I would have bet on Ogilvie against the field, myself.

Not feeling much like fishing, I sat down and watched Black cover Miller's run from the gravel bar to the undercut bank with that little 8-foot rod of his. I was thinking about that scene up at Charlie's until it struck me with a wallop that this Homer Black had taken four nice brownies and released them and was into his fifth. Then I saw why. He was shooting his dry fly right in hard against the overhanging bank where the swallows nest and letting it drop to the water with enough slack in the leader where it fell to give him a good long float without any drag. I figured I was casting my limit and doing a swell job of fishing when I dropped my fly five feet short of the bank with my 9-foot rod and got a few feet of float before the drag started the fly to skidding.

That gave me an idea. The 'Kill is one of those crystal-clear streams where the fish can see you a hundred feet away. The average fisherman coming down here doesn't get much and soon gives up in disgust. It takes long casts and a quiet moving man to take the brownies. The current is deep and slow. Ripples will carry a long way and they've put down a lot of fish for the dubs, too. I thought of the Old-Timer. He was the biggest fish in the valley without a doubt, and I questioned whether any of the men up at Charlie's would try for him. They'd all tried too often and failed. He'd been hooked enough, but it was always by one of the locals that went down with a big gob of nightwalkers, heaved them out, and just sat and waited for three or four hours until he got around to taking them. They always lost him because it was too far to get a bait over to him from the far side and from the near bank he always swung down into the brush pile by the deep eddy below his hangout and was off in jig time. As I watched Black I knew he could make that long cast.

Fish like the Old-Timer don't feed much, but if tomorrow turned out to be a good day and the thing did work out ... well, it was worth a try. I waited till Black released his fish and called him over. We went up to the pool below the second covered bridge and I showed him where the big trout lived. While we spoke there was a heavy slosh just where I said he always fed when the mood was on him and part of that broad brown back of his showed above the water. He came again and a third time while we watched. "He'll go ten pounds, Mr. Black!" I whispered with a quiver in my voice like there always is when I see a fish that size.

"Maybe, but I think you're a little high," he nodded. "Anyway, I think he'd take the prize all right."

Not many trout fishermen would stand there and watch that kind of a fish rising without making a cast or two, because Lord only knows when a fish that big will take a notion to rise again. To pass up such a chance meant a sacrifice and I knew it but it wouldn't help the Dunn kid if we took the Old-Timer today. The bet was on the largest fish caught on Decoration Day—and remember, Dunn would win if Ogilvie didn't get the big one; it didn't matter who did.

It was pure torture for both of us to watch that fish feed. I could count on the fingers of one hand the times I'd seen him rise to the surface before, but that day, while we watched, he came up more than a dozen times. I couldn't stand but so much of it and I said, "Let's get the hell out of here before I start to fish for him myself," and we went on back to Charlie's.

The next morning, contest day, was disappointing. The wind was in from the east in squalls and a little thunder was rolling around and echoing through the valley. All anybody got that morning was wet. Ogilvie was the only one who didn't stir out of the house. He checked pretty closely with his pocket barometer and just said, a couple of times, "Let them go out and get soaked if they want to. I'll take a winner this afternoon when this clears off." He had his lunch around eleven-thirty and sure enough, the skies cleared up just as the rest of them were sitting down to eat. That gave him half an hour's start to pick his pool while the others ate and changed their dripping clothes.

Just following a hunch, I stopped off and looked in at the bend and there was Ogilvie with a fish on, and a good one. I watched him land it from the high bank. That fish was all the net would hold and my heart sank when I saw him stretched out on the sand. He was good for five pounds, sure. I noticed something, though. Ogilvie put his back to me when he took the hook out. By the time I got down through the alder thicket Ogilvie was ready to show me the fish, a deep old male with a hook bill and heavy dark spots. As I came through the thicket I thought I saw a little splash at the edge of the slack water. That didn't seem quite natural. It was dead water and no place for a trout to be rising.

After Ogilvie had gone I went over to the spot. Lying in the shallow water was a 7-inch trout that was dead and pretty well scarred up. He'd been swallowed and there was a hook mark through his upper jaw, a mark from a pretty big hook. There it was! He'd hooked a small trout on a big fly, perhaps one of those low-water salmon flies he'd been showing around, and then played him in front of the big one's hangout.

If Ogilvie'd been there I'd have said a lot, probably, but he wasn't and the more I thought it over the less sense I could see to making that kind of a fuss. It was none of my business. I wasn't in the contest. And even if I did tell what I'd found Ogilvie'd deny it and they'd give him the prize anyway. All I'd do would be to make a bad situation worse. According to the letter of the rules he'd taken his fish on a fly in one way, I suppose.

I was feeling pretty glum about it as I went on down to the pool below the second covered bridge. Black was sitting up on the high bank and watching. He knew that if Old-Timer were on the feed he'd show himself somewhere and if he wasn't, any casting that was done would just put him wise and queer the chance of ever getting him to take a fly.

I told him about Ogilvie's 5-pounder. The Old-Timer was the only fish I knew of in the river that would weigh more. We didn't talk much as the time went slowly by. Black had gone into the field and caught a bunch of crickets. Every so often he'd take the path upstream and cut in above the pool, wade out, and throw a couple of them where they'd float down near the Old-Timer. When nothing happened he'd come back and sit down again.

The wind dropped entirely and the air was warm and still as the sun went down behind the long green ridge with the grove of pines on its crest. There was no other action because the Old-Timer always kept the run cleared of other trout. There wasn't much time left because the contest deadline has been nine-thirty ever since the old Judge came in a few minutes after midnight with a 3-pounder that would have won over Ogilvie's fish if there'd been no complaint about the time.

Then the Old-Timer rose. Black slid down into the water and spent a cautious couple of minutes moving out into the current. He was a tall man, and rangy so that he could stand a little farther out in the current than I'd ever seen anyone get before. He had on a light-colored fly, a fuzzy one that was all whiskery and uneven with a heavy body and a bushy tail. It looked like too long a distance from where he stood, almost up to his armpits, at the edge where the bar dropped off to the spot where Old-Timer had risen. Eighty feet, when a man tells the truth, is a long cast and when he's up to his breastbone in water and using an 8-foot rod it's . . . well, a miracle.

I remember watching so hard my eyes got a little watery just as he was casting but they cleared in time to see that fly flutter down about three feet above the place the rise had been. Nothing happened. The second cast was a little farther upstream and came right down over the same spot. I noticed that his line was sinking, which meant that he had to bring his retrieve pretty well in before he could pick it up off the water.

The third cast was just about where the second had been, twelve or fifteen feet above the Old-Timer. I was watching the fly as it floated down, and I couldn't help a groan when I saw it pull under the surface just as it passed over *the* spot. My eyes swung down to where Black was standing and I saw that he'd done it purposely. A heavy slosh in the water pulled my eyes back to the deep water and there was a heavy swirl where the Old-Timer had risen or turned, just under the surface. Then I heard the reel sing.

I looked at my watch. The hands showed five of nine. Allowing for a five-minute trot back to Charlie's place it gave Black just half an hour to bring in his fish. It was a tall order. Black headed right downstream along the bar on a dead run and by the time the Old-Timer made his bid for the brush pile Black was well below him and the fish had to buck the current. I think that was what turned him. Anyway, he tried twice and didn't make it either time. After the second attempt he seemed to lose his spirit and it was only a little while longer before he showed the yellow and white of his side and belly as Black turned him at the end of a short spurt. He tried the old trick of rolling in the current and then gave up.

Black's net wasn't any use with a fish of that size. I didn't have any tackle with me that day and even my big net wouldn't have been any good. While the little beads of sweat were coming out on my forehead Black walked back onto the bar and drew the Old-Timer into the shallow water where he couldn't stay upright and flopped around long enough to let him take a few quick steps forward and, bending over, close one of his big hands over the fish's neck right behind the gills to carry him to the safety of the dry gravel.

My watch said twelve after nine. I held it to my ear and it was still running. I wound it a little and found it was almost tight. I had to believe it. Seventeen minutes!

Black was taking the fly out. He started to put it in a little sponge he carries on his fly vest and then handed it to me instead and said, "Here's a souvenir for you, Al." It went right into my hatband where you see it now, and we were off down the trail.

If I hadn't crooked my elbow that fish's tail would have

dragged on the ground. Before I was postmaster I used to work in Clarke's Store. That's where I learned the heft of things. The Old-Timer was good for seven pounds and a half. We kept hurrying along the trail and neither of us spoke until we were almost back to Charlie's. As we got there in early darkness Black said, "Suppose you wait outside a minute with the fish while I go in and let Ogilvie have his moment of gloating before you bring him in." So I propped my back against the woodpile and waited.

In a couple of minutes he came out again and his face had a big grin on it. "We won't need the Old-Timer," he said. "Young Dunn just came in with a fish that's an ounce and a half heavier than Ogilvie's and the old boy is fit to be tied."

He picked up the Old-Timer and laid him under a couple of lengths of wood on the pile and continued, "We'll leave him here till you're ready to go. Carry him over to your place tonight, won't you? I'll take him along with me when I leave in the morning and we won't say anything about this to anyone."

It was his fish and I liked him so I just nodded. We went in together.

That was the kid's night. Judging by the grins on all the faces around everyone else seemed as happy as he was. Old Ogilvie had gone up to bed leaving the six rods lying out on the table. Still, I don't think any of them was any happier than Black as he sat there quietly, smiling and not saying much.

The kid's fish had come out of Russell Pool. I never found out what he took it on, and it never seemed to matter. All I know is that old Ogilvie's been a lot nicer guy to have around since then. You see, the kid gave him back his two pet rods.

I put the Old-Timer on ice that night and packed him cold in dry ferns for Black to take along with him the next morning. Like he said, I never mentioned it to a soul. The funny thing about the whole business is that Charlie told me before Black left he promised to send up a big mounted brownie he had home to fill up that space over the mantel where the moosehead used to be. About a month later a 7^1/$_2$-pound brown trout, mounted on a long mahogany panel, arrived by express and it's hanging over the mantel at the lodge right now.

[1943]

35

Steelhead and Atlantic Salmon

If I'm not near the fish I love, I love the fish I'm near. All that means is that I like many different kinds of fishing. I've gone very happily to the Northwest after steelhead and just as happily northeastward for Atlantic salmon. I may be surf-casting for striped bass in November and then thinking about the flies I'll use for next season's brown trout while I'm driving home. I would hate to miss any of it. Just as I'd hate to choose only one fish.

As Wulff points out in this chapter, however, many people do rate their favorite fish as tops among game-fishes. Among fly fishermen, especially, the most volatile arguments always seem to concern steelhead and Atlantic salmon. The discussion sometimes even gets into social stereotypes: the roughshod and crude northwestern steelheaders (as perceived by some Easterners) and the uptown tweedy, snobbish Eastern salmon fishermen (as perceived by some Westerners). Neither characterization is true, of course, but before getting into further trouble, let's join Wulff for a look at the fish themselves.

Anglers are always naming *their* favorite gamefish as the champion of all gamefishes. Practically every fish in the book has been named by someone as the best of all and usually with some good reason. And, as usual, one man's meat is another man's poison.

Black bass used to be named top fish with an accolade: "Inch for inch and pound for pound, the gamest fish that swims." Yet whenever both trout and bass were available to anglers, as in Maine, the trout were the preferred fish. The trout-fishing enthusiasts claimed that most of the bass proponents had never caught a trout or an Atlantic salmon and, at best, were going on hearsay and were hardly qualified to make a fair comparison.

There will always be good arguments both for and against those fish that are in common contention. The speed of the bonefish is dazzling, but tarpon advocates will point out that bonefish aren't very big and, moreover, they don't jump. A trout fisherman will say, "Neither of them is caught in running water, which makes the capture of any fish much more exciting." A bass fisherman puts in: "A bass hits a lure more savagely than any other fish," and finds plenty of support for that statement.

Trout fishermen can contend that "bass will take anything they can get into their big, bucket mouths. They're nowhere near as selective or as difficult to hook or as demanding of small hooks, delicate tackle, and playing skill as trout are. Ever watch one of those bass pros bring in a fish? It's strike, splash, splash, and bump on the bottom of the boat. They call that *playing* a fish?"

The Atlantic salmon anglers say, "Trout and all the other top contenders are 'feeding' fish and can be caught by appealing to their ever-recurring need for food, while Atlantic salmon in the rivers simply cannot digest any food, and so to catch them, the angler must reach deep into their minds to stir a memory or cause an instinctive reaction, something that makes salmon angling a lot more challenging."

The Atlantic salmon tends to be rated at the top by those anglers who have fished widely for all game species, yet there are many challengers, and here I'll consider a challenge by one of the best, the steelhead trout, comparing the virtues and weak points of each fish, their similarities, and their diversities as fairly as I can.

Both fish are caught in the running waters of big streams with dramatic flows. Both jump with abandon. Both are caught, normally, by an individual angler without help from anyone else. (Outside help diminishes the angler's difficulty and reduces the skill required.) I'm considering here only the angler who fishes alone.

Steelhead *feed* in the rivers, often following the Pacific salmon runs in from the sea to feed on the salmon's eggs when they spawn. Nature can't let the Atlantic salmon feed in their rivers because there is no real food supply available, and if they were to maintain their strength by feeding as ferociously as they do in the sea, they'd eat up their own young, which usually stay in the stream as fingerlings for three or four years before making their first migration to the sea. Nature solved this problem by taking away the river-returning adult salmon's capability to digest food and with it, of course, their hunger.

In comparing the strength and speed of these cousins within the *Salmo* genus, the rainbow and the Atlantic salmon, one must consider the fact that the Atlantic comes into the rivers after a long sea-feeding migration so supercharged with energy that he can go for a period of months, sometimes almost a year, without taking any food. Obviously he is stronger when he comes in the stream than is the steelhead or seagoing rainbow, which doesn't store up strength to the same degree and can renew its strength while in the stream by day-to-day feeding.

The other side of the coin is that the steelhead *can* renew its strength while in the rivers. While the Atlantic salmon is comparatively stronger than the steelhead upon entry into the rivers, from that time on the salmon's strength is on the wane, but the steelhead's is being maintained at a good level. After a month or so in the river there will come a point where their energy levels will be equal, and following that the salmon's energy level will be lower than that of the same-size steelhead. It makes a difference, then, whether the salmon you choose for your comparison has just come into the river and is at his peak or has been there for weeks and is getting stream weary.

The Atlantic salmon is unquestionably harder to catch. A salmon can go through the entire fishing season without having the desire or the need to take any food or any fisherman's lure. His response to a fly is most often considered to be a deep-seated reaction to his stream memories when, as a fingerling, he fed on insects in the stream. The flies he responds to are very small in comparison to his bulk and are always being attacked by the very fingerling salmon that match his state before he went to sea. The small hooks in relation to the salmon's bulk demand greater skill of an angler. One group of fishermen I know has recorded some sixteen salmon of over 20 pounds each taken on #16 single-hook flies, the largest being 27 pounds, and this, they believe, is a greater hook-size-to-poundage ratio than any steelhead angler has faced.

The Atlantic salmon takes flies from any angle, and the fly may be either floating freely or moving in any direction. Steelhead are more patterned in their taking of a fly or lure, and that brings us to the methods of fishing. By law on this continent, the Atlantic salmon can be taken only by fishing with an unweighted artificial fly in the accustomed manner. Fly fishing is a more demanding method of fishing than either spinning or bait casting. Ask anyone who has switched from spinning to fly casting if he found it just as easy. To compare spinning and fly casting as a method of fishing is like comparing checkers to chess.

In a comparison of the fish's gameness and sporting qualities, an angler could use the same method, fly casting for both fish. The difference here is that when the Atlantic salmon are dour and lying deep, they are relatively safe from fly-fishing-only anglers, while the big steelhead, lying deep, are presented with a bait or other lure sinkered down to their level so that to take it they have only to move a few inches. The Atlantic salmon, lying deep, must move energetically from his lie near the bottom to the surface waters in order to take a fly. Consequently, in the steelhead rivers, most of the big fish are taken before the conditions are good for fly fish-

313

ing, while in the salmon rivers, when good fly-fishing conditions come along, practically all the fish are there to fish for.

When you finish one of these analytic comparisons, you find that it is largely academic. What Atlantic salmon angler would turn down a chance to fish a magnificent steelhead river with the sound of moving water all around him, the current pressing hard against his thighs, and the big trees throwing shadows on the sunlit pools, just because, in his mind, the Atlantic salmon was a better fish. Would any steelhead proponent in his right mind let his certainty that the steelhead was top fish keep him from enjoying a salmon river, if he had the chance?

There are other differentiating points to consider, depending upon particular fish and the particular experience of the individual angler, but the foregoing is, I think, a fair basic coverage. One final word. The only anglers capable of judging the sporting qualities of different species are those who have caught dozens of each kind. A fish or two caught at a certain time or place will rarely be representative of the species as a whole. It is a worthwhile project to catch enough of all the top-rated species to be able to have a personal feeling about each one and a sense of justice when making judgments. Join the club and enjoy yourself—and don't forget the bonefish, tarpon, bass, and the others along the way. And, if you really want to go the whole route, learn to evaluate the big-game fish of the sea by the problems they give to the *teams* on the sportfishing boats that capture them, and you'll have an endless amount of great sport to look forward to.

[1981]

36

This Was
My Alaska

Everything about Alaska seems to me larger than life.
Even when viewed from an airplane, the vast expanses
of wilderness stretch into tomorrow. The moose and
bears are both immense, huge in the distance and
beyond belief when encountered close-up. Even the
trout I've taken here have been far larger than those I've
caught elsewhere. And given his extraordinary accom-
plishments, it somehow seems fitting that Lee Wulff
started out here as well.

Alaska is now described by some outfitters as the
very last of the very best fishing in North America. But
the really good fishing, especially for trout, is confined
to a few limited areas of this vast region, which already
are seeing more and more anglers. As Wulff himself
once said, even yesterday may have been too late. If you
can go, go now!

It was like a daydream. Waters were swirling around my
waist, making that special sound they make when they slide
right over my chest waders. I could feel the pressure of the
water at my back, firm and solid, as I held my footing for the

cast. The banks on both sides were overhung with high grass and great pieces of turf hung down, dragging the grass into the flow. There were patches of willows and scattered birches and spruces along the banks, some still secure, other succumbing to the undermining process and hanging from the bank into the stream.

I could picture the insects, even the mice and moles, tragically caught in the shifting sod and sliding down into the steady undercutting sweep of the run, helpless before the trout that lay there. There were indentations in the bank, cutout places between the tangled logs that still clung to the soil.

In each of these cut-bank pockets, I knew a trout would lie. It would be a big trout and a hungry one. A trout that would not quibble as to whether the fly was a #6 or a #2 or a #4, or worry whether the hackle was a true Andalusian blue or a blue-dyed white hackle from Fresno. I knew that just a few yards farther downstream, in the next bank pocket or under the next leaning log, there'd be another, just as eager to rake a fly. These dream fish would be primeval trout, untutored by many releases or escapes from an angler's fly. They would strike with the sure abandon of the king of a prime pocket of water. Then, being rainbows, they would shake their heads and leap in bewildered fury. They would run out into the open water and then dog their way back to the bank where the snags would worry me, where I'd have to slack off and hope their love of speed and the open reaches would call them back to the main flow where I could tire them out.

It would take a long cast but they would take the streamer I had just tied on, a beautiful big Kulik Killer on a #2 hook of flashing gold. And when they finally came in with appropriate reluctance to be released, my fingers would take the hook and set them free.

I knew, before I cast, exactly what flow of power it would take to reach the first fish. It was like being in a dream . . . but it wasn't a dream. It was real. I was back in Alaska again.

I had just stepped into the American River. I could touch the flowing water and feel its coolness. I could see the eddying

316

sand and silt that the current picked up every time I moved a foot. I could hear the birds and see the trails of the great bears on the banks, feel the wild loneliness of the land around me. I was back in Alaska again, and it was just as I'd dreamed this homecoming would be.

Although, according to the Department of the Interior, I am not a "native Alaskan" I was born at Valdez at 2:00 P.M. on the tenth day of February 1905, just as the steamship *Excelsior* was steaming into the bay and sounding her whistle to alert the town's inhabitants. My earliest memories are of fishing. My mother used to tell me that I was fishing with a bent pin on a piece of string as soon as I could crawl the fifty yards to the "crick" behind the house.

Valdez was a great town for a fisherman's boyhood. The streams had great runs of trout and salmon, and there was a good smelt run in the winter. From the bay we could catch not only salmon but cod, flounder, and halibut. Each fall, when the salmon and trout runs were on, every family in town wanted to salt down at least a couple of barrels of those fish, and a kid who liked to catch fish could fish endlessly and never catch more than his family and his neighbors needed, no matter how many he caught.

There were hundreds of sled dogs in town, and if you add the needs of the dogs to the human demands in that town of 1,700 souls, the total was staggering. There were no game laws. There was only a vital need and a seemingly endless supply of fish, runs of trout and salmon that streamed into the fresh waters over and beyond the take of the canneries that operated farther out in Prince William Sound.

Early fishing memories come back across the years when I let them. Memories of early summer days when the fields on the way to the two-mile creek were covered with a mottled red blanket of Johnny-jump-ups and shooting stars. But I took only fleeting notice of the flowers. My interest was in the rivers and the fish.

In spring there were only trout and salmon parr in the streams. This was the time when fish were few and hard to catch. We young fishermen carried some hooks and a length of line. I'd find a place where a log or tree leaned out over a pool and I'd quietly let my line down to where the trout or parr were moving in the slow current. I'd twist the line to adjust the small single hook and wait till a fish swam over it. Then I'd yank. The yank would carry the small fish right out into the air and somewhere up on the bank.

From there on my fishing was more conventional. Now there were two eyes for bait and I'd add a sinker to the line and, swinging it over my head, send it out to the deep eddies to rest on the bottom where the bigger trout were. Each fish caught had two more eyes to take out, so the supply of bait from that point on was never ending.

Fishing with hook and line was fun but there were other methods of catching fish that were more certain and equally entertaining once the main runs came in. These called for different gear and much more stealth and skill. I could fasten a short length of soft copper wire to the end of an alder pole. Forming the wire into a loop a little larger in diameter than that of the trout I was trying to catch, I would move it down cautiously over the fish's head and fling him out onto the bank. The trout were wild, and the problems of seeing them, then stalking carefully and finally getting the snare in place, were far more challenging and effective than the simple method of throwing a sinker and bait out into the pools.

We made gaffs with a 14/0 shark hook wired to the end of an alder or a bamboo pole. In gaffing the fish we liked to see them first and, as with a snare, drift the gaff gently into position and yank it into the fish. A gaff would bring ashore bigger fish than we could take with a snare, because the soft copper wire wouldn't take the heavy weight and hard twisting. The great value of the gaff lay in its effectiveness in cloudy or turbulent waters. Even though the fish couldn't be seen, if you could read the water and your stroke was good, you could connect with fish.

By the time I was eight, I was proficient with the hand line, spear, snare, and gaff. I was wet to the hips all summer long, either wading wet or soaked over the tops of any boots I wore. We'd wade down a stream, and when the trout that had congregated in the tail of the pool tried to race past us to get to safety we'd strike them with a spear or nail them with a gaff. It took a lot of judgment. We had to be able to see the fish in the twisting eddies (something most anglers never have to learn to do), then, as a trout became a fleeting shadow sweeping by at full speed, we'd strike him with a spear or gaff while allowing for the reflections and refractions and the speed of the water. As with the old market gunners, once you really became skillful you were so deadly that your catch was basically limited only by the number of fish in the waters you worked.

The commonest method of taking salmon during the run was by snagging with a 3/0 treble on a heavy line tied to the end of a 15-foot bamboo pole. Such an outfit gave one a 30-foot reach, and when the fish were thick the catching was easy. Most of the citizens who were looking for their barrel or two of salmon caught them that way. I thought snagging was too haphazard, and liked it even less when, in my ninth summer, I hooked a big coho on the back fin, pulled back hard, and then had the hook pull loose. The big tackle snapped back across my shoulder, looped around my neck and dragged a hook-point across my open left eye, directly over the pupil. For the better part of a year I had a white scar there, long enough to be a good reminder.

The year I was ten, most of my fishing was done with a character called "Slop Jack." He was the town indigent and handyman. Small and cheerful, he hauled garbage and did odd jobs at the saloons. He boozed a bit, never seemed to have a dime, and lived alone in a small weatherbeaten shack. Slop Jack's main industry, and the one that tied us together, was feeding the sled dogs in the summer.

To most sled drivers, their dogs were just a nuisance in the summer. They required food but they couldn't be worked when there was no snow. So Jack boarded them and fed them during the summer. What better ally and companion could he have than a fishing-freak kid who'd go along for just a little gear, an occasional bag of fruit or candy, and some wonderful free lunches that came from the saloons where Jack carried out slops.

Spearing, I think, was the prime sport of all. It was more exciting and more deadly than any other method. Anyone who has ever become good at it realizes that it became too deadly to be allowed as pressure on the fish increased. I'm glad I lived at a time when I could learn and enjoy it. Jack and I would work a stream together, sneaking upstream on the banks on each side and spearing the fish we could see from shore. Then we'd wade back down, side by side, taking as many of the fish we hadn't seen on the way up as possible.

Jack was not my only older fishing companion. A friend of my father's, a guard at the local jail named Rosy Roseen, also took me under his wing. Rosy was a displaced Englishman and a devoted fly fisherman. I'll be forever grateful for the introduction he gave me to fishing with a fly.

In my ninth and tenth summers I spent a good many hours with him, using first a bamboo pole with wire guides and waxed mason line attached to a 6-foot, three-fly silkworm gut leader. In my tenth year I had a combination lancewood and greenheart rod and a fair assortment of flies, some of which I'd tied under Roseen's supervision. When the big runs weren't on, I divided my time between the superb sports of spearing and gaffing with Jack and casting flies for the smaller fish with Rosy.

Such were the days of my youth. Then calamity seemed to fall, and my father gave up the newspaper he ran in Valdez and moved the family down to the States, where my fishing in New York and Pennsylvania, and later California, was far, far different.

While I was reminiscing about my youth I was fishing today's Alaskan dream, a thirty-rainbow day on the American River with a few Arctic char thrown in for good measure. Our group met at 4:30 where the river flowed into a lake, and with my companions, Dean Hadcock, Jerry Jacob, and young Bill Jacob, I climbed aboard the Cessna and flew back to Kulik.

I had made that trip to Alaska to be with Jerry Jacob and, in memory, with his father, Jake, a longtime friend with whom I'd often fished the wild trout and salmon waters of Labrador. Jake was a man who loved deeply, both his friends and his fishing places. His angling was worldwide but best of all he loved this Kulik area, the river valleys, the big brown bears that walked the banks and sometimes watched him fish, the bright flashing rainbows that struck his flies. Each year, with a group of friends, he came back to the Kulik area in September. Each year, too, he asked me to join him but that had been a bad time and I hadn't been able to make it— until this year. I'd worked out a way to be free and join him in September. When I called to tell Jake he could count on my joining him, Jerry had answered the phone. I said, "Jerry, tell your dad I'm going to fish with him in Alaska this year come hell or high water."

Jerry said quietly, "You can't fish with Dad, Lee. He passed away three weeks ago." He paused, then added quickly, "But you can come and fish with us. I'm taking Billie for the first time. He's twelve now and he'll be as pleased as I will if you'll join us."

So I joined Jerry and Billie and their friend, Dean Hadcock, another wide-roaming fisherman, to make the pilgrimage that Jake had loved so much.

On a quiet morning, soon after our arrival at Kulik, Jerry and Billie climbed to a long ridge that overlooked the river. There, as he'd wanted it, they put Jake's ashes in a cairn that watched over the valley where he'd found a high point of happiness. When they came back to camp Jerry said simply, "Let's go fishing," and we got into our waders and fished the Kulik.

One day the plane took us to the Battle River, beaching where the Battle flowed into the lake. We made our way over soggy sand to the inlet. The others took the tundra trail to meet at the river a mile or so upstream. I inched my way across to an island with an occasional drip coming over my waders. From there I worked up the main branch of the river through some low and swampy ground.

Working upstream on a big river, where the banks overhang, is awkward. The steelhead weren't seriously interested in dry flies, and trying to work a wet fly or a streamer while backing upstream doesn't give the fly the same teasing approach to a fish he'll get if it gradually moves down into his vision from upstream. I leapfrogged upstream for a quarter mile of fresh water and fished down till I reached the spot where I'd started.

There was none of the rich deep soil we'd found on the American River along these banks. This was rock and gravel with only an occasional pocket of settled-in sand. The water was sparkling clear instead of having the milky limestone look of the American. There appeared to be far less food for fish, too. The major salmon runs were over, and only a few carcasses lay in the water or lined the banks. I didn't expect to find too many rainbows hanging on. An hour and a half of fishing gave me neither sight nor feel of a fish.

It's a long way to these wild, uninhabited streams of Alaska, and it's a little surprising to find, after you've dreamed or remembered so long, that it's usually feast or famine. Strike a river when the run is in, and the action is hot. Hit it after the run is over, and it can be dead. I hoped for a rainbow straggler and kept on fishing . . . and let my mind flash back.

It was the summer of 1923. I was back in Alaska on my summer vacation as a sophomore at San Diego State—to drive a Model-T Ford truck over the road from Valdez to Fairbanks, to work as a stevedore on the Valdez dock, and to have a hunting trip in the mountains back of Rapids on the Fairbanks road. Late in August we took the S.S. *Alaska* to Seward to meet the first train to come over the brand-new Alaska Railroad, with a fishing trip afterward. The track had finally been laid all the way to Seward, but the grades south of Anchorage were so steep that the inaugural train had to be broken down to two cars, leaving the others in Anchorage and hooking on two engines for the two-car train. When the train pulled in we were part of the small crowd on hand to shake hands with President Harding and his secretary of commerce, Herbert Hoover.

While President Harding went on by ship to sickness and death in San Francisco, my father, his friend Judge Wickersham, a pair of guides, and I boarded the train for its trip back to Anchorage. Our guides were Andy Simons, one of

Alaska's most famous, and Henry Skilak. We left the train with our canoes and duffel for a trip down the Kenai and up Turnagain Arm to Anchorage.

Judge Wickersham made periodic trips to check the lesser settlements and the backcountry of his district. Dad, an old friend from his newspaper days, had been invited to go along and he'd rung me in to give me what Judge Wickersham (who, like Dad, could take fishing or leave it) had said would be the best rainbow fishing he could offer. The trip had been planned for a long time and I was prepared for it.

I'd been tying flies through the winter months and among them was a brand-new idea in flies. It was the *streamer*. I'd copied it from a photo in that year's Abercrombie & Fitch catalog. It was called the Rooster's Regret and was made with a few hackles wound around the shank behind the eye and four long hackle feathers streaming out behind the hook for a startling innovation. The catalog said it was designed for the fighting smallmouth of the Belgrade Lakes but that big trout, too, would take it. I meant to find out.

Our first camp was at the mouth of the Russian River where its clear water poured into the cloudy Kenai. This was my father's promised Rainbow Heaven. Andy caught trout after trout on his salmon eggs for a total of sixty-four in our two-day stay. I caught three times as many, mostly on the newfangled streamers, and one of my fish was by far the biggest. Big enough, it turned out, to take a *Field & Stream* prize that year.

Two days of pure delight on the Russian and then we took our outboard-powered canoes and went on down the Kenai and up the arm to Anchorage, where we found a few saloons, a church, a small scattering of houses, and, as an added attraction, a cow moose walking down the street.

My musings on the past were interrupted by a solid and unexpected strike—and the leap of a 4-pound rainbow. In the Battle's fast flow he put on an exciting display before I brought him in and released him. Then there was more time for musings. I checked the bear trails and scanned the hillsides but I saw no bears. I listened to the gulls. I watched an eagle. A flock of ptarmigan landed at the stream edge but, for the rest of the morning, I didn't draw another strike. It wasn't till noon, when I had the rest of the group in sight upstream, that another fish struck.

This one was a male, beautifully colored, weighing close to 10 pounds. When I brought him to the campfire where the others sat, I found that Dean had caught his twin, a silvery female. They were a beautiful pair. Dean was as elated as an angler can be. His was a bright new moment. Mine was an echo of an old memory.

For our last fishing day we flew back to the American River. Billie was working down ahead of me with a big orange Woolly Worm he had tied the evening before, under my tutelage. He was a quiet boy, old for his twelve years, and very keen about fishing. Jerry had given him a good outfit to use, one of his impregnated split-bamboo rods with a matched line and leader. He had picked up casting easily and was fishing his fly well.

Fishing parties had been flying in to the American almost daily and although the fish had been plentiful and eager on our first visit, they now seemed scarce and very reluctant to take a fly. A lot of the river's stock of rainbows had undoubtedly been caught and released, for, like ourselves, the other parties brought few fish back to camp. As a result we weren't going out in a blaze of glory. I was acutely aware that Billie hadn't caught a very big trout and I kept hoping he'd get one he could be proud of.

I was watching his fly when it bounced off the far bank and dropped to the water just ahead of a half-submerged log.

"Nice cast," I said to myself under my breath.

Then I saw the swirl and sensed rather than saw the lift of his arm and the tightening of the line. My eyes had stayed on the swirling water, for there was a long bright rainbow flash near the log.

For an instant the reel made no sound and all action was frozen. Then the reel sang and the fish raced downstream, leaping as he went. He was a good, big fish and I felt a warm ray of hope for Billie.

Just then I had a strike. A 2½-pound rainbow, like the half dozen we'd caught already, hit the fly and zinged out across the pool. He completely absorbed my attention by ending up in a tangle of sunken branches.

Periodic glances told me that Billie was still fast to his big fish and was slowly wearing him down. While I waded out and gingerly pulled and twisted the snag enough to free my fish, Billie had worked down under the high overhanging bank as far as he could go. He was wedged in against the wet earth wall on a slim shelf under a tangle of willow branches.

My fish was played out and I reached down to free him, so that I could go and help Billie, when I heard his call.

Pulling the hook free quickly I rushed toward him. He was half-standing, half-falling back against the willows. He had the big rainbow in his arms and he was shouting, "The hook's come out. He's loose! He's loose!"

Handling a big, lively, and slippery rainbow isn't easy even for a grown man and Billie was losing his grip. We carried no nets but I had my rod in my left hand and the fly I'd just removed from my fish in my right.

Reaching Billie, I hooked my fly into the rainbow's mouth with a quick motion milliseconds before he slid back into the stream. I handed the boy my rod and picked his up from the mud where it had fallen.

The rainbow rested upright in the shallow water, fanning his fins a little. "Billie," I said, "that's a beautiful fish. He's about as big as any we've taken on this trip. He'll look great on your wall at home."

The boy just stood there for a moment, looking at the tired fish. He just stood there, watching, then he added, "Grandfather Jake always said, 'It's the big ones we want most to catch that we should leave in the rivers to breed more big fish for us.' He said the smaller ones may never grow into a really big fish like this one."

This time my mind went back to the pristine Labrador brook trout waters Jake and I had pioneered in my seaplane and how great that fishing had been. Together over the years, we'd watched the runs and the fish diminish in size to where

325

2- and 3-pound fish were "trophies." They'd cleaned out the big ones and left the runts to breed. I could picture Jake telling all this to the boy.

Bill spoke again, "You *helped* me, too. I know I'd have lost him if I'd been here alone."

He bent down over the fish and worked my fly out of his mouth. Then he gave him a little push. With a lazy sweep of his tail the big rainbow moved out into the flow and disappeared.

Jake, whose mortal remains were finally at rest on the ridge over the Kulik, had taught his grandson well. I wished with all my heart Jake could have been there at that moment. Come to think of it, he was.

[1977]

37

Dan Bailey and the Great Depression

Although Dan Bailey died in 1982, the business he built in Livingston, Montana, as Dan Bailey's Fly Shop has grown into one of the world's largest fly-fishing retailers, now run by Dan's son John. Dan's influence on western trout fishing is indelible. He was a major influence in modernizing western trout fishing during and after World War II. And, although the famous Muddler Minnow was developed elsewhere for brook trout by Don Gapen, it was Bailey who gave the fly its most enduring and successful form.

Bailey started a tradition in his shop of a "Wall of Fame" where outlines of large trout caught in the area were mounted on the wall together with the angler's name. John McDonald, a 1930s crony of Bailey and Wulff in Greenwich Village, once described the origin of the wall for me in a magazine article, noting that he and Dan had traced fish on the wallpaper of a cabin they shared in the Catskills. It's my understanding that John finally went back to the cabin and removed that portion of the wall, sending it on to Livingston, where it most properly belongs.

Among the great memories of my very early days of angling are those shared with Dan Bailey. Dan and I fished together a great deal back in the early 1930s. Dan was a science teacher at Brooklyn Polytechnic, and I was a free-lance artist. We both lived in the Greenwich Village section of New York City.

It is hard to imagine two more dedicated anglers. We opened the season in the Catskills even if there was snow on the banks of the Beaverkill, or the winds of the Esopus Valley froze our fly lines in the guides of our rods. We fished every free moment, and I can remember how great the fishing was.

We camped out and lived simply, for those were the days of the Great Depression. I remember one rain-soaked week in late June spent at the Wilmington Notch Camp Grounds on the Ausable with our long-suffering wives, both named Helen. We huddled in our tents and cooked food on campfires sputtering in the rain. The river was high, of course, but we had wonderful fishing. I recall that the front half of the felt soles on my waders came loose, and I held them in place with big rubber bands made of a section cut from an old inner tube stretched around the front of each foot. That made the wading slipperier than at any other time I can remember.

Because of the high, rushing waters we gave up on flies, except for large streamers. We fished with live stonefly nymphs most of the time—and amazed the rest of the campers with our catches. One day we left the Ausable to fish the Saranac, and each brought back a brook trout that was close to 4 pounds, having released many lesser ones.

On another day we drove over to Miller Pond in the Saranac Lake chain, a shallow, uninhabited lake with many brush piles and rocky ledges. We caught a lot of smallmouths, many in the 4-pound class, and the occasional much larger northern pike.

It was Dan who was with me when I first fished with my then-revolutionary bucktail-winged and -tailed flies on the Esopus in 1930. And it was Dan who wisely counseled, "No. Don't call them the Ausable Gray, the Coffin May, or the Royal Bucktail. Call them all *Wulffs.*" We were both tying flies in our spare time to augment our Depression-shrunken incomes. That fall Dan and I worked out the full ten patterns of the Wulff series so that he'd have a complete coverage of this new type of fly to sell.

Between fly-tying sessions, Dan and I had the idea of starting a fly-fishing school. Ray Camp, rod and gun editor of *The New York Times*, was a good friend, and he announced the availability of the class in his column. We held the first session in my apartment, and there turned out to be only five people attending. Ray Camp was there. So was top angling writer John McDonald, one of our good friends. We had one student-customer: John McCloy, later to become one of President Franklin Roosevelt's trusted European troubleshooters. Dan and I filled out the five. Our first session was our last.

An amusing incident comes to mind. Dan and I and our wives had met Preston Jennings and had been invited to his home for dinner. Preston was then writing articles about trout-stream insects. He was somewhat aloof, and had never talked about his business or anything personal except fishing. Helen Bailey had noticed an article in the *Times* that morning wherein a man named Jennings, an exterminator, had solved a bug problem that had plagued a Bronx apartment complex. She felt she had discovered Preston's other life and was determined to ask him about it. She did.

"Tiny" Jennings, Preston's wife, just laughed—but Preston was as thoroughly outraged as anyone could be. He was much older and much more dignified than we and we felt very small for the rest of the evening. But, as Helen said, "At least we found out what he does when he isn't fishing!" It turned out that he worked for Frigidaire refrigerators. As time went on we became good friends.

In 1932 and '33 I had a beautiful little Marmon coupé with a rumble seat (Lord, how I wish I had it now!) just to go fishing in. I parked it at a garage a block from the 247th St.–Van Cortlandt Park subway station, at the north end of the Seventh Avenue line, at a monthly rate of $12. We'd ride the subway from our apartments in the Village to the garage and then drive to the Catskills or the Green Mountains to camp out and fish. We'd come home late of a Sunday night, tired but happy, park the car, and make the long subway ride back to our apartments. We got some strange glances on the subway because instead of carrying duffel bags we simply stuffed our cooking utensils, wading shoes, blankets, and things into our waders and tied them tight at the top. Getting on at the end of the line as we did, we found plenty of empty space, so we'd sit with our gear-stuffed waders between us. The wader feet were on the floor of the car and the seat of the waders beside us, like a human cut off at the chest. And we'd get the strangest glances of all when we'd arrive at our station and lift the waders to a piggyback position to carry them out and into the streets, rod cases in one hand and sometimes a creel containing a few late-caught trout bedded on ferns in the other.

In 1933, I spent July and August on an Atlantic salmon trip, camping out on Nova Scotia rivers, and from then on went north each summer, going after salmon or big bluefin tuna. Dan began to go west to Montana for *his* summer fishing, but we still spent many of our spring weekends on the Catskill rivers or the Ausable or Battenkill until, in 1938, Dan moved to Montana to set up his tackle shop and fly-casting business.

Dan was a hard and avid fly fisherman, yet a very friendly and gentle man. He had great warmth and charm and a deep integrity. And a fierceness for what was right. I remember how his eyes blazed when, during my trip west to fish with him in 1941, he discovered that Frenchie, one of his store workers, was stealing both flies and money from the till. Though Frenchie towered over Dan like a heavyweight over a bantam, he went out of the door cowed and cringing, never to return.

That year I fished with Dan on fabulous Armstrong Creek, then a little-known stream. I have never had such dry-fly fishing before or since. At that time the stream ran freely from its upwelling spring at Armstrong's ranch through Depew's land, emptying into the Yellowstone. When the waters of the big river warmed up in summer, the big browns and rainbows from that great flow came up into the cooler waters of spring-fed Armstrong Creek in amazing numbers, augmenting the trout already there. It was something never to be seen again. Later, Depew blocked off his flow to the big river and to Armstrong's section. There were fewer fish for more fishermen, yet it is still one of the world's best trout streams.

Before he decided to give up teaching and move to Montana, Dan had explained that western dry-fly fishing was in its infancy. He said that most Westerners, if they fished dry, fished with either a Brown Hackle or a Gray Hackle, simple flies that cost only 15 cents. Although he would charge the eastern price of 25 cents a fly, he was sure that the hatch-imitative flies of our eastern fishery would be so successful he'd have a good business opportunity. And he was right. He took our eastern flies to Livingston and changed the face of western fly fishing.

Those were wonderful days, and I am fortunate to have lived through that great period of angling development with some of the pioneers who gave us so many of the techniques on which our modern fly fishing is based.

[1986]

38

No Greater Disappointment

All fishermen, and most especially young ones, will believe anything that carries the promise of more and bigger fish. Tackle makers, of course, are well aware of this and always have been. Even the few very early eighteenth-century tackle advertisements that appeared in the American newspapers of the time offered hooks, lines, and leaders that were the "newest and best."

This long tradition of hyperbole reached its zenith with the late George Leonard Herter of Minnesota, who in his mail-order catalogs of the 1950s offered nothing that wasn't new, unusual, effective, and invented by himself (whether or not it actually was). As a youngster glowing over those catalogs I often found that "unusual" was the only attribute that applied when the box finally came and was opened.

Given the very large population of anglers in this country, it's only fair to assume that it was fishermen to whom P. T. Barnum alluded in noting, "There's a sucker born every minute."

The moment I saw it, I knew it would be deadly. I pictured it chugging its way across the surface of Murray Lake and pulling up those old granddad bass to let me bring home a stringer that would knock the eyes out of the gang.

The year was 1922, and there in the South Bend Bait Company catalog was a picture of a "nite-luminous" Surf-Oreno. The photo showed a white lure on a black background with sharp white lines radiating from it. The caption said that all that was required to make it glow brilliantly for many minutes was to hold it briefly in the beam of a flashlight. I'd make that ghostly glowing "thing" splash its way along the edge of the weeds. Holy Smoke! It would drive those bass crazy.

The catalog reached me in January. The bass season opened at 12:01 A.M. on April 1. That gave me plenty of time to send to Indiana and get two of the lures. It gave me a long time to dream about them before I could cast them to the bass.

In due course the lures arrived, floaters with propellers to spin fore and aft. I couldn't wait for dark, but took the lures and a flashlight into a dark closet and made a test. Sure enough! The lures glowed brightly with an eerie purplish light. It wasn't a wholesome milky-white glow like a firefly, but I didn't figure the bass would care—and in San Diego there weren't any lightning bugs for them to compare the glow color with, anyway.

In the intervening weeks before the season, I practiced on the lawn with my old bait-casting rod and my new take-apart Meisselbach free-spool casting reel that would let me throw a lure a mile if I thumbed it perfectly but would give me a backlash quicker than I could wink if I didn't. I wondered if I was wise to use so tricky a reel in those first dark hours of fishing when I couldn't see what I was doing and when digging out a backlash under a flashlight's beam could take a long long time. My old South Bend sounded like a coffee grinder. I knew I could cast farther with the free-spool reel and decided to chance the backlashes. Besides, I would carry a spare 50-yard spool of 20-pound-test Black Oreno casting line just in case I had to give up and cut a tangle to clear the reel.

My father agreed to let me have the car to go fishing if I had it back at the house by nine o'clock in the morning.

Everything was set. I didn't take off my clothes that night. I just lay down on the bed, but couldn't sleep anyway because of the anticipation. At eleven I took my tackle and left for the lake.

Murray Dam was only about three miles out of town. When I reached it there were a few other fishing freaks who couldn't wait till daylight renting flat-bottomed wooden boats from the livery. There were no outboards in those days, and the sounds of splashing oars could be heard as each fisherman headed out for his favorite spot.

The lake was a little more than a mile across and, as always, the best fishing seemed to be in the farthest coves. Leaning into the oars, I headed across the lake for a section of the shore where the water deepened sharply and where I'd caught the biggest bass in the past. It was a quiet night, moonless, with clouds and a few stars. I could see the dark shadow of the shoreline as I closed in, slowing my oar strokes and finally sliding into casting range with only a soft whispering of water against the hull.

I laid the new lure under the seat and shone the flashlight on it at an angle that would keep the light from shining on the water. At the end of a minute when I switched back to darkness again, the lure glowed brightly with its eerie light. I cast it out, carefully, and not the full distance, avoiding any chance of a backlash. I not only heard it splash, but I could also see the tiny speck of light on the surface. I let it lie still a moment while my heart pounded, then started it on a chugging course back to the boat. I was keyed up, tense, and ready for the strike. It never came.

Not only did that first cast come back untouched by a fish, but so did the hundreds that followed. From midnight till dawn I cast and cast and was finally convinced that my super lure was a dud. Dawn had broken and the sun was about to hit the hilltops when I finally gave up hope. By that time I could hardly notice any glow from the freshly flashlighted luminous plug as I reeled it in. It looked just like an ordinary white surface plug. One more cast, I thought, and I'll change to a regular red-and-white Bass-O-Reno.

Halfway through the retrieve a bass came up and struck,

334

a 3-pounder that leaped well and finally came to the net. It was the end of a dream. My wonderful "nite-luminous" lure would work in the daytime, but not at night.

In a daze I kept on mechanically covering the water. Between that first strike and the time the sun showed eight o'clock in the cloudless California sky, I had three more strikes on the nonglowing glow plug and netted two more bass, both between 2 and 3 pounds.

Rowing back across the lake to the car, I pondered on the fickleness of fish and fishermen. I had thought and dreamed, but not "just like a fish" in judging that lure's capabilities. I could sense, too, that I'd have other such surprises in the future, but I can remember no greater disappointment.

[1980]

39

Rivermen Remembered

The woodsmen's sons leave as soon as they're able, south a little for a second shift in the pulp mill with a warm house and wages or else a shoe factory, where they'll sew the soles of the bankers who keep their wages low. "There's no future for me in the woods," they'll say, and then be gone. So with the erosion of wilderness the skills once honed fine for living there disappear also.

Life in the north country, for those who live there all year, isn't all adventure and romance by any means. Hard-grinding poverty characterizes many rural areas, and it's a crucible that either creates a superb spirit or drives one south in search of a paycheck. Among those who remain is often a very strong and quiet pride, a feeling that may find no more wonderful expression than working a loaded canoe through a maelstrom of white water.

Rupert Brooke, a British poet who died in World War I, wrote, "These I have loved:/White plates and cups, clean-gleaming,/Ringed with blue lines;/ . . . and the rough male kiss/Of blankets; . . ."

When I look back on the things I have loved, there runs through them, as surely as the songs of the birds and the smell of northern spring, the poling of canoes on our continent's northeastern rivers. I can picture well-loaded canoes—each hanging in the rough water like a bird hovering above a wind-tossed branch—edging slowly to one side or the other until the riverman is ready to lift his pole and glide down a rock-free stretch. Again and again he must catch and hold the canoe in the current with his pole, maneuvering laterally from time to time, before he slides safely down to smooth water.

I hear the strident voices of the timid savers-of-others saying, "It isn't safe. No one should ever stand up in a canoe."

Perhaps *they* shouldn't. To pole a canoe, one *must stand* with excellent balance—and then be able to take that tippy craft through white water that most canoeists would not or could not paddle down. Poling a canoe—either up or down a river, a method that will take a load where no other craft could take it—calls for special strengths and skills. Being a passenger in such a poled canoe is like watching a superb horseman ride through a steeplechase or over rough country behind the hounds.

Even through a gentle flow it takes a special sense of balance to pole upstream. The proper place to stand will depend upon the amount and placement of the canoe's load. One must push precisely in the right direction with enough power to overcome the speed of the water and to counter the force of any stray gusts of wind. One can brace the bottom-holding pole against the gunwale of the canoe and literally pry the craft from one stream position to another. In treacherous water the poler must look well ahead and plan a course that will take the canoe up or down the safer water between the dangerous rocks and eddies. The canoe must be under positive control at every instant. Lose control, and the river will scatter your gear and bend your canoe around a rock.

Coming downstream, a paddle can deal only with the unstable, moving water. Nothing but a pole can tie the canoe to the streambed and let it move only where the water is smooth enough and deep enough for safety.

The canoe came from the Indians in the great wild areas where slow rivers and lakes interlace unbroken country. Canoes carried men and their equipment quietly and beautifully by paddle through those myriad highways of the wilderness. The rough and rocky salmon streams of the northeast could not be paddled. Out of necessity the rivermen took to poles. Upstream and down, each trip a constant battle for balance, the riverman might cover twenty miles or more in a single day. The most able canoemen poled alone in canoes about eighteen feet long. Longer canoes were often handled by two men, one front and one rear, but the most difficult runs were made by a good man working alone.

One of the great canoemen of my memory was Charlie Bennett. He was of medium height with broad, sloping shoulders and stout, strong legs that gave him a low center of gravity. Charlie could pick up a 300-pound caribou stag and walk with it on his shoulders across a mile of muskeg to a waiting canoe. His strength was amazing. We carried loads of heavy stuff in those eighteen-foot Peterboroughs—canvas tents, canned goods, camera equipment, and the like that brought the gunwales to within a few inches of the water. I'd sit in the front of the canoe, and he'd stand, solid as a rock, halfway between me and the stern with most of the load between us. He'd push up through a slight eddy where a submerged rock took away some of the current's speed, hang there briefly till he was perfectly poised and then, with a few powerful thrusts with the pole, drive us up through a racing run to another slow spot where he could hold and poise us again. I could feel the movement of the water through the flexible skin of the canoe. I could sense the sureness of his poling and recognize the time it had taken and the aptitude required to have made him what he was.

He would sweat and smile as he came up through the hard ones. I knew how he felt then. Like I felt when I traveled a mountain trail with a good pack, found my second wind, and pushed ahead of my trailmates on the climb. He was good, and he reveled in taking his canoe through rapids where the others had to portage. It was with men like Charlie—and tall, broad-shouldered Bruce Nichols of Newfoundland's Humber River—that I realized how wonderful poling a river could be, and that for them it was a sport and not a labor.

I remember a run down Harry's River in Newfoundland. Charlie brought our canoe down first, and we pulled off into the eddy at the bottom of the white water to wait for the second canoe. Filmmaker Vic Coty was in it with his cameras and half of our food and equipment. His guide had been playing down Charlie's skill with a pole in favor of his own. As they came down, the guide's pole caught between two rocks on the bottom, and he couldn't extract it. He tried to hold his place in the river, but his pole bent like a willow in the wind, then snapped. The canoe was like a car skidding out of control on an icy road. Camera, film, groceries, sleeping bags, tent, and tackle spilled into the stream. Charlie got into his canoe to follow the stuff that floated. Having waders on, I went out to pick up what I could of things that washed into shallow water or sank within reach. Vic and Bob clung to their canoe until they hit shallows and could wade ashore. It was a real disaster, and from that moment on Vic's guide bore the nickname "Whitewater Bob."

I fished too much to take the time needed on the river to develop a great skill with the pole. Only one man I can recall might disagree. We were coming down Western Brook after a trip to explore the magnificent gorge at its head. Mark Roberts, a trapper and guide who, like most Newfoundlanders of that time, couldn't swim, had been amazed at my swimming in the cold lake water. He'd begun to think I was something special. But what really set it up for him was our trip back down the river. Mark was no canoeman, so I put him in the bow with a paddle and said, "If we come close to any rocks, push off enough to let us pass by."

At the first rock we came to, Mark reached out and gave a hell of a push. To steady us I drove the pole to the bottom hard, and it caught between two rocks. Then the current threw the canoe hard against the pole. The water was deep and the pole was short. The top of the pole caught in the drawstring loop of my waders. The pole bent under the strain and, acting like a catapult, flipped me into the air.

By some miracle I landed on my feet on a rock next to the bow of the canoe. I calmly reached out and, taking the gunwale, passed the canoe along. I picked up the floating pole and, as the stern of the canoe came alongside, stepped into my poling position, and we continued on down the river. I never explained to Mark that my wild somersault was an accident and a near disaster (I could have hit my head on a rock), and he lived out his life thinking I was the most fantastic riverman of all.

Perhaps the finest canoe balancing I ever saw was down in Panama, where I saw five native fishermen standing up in a line in a fifteen- or sixteen-foot dugout canoe crossing a bay. The front man and the tail man were using long paddles; the others just stood and balanced, no one touching another. That's like the Wallendas on a high wire.

I brought home one of the native dugout cayucas—a thirteen-footer—and have used it on ponds and lakes for fun. It is beautifully round on the bottom, with not the slightest suggestion of a keel. I usually wear swimming trunks when I get into it. Sometimes I don't get more than fifty feet, standing up and paddling, before I go into the drink.

It is becoming harder and harder to find any of the old rivermen who know how to tame a wild river with a canoe and a pole. They're a dying breed. Outboard motors, particularly the jet type, have made rough river travel easier and faster. One no longer has to go through the long hours of learning and developing the powerful poling muscles to be able to travel through the rocky runs.

I can recall the pleasure some of us had when we made a long, hard upstream run to some otherwise inaccessible fishing pools with an outboard jet for the first time. Between early breakfast and late supper at the main camp, we had an afternoon of fishing on those wild pools that, in the old poling days, would have taken one day to get to, called for an overnight camp with its load of duffel, and another half day to come back.

We'll always have level-water canoe paddling and downstream paddle runs though some white waters, but no paddle will take a canoe where a pole can make it go. Like the great log drives and the men who could walk like cats across them as they floated, the poles and the poling canoemen are passing into time.

Last summer, at Fred Webb's camp on the Tobique in New Brunswick, Noah Ruff poled me upstream and down between the salmon pools. It was great to have that wonderful feeling of balance and security in potentially dangerous waters. When Fred comes down to the Harrisburg Sportsman's Show this winter, he'll bring me, atop his station wagon, one of Noah's poles. It will be one of those he used last summer, a spruce stick that grew straight and tall with little taper for its eleven-foot length, and shod with a soft iron shoe that will hold well on streambed rocks.

One day next spring I will take that pole, my tackle and canoe over to the Delaware, which is a mild and gentle river, but with a few swift runs to make it interesting. I will pole my way up through good trout water, stopping now and then to cast a fly. I will lunch on the shore to watch the water and to rest my weary arms. In the twilight I will come sliding downstream, hanging in the swift flows for a few moments, now and then, as I choose my path. And I will dream of the great rivermen I have known. I will hope, perhaps, that somehow today's young people who are dedicated to canoes and paddling will discover the joys of poling and either learn the game from the few old-timers that remain or through their own trials and errors. It is a skill far too valuable for us to lose.

[1979]

40

The Shushan Postmaster

This particular chapter once inspired me to a dark deed on a dark night, which I haven't repeated. Having been bass fishing earlier on this particular day, my plug tackle was still in the car as I finished fly-fishing the evening rise on a stretch of the Battenkill once fished by Wulff and Al Prindle. I had edited this article for inclusion in a magazine only a few days before, so it was fresh in mind as I put away my fly rod and returned to the now-dark river with a bait-casting rod and bass plugs.

It wasn't long before I had a strike on a big swimming plug, and the line went whizzing off the reel as an unseen, but obviously large, trout ran to the end of the pool. The hook pulled out before I ever saw the fish. Atherton was right, I remember thinking then as I thought also of this chapter. It just didn't seem as if I was playing fair, and ever since then I've fished the 'Kill with trout tackle only.

The most memorable of all my fishing companions was Al Prindle, the Shushan postmaster. My first sight of Al was on the Battenkill in east-central New York in the year 1931. I saw him ahead of me there, fishing three wet flies on a 6-foot leader in the customary fashion. I was coming downstream behind him and moving faster than he was. As I drew near, he had a strike, and I saw the flash of a silver belly as his rod-bending response lifted the 8-incher out of the water and back into the grass of the sheep pasture behind him. The trout had come unhooked on his flight through the air, and as I reached him, Al was down on his knees searching in the grass for the trout.

"I lose more fish in the grass, I guess, than I do in the river," was his comment. We both looked and soon found the wriggling trout, which he slid carefully into his already half-filled creel.

Al Prindle was one of the few Democrats in that Republican stronghold. He was also a veteran of the Spanish-American War, and it was natural that he should become postmaster when the Roosevelt landslide of 1932 brought the Democrats to power. Al arranged things so that his wife, Anna, could always take over the postmastering duties at a moment's notice, and whenever I came through the door after a hard five-hour drive up from New York City, he was free to go fishing with me.

Al was a roundish man of medium height with a sharp Vermont accent and a ready sense of humor. Soon after I met him, we were fishing together practically every weekend. That went on for years until I moved up to live on the 'Kill because of its trout and the beauty that surrounded them.

Early on I gave Al a copy of George LaBranche's *Dry Fly in Fast Water*. The following weekend he wasn't at the post office but was already out on the river when I rolled in from New York. I found him belly deep in the Russell Pool, and it looked as if his creel was a bit heavy.

"How's it going?" I asked.

"Fine! That fellow LaBranche knows a mite about fishing. I've got eight so far."

"What does he know that you didn't?" I asked.

"Why, creating a hatch! I never thought of it before. But,

today I put on all three flies the same. All Leadwing Coach-men. And he's right. They see the first swim by [here he made a fluttering movement with his hand] ... then the second ... [another hand movement] ... and by the time the third one comes along they get excited and strike [here the hand closed in a vicious grab]. Caught every one on the tail fly!"

Soon after I'd started wearing that first fly vest I sewed up for myself, I came up to find him in the river. He had put on his old hunting vest with a couple of red 12-gauge shells still showing in their elastic holding places. It was longer than my fly vest, and the side pockets and game pocket were half under water. But he had fly boxes in the upper pockets and two fly-filled pieces on sponge safety-pinned to his chest. Where I had small scissors hanging inside my left vest front, he had a foot-long pair of shears hanging from another safety pin.

Al took readily to the new techniques that were develop-ing in fly fishing. He was born to fish, and he loved it. He shifted largely to dry flies and the new nymphs although he had a hard time softening his strikes to accommodate the very small hooks. He read all the books I brought, and while resting on the banks, we discussed the writings of Hewitt, LaBranche, Dick Hunt, Dr. Burke, and many others.

Catching fish was his goal, and when the Battenkill was high and discolored, we fished Black Creek for northern pike with plugs or went to one of the ponds nearby to fish for bass with streamers or bugs. That's when I learned he had an unreasoning fear of snakes.

We were fishing Dead Pond for bass. I saw a water snake swimming, his head just breaking the surface about fifty feet away. I cast over with a double-hooked streamer and snagged the snake an inch or two behind the head. Water snakes kill fish, and I planned to end his fish killing. As I brought the snake close to the boat, Al stood up and said, "If you bring that thing into the boat, I got to get out over the side. I can't stand 'em. And I can't swim!"

I brought the snake in just close enough to cut the leader and sacrifice the fly.

Al didn't put back many fish, and he loved to catch the big ones. He never gave up the use of worms or minnows and tried to fish, always, with whatever fly, lure, or bait would catch the most fish. I didn't do the river a favor the day I suggested to Al that if he really wanted to catch big trout, he'd fish at night with a bait-casting outfit (spinning had not yet come onto the scene) and a Heddon Spook or a Pikie Minnow. I didn't like fishing the 'Kill at night because fly fishing loses most of its precision and beauty when you can't see to cast or wade, but Al loved it.

Soon he was catching a lot of big trout. I had moved up there by that time and had to spend a lot of my time working. Al would drop by when I was working late to show the wonderful results of his nighttime plug fishing. It bothered me a little, but it bothered my good friend Jack Atherton, who had come up to live on the Battenkill, too, a lot. He hated to see all those beautiful big browns coming out of the river for keeps even more than I did. He'd get tense and resentful every time he saw Al with a plug rod or saw his car parked by the stream at night. I guess I blamed myself a little more than Al and felt a little more forgiving.

I sold a picture or two of Al for magazine covers, and Norman Rockwell, another neighbor, used him for a calendar and a *Saturday Evening Post* cover. He developed a bit of fame as the Shushan Postmaster. I came to spend more and more of my time fishing for Atlantic salmon and eventually spin fishing came, and the fishing on the Battenkill deteriorated badly to the point where I moved to New Hampshire.

Al is long gone now, fishing the heavenly streams, I hope. I'll never forget his telling me once that Anna had arranged for his funeral and hers well ahead of time. It was paid for in advance.

"She's made the arrangements with Larry Stone, the undertaker in Salem," he told me. We both knew Anna loved all animals and didn't hold with the deer and partridge hunting we did, so I wasn't surprised to hear him continue, "Anna at least wants me to end up dignified. In my best black suit and a white shirt and tie. But I talked to Larry, and he's promised to put an old three-fly leader in my hand, tucked away half up the sleeve so no one can see it. I gave him the leader, and all three flies are Leadwing Coachmen. I wouldn't want to go on that trip unprepared."

[1982]

41

The Price
of a Payne

Among those who scour the countryside for antique fishing tackle, the ideal find is a collection that belonged to what I call a country-club fisherman. He could afford to buy the best, and his fishing peers dictated that Leonard, Payne, Gillum, and other masters be well represented in his rod rack. But the same fellow did most of his fishing from an armchair over martinis, which means that his best tackle will be even now in virtually unused condition.

The opposite of this will be a collection of fine tackle that belonged to a really active angler. It's a safe bet his rods will be worth far less in the collectors' market. Rod tips will either be slightly short or wrapped over with thread where once broken. The once gleaming nickel-silver hardware will be dented and corroded, and the rod grip may be deformed where he once used a jackknife to make it better fit his hand. Although a Vermont snow is falling as I write this, I was able to confirm the damage by checking my closet.

I'd just bought a new Payne fly rod from my friend Max Malay at Folsom Arms in downtown New York. It was a beautiful thing, just under 4 ounces, a two-piece rod 8 feet long. A 2 percent discount for paying cash brought the price down to $49. I was walking on air. I had a rod like one Hewitt fished with, and George LaBranche and Guy Jenkins. I was going to get somewhere as a fly fisherman.

As I rode the subway back to my Greenwich Village apartment I could picture the sheer beauty of that slender rod in action with a Hardy King Eider double-tapered "C" line flowing out over the Beaverkill or the West Branch of the Ausable. It was January, and I had a long time to dream before that could happen.

Not only did I dream, but I vowed to cherish that rod as no other rod I had ever owned. The Granger, the Heddon, the old Abbie, and Imbrie Centennial had ended up with many scars of battles with the fish and the weather. I would keep the Payne silky smooth, dried and waxed after each encounter with the elements. I would be ever so careful not to let any carelessly cast flies strike that lustrous, flame-toned bamboo finish for which Payne was famous.

A streamer cast at high speed and thrown off course by a sudden gust of wind can hit a rod at close to a hundred miles an hour, and if the point of the hook is forward, it can penetrate and weaken, even shatter, one or more of the precisely glued segments of bamboo. I had had it happen once before on a Granger tip, leaving it bent and weakened. No streamers, then. If I used them at all, it would have to be with the greatest of care. The lead shot I sometimes clamped to my leader to take a fly down where the fish held in the eddies and pocket water could snap a tip even more easily than a streamer. I'd have to keep the old Granger, then, as a backup for rough work if I knew that was how I was going to fish.

Spring brought the Catskill fishing. The hatches were early, and only once or twice did I feel the need to get down with a split-shot, and I cast them carefully. The Payne performed perfectly. Even my two-week vacation in late June at By Blanchard's boardinghouse on the Ausable went smoothly. I used streamers sparingly, even though I loved them then, ahead of their time of popularity. The Payne was a pure delight. Until the last day.

It was a dull morning when nothing was rising, and I could coax only a few small fish to take a gray-bodied nymph. In desperation, I put on a streamer, rose a big trout, and on my hasty follow-up cast, the fly touched the rod tip as it whizzed out on the delivery. The fish took and I played it to the net. Then I looked at the rod. There was a tiny nick in the finish a foot above the ferrule. Off came the streamer with a feeling of shame that I'd marred my beautiful rod, even though the hook point had only penetrated, perhaps, a thirty-second of an inch.

Changing to dry flies I worked upstream toward the slower waters near the ski jump, pausing at a pool where a slow flow eased by a high dirt bank into and out of which swallows were flying. Their nests or burrows were about a foot below the grassy sod and about five feet above the dry gravel of the streambed. No fish were rising so I sat on a rock to watch. A swallow would disappear into a hole with bugs in her mouth and come out again half a minute later empty-mouthed. There must have been a hundred holes, and a hundred swallows sweeping the air for insects above the pool.

A flash of dark fur showed up at the edge of the grass, and a mink slid down from the overhanging sod into one of the holes and disappeared. A minute later he came out, climbed up into the grass again, and dropped down a few feet away to enter another hole. By the time he'd entered and left the fourth hole, I felt that he was going to eat every young swallow in the colony, and outrage built within me.

As he disappeared into the fifth swallow nest, I leaped to my feet and dashed over to confront him when he reappeared. There I stood, facing the hole at eye level with swallows filling the air with their cries, when the mink's head appeared. He paused just inside the hole, beady eyes staring into mine in an instant that is frozen into my memory. I had no plan of action. I'd moved impulsively. I stood there with nothing in my hands but the Payne. I raised the butt to strike the mink when he came out, then paused, realizing it was my precious Payne, with which I couldn't swat a fly without fear of damaging it.

In that moment of indecision, the mink leaped forward

and down to the ground at my feet and started running upstream over the dry gravel. Instantly I was in pursuit, waders rustling and heavy wading brogues pounding the gravel, hoping, I think, to mash him into the stones. It was close. For a few seconds I gained, then the mink drew ahead. Where the high bank lowered he leaped into the grass and disappeared.

That night I smoothed out the streamer nick, waxing and polishing until it was almost unnoticeable. But something had changed. The rod was fishing me, not I the rod. A few weeks later a friend offered me what I'd paid for it in spite of the tiny nick, for Paynes were back-ordered and hard to get. After some soul searching, I let it go—and spent the money on a three-piece Heddon (fifteen bucks), a secondhand Hardy St. George for left-hand reeling, an extra line, and a lot of hooks and materials for flies. My fishing became a happier thing. I cast with abandon, caught more fish, nicked one of the tips with a streamer, and didn't let it worry me. The Heddon lasted a good long time and helped me catch a lot of trout and a few Atlantic salmon before I gave it to one of the kids.

But as time went on I came to feel that a good rod can and should take all the work an angler can give it as long as there's no abuse in its handling. Years later there came another rod I loved. Wes Jordan of Orvis made it up for me on my special design. It was impregnated split bamboo, 6 feet long and all one piece, well under 2 ounces. It had something I think no rod had ever had before in the same degree: maximum delicacy with enough power to cast an HCF (WF7 to you of the modern era) as far as or farther than the longer rods I had cast before. I loved it and I made it work hard, but always within proper limits when full power was applied. With it I caught hundreds of Atlantic salmon. It never faltered, and at the end of six years I retired it to use other designs in which I was interested, but even now I have it as a standby to fish out of love for the old familiar feel of bamboo and the many memories it carries.

Had I been as wise at the time of the Payne as I was with the 6-footer, I probably would never have nicked that dream rod with my streamer. Somewhere in between I had decided to make *all* my casts as perfectly as I could. I always made it a point to drop my rod and take up all the slack before I started any back cast, instead of starting the cast from halfway up and counting on making up for a poor back cast with an extra load of power on the forward cast that followed. I learned to cast smoothly with a constant pressure on the rod from the moving line. I learned to sense the slightest wind on my cheek and to adjust my casts instantly to a changing flow of air.

Good tackle should be a pleasure to own, a pleasure to use, and something that brings your angling closer to the point of perfection. But just as a fisherman dreams of good tackle, good tackle demands something in return. Unless the angler brings his casting and fishing techniques *up* to the quality of the tackle, he's missing something to treasure. Fine tackle is designed to be fished. Happy is the angler who has the skill and the wisdom to use and enjoy the best.

[1979]

42

The Wheel of
Fortune

*I can remember years ago seeing a photo of Joan Sal-
vato in a fishing magazine and thinking at the time:
Gee, what a pretty woman. Her fishing, of course, was
all the more impressive. It was many years later that we
finally met, and I remember very clearly, Wow, she still
is! flashing through my mind as she introduced herself.
As we've become friends, I've found her to be a fine
person and found, too, that my initial impression was
much more than skin deep. As a tournament caster and
angler, she'd firmly established her own credentials as a
world-class fisherman before marrying Lee twenty-two
years ago. It pleased me a great deal to have my photograph of her casting on the cover of her new book,* Fly
Casting Techniques *(New York: Nick Lyons Books).
When I was publishing Lee Wulff's column on the back
page of* Rod & Reel *(where it still appears, in addition
to Joan's fly-casting column on the inside pages), he
and I often used to hash over what he might cover in
the next or a future issue. One day I asked him how he
and Joan had gotten together, and this chapter was the
answer.*

I think sometimes of the debts I owe to people I have never met, but who have made my life richer or happier through something independent of any action of mine, like the unknown deer hunter who spooks a big buck that comes your way. The other day I heard that old song, "Wheel of Fortune," and thought of Kay Starr and the debt I owe her. As it was for millions of other Americans, her "Wheel of Fortune" was one of my favorite songs. Most of us who listen rarely see or meet the great singers. In 1966, as a producer of segments for the "American Sportsman" television series, I thought I would meet Kay Starr. I had learned that she might be interested in outdoor sports, so I asked our office to see if she'd star in a giant-bluefin-tuna segment I had planned for that summer. I wanted an attractive, feminine female to capture a tuna far bigger than she was, to show how, although she might be inexperienced, she could, under a captain's direction and with a good crew, become a successful big-game fisherman.

Word came back that she'd accepted the assignment just as I took off with Curt Gowdy to film the catching of big brook trout in my then-secret water of the Minipi Basin in Labrador.

When Curt and I came out of the Labrador bush, and I was ready to move to the east coast of Newfoundland to work on the tuna film, word came through that Kay Starr had a minor illness and had to go to the hospital for a checkup instead of coming up to fish for tuna. However, New York was sending up a substitute. She was Joan Salvato, casting champion for many years, who traveled and demonstrated casting for the Garcia Corporation.

I'll have to admit to being very disappointed. I'd wanted a national celebrity—and I'd wanted to meet Kay Starr. Joan breezed in with excitement in her eyes and an eagerness that was refreshing. Although she'd never been big-game fishing before, she told me she'd read the IGFA rule book and that nobody was going to touch the tackle while she played a fish, so that if she did happen to catch a record fish it wouldn't be disqualified. The tuna she caught, a 572-pounder, wasn't a record, but it looked monstrous against her 122-pound figure when it came finally aboard.

She took the problems of the fishing and the filming with a smile. During the slack periods we talked of fishing, friends, politics, and life in general. I sensed in her a firm integrity and I realized she had a deep feeling for the wild things. At the end of a week she went back to her world, and I stayed on to do another film in Newfoundland.

The following year when the "American Sportsman" needed a fly-casting film, Joan was selected as the caster, and I was sent to Florida to produce it. It was a difficult job because another producer refused to give up the crew on schedule, holding it in the field with him until I was left with just one day and a half in which to complete my film. Again, Joan was quiet, efficient, and sparkling on camera. The film won a Teddy award. I knew then that if there ever was the perfect wife and companion for an outdoorsman, it was Joan.

The year turned its cycle and the "Wheel of Fortune" went on spinning its schemes. Nineteen sixty-seven was a great year for me. I took two world records, a 50-pound-test-line tuna and a 12-pound-leader-test fly-rod striped marlin. More important, I made my finest catch of all. Joan became my bride. I'll always be grateful to Kay Starr and her "Wheel of Fortune" for the happiest years of my life.

[1980]

43

The Wealth
of Age

In this almost-end-of-the-book chapter, Wulff reflects on the pages past—in this book and in his lifetime—and finds himself better off than ever. The reasons may please you as they please me; at some point in your life you may share them.

Don't, however, write him off. He's fishing more different pools right now than I'd care to handle at my own substantially younger age. For one thing, the fame achieved by Lee and Joan through their angling lives has made their home (and telephone) something of a mecca for anglers all over the world. Both phone and doorstep continue to get plenty of wear these days. Much of their time is spent deciding where to fish next and making the arrangements, and I'm never sure in talking with them what adventure I'll hear about next. They're both still actively writing and lecturing, and the Wulffs, as ever, are a fountain of new ideas.

From the front cover of the magazine, a big caribou bull stared at me. In my youth, that would have set me dreaming of going on a caribou hunt. Instead, my mind flashed back to

Jim John and what he called the "harvest fields" of the upper Gander River in Newfoundland. The year was 1940, and I was thirty-five.

Jim was a full-blooded Micmac Indian. His home was on the south coast of Newfoundland some seventy miles away. He was one of the best guides in the province, and he had brought me to this, his favorite hunting area. We had a few days of fruitless hunting behind us when we spotted a stag (the Newfoundlanders use the English *stag* for males instead of the American *bull*). The animal was about a mile away, and he looked good through the binoculars. If we hurried, Jim said, we could intercept him, and we took off.

We were making a film, so there were three of us on the lookout point—Jim, my cameraman, and I. Halfway along, the cameraman gave Jim his magazine camera and promised to come with the big camera and tripod as soon as he heard a shot. Jim was over fifty then, but he was still a traveling fool, and we ran more than we walked across the rough going till we came to a jutting finger of the forest that penetrated the muskeg. We were still breathing hard when the caribou came into the open just where Jim, knowing the caribou trails, knew he'd show. The bull stood there, a little more than one hundred yards away. He looked just like the caribou on the magazine's front cover. He was facing us and staring right at us.

It was a tableau. None of us moved, including the caribou. I looked along the iron sights and thought: If I shoot now, I may hit the head or antlers and spoil them and the pictures. Should I wait? If I do, will he bolt and leave me with a running shot and a poor chance for a clean kill? The seconds ticked by.

Slowly, the antlered head started to swing, a sign that he was ready to run. Without a word from me, Jim started the camera. I heard it running, and as the head lifted and the antlers cleared the white of his neck, I squeezed off the shot.

The bullet hit the spine in the neck, and he dropped in his tracks. It was a lucky shot under great pressure. Anything other than an instantaneous kill cannot be shown in a film.

That's just one of the animals I remember when my thoughts turn to caribou country. In memory, I recapture the look and smell of the yellow muskeg and the red blueberry barrens lying between the patches of dark timber. I close my eyes, and I am there.

The wealth of old age comes in having past reality to reflect upon instead of future uncertainty to dream about. It lies in knowing firsthand instead of relying on the word of someone else to make decisions. It comes from having done most of the things you really wanted to do at least once and knowing those you enjoy most and want to do again and again. It lies in wisdom, which can only come from experience. Knowledge is something youth may have as well as old-timers. Wisdom comes from testing mere knowledge and being able to use it effectively.

Physical things, too, can be the gift of age. I remember 1938 and a fishing trip in the northern bush. The black flies were as thick and as fierce as I ever remember. The fly dopes of that day were not very effective and in a few days, we ran out of them. My guide said, "Wait long enough, and you'll get used to the bugs like I am."

He was right. I was bitten so much that I grew nauseated and felt physically ill for two days. He called it "fly fever."

Then the miracle happened. After that, I could watch a black fly bite me and feel no pain. The fly would go off leaving a tiny, round, red mark on my flesh. Within a day the red spot would turn black. There was no swelling, and by the third day, even that small black reminder of the fly's visit was gone. That immunity is still with me, though perhaps not to the same degree, and I'm seldom bitten. When others around me are complaining of bites, I'm comfortable and disdain fly dope. It's truly a gift of having lived and experienced.

I was about forty-five when I admitted to myself that my muscles would never again be what they once were and that I'd have to start using my head to make up for their failings. I couldn't race full tilt across a bog to intercept a caribou. I couldn't lift and carry as much or more than anyone else in the party and race to be the leader on the trail. Thinking becomes harder when good muscles have previously given you a great advantage, but thinking helps you to do your share of the physical things when you grow older.

I had the first light seaplane in Newfoundland or Labrador. Flying a floatplane let me fish the then-uncharted rivers, and I fished them before the other planes came and today's crowds moved in. As a result, I have a special sense about playing Atlantic salmon that came only with time and long experience. I have caught at least 3,000 salmon, and the total may be 4,000. I can watch one of the old movies of me playing a salmon in the late 1930s and see how much my tactics have changed. I've learned how well angle and pressure changes can be used to control a fish's runs and his position in a pool. I have learned that in playing stream fish, the best position for the angler is downstream of the fish so that it fights not only your pressure, but the flow of the stream as well. I used to race downstream to keep ahead of the fish, relying on my fleetness of foot and balance to get to the right places. With time, I learned to use only light pressures so the fish stayed in the pool, instead of pressuring them into wild, downstream runs, and I brought them in more swiftly than before.

With the big fish of the sea, there was a greater need to use my strength efficiently. I learned to work with static pressure so that the boat traveled on the same course and at the same speed as the fish as often as possible. The line neither comes off the reel nor is reeled in, so that maximum strain can be put on the fish with the minimum of effort. I learned to break down the fish's will to resist.

At forty, when my muscles were beginning their downward slide, it would have been hard to imagine that at seventy-two I'd be able to set a new 80-pound-test-line-class record for giant bluefin tuna. I had to play that fish for two hours and fifteen minutes, and I did it more with my mind, or just as much, as I did it with my muscles. That 895-pound record fish has been bettered, but as I write this, I'm in my seventies, and I'm still trying for a tuna record. I came close to a new record in 1982, when I was seventy-seven, with a 960-pound bluefin tuna I caught in Nova Scotia. After fifty it is an interesting game to see how much you can accomplish with a minimum of physical effort.

Fly casting, like many other things, is a matter of skill and timing—of easy rhythm rather than power. Such things can be enjoyed all through life and perhaps most of all in the more relaxed years of age. Paddle easily. Climb slowly. Choose the right places from the experience of other days, and enjoy the view to the fullest.

I have been fly casting since I was nine, but it was not until I was over forty and started flying a light seaplane that I really learned to cast a fly into the wind. Newfoundland, the old pilots told me, was too windy for a light plane like my J-3 Cub, but the Cub and I survived and I learned to live with wind.

The gales would pour viciously over the mountains and beat down hard on the lakes and bays I had to land on. Watching, I saw that winds are rarely constant. They flowed over the earth like water over a rapid run, gusting along at varying speeds. I used to look down fearfully at the pattern of hard, black squalls in which I was about to risk my airplane and my life. Then it dawned on me that the way to beat the wind was to land into the wind at the tail of one of the black squalls. The wind was strong, and my ground speed was slow when I approached. Then, just as I lit on the water, I'd enter one of the slack wind periods and my plane could settle quickly onto the water.

And that's the best way to cast a fly into the wind. Let the tail of a gust take your line out on a hard back cast, and then, in the lull that follows, drive hard into and through the relatively calm spots behind the gust. Casts should be timed to the wind. Though you can't make as many casts as you can on a calm day, it's possible, without too much effort, to fish quite effectively when most anglers have retreated to the taverns.

When it comes to deer hunting, it's obvious that the older hunter has to slow down. He can't cover the terrain he did in his youth. However, his growing experience should give him a better understanding of the animal so that he will be at the right places at the right time more and more. Most of the time, he can plan to signal a friend to help drag out the deer.

Failing that, he can often shoot where the dragging is all downhill. Old bird hunters, too, manage to get their share of the game, using slower-working dogs that cover the ground more thoroughly, and they know just when, in a bird's flight, is the best time to shoot.

An old man can build up out of his years a fund of knowledge that stands him in good stead when there are decisions to make. Watching trout in the small brooks as a boy, I learned that the hardest strikes always come when two fish are racing each other to get the bait. Whenever I encounter an extra-hard strike, I still remember those racing trout of boyhood. As quickly as I play one fish, I cast back to the same spot, because another hungry fish should be there.

When I went up to Newfoundland in 1938 to pioneer that island's tuna fishing for the government, I knew the fish were big, and I hoped to set a record. I used stout hooks and stainless-steel wire cable leaders headed up with a large bright-brass swivel. I only hooked one bluefin that looked like a record breaker. I tossed a mackerel bait to that monstrous fish and watched him take it and race away just under the surface in smooth water. Then I saw his companion, equally large, rushing alongside. My line went slack. My tuna's friend had snapped at the flash of the big brass swivel and the bright bubble of air it made as it raced through the water. The second fish cut the doubled line. Since then, I've used no swivel at all or the smallest, dullest one I thought would not break before the leader did.

All of us are seeing things now that will vanish with the changing world, leaving those who hold such memories with a deeper realization of the inevitability of change. I had heard that the old north-woods trappers could build their cabins without a single nail and with an ax as the only tool. One of the great north-country guides built a cabin for me. I helped him cut and peel the poles of spruce and fir and then notch and place them. Using pressure and pegs and undercuts to hold things together or to hinge them, he made a beautiful cabin. Its roof was of birchbark overlaid with soil on which he planted sod to hold the whole thing steady. It was a beautiful cabin that I think is still standing. Its creation gave me a sense of similar skills our civilization has already lost.

Another wonderful thing that makes the late years great is that your kids grow up and go off on their own. They were so big a part of your life that the change when they go is a dramatic one. You would have thrown yourself in front of an oncoming car to push them out of harm's way. You had them in your mind in all your waking hours. They gave you a lot of pleasure, and you'll always remember the towheaded three-year-old—now forty with hair as black as yours once was—catching his first sunfish with squeals of pure delight. You remember flying back to a salmon camp and looking down to see his ten-year-old brother standing in the river. You watched the salmon he was playing, his first, leap in a splash of spray and sunlight.

When they were small, you worried that they'd fall into the Battenkill and drown. One of their playmates in the village had done that. As they grew up, you wondered at night if their delayed return meant that they'd been in an accident, and you had a twinge of fear if the phone rang in the wee hours and they were still out.

When they finally went off on their own, there was a great sense of loss at first. Then you realized that bringing them to maturity as good, healthy citizens was your real goal and that you had achieved it. They are no longer the kids you cuddled. Now they are grown-ups you love in different ways. And you've passed on to them an understanding of the wild world that endures.

Mature, experienced people do their best creative work. It is a time to enjoy with the richness of friends, doing the things you most want to do.

There is a wealth in having sat around many campfires in a multitude of camps. It lies in the friends you make. When you have lived with them on the waters and in the woods and time has seasoned the friendship, it is far more secure and satisfying than those that develop casually, each person showing the other only a part of what he is. It may be that the greatest wealth of all lies in our friends.

Old friends can wade a trout stream together or walk a woodland cover and encounter not just the fish or the game of that day but also the memories of other days and other places. They've taken the bitter with the better and found it all rewarding.

The years beyond fifty have been by far the best of my life. I've had the physical capacity to do a great many things and the judgment to do them better than ever before. I haven't had to do anything I really haven't wanted to do during those years. I know I put my heart fully into each effort. Because of maturity and depth of interest in what I do, whether writing, making films, or playing a fish, each thing I do should be more complete and better than the things I did in my energetic youth.

It is good for the young to realize how rewarding the over-fifty years can be—years when the mind has sorted out the things of greatest value. When I look back, it seems I spent my youth and middle age preparing to enjoy my final years.

[1983]

44

Small Explorer

This is one of the few poems, if not the only one, Lee Wulff ever wrote. At least I've been through everything of his I could find in my own library and various others, including his own basement, and not found another.

Knowing the ages of his sons, I date this to about 1937. The poem is about beginnings, and I suppose I might have used it at the beginning of the book instead of the end. But we've only begun with this book to explore the many works Lee Wulff has already produced, and I look forward to the ones he hasn't written yet. So we'll end this book with a beginning and hope for more—leaving the table, as my grandmother advised, still a little bit hungry.

He crawled into my studio today,
This son of mine just ten months old,
To stare about him,
Bright eyes round with wonder.
He stopped . . . and crawled . . .

And stopped again to sit a little while and look.
And when his eyes had taken in
The first fresh newness of the scene
He let a tiny "Ah" escape
As if he found it good.

The metal standard of my desk,
A thing of beauty I had long forgotten,
Caught his eye and held it.
Curiously then,
He scanned the tall round column
That holds my paper scraps,
As beautiful for him
As any obelisk rising to the skies
In honor of some great ruler
Long since dead.

One small finger bent
Against the lushness of the rug
To feel its softness,
To pause and marvel,
Little dreaming of the craft within
That began with rough grass mats
Upon a dusty cave floor
When early men were cold.

The long white drapes,
Hanging almost to the floor,
Lit his eyes with pleasure.
He moved to touch them,
Lightly first, then
To take them in his baby fists
And start to rise.

And who was I to take him up
And put him in his pen,
His well known world,
When all this lay before him?
Too soon he'll learn to care

Lest eager hands be bruised.
And all the world
Will try to mold
Him like the rest
With things he must
And must not do
Until his mind is numbed
To freshening thought.

Grant that I may live, myself,
With eyes on new and different things
To be his guide
And an example
So that growing up may teach him
To be safe from hurt but never fearful
To seek out new worlds.

[1937]

Index